HEAVEN IS A GAY BAR
Bryan Foreman

BForeman Books | Oklahoma City, OK
ISBN: 978-0-692-88011-1
Card Catalogue Number: 2017906365
Title: Heaven Is a Gay Bar / Bryan Foreman
Digital distribution | BForeman Books, 2017
Paperback | BForeman Books, 2017

DEDICATION

I dedicate this book to my family and all my friends, old and new, plus those who are no longer with us.

CHAPTER ONE

August 26, 1994—I was diagnosed with type 2 diabetes back in November, just before my thirtieth birthday, and it'd been a nightmare ever since. The doctor put me on Glipizide and insulin, but neither appeared to be doing much good. My blood sugar was still out of control, and now it was at an all-time high—a whopping 350 mg/dl at last check. So I took off work that morning to see a specialist.

Checkups were usually painfully awkward for me, but this one exceeded all expectations. The old guy had me take off all my clothes and lay down on his exam table. Then he proceeded to examine every inch of me from head to toe. Maybe it wouldn't have been so bad if I wasn't so disgustingly overweight and didn't have one or two peculiarities that made me different than other boys. Then again, probably not. I felt like I was being probed by aliens!

The mad doctor came to a sudden halt when he reached my groin area. *Oh, God... here it comes,* I thought, just as I felt his gloved finger touch my scrotum—right where my left testicle should've been.

"What's goin' on down here?" he asked curiously.

"I had the mumps when I was twelve and my ball shrank," I replied, embarrassed. "The doctor told me I'd never have children."

"That's not true!" the old man said. "All you need is one!" He gave my right testicle a swift poke, causing me to wince. "And this other fellow seems healthy enough!" He then tapped me on the penis. "How 'bout this guy? Any problems with him?"

"Yes," I said.

"Yes?"

"It doesn't work."

"No erection at all?"

"No."

"And how long has this been goin' on?" he asked.

"I don't know... a year, maybe," I replied.

"Does your primary physician know about it?"

"Not yet."

He smiled, bewildered. "And what does the missus have to say about it?"

"There's no missus," I replied.

"You're kiddin'... a hoss like you?" he exclaimed. "You better get on the ball, son!"

"I know," I sighed.

He stepped to the front of the table and looked down at me with a grim expression. "The impotence is from the diabetes," he said. "It damages the blood vessels, causing them to constrict... which reduces blood flow to the penis. But I also suspect that your testosterone level is low. That probably has somethin' to do with it as well. Have you felt a lack of energy lately? Any problems sleeping?"

I shook my head.

"Well, I'm gonna take a blood sample from you before you go," he said. Then he laughed at me and added, "But, you know... there's medication you can take for that! You don't have to live like a monk!" He looked dead serious again. "Now, as far as the diabetes is concerned... you need to lose about a hundred pounds. Have you tried losin' weight before?"

"Practically my whole life," I scoffed.

"We'll start you out on a sixteen hundred-calorie diet," he said, "and see how that goes!" He walked back down to the other end and stood over my feet, staring down at my long, yellow toenails with a big grimace. "Look at these bear claws!" he said, shaking his head. He pulled a pair of toenail clippers out of his coat pocket and went to work on my left great toe. "You need to take better care of your feet, kiddo!" he said. "The last thing you want is an infection! All it takes is an ingrown toenail and there goes your toe!"

He trimmed every single one of my toenails for me. Then he had me put my clothes back on and drew up some blood. When it was all over, I stormed out of the building, hopped into my little Dodge Neon, and let the expletives fly.

"Are you fuckin' kiddin' me?" I exclaimed, tossing the prescription and sixteen hundred-calorie diet sheet into the other seat. "What the fuck was that? The goddamn pervert!"

He wanted to see me again in two weeks, but there was no way I was coming back. I'd never been so humiliated in my life! I felt like a total piece of shit! *No one should ever have to see me without my armor!* I thought.

I was back at the jobsite just twenty minutes later, yanking sheetrock off the wall piece by piece and tossing it on the floor behind me. I remodeled office spaces for a living, me and nine other guys, working for my father—a successful commercial contractor and the proud owner of Oldman Construction. I'm Benjamin Oldman. Most of my colleagues preferred the building back process, putting up new walls. But demolition was my forte! I liked tearing things down, bashing holes in the wall with my hammer, and kicking in metal studs. There was no better way to vent out my anger and frustration. I soon forgot about my humiliation at the doctor's office—'til a couple of coworkers came over and started working alongside me.

"So, Big B... what did the doctor have to say?" said the tall, swarthy-looking gentleman, Sean Grasso. "Are you gonna live?"

I just looked at him and smiled. Then the shorter fellow with the blond hair, Matt Ross, asked me if I wanted to meet them at the strip joint after work—or the "titty bar," as he referred to it. They were always trying to talk me into going to that place. I wasn't sure if they were just being friendly or if it was some malevolent scheme to corrupt the boss's son. I often wondered why they even bothered talking to me at all. It wasn't as if we had anything in common. They were a few years younger than me, mid to late twenties, and good-looking. They liked to wear tight clothes to show off their buff bods—Sean in his sweaty white tank top and cut-off shorts and Matt in his gray muscle shirt and ripped jeans. He also wore a blue Dallas Cowboys baseball cap—around the clock, it seemed. I, on the other hand, was a bit overdressed for the summer weather in my long-sleeve flannel shirt and baggy jeans. I respectfully declined Matt's invitation. I told him I already had plans.

"Oh, yeah... I forgot," he smirked. "Friday night... movie night. What are you gonna go see?"

"*Natural Born Killers!*" I said excitedly. "I might even make it a double feature! I'd like to see *Forrest Gump* again!"

"That good, huh?" he said.

"Yep! Want to see it with me?"

"I think I'll pass." He sighed. "Enjoy your show."

After a long, hard day in the trenches, I drove straight home—to my Fortress of Solitude. Actually, it was just a little one-bedroom apartment. But it had everything I needed to tune out the real world at the end of the day: two TVs, a hi-fi stereo, a massive collection of movies on VHS, and even a word processor—so I could create my own fantasies. Currently, I was working on a screenplay.

I ate a couple of TV dinners in front of the big screen TV, then hurriedly got myself ready for the big night. I showered, shaved, threw on a nice dress shirt and a pair of slacks, brushed my hair in front of the mirror, slicked it back with some gel, and sprayed a smidgen of Old Spice on both cheeks. Moments later, I was off to the local multiplex to catch the new releases.

Natural Born Killers was a total disappointment—too violent and mean-spirited for my taste. So I sneaked in to see *Forrest Gump* afterward, and it was even better the second time! I'd always been a sucker for a good love story, especially the sad ones that ended in death. I liked what the movie was saying about love being eternal. As I sat there with my eyes glued to the screen, almost on the verge of tears as I watched Forrest talk to Jenny's tombstone, I heard people snickering and giggling behind me. And it didn't take me long to surmise that they were snickering and giggling at me. Tuning them out as best I could, I suddenly felt a Milk Dud strike the back of my neck. I knew it was a Milk Dud because the next one missed and landed in my lap. The third one was another direct hit, however, thumping me against my crown. It took me right out of the movie and back to my adolescence when I was constantly being laughed at and getting food thrown at me. Needless to say, I was a little angry and deeply hurt. But I didn't turn around and confront them. I just sat there and took it like I did in high school, middle school, elementary school, and even kindergarten. At least the college kids were a little more reserved!

The scoundrels got up to leave during the final scene, but not before kicking the back of my chair really hard. I turned around to see them scramble down the aisle. They were a group of high school kids, just as I'd suspected. Yet I didn't suspect them all to be girls!

Saturday morning, I resisted the urge to go back to the multiplex and watch movies all day, opting to stay home and work on my screenplay. Orson Welles was just twenty-four years old when he produced, co-wrote, directed, and starred in *Citizen Kane,* arguably the greatest movie of all time. And here I was at thirty, still struggling to master one talent while busting my ass in the construction business and watching movies on the side. I didn't want that to be my life twenty years from now, when I was fifty. I wanted to make my mark somehow and be somebody. Currently, my dream was to be a brilliant screenwriter—the Paddy Chayefsky of the nineties! Then maybe people would treat me with the respect I deserved and kids would think twice before throwing candy at me!

My screenplay was a routine cop thriller, riddled with tired clichés and shoddy dialogue. But at the time, I thought it was gold. I sat at the writing desk inside my bedroom and typed away for hours, with the little TV on mute and Debussy playing on my cassette player for inspiration. Both electronic devices sat high on a shelf above the desktop. I produced ten pages by nightfall while consuming a large bag of Cheetos, half a bag of potato chips, a two-liter bottle of Dr. Pepper, and an entire package of Oreos. Talk about feeding my creativity!

The next day, I produced six more pages. Then Monday reared its ugly head and I was back to tearing down walls alongside Matt and Sean, who kept boasting about their incredible weekend and the two strippers, Domino and Skye, they'd met at Baby Dolls on Saturday night. According to Sean, they went to Domino's house after the club closed, partied with a bunch of strippers, and had an orgy on the living room floor.

"You missed out, bro!" he said to me with a big, goofy grin. "I was fuckin' four women at the same time!"

I just smiled and said, "That's nice. I'm happy for you." Though secretly I was wondering how that was even physically possible.

I got it! It was their first orgy, so naturally they were still excited and couldn't shut up about it. But they gradually wore me down with their endless talk of perky breasts and wet vaginas. It made *my* weekend seem like a Shakespearean tragedy in comparison. Then Matt had to bring his penis into the conversation.

"It's gotta new nickname!" he said. "Skye and Trixie kept callin' it the beer can! Hey, Matt... bring that beer can over here, will ya?"

Sean skeptically shook his head and laughed. "It ain't the size of no beer can," he said. "A smoked sausage, maybe!"

The Kid came up behind us with a trash cart to pick up our mess. I had no idea what his real name was. We just called him Kid because that's what he was—a scrawny, rambunctious teenager fresh out of high school.

"Could you faggots hold it down over here?" he said. "You're makin' us all sick!"

"Shut up and get back to work, Kid!" Sean snapped at him. "No one wants to hear your two cents!"

He then proceeded to tell us about *his* amazing cock and how he was able to sustain an erection for hours on end.

"You should see a doctor about that!" Matt quipped.

I was sweating bullets, meanwhile, and it wasn't just from the heat. *Are we gonna start comparin' dicks now?* I wondered, furiously yanking sheetrock off the wall and throwing it in the Kid's trash cart. Just when I thought the topic had come to a close, the two old guys working together on a separate wall decided to chime in.

Homer, a fifty-nine-year-old man with a thirty-year-old girlfriend, said, "Last night, Sheila stuck a string of beads up my ass and pulled 'em out just as we were fuckin'. It gave me a stiffy like you wouldn't believe... and a hell of an orgasm to boot!" He then spit a wad of chewing tobacco on the floor to complete the effect.

"Been there, done that!" said Tim, a man in his late forties and the job foreman. "Has she tied you to the bedposts yet? That's how me and the old lady roll!"

Jesus! Is everyone having sex but me? I thought. It didn't seem fair that I was missing out on such a basic human need, especially since no one longed to be with a woman more than me. But I suppose wasting my weekends away in a movie theater wasn't helping much, living vicariously through the characters on the screen when there were plenty of real-life adventures to undertake. Something had to give! I was losing my humanity to the silver screen!

Slipping my hammer into my tool belt, I turned to Sean and Matt and said, "Are y'all goin' out *next* Saturday?"

"Why, you wanna come?" Sean said excitedly.

"Actually, we're goin' back out there tonight!" Matt said.

"Tonight?" I replied, slightly daunted. "But it's Monday!"

"And your point is?" Matt said.

"I've gotta be here at eight o'clock tomorrow!" I said.

"So do we!" Sean shrugged.

"Don't worry, Cinderella!" Matt laughed. "We'll get you home by midnight. So, are you in or out?"

"I'm in!" I replied, without giving it any further thought.

And that's all it took. Just one bold and impulsive move and I was on the road to corruption.

That night, we all met at Sean's house and got drunk before we went out. Actually, Sean and Matt got drunk. I nursed a bottle of Molson Ice for a whole hour. I couldn't stand the taste of it. The house looked like your typical bachelor pad. It had a big, spacious living room for dancing, orgies, and what have you; two bedrooms upstairs, in case a couple of us got lucky; a pool table, pinball machine, and jukebox in the den, and a hot tub out back. We were all spread out in the living room, Sean in his Archie Bunker chair, aimlessly flipping through channels on the big screen TV, and me and

Matt on opposite ends of the couch. I felt slightly uneasy. We weren't all that close, and I knew very little about them, except that they were really good friends and they'd known each other long before *I* ever met them. They came looking for a job together a couple of summers ago and Dad had hired them both on the spot.

At least I got to know Matt a little better as he sat there guzzling his beer. He talked about his younger years, his early twenties, I presumed, when he left home and headed east in search of greener pastures. He spent some time in Chicago and New York City. But ultimately, he settled down in Miami, Florida, met a girl, and fell in love, which led to two blissful years of sizzling-hot romance fueled with sex and drugs. I'm paraphrasing, of course.

"It was the best two years of my life!" he said remorsefully.

And here I thought he was just another simple hayseed, a meat-and-potatoes kind of guy, whose only passions were naked women and beer.

"I'd be with her right now," he continued, "if I hadn't caught her cheatin' on me! I beat the shit out of the guy and hightailed it back to Oklahoma to avoid an assault and battery charge." He laughed impulsively. "I almost killed the bastard!" he said. "Now I'm a wanted man... hiding out in my mom's basement!"

"Well, that's life," Sean grumbled. "Why don't you shut up and watch TV? You're bringin' us down with that Miami shit!"

"Maybe I would, if you'd take your goddamn finger off the remote!" Matt retorted.

That was another thing I learned about the pair that night—get a few beers in them and they start bickering at each other like an old married couple.

After they were pleasantly soused, we hopped into Sean's tan Suburban and headed to Baby Dolls. Matt sat up front in the cockpit with Sean, both still chugging down Molson as we shot onto the highway with the stereo blasting. I sat in the back seat filled with trepidation, suddenly wondering what the hell I'd gotten myself into.

Matt turned around in the passenger seat and said to me with a drunken slur, "Yeah, you'd love it there in Miami! Have you ever been anywhere outside of Oklahoma?"

"My parents took us to Six Flags once," I replied.

"Which one?"

"Texas."

He smirked and said, "Go to Miami, bro! Everything's ten times better there! The food's better, the women are sexier, the nightlife's more exciting, and the liquor stores never close!"

"Wow!" I replied.

I was reminded of how much I hated strip joints the moment we stepped into the place. Motley Crüe's "Girls, Girls, Girls" was playing very loudly over the PA system. I despised '80s metal. And much like the construction site, the room was chock-full of crude, rowdy, tough-talking men. I recognized two of them almost instantly—a young electrician named Sammy and his sidekick, Alfonso. Sean and Matt waved at them and led me to their table, just inches away from the stage. The two Latino men were still in their dirty work clothes, suggesting that they'd been sitting there for hours. Sean and Matt said their hellos and we all sat down. Matt sat next to Sammy and began talking in his ear. Though I couldn't hear what they were saying, I was pretty certain that they were talking about me, the way they kept glancing at me from across the table. No doubt, it had something to do with me being a first-timer. I decided to ignore them and concentrated on the woman pole dancing on stage. She was young and beautiful but in a manufactured sort of way, with her dark tan, perfect boobs, and rainbow-colored hair. I was captivated by her nonetheless. The last time I saw a woman naked was in college. And that, too, was at a strip joint.

Looking away from her for a split-second, I noticed everyone at the table laughing at me. *Why am I so damned amusing?* I wondered. Matt stood up and stuffed a dollar bill in the woman's G-string while Sean summoned a waitress over and ordered a pitcher of beer for the table.

The song ended and another stripper took the stage, dancing to Nine Inch Nails' "Closer." She was more exotic-looking than the last—long, dark hair, naturally dark skin, and a perfectly toned body. She was the kind of woman most men would kill for. But I didn't care for exotic any more than I cared for the plastic Barbie doll look. I always preferred someone more average-looking, a plain Jane or the girl next girl type... better yet, a housewife! June Cleaver would be perfect for me—if she wasn't a fictional character. That was why I hardly ever went to strip joints or watched video porn. The women were too perfect and unattainable... and I wanted the real deal.

Suddenly, the stripper with the rainbow-colored hair stepped out onto the main floor wearing a pink negligee. Matt stood up, waved her over to the table, and whispered something into her ear while handing her twenty bucks. Having already slipped her a dollar bill, I thought he fancied her and was getting himself a lap dance. She walked off for a few minutes and came back just as Def Leppard's "Foolin'" began to play. Only, she walked right past Matt and came straight for me, catching me completely off guard.

"Scoot your chair back, hon!" she whispered in my ear.

I scooted back in my chair several feet, allowing her to get between my legs and dance provocatively while stripping down to her G-string. She rubbed her bare breasts against my face and her ass against my crotch. Yet I pretended not to take any pleasure in it, knowing that everyone was watching.

Looking a little perplexed, she put her arms around my neck and whispered in my ear, "You can touch me if you want!"

I didn't want to disappoint her, so I suddenly let go of my inhibitions, closed my eyes, and began running my fingers all over her body like I was playing a musical instrument, practically making love to her with my hands and breathing in her perfume as she rubbed up against my face. My friends were probably laughing at me, but I didn't care. It was the closest I'd ever come to having sex, and I relished every second of it. All of a sudden, there was a tingling sensation in my groin area and I felt my penis move ever so slightly. It thrilled the hell out of me to know that there was still some life down there!

"Thank you, God!" I shouted with joy.

The woman kissed me on the cheek after the song ended and swiftly walked off. I saw the amused looks on my friends' faces as I scooted my chair back to the table.

"Now *that* was a lap dance!" Sean remarked.

"And worth every penny!" Matt added. He smiled and winked at me. "Don't say I never gotcha anything!"

The two were still talking about it at closing time a few hours later, walking out of the club with Domino and Skye on their arms.

"I can see tomorrow's headlines!" Matt jested. "Bear Mauling Inside Titty Bar!"

They all had a good laugh over it as I walked behind them, slightly embarrassed but also a little proud of myself. It was two thirty in the morning when we got back to Sean's house. Matt invited me to come in and party with them, but five was a crowd—particularly when it came to orgies. Besides, I had to be at work in five and a half hours.

CHAPTER TWO

My surprise lap dance was the top news story at work the next day, thanks to Sean and his big mouth. He announced it to the entire crew while we were busy tearing out a room, telling them how I turned from mild-mannered Big B into the Incredible Hulk in a matter of seconds.

"He was all over that poor girl!" he said. "He even got inside her G-string and stuck his fingers up her pussy!"

Everyone stopped working and looked at me in disbelief.

"Is that true, Ben?" big, bushy-bearded Tim asked me. "Did you stick your fingers up her pussy?"

I didn't want to disappoint them by telling the truth, so I said, "Yeah!"

"I'll be damned!" Tim laughed.

You didn't wash those fingers, did you?" Homer said to me with a sly grin as he spit.

He was just being his usual crude, disgusting self. But I gladly played along this time, taking a whiff of my fingers and pretending to be intoxicated by their smell. They all immediately looked away and went right back to work, which wasn't quite the response I was hoping for. *Uh-oh,* I thought, and slowly turned around to see my father standing right behind me, giving me his signature stern father look. Stanley Mathias Oldman, or "Stan the Man," as he was fondly referred to, was a tall, thin, balding man in his early fifties, blue-eyed, and handsome for his age. He looked nothing like me, in other words. His nice, clean shirt and fancy bow tie meant that he probably wouldn't be staying long.

"Benji!" He nodded. "Haven't seen you in a while! Whatcha been up to?"

"Nothin'... just workin'," I answered rather stiffly.

"Your mother wants you to stop by the house tonight and have some supper with us," he said. "She's fixin' your favorite... Mexican meatloaf."

"I can't," I quickly blurted out. "I gotta work tonight."

"Work?" he said, studying me curiously. "You're not moonlightin', are you, son?"

"No... I meant my screenplay," I replied. "I'm working on *it*."

"Oh, I see," he said, nodding disappointedly. "Some other time, then."

He rushed off to meet the new tenant and his subcontractors, who'd just walked into the building. Matt sidled up to me and spoke in my ear.

"What's wrong with you?" he kidded me. "Are you too good to spend some quality time with the folks?"

"I see 'em all the time!" I exclaimed defensively. "Thanksgiving, Christmas... any time there's a fuckin' birthday party—"

"Whoa! Calm down there, big'n!" he laughed. "I'm just fuckin' with ya! We're goin' out again Thursday night. You comin'?"

"*Hell* yeah!" I replied. "Baby Dolls, right?"

"Actually, I thought we'd try the nightclubs first," he said. "Shenanigans... ever been there?"

"No," I replied.

"It's kinda swank," he said. "You gotta suit?"

"Huh-uh."

"Buy you one, bro!" he said, slapping me on the arm. "Your old man pays you enough!"

I did more than just buy a cheap suit that evening. I decided to reinvent myself by coming up with a whole new look, something unique that was all my own—a look that would make me stand out for a change.

Thursday night, I showed up on Sean's doorstep wearing a black sports jacket over a black t-shirt, black slacks, black socks, and black shoes. I thought I looked pretty cool. I was the new man in black! Yet, with my dark, wavy hair, dark eyes, and slightly pale complexion, I looked more like an overweight Goth rock star.

"Hey, look... it's Trent Reznor!" Sean joked as he let me in.

He was wearing a dark-blue double-breasted suit, while Matt sat on the couch in a gray sports jacket, white t-shirt, faded jeans, and his Dallas Cowboys baseball cap, of course. It was as if we were kids playing dress-up. Sean made me delicious drinks from the blender, strawberry daiquiris and piña coladas, so I could get pleasantly soused as well. We drank and bullshitted for an hour, then took off in the Suburban. I wasn't a staggering drunk just yet, but I was definitely numb.

Shenanigans was an upscale joint located on the first floor of the Marriott Hotel. Entering the hotel lobby, we stepped up to the club entrance, paid the cashier, and walked into an expansive, luminous room full of well-dressed, pretty people. Over in the far corner, a live band played in front of a crowded dance floor. And, straight up ahead, right smack-dab in the middle of the room was a large, circular bar. My friends and I made a beeline for it. Matt ordered our beers and collected money for them. Then, once we all received our drinks, it was every man for himself. Sean headed for the dance floor and went from table to table, asking women to dance. Matt wandered off to the other side of the bar to do his shopping, leaving me standing alone and petrified with my back pressed up against the bar as if I was anchored to it. People kept rushing past me like cars on a busy freeway as I looked straight ahead toward the dance floor and the stage directly behind it. The cover band consisted of four skinny white guys wearing flashy suits, shades, and huge afro wigs from the '70s—everything but the blackface. They would've been more tolerable had they not been playing one cheesy song after another. At the moment, it was "Brick House" by the Commodores. I felt a tap on the back of my shoulder and turned around to see a muscly, young bartender glowering at me.

"Hey, buddy... you wanna move away from the bar?" he shouted over the loud music. "People are tryin' to order drinks here!"

"Sorry!" I replied, and walked off.

Carefully weaving through the crowd, I headed to the back of the room and stood against the wall with several other male customers who looked utterly miserable. Now that I was away from the herd and more relaxed, I focused on all the beautiful women walking around in dresses and tight miniskirts, some flashing their big, bubbly smiles at me as they walked past—others turning their noses up at me. The dance floor was farther away now, but I happened to notice Sean and a young woman dancing together. Actually, she did all the dancing—quite animatedly, in fact. He just stood there with his feet glued to the floor, swaying back and forth to the music and barely snapping his fingers. I found it very amusing. I'd never danced a lick, but I knew I could do a better job than that—given half the chance! Matt suddenly ran into me while making his rounds and looked surprised.

"What are you doin' back here?" he shouted.

I shrugged and took a sip from my bottle.

"You're supposed to be helpin' us round up some girls," he said, "so we can take 'em back to Sean's place! Did you get a phone number, at least?"

I hung my head in shame. He laughed and slapped me on the shoulder.

"Just kiddin', bro!" he said. "I shouldn't have left you on your own!"

"Are we goin' to the strip joint after this?" I asked him with pleading eyes.

He firmly shook his head. "That place is no good!" he said. "Nothin' in there but skanks... and all they want is your money! We need to find you a woman!"

I was infuriated at him for thinking that he knew what was best for me.

"You've been tryin' to talk me into goin' there since... forever, it seems!" I shouted. "Now you're tellin' me it's no good?"

"Yeah!" He nodded.

He turned his head and saw the sexy redhead sitting alone at the bar.

"See that?" he said.

"Yeah!" I replied.

"I'm gonna get her number!" he said very confidently. "Watch and learn, Grasshopper!"

He strutted up to the bar, casually sat down next to the young woman, and began talking to her. I marveled at how easy it was for him. I could never do that, just walk up to a complete stranger and strike up a conversation—especially a female stranger. She seemed interested in him at first, both of them smiling and chatting away. But then she sternly shook her head and, concentrating on her lips, I clearly saw her utter the word no. I felt the sting of it right along with him— probably more so, in fact. It was the very reason why I'd never try to sell myself to anyone—that constant fear of rejection. Matt continued talking to her for another minute or two, perhaps pretending to be okay with her answer. But I noticed a slight frown as he got up to leave.

"I'm havin' an off-night for some reason!" he said, walking up to me. "I don't get it! There's a full moon out... and I'm lookin' pretty damn good tonight! I look good, don't I?"

"You look *damn* good!" I assured him.

"Thanks, man!" he said. "So do you! Black's definitely your color!" We just stood there admiring each other's looks 'til it got a little awkward. "Okay... so if it ain't us, it must be them!" he said resolutely. "We need to get the hell out of here and find another bar! The women in here suck!"

"Baby Dolls?" I said excitedly.

"Would you forget about Baby Dolls?" he snapped at me. "That place is beneath you!" He stepped away and motioned for me to come along. "Let's go find Sean!"

Sean was having much better luck with the womenfolk than Matt, so it took some convincing to get him to leave. Yet Matt got his way in the end, and we were off to the next watering hole.

"Where would you like me to take you, sir?" Sean quipped as he drove us out of the parking lot and toward the intersection. "Back to the titty bar?"

"Oh, I don't know!" Matt replied. "I thought we'd try somethin' new."

"What the fuck are you talkin' about?" Sean grumbled. "We've been just about everywhere in this sorry-ass town!"

"I can think of *one* place we haven't been to," Matt said with a sly grin.

"Huh-uh! I told you, we're not doin' that!" Sean vehemently exclaimed. "I'm not takin' you to Club H!"

"The gay bar?" I blurted out in the back seat, shocked that Matt was even suggesting it.

"Yes, B... the gay bar," Matt said, still focusing on Sean. "Why not?"

"'Cause I ain't no fudge-packer!" Sean exclaimed. "That's why not!"

Matt laughed. "Neither am I!" he said. Then he turned around and looked at me. "Are you a fudge-packer, B?"

"No!" I replied.

"Well, we've got that straightened out," Matt said. "None of us are fudge-packers. Good thing there's plenty of straight women in there."

"You don't care about the women," Sean scoffed. "You just wanna get high!"

He mockingly put his finger to the side of his nose and sniffed a couple of times.

"When in Rome," Matt shrugged.

"I thought you was through with that shit!" Sean said.

"Well, maybe it ain't through with *me!*" Matt replied. "Stop bein' a pain in the ass and let's just go check it out."

Sean huffed and made a sharp left turn at the intersection, taking us to Gay Town, I presumed. Matt turned the music up and we soared down the Northwest Expressway listening to U2's "Even Better Than the Real Thing," getting off on Pennsylvania Avenue and making a right turn onto 39th Street.

Just up ahead was an old, rusty metal building with a large neon sign above the entrance that read: "Heaven." People naturally referred to it as *"Club* Heaven" so as not to confuse it with the actual place. And some folks called it "Club H," kind of as an inside joke, since "H" also stood for heroin and that's where all the drugs were. Other gay establishments aligned both sides of the street, including a lesbian bar, a leather bar, and an afterhours dance club. There was even a diner and a hotel somewhere in the vicinity. Collectively, it was known as the gay strip, but we just called it Gay Town in our neck of the woods—or Queer Town, depending on who you were talking to.

The Club H parking lot was completely full, so we parked in an alleyway directly across the street. I could already hear the music pounding as we got out of the vehicle and crossed the street, and I instantly recognized the tune. It was an old disco favorite from the '70s—George McCrae's "Rock Your Baby." Its loud, pulsating beat filled me with excitement before we even reached the metal doors.

We paid the five-dollar cover charge inside the vestibule, got our hands stamped, and stepped through a green curtain, entering a dimly lit room full of shirtless men—with a handful of women and shirted men scattered here and there. I also saw lots of drag queens walking about, many of them huge and manly looking, wearing sparkly dresses and big-hair wigs. There were even a few people in more elaborate costumes, like the club kids in New York City I'd read about somewhere. I spotted a fairy princess, Batman and Robin, and a white rabbit.

I walked very closely behind Sean, shielding myself from all these freaks. Matt was so far up ahead that we suddenly lost him in the crowd. We walked straight up to the bar and ordered a couple of drinks.

"These people are from another planet!" Sean shouted at me over the loud music.

"It's different!" I shouted back.

"Yeah, that's an understatement!" He laughed.

A young shirtless man stepped up beside him and whispered something in his ear.

Sean scowled at him and shouted, "Get the fuck out of here!"

The man walked off with a stunned look on his face. Two minutes later, another young man started coming onto him, and he immediately sent *him* on his way as well.

"That's it!" he said to me angrily. "If one more faggot comes onto me, I'm clockin' his ass!"

Yet, just as he said it, he saw a creepy-looking, older man giving him a lascivious wink at the end of the bar.

"I'm gettin' a really bad feelin' about this place!" he said. "Let's go find Matt and get the hell out of here!"

I turned around and followed him through the crowd. We spotted Matt sitting at a table with a handsome black man. Both were sipping Mai Tais and appeared to be engaged in pleasant conversation.

"What the fuck!" Sean exclaimed, walking up behind Matt and tapping him on the shoulder.

Matt turned around and smiled. "Hey, I want you to meet Tony Orlando!" he said. "Not to be confused with the singer, of course! Don't ask him where Dawn's at!"

He introduced the two men to each other and then introduced me. Tony looked to be in his early to mid-thirties and was well-built, wearing black studded leather pants and a matching vest over his bare chest.

"How you boys doin'?" he said to me and Sean in his suave, Lando Calrissian voice.

"Eh," Sean answered, making a so-so gesture with his hand.

Matt reached over the table and grabbed Tony's muscular bicep. "Look at the arms on this guy!" he exclaimed. "We're gonna start workin' out together!"

"Can I talk to you for a sec?" Sean said to him, deeply appalled.

Matt got up and they stepped away from the table. I huddled up with them as well.

"What the hell are you doin'?" Sean scolded Matt.

"I'm gettin' us some party favors!" Matt exclaimed. "What the hell do you think?"

Sean laughed and shook his head.

"Tony says he can score us some coke later," Matt said, "but right now he's got some really good E! I just took one!"

"What, ecstasy?" Sean exclaimed.

"Yeah, man!" Matt replied. "Me and Miriam did it a few times when I was in Miami. That shit was awesome! Give me fifty bucks and I'll get you hooked up!"

"Are you fuckin' serious?" Sean exclaimed. "There's no way in hell I'm doin' that shit!"

"God, you're such a control freak!" Matt smiled. "Loosen up... live a little! Do you wanna have a hot tub party or not?"

"Yeah! I *do!*" Sean replied.

"Okay," Matt said. "First we get the coke, then we get the girls and take 'em back to *your* place!"

"I don't need coke to get women!" Sean stubbornly replied.

"Not to get 'em, you idiot!" Matt exclaimed. "To keep 'em! Women like coke!"

"They also like pot!" Sean retorted. "Get us a couple of dime bags and let's bail!"

"You can get pot anywhere, dude!" Matt said, and rushed back to the table.

"I need another drink," Sean sighed. We headed for the bar.

We sat there for nearly half an hour, drinking Kamikaze shots with our beers. It didn't improve the taste any. Sean kept giving people the squinty-eye so they wouldn't come on to him anymore. He guzzled down his fifth beer and slammed the empty bottle on the bar.

"That's it!" he said. "Let's go get him!"

We got up and walked over to the table, which was now occupied by three women.

"Where the fuck did they go?" Sean exclaimed.

We turned toward the dance floor less than ten feet away and there they were, dancing with two Asian-American girls in tight miniskirts.

"Un-fuckin-believable," Sean muttered, and shook his head.

"I guess he forgot about us!" I said.

We walked up to the very edge of the crowded floor and just stood there scowling at them 'til Matt suddenly took notice. He immediately ditched his new friends and ran up to greet us, throwing his arms around Sean and giving him a big hug.

"Who the hell are you and what did you do with my friend?" Sean cringed.

"*That's* funny!" Matt laughed, finally pulling himself away from him with a creepy smile on his face. "Don't you just love this guy?" he said to me.

"Sure do!" I replied.

"It'n he funny?"

"Oh, he's a riot!"

"So where's the coke?" Sean asked, looking at Matt very sternly.

"What coke?" Matt replied.

"The coke you were supposed to get for us!" Sean said. "First the coke, then the girls... remember?"

"Oh, yeah!" Matt replied. "Tony's workin' on it!"

"Yeah, I can see that!" Sean scoffed, looking directly at Tony, who was still dancing merrily with the two women.

"He's got plenty of pills on him!" Matt said. "The coke should come later anyway... when you're comin' down from the E!"

"Yeah, well... I ain't no e-tard!" Sean exclaimed. "Come to think of it, I ain't much of a cokehead either—"

"*And* you ain't a fudge-packer!" Matt grinned. "Got it!" He then turned to me and said, "How 'bout you, big guy? You ready to party? It's some really good shit!"

I fearfully shook my head, just as I'd been programmed to do my entire life. Even as far back as preschool, I was taught that drugs were evil and I should always say no to them, no matter what.

"Suit yourself!" Matt said. "It's *your* loss!"

"Matt!" his female dance partner shouted at him. Looking toward the dance floor, he saw them all waving at him.

"Later, gentlemen!" he said to us and rushed back out onto the floor.

We watched the four of them dance to M People's "Excited," Sean with the look of betrayal in his eyes and mine filled with envy, noting the ecstatic look on Matt's face—and all the faces around him. A mirror disco ball twirled above their heads, flashing multi-colored streams of light over their sprightly bodies and making them shine like joyous, heavenly creatures. And to think that I could've been one of those creatures if I'd had a pair of balls—instead of one and a quarter. I looked over my shoulder and noticed a whole other crowd of people staring down at me from the upstairs balcony railing—drag queens, club kids, butch women, bare-chested men, and the like—and suddenly I realized that it wasn't such a bizarre and scary place after all. It suited my sensibilities perfectly, in fact. The room was dark and mysterious; the music was new and exciting and, at times, old and nostalgic... and the people were misfits and eccentrics—not so unlike myself. *Could this be home?* I wondered.

The two Asian-American girls abandoned Matt and Tony about halfway through the song, rushing off to the restroom, it appeared. Matt simply shrugged it off and started dancing with Tony, which was the final nail in the coffin as far as Sean was concerned.

"Let's go!" he said. "I've seen enough!"

I turned and followed him to the exit. The mood was very somber as we drove away. I sat quietly in the passenger seat, afraid to say anything.

"We never should've gone there," Sean muttered. "He just wasn't the same when he came back from Miami. I tried to keep him happy with the booze and the strippers. But, even then, it was Miami this, Miriam that... and he kept goin' on and on about all the gay bars they hung out at... that and the goddamn coke! Fuckin' Miami!"

CHAPTER THREE

I had to choose a side, now that Sean and Matt were at odds with each other... and I chose Matt. I just wasn't a Shenanigans kind of guy. We met at my place on Saturday night, had a few beers, and went to Heaven in my Dodge Neon. I sat at the bar and forced down another beer, trying to get my courage up, while Matt rushed over to the leather bar across the street to look for Tony and hopefully purchase some pills. Part of me wanted to do the stuff and another part didn't. But I promised Matt that I would, and there was no backing out now. He walked up about twenty minutes later, smiling like he had a million dollars in his pocket.

"We're in business, bro!" he said. "Here, take this!"

He scooted in closer and slipped me a pill underneath the bar.

"Did you take yours already?" I asked.

"Yep!" he said.

I popped it in my mouth and quickly washed it down with my drink. Then Matt plopped down on a bar stool and we sat there waiting for the fireworks to go off, frequently exchanging glances.

"Feelin' anything?" Matt asked after ten minutes slowly ticked by.

"No," I replied. "Are you?"

Matt shook his head and sighed. Yet, within the next five minutes, he was up on his feet and bouncing all over the room so fast that I could hardly keep track of him. I got so bored sitting there by myself that I finally stood up and walked over to the dance floor to watch other people having a good time. Sure enough, there was Matt, right in the middle of all the action with Tony by his side, dancing with their two Asian-American friends. They all had the same ridiculous smiles on their faces as they had a couple of nights ago. *Great, everyone's gettin' off but me!* I thought.

Matt looked over at me and shrugged. "Feeling anything?" he mouthed.

I disappointedly shook my head at him. It looked like I was in for a lonely, boring night on the sidelines when, all of a sudden, a huge wave of euphoria swept over me, causing me to smile uncontrollably. Unable to stand still, I walked along the edge of the dance floor, brimming with confidence as I weaved in and out of the crowd. I swiftly made my way to the other end of the room and came to a standstill again just inches away from the floor. The next thing I knew, I was bobbing my head to Lipps Inc.'s "Funkytown." I noticed Matt laughing and gesturing me to come out and join them. I just smiled and shook my head.

"That's okay... I'm doing fine right here," I muttered to myself.

"All right, people... it's Saturday night!" the deep-voiced DJ said into his microphone. "Get your manginas out here and dance, you lazy fuckers!"

I looked into his booth upstairs in the corner of the balcony, but the tiny room was dark and all I could see clearly was a lit cigarette dangling from his lips. He was the invisible man.

"Yeah, that means you, big guy!" he said.

Realizing he was talking to me, I suddenly burst out laughing. Meanwhile, "Absolutely Fabulous," by Pet Shop Boys, began to play, and people stormed the dance floor. It had such an infectious melody and heavenly beat that I started shaking my hips and broke into a little soft-shoe routine. I then placed one foot on the dance floor as if to test the water.

"Oh, what the hell?" I said, jumping completely in and dancing all the way up to Matt and his friends.

Matt was so surprised that he could barely keep dancing while the other three welcomed me with warm smiles. I even surprised myself, having never danced before in my life. And here I was dancing like a seasoned professional with a style all my own—lots of leg action and fancy footwork. I was a cross between Zorba the Greek and Michael Flatley, the Lord of the Dance. Matt and the gang immediately formed a circle around me, since I didn't have a partner. But, being strictly a one-man show, I soon broke free from them and gradually made my way across the entire floor.

"This is it, boys and girls... last song of the night!" the DJ said, followed by boos and moans.

Then everyone clapped and cheered as he played yet another exciting, beat-driven tune, "Dreamer," sung by Livin' Joy. More people stormed the dance floor, filling it to the brim, while I became even more animated and danced like a wild man. It managed to attract the attention of two shirtless gay men, who basically turned me into a human sandwich, one gyrating closely against my tush—the other against my crotch. Other bare-chested and tight-shirted men began dancing around me 'til I found myself completely surrounded. My boundless energy just kept drawing them in like moths to a flame.

"Made it, Ma!" I shouted with joyous laughter as I looked up at the rotating ball and multicolored lights shining down on me. "Top of the world!"

Suddenly, the song ended, the lights were turned up, and everyone stopped dancing.

"Th-th-th-that's all, folks!" the DJ said. "Let's start headin' for the exit!"

I just stood there with a face full of sweat as people began walking off the floor. I couldn't believe that it was already over. I was just getting started! Matt and Tony were talking to their female partners less than ten feet away. Matt noticed me and quickly walked up.

"Feelin' it yet?" he joked.

"Oh, yeah!" I replied, and we both laughed.

"What did I tell ya?" he said. "Huh? Pretty good shit, it'n it?"

"Mmm-hmm," I replied. "I'm startin' to come down a little, though."

"Oh, here's your other one!" he said, reaching into his pocket. He pulled out a little baggie with one pill left in it and handed it to me. "You'll get a better high if you chew it up and swallow it," he said.

I took out the pill, popped it in my mouth, and ate it. It tasted awful, but that seemed like a small price to pay for what would come after.

"I'll have Tony get us some more!" Matt said, waving and whistling him over. "Okay, give me some more money! Fifty bucks should do it! No, better make it seventy-five!"

I swiftly pulled out my wallet and forked over seventy-five dollars, no questions asked.

"Hey, B!" Tony said as he walked up. "Or, should I call you John Travolta?"

"No, I'm Fred Astaire!" I retorted.

"Hey, we need more pills!" Matt said to Tony, and slipped him the money.

"I'll see what I can do," Tony said.

"All right, boys... to the Inferno!" Matt exclaimed, and led us to the exit. "The girls said they'd meet us there."

The Inferno was an old warehouse building right next to Heaven. It was about the only dance club in town that stayed open 'til six in the morning, playing nothing but hardcore techno music. We got in half-price with our Heaven hand stamps and entered a large, nearly pitch-dark room filled with loud, throbbing music. Pushing through the crowd, we stepped up to an oblong dance floor illuminated by flashing strobe lights and kids with glow sticks. I would've felt old and out of place if it wasn't for my ecstasy high, seeing all the sprightly twenty-year-olds dancing before me and gathered all around me.

"I'm gonna see if I can find us something!" Tony said to Matt, and went to look for a drug dealer.

Soon after, the two Asian-American girls came up to Matt and put their arms around him.

"B, these are my girls!" he proudly exclaimed. "Simone and Desiree."

They were twentyish, petite, and very sexy in their short skirts. They could've passed for sisters, but they assured me that they weren't. Desiree asked me if I cared to dance with them. I respectfully declined. So they doubled-up on Matt, grabbing his hands and pulling him onto the dance floor. As I watched them dance, a second huge wave of euphoria hit me like a tsunami and I was right back in the spotlight again, dancing alone to some deep, dark techno-trance song that seemed to go on forever. I once again caught the attention of my fellow dancers with my quirky dance moves. A group of young girls wearing tie-dye t-shirts, glow necklaces, and glow bracelets circled around me and danced with me for a while. Three songs later, a beautiful black woman in a sexy beige dress and gold sandals invaded my space and started dancing with me. But eventually, I was back to dancing alone—and yet I wasn't alone. I felt more of a community spirit out there on the floor than I ever did inside a darkened movie theater. Matt and Tony were dancing with the girls just a few feet away. Tony smiled and winked at me, and Matt gave me the thumbs up.

"All right!" I exclaimed, dancing more excitedly and aggressively.

Eight or nine techno songs later, the dance floor was far less crowded, and Matt and the gang were watching me from the sidelines, only his entourage appeared to have grown slightly. He had Simone and Desiree on one side of him and a new girl on the other, while Tony stood next to an equally handsome white guy. It seemed that my novelty act had finally worn out its welcome. They all looked bored, even a little irritated. Matt tried to wave me off the floor, but I simply closed my eyes and ignored him, determined to dance the night away. When I opened them again, I was surprised to see him standing directly in front of me.

"Man, you're sweatin' your ass off!" he laughed. "Haven't you had enough? It ain't a contest, you know!"

I continued swaying and bobbing my head. "I don't wanna stop!" I said.

"Yeah... I feel you, buddy," he replied. "But you're gonna have to at some point! Come on, we're all goin' to Tony's. He's havin' an after-party!"

"Y'all go ahead!" I said. "I'm stayin' here!"

"We need you to take us!" he replied, which was obviously a ploy to get me off the floor.

"Am I the only one with a car?" I exclaimed.

"Well, Tony doesn't drive," Matt replied, "and I came with you... so, yeah!" As if he were my keeper, he added, "I'm not leavin' you here like this. You need to stop before you have a heart attack!"

I reluctantly came to a standstill and followed him to the sidelines.

"B, we thought you'd go on forever!" Tony said to me. "You're like the Energizer Bunny out there!" He introduced his blond, blue-eyed boyfriend to me. "This is Neil," he said, putting his arm around the man's waist.

Neil nodded at me and managed a smile, but I could tell he wasn't all too pleased to meet me. And he kept leering at Matt like he was the Antichrist. He was a foot taller than Tony, though not as buff, and appeared to be slightly younger—late twenties, maybe—wearing cargo pants with a tank top. Matt introduced me to the new girl next, a blonde-bobbed, saucer-eyed little firecracker named Laura, in her mid-to-late twenties, dressed in a slinky tube top and khakis.

"Hello," I said to her very politely.

"You're all wet, dude!" she grinned.

"All right, people... let's go to Tony's!" Matt shouted, once again leading the way.

I thought everyone would split up once we left the building, yet they all continued to follow Matt, Tony, and me to my car parked across the street. Why they'd choose me as their designated driver was a bit of a mystery, seeing as how I was too fucked-up to stop dancing. We even managed to pick up two more brave souls along the way—friends of Tony's who were looking for a ride and an after-party. *How do you fit nine people into a Dodge Neon?* I wondered, and immediately laughed it off. I felt like I was in my favorite Fellini movie, *La Dolce Vita,* and I was Marcello Mastroianni, leading a band of odd Felliniesque characters to the next party. All I needed was a pair of shades.

"Can you drive?" Matt asked me as we were crossing the street.

"You bet!" I smiled.

"Okay, give me the keys!" he said, holding out his hand.

"Why?"

"Because I don't want to end up in a ditch somewhere! Hand 'em over!"

I removed my car keys from my pocket and threw them at him. He walked up to the car, opened the door, and let everyone pile into the back seat except for Laura and me. We walked over to the passenger side.

"Go ahead and get in, hon!" she said to me as I opened the door. "I'll just sit on your lap!"

I hopped in and she climbed onto my lap, barely managing to pull the door shut.

"I bet we could fit twenty more clowns in here!" Tony quipped in the back seat, now that we were crammed in like sardines.

Matt quickly started up the engine and pulled out of the alley.

"Man, you're soakin' in it!" Laura said, running her fingers through my sweaty hair. "Do you want me to lick the sweat off your face?"

It was by far the sickest and most perverted question I'd ever been asked. Still, I thought it over for a second.

"I'll do it!" she laughed.

Then she leaned in and gave me a quick lick on the cheek. I didn't know what to make of her after that. *Is she one of those chubby chasers I've always heard about?*

"Turn on some fuckin' music!" Simone shouted from the back. Matt reached over and turned on the radio, which was set on a classical station.

"Turn it to somethin' else!" Desiree demanded. Apparently, she wasn't in the mood for Beethoven's Ninth.

"All you're gonna get in this redneck state is a bunch of country crap!" Matt grumbled while he turned the dial from one country station to the next. He finally gave up and left it on an old Johnny Cash tune.

"This is good!" I said.

I reached over to turn it up and we all started singing along to "Ring of Fire."

Tony lived in a little three-bedroom house just a mile away from the club. Matt parked the car in the driveway and everyone crawled out. Three people were already sitting on the couch when we walked in, snorting lines of cocaine off the coffee table.

"That's what *I'm* talkin' about!" Laura exclaimed and went to join them, along with Tony's two gay friends. The rest of us walked through the living room and headed straight for the hall.

"Where are we goin'?" I asked.

"To the bedroom!" Matt declared.

"To do what?"

"What do you think?"

The word "orgy" flashed through my brain in huge red letters, forcing me to a sudden halt in the middle of the hallway. I could just picture them all laughing at me because I couldn't get it up, this only seconds after being sickened by the sight of me naked. It was one horror show I wanted to avoid at all costs. Matt immediately turned around and came back for me.

"We'll be in there in a second!" he said to the others as they entered the last room on the left. He looked at me with a puzzled expression and said, "What's wrong? Don't worry, Tony and Neil are just gonna watch!"

"I think I'll just stay out here," I said, trying not to make a big deal out of it. I was already feeling good, after all.

"Don't get all shy on me now!" Matt said. "You thought dancin' was fun—"

"I'm not ready for that!" I exclaimed.

"What do you mean you're not ready?" he asked with a surprised laugh. "Wait... you mean you've never—"

"I'm saving myself for the right girl!" I explained to him, even though it wasn't entirely true.

"Okay... I can respect that," he said. "I don't necessarily agree with it. What's wrong with a little casual sex now and then? But hey, to each his own. Why don't you come on back? It'll probably be a while before anyone takes their clothes off. We're just gonna snort a little coke, maybe smoke some crack, and see where it takes us."

"Nah, that's okay," I replied. "The pills are all I need."

"Suit yourself," he said. "Oh, that reminds me!" He reached into his pocket, pulled out two pills in a baggie, and handed it to me. "Enjoy!" he said, and rushed off to Tony's bedroom.

I bet he tells everyone I'm a virgin, I thought with a heavy sigh. I took a pill out of the baggie and chewed it up. Suddenly, the door to the first room burst open directly in front of me and a fair-skinned, elfin beauty with green bedroom eyes and short-cropped brown hair stepped out, dressed like a bohemian in a dark-purple cable-knit sweater and bell-bottoms. There was something very unique and refreshing about her appearance. She gave me a strange look and headed for the living room. I decided to follow her. I walked over to a large fish tank against the living room wall and watched her sit down next to Laura. They prepared lines of coke together. Then she borrowed Laura's straw, snorted a couple, and immediately got up to leave. She gave me another strange look as she passed me by, heading straight to her room and shutting the door.

Fifteen minutes went by in a flash. The living room was much more crowded, and I was still standing against the wall, feeling a third wave coming on. The bohemian girl stepped out of her room again and entered the living room.

"Why are you staring?" she said to me as she walked past.

"I didn't know that I was!" I shouted at her back.

She stopped and turned around for a second.

"It's very rude, you know!" she said with a flirty smile.

She walked up to the coffee table, knelt down, and snorted a few lines while chatting with the people on the couch. Then she stood up and headed for the hall.

"You're still staring!" she said to me and kept on walking.

I think I like this girl! I thought, grinning from ear to ear. She left the door open this time, so I sauntered over to the hallway and peeked inside. She was sitting in the middle of a twin-sized bed with four men seated around her, passing a bong around. They looked like modern-day hippies with their long, unkempt hair and scruffy t-shirts. One of them looked up and saw me.

"There's a guy standing in front of your door," he said to the bohemian girl.

She looked at me and laughed. "Oh, don't mind him," she said. "He's harmless... I think! He just has a staring problem."

She studied me curiously. Then the tall, skinny, bearded hippie with horn-rimmed glasses got up and shut the door in my face. I walked back into the living room and found a new spot to stand in on the other side of the fish tank and just a few feet from the front door. The door to Tony's bedroom finally opened and Matt stepped out to check up on me.

"Are you doin' all right?" he asked as he walked up.

I nodded and smiled.

"Why aren't you mingling?" he asked. "At least go sit down for a while... take a load off!" He pointed toward the empty recliner in the far corner of the room.

"I'm fine," I said.

"You want me to go away and leave you alone, don't you?" he smiled.

Smiling back at him, I noticed the bohemian girl step out of her room again.

"Who's that?" I asked, pointing her out to him before she walked into the kitchen.

"That's Barbie... Tony's roommate," he said. He looked at me and laughed. "Don't you be gettin' any ideas, now!" he said. "She's as wild and crazy as they come!"

We watched her come out with two Coronas in each hand and go back into her room.

"If you need anything, you know where to find me," Matt said, and headed back to Tony's room.

The crowd grew even larger by the minute as newcomers kept pouring in. A whole group of revelers congregated directly in front of me, pinning me against the wall, at which point I noticed a black drag queen making eyes at me from across the room. She was one female impersonator I didn't want to mess with, standing over six feet tall with a sinewy build. She could've been a professional athlete for all I knew. *Time to mingle!* I thought, and dashed through the crowd. I sidled up to a middle-aged man and three young women carrying on a conversation in front of the TV. They took one look at me and broke out laughing.

"Are you rollin', sugar pie?" the man asked. He looked just like John Waters with his slight build, thinning hairline, and pencil-thin mustache.

I simply nodded.

"You poor thing!" he said. He pointed toward the empty recliner. "Why don't you go sit down over there and dry off?"

Yet I just kept staring at him.

"You be a good girl and run along now!" he said, gesturing for me to go away. "Shoo!"

I slowly backed off, neither offended nor humiliated. For once, I could be myself without having to worry about what anyone thought of me. If I wanted to look another human being in the eye and smile like an idiot, then so be it. Their laughter and ridicule couldn't hurt me. I was invincible. I walked up to the recliner and sat down as people kept suggesting to me, but only because my communication skills appeared to be lacking in my present state—and mingling was never my strong suit. Laura seemed to be having a blast over on the couch, snorting up line after line while swapping jokes with the two men seated with her. She and I exchanged glances.

"Hey, Benny... have you met Rog and Skippy?" she shouted over Al Green playing on the stereo.

"No!" I shouted back at her.

"They're a hoot!" she exclaimed, and made the introductions.

Both men appeared to be in their late thirties or early forties and were primly dressed in polo shirts and slacks. Roger was a dead ringer for Steve Martin with his handsome yet slightly comical face, slender frame, and prematurely gray hair, while Skippy was more of the George Costanza type—short, stocky, semi-bald, and wearing glasses. Apparently, they were movie buffs. Roger started talking about all the summer movies he and Skip had seen recently, *The Lion King* being his favorite and *Forrest Gump* his least favorite—surprisingly enough. He said the movie was a total piece of crap.

"I loved every single frame of it!" I quickly butted in. "It's gonna win Best Picture!"

"Oh, please!" Roger scoffed.

"And I'm gonna suck Kurt Russell's dick!" Skippy added, causing Laura to laugh hysterically.

"I betcha Tom Hanks wins Best Actor, too!" I said, undaunted.

Roger smiled and shook his head. "Hanks already won his Oscar for playin' a gay man!" he said, using air quotes with the word "gay," as if the actor had done his people a disservice. "They're not gonna give it to him twice in a row!"

The whole conversation felt a bit surreal to me. I vowed to never set foot in a multiplex again and yet here I was, talking movies in a crack house of all places, proving that they'd always be a part of me, no matter what. *Uh-oh, what's this?* I thought, watching the black drag queen sashay up to my chair in her gold sequin gown, white high-heeled pumps, and dark bouffant wig. She stood over me and smiled.

"You showboat!" she said in a deep yet feminine voice.

"Excuse me?" I replied.

"I saw you out there dancin'!" she said. "You were on fire! Do you mind if I sit down for a minute? These shoes are killin' me!"

"Not at all!" I said, and started to get up.

"Stay seated!" she demanded. "We can share... unless you're afraid I'll bite!"

"No, jump on in here!" I said, pretending to be okay with it.

I scooted over as far as I could and she tried to squeeze in beside me, her large body overlapping mine and crushing my leg.

"Are you gonna catch my act tonight?" she asked.

"Huh?" I replied.

"The floor show, silly!" she said, playfully bopping me on the head.

"Oh, that!" I exclaimed, even though I had no idea what she was talking about.

"We're either lip-syncin' to 'Baby Love,'" she said, "or 'Where Did Our Love Go?' We haven't decided."

"So you're a Supreme," I said.

"Mmm-hmm," she replied.

"Which one?"

"Which one do you think?"

"Diana Ross?"

"Of course!" she said. "My name's Porsche, by the way." She extended her hand and I shook it.

"I thought you were Diana," I said, confused.

"That's just a character I play," she said. "One of many. I've been Sarah Vaughan, Nina Simone, and even Billie Holiday. Right now, I'm into Motown. And what shall I call you?" she asked.

"You can call me Benjamin... Ben, actually," I replied.

"Okay, Benjamin Ben Actually," she said. "So are you comin' tonight, or not?"

"Yeah, I'll be there!" I replied, flat-out lying to her. "Shouldn't you be restin' up for it?"

"Honey, I've got enough booze and crank in my system to keep me up for days!" she said. She raised her hands in the air and added, "I'm a twenty-four-hour party girl! Haven't you heard?"

She then proceeded to tell me her life story—growing up as an only child in Bugtussle, Oklahoma; her love for jazz, blues, and Motown music, which began at an early age; her strained relationship with her parents, who were unable to cope with her being different; being bullied and made fun of at school.... It was a story I knew all too well. I kept nodding at her and pretending to be interested. But the whole time I was thinking, *I've got a two-hundred-and-twenty-pound drag queen sitting on my leg,* and *How did it all come to this?*

Barbie looked at us and laughed to herself when she stepped back into the room. *Damn! Now she thinks I'm gay!* I thought, watching her kneel in front of the coffee table and snort some more lines.

"I don't know," Porsche continued. "Sometimes I feel like a total fraud. Most of my friends either *had* sex changes or they're savin' up for one. But I'm still undecided. Sure, there's times when I feel like cuttin' the damn thing off, but it comes in pretty handy when you're swingin' both ways. I love to pleasure a woman almost as much as I enjoy being pleasured by a man. You see what I'm sayin'?"

This gal's certifiable! I thought as I continued nodding at her like a bobblehead doll. *Is it just me, or is she deliberately tryin' to make me nauseous? She's probably gettin' her rocks off watchin' me squirm! I've gotta get out of this chair somehow! I look fuckin' ridiculous sittin' here! Not only that, she's messin' with my high... talkin' about her creepy sex life and cuttin' her dick off! Nobody wants to hear that shit at a fuckin' party!* Thank God, Neil stepped in to save the day.

"Hey, Porsche... Tony needs you in the bedroom!" he shouted across the room and rushed back into the hall.

"Gotta go now, sugar!" she said, playfully mussing my hair and lifting herself out of the chair. "Duty calls!"

That must be some orgy they're havin' back there! I thought as I watched her leave. *What the hell do they need a drag queen for?*

Barbie gave me a quick glance before she stood up and left the room. Since there was no way of meeting *her,* I decided to enjoy the rest of my high in total solitude. I got up and slowly made my way to the front door, walking out as people were walking in. Suddenly, it was very quiet and peaceful, and the warm night air felt good against my skin. The driveway and both sides of the street were full of cars, I noticed, as I stepped into the middle of the yard. Matt, Tony, Porsche, and Barbie stepped out an hour or so later and caught me lying in the grass, contentedly staring into space. They all huddled around me and looked down at me with curious faces.

"What the hell are you doin' down there?" Matt asked. "Are you okay?"

"Yeah, I'm fine," I said.

"You had us worried there for a second, B," Tony grinned. "We thought you were dead."

"Nope, just chillin'... gazing up at the stars," I replied. "There's so many!"

Tony and Barbie looked at each other and laughed.

"B, have you met Barbie?" Tony asked.

"I don't believe I've had the pleasure," I said, gazing up into her green eyes. "How you doin'?"

"Not as good as you, apparently," she quipped.

"Why don't you get up from there and come inside before the neighbors see you?" Matt snapped at me.

"Nah, I think I'll just lay here for a while," I said.

"You sure, B?" Tony asked.

"Yeah."

"Okay, whatever," Matt sighed. "But you better keep your knees up, so no one will mistake you for a corpse!"

"Roger that," I replied, though I continued to lie flat as they started to walk off.

"Hey, Matt!" I exclaimed.

He stopped and turned back around. "What?"

"I don't want this feeling to ever go away!" I said. "Take everything... my money, credit cards, the big screen TV... and bring us back a shitload of pills, enough to last us through the rest of the year!"

"We'd just end up doin' 'em all in one night!" he said.

"Yeah, but what a night!" I grinned.

CHAPTER FOUR

I woke up on Tony's living room carpet, having absolutely no idea how I got there. The sun was shining through the window, and I could hear people talking in another room. I got up and went to investigate. Stepping into the kitchen, I found Matt sitting at the bar with Porsche, Simone, and Desiree. Porsche was snorting cocaine off a plate.

"Well, good morning, sunshine!" she said to me as I stood in the entrance. "Would you care for a line? It's the breakfast of champions!"

"No, thanks," I said, and looked at Matt. "Are you about ready?" I asked. "I need to get home, so I can write."

"All right, girls... you heard the man," he said to Simone and Desiree, sitting on either side of him. "Time to hit the road!"

We stepped out of the house moments later, jumped into the car and took off, me behind the wheel and Matt keeping the girls entertained in the back seat. I felt like I was running a taxi service. I dropped his playmates off next to their little yellow Corvette sitting alone in the Club H parking lot. Then Matt hopped up front and slumped down in the seat as I drove off.

"So what's Barbie's story?" I asked.

"She works at the T-Bone with Tony," he said, sounding annoyed by the question.

"They're just friends?" I asked.

"Tony's one hundred percent gay," Matt said. "So I'd say yeah... just friends."

"Why is she livin' with him?" I persisted.

"Tony was lookin' for a roommate, she needed a place to stay... end of story." He sighed. "Oh, wait... there's something else you should probably know." He suddenly raised up, got close to my ear, and cupped his hands around his mouth as if speaking through a bullhorn. "She's a fag hag!" he exclaimed. "She hangs out with gay guys because she can't handle a real man!"

I gave him a disapproving glance as he slumped back down in the seat.

"I'd say that's a *huge* red flag... wouldn't you?" he laughed. "I wouldn't get too attached to these people," he said. "All they do is party. That's about all they're good for, and it's the only reason we're hangin' out with 'em. We're just havin' fun... right?"

"Yeah, sure," I replied.

I drove into the parking lot and parked in front of my apartment building.

"I need to ask you a favor," Matt said before we got out.

"What?" I hesitantly replied.

"Let me crash here for a while."

"Man, I don't know—"

"I don't wanna go home just yet!" he swiftly butted in. "The bitch'll chew my ass off for stayin' out all night!"

"You're talkin' about your mom, right?" I said, taken aback.

"Yeah!" he replied. "She's a real ballbuster, that one! And I'm too tired to put up with her shit right now! Just a couple hours on your couch... that's all I'm askin'!"

I looked down with a heavy sigh, disturbed at the very thought of having my Fortress of Solitude disrupted.

"You're welcome to come in and talk or whatever," I said amicably. "But I can't afford any distractions once I start writ—"

"I'll be very quiet, I promise! You won't even know I'm there."

"Like I said, you're welcome to come in for a little—"

"Nah... forget it, Shakespeare!" he sighed. "I wouldn't want to stand between you and your masterpiece. The bitch gives me any trouble, I'll just punch her in the face."

I looked at him, confounded.

"Just kiddin'!" he laughed. "It'll probably be the other way around."

We got out of the car and he walked over to his Harley sitting a couple of spaces down. He peeled off his gray sports jacket and stuffed it into the saddlebag. Then he pulled out his stars and stripes helmet and put it on. I headed upstairs as he roared out of the parking lot, feeling like a heel for turning him away. But there was a time for work and a time for play and never the twain shall meet.

I managed to write about a page and a half that afternoon before the phone rang. I got up from my desk and walked over to the nightstand to grab it.

"Hello?" I answered.

"Hey, what's up?" Matt said.

I could hear his mother yelling at him in the background.

"Just a minute," he said, and yelled back at her in a muffled voice, "Would you shut the fuck up? I'm tryin' to talk! Okay, I'm back. You there?"

"Yeah," I answered.

"I really need to get out of this shithole," he said. "We should go out again tonight."

"Gee, I don't know," I muttered. "Tomorrow's a workday—"

"We'll go easy this time," he said. "Have a few drinks, talk to some girls... no pills."

I hesitated to give him an answer.

"Barbie will be there," he said. "Tony says she never misses a floor show."

"Okay, let's do it!" I said.

I churned out six more pages while consuming three-quarters of a large Domino's pizza, half a two-liter bottle of Pepsi, an entire bag of Little Debbie mini powdered donuts, and a half-gallon of milk. Then I shut down for the night, put on a white, long-sleeve shirt and a pair of blue jeans, and went to pick up Matt at his mother's place. They lived in a small, weather-beaten house in an old, run-down neighborhood. *What a dump!* I thought as I gazed at it for the first time, feeling a little more sympathetic toward ol' Matty Matt. He also decided to dress down for the evening, walking out to the car in a black, short-sleeve muscle shirt and ripped jeans.

The floor show was already in progress when we arrived at the club. Every Sunday night at nine o'clock the drag queens took over the dance floor, which was now a stage, and impersonated famous female singers and movie stars—most of them dead and gone. But there was usually a Barbara Streisand, Liza Minelli, Celine Dion, or Madonna in the bunch. Club H was famous for their floor shows. They attracted customers from all over the state and beyond—gay and straight people alike. It was like a circus for grown-ups! We stepped up to the bar and ordered Long Island Iced Teas, just to try something different, and then walked over to the enormous crowd standing in front of the dance floor—or stage, rather. The room was dark, and Marilyn Monroe stood in the spotlight, singing "Diamonds Are a Girl's Best Friend" while people whistled at her and threw roses on the stage. I found it all very fascinating. Matt let out a big yawn.

"I don't know about you," he said, "but I'm feelin' a bit tired! Couldn't get much sleep with the bitch screamin' at me all day. I need to put a padlock on that basement door."

"You're the only person I know who refers to his own mother as a bitch," I felt compelled to point out to him.

"If the shoe fits!" He shrugged. He yawned again. "Yep... I'm definitely gonna need a little pick-me-up. I think I'll mosey over to Saddle Tramps for a minute, see if I can find Tony's dealer!"

"Which one's Saddle Tramps again?" I asked.

"The leather bar," he replied. "You wouldn't like it. Only hardcore gays go in there."

"Is it like the one in that Al Pacino movie?" I asked curiously. "I forgot the name of it. He plays an undercover cop."

"I don't know what you're talkin' about," he said, "but don't mention five-0 in this place! It makes people nervous! Do you want me to get you somethin' or not?"

"No!" I answered sharply. "And you shouldn't do it either. Dad's liable to fire your ass if you miss any more days!"

"Don't worry about it!" he snapped. "I'm just gonna do one!"

I sighed and reached into my pants pocket. "Might as well get me one too," I said, pulling out my wallet and handing him twenty-five bucks.

"Be right back," he said, and quickly took off.

I watched as a Marlene Dietrich look-alike took the stage and began lip-syncing to "Lili Marlene." Out of the corner of my eye, I noticed someone walk up beside me and could feel him staring at me very intently. *Who is this asshole?* I thought, finally turning my head and looking the fucker straight in the eye. I was shocked to see that it was Barbie smiling at me in a brown floppy hat, fringe poncho, and knee-high boots. She laughed as soon as our eyes met. And that, too, was a surprise, for it was a big, hearty laugh—almost a cackle, but an endearing and infectious one.

"It took you long enough!" she said. "Is this your first floor show?"

"Yeah!" I replied.

"I take it then that you're not gay."

"Nope, I like women," I replied. "I mean, I *really, really* like women."

"I believe you!" she laughed.

"How 'bout you?" I asked.

"You mean, do I like women?"

We both laughed.

"Hate 'em," she answered. "Most men, too."

"So you're a misanthrope," I said.

"Not yet," she replied. "Gettin' there, though. Give me a couple more years."

"How old *are* you?" I asked.

"Twenty-one. How old are *you?*"

"Thirty."

"You're kidding!" she said, looking surprised. "I figured you were *a lot* younger!"

"I still get ID'd," I joked. "Is that a problem?"

"What, that you're old?" she said. "It's okay with me if it's okay with you. Just seems a little odd that you're still doin' this. Shouldn't you be at home with the wife and kids?"

"Haven't got to that point yet." I shrugged. "I guess I'm a late bloomer. I've just now discovered X and partyin' 'til three."

She studied me very closely and said, "You're a Scorpio, aren't you?"

"How did you know?" I replied.

"You look like one!"

"How do Scorpios look?"

"Odd," she said, "but kinda sexy... and a little mysterious. They can also be extremely possessive... and obsessive!"

"What sign are *you?*" I asked.

"Aries," she replied. "We're very incompatible, you and me... like fire and ice."

"You don't really believe in that stuff, do you?" I asked.

She nodded. "I also read tarot cards... and dabble in witchcraft!"

"Really?" I said, taken aback.

She laughed. "Don't worry, I'm a good witch!" She started to walk away. "I've gotta meet some people upstairs," she said. "Tony's havin' an after-party later if you want to come!"

"I'll be there!" I said very enthusiastically and watched her leave.

Marlene Dietrich began singing "Falling in Love Again" as I turned back around. She walked off to enormous applause afterward and then Ethel Merman came bouncing onto the stage, singing "Anything Goes." She followed with "There's No Business Like Show Business" and everyone clapped and sang along. I'd never seen anything quite like it. *Yep, definitely a community spirit!* I thought, feeling completely at home.

Things really took a turn for the bizarre when Porsche and her fellow Supremes finally hit the stage in their matching peach feather gowns and began lip-syncing to "Baby Love." *Holy shit!* I thought, appalled yet unable to look away. Porsche, AKA Diana Ross, wasn't quite as tall as the other two but was a little more attractive. And they all looked like they could play for the NBA. They looked like the Supremes from another planet or the Bizarro World—to give DC Comics a shout-out. Matt suddenly returned, stepping up close beside me and surreptitiously handing me a pill. I immediately popped it in my mouth and washed it down with my Long Island Iced Tea.

"What the hell are we watchin'?" Matt asked in horror as he looked toward the stage.

I simply shrugged. The Bizarro Supremes did their one song and walked off to uproarious applause, cheers, and whistles. Then Whitney Houston came out to close the show with "I Will Always Love You," after which the disco ball was lit up and people swarmed the dance floor.

"Okay, boys and girls... time to put on your dancin' shoes!" said the omnipotent DJ.

I remained on the sidelines and finished my drink while Matt headed over to the bar. Porsche and the other two Supremes stepped up to me from behind, catching me completely off guard.

"You made it!" Porsche said with an excited grin.

"I said I would, didn't I?" I replied.

"Well, what did you think?" she asked.

"I loved it!" I said. "You were great!"

"You're a doll!" she said as she leaned in and gave me a hug.

She then introduced me to Mo'Nique, AKA Mary Wilson, and Kaneesha, AKA Florence Ballard, and persuaded me to join them on the dance floor, just as my pill was kicking in. We walked onto the crowded floor and started dancing to Hot Chocolate's "You Sexy Thing," Porsche paired up with Mo'Nique and me with Kaneesha. At six foot and damn near three hundred pounds, I wasn't exactly what you'd call little. But all three transvestites towered over me like I was a gerbil. I noticed Matt standing in front of the dance floor with a beer in his hand, giving me a strange look and shrugging his shoulders.

"What the fuck?" he exclaimed, and I had no trouble reading his lips.

I shrugged back at him and kept on dancing. After Hot Chocolate, the DJ began playing "In and Out of Love" by the real Supremes.

"This one's for you, ladies!" he said.

Porsche looked up into his dark booth and blew him a kiss. About halfway through the song, Matt came rushing onto the floor and grabbed my arm, bringing me to a stop. I could tell by the crazy look in his eyes that he was rolling his ass off, as was I.

"Come on, I need to talk to you!" he said, and tried to pull me away.

"That's very rude, Matt!" Porsche scolded him.

"I'll bring him right back!" he assured her, and escorted me off the floor.

"What the hell do you think you're doin'?" he snapped at me.

"Dancin'!" I replied. "What are *you* doin'?"

"Savin' your ass!" he said. "You've gotta be careful on this shit! You don't want people to get the wrong idea. Only dance with real women from now on!"

"There ain't a real woman in this place!" I scoffed. "You said so yourself! All you're gonna find in *here* are bull dykes, switch-hitters, and fag hags!"

Matt nodded toward a group of girls sitting at one of the tables behind us. We exchanged glances with them, and they all laughed. Matt looked at me very sternly and said, "Let's go!"

"Why not?" I replied, pretending to be Warren Oates to his William Holden in *The Wild Bunch.*

It was at least one movie Matt was familiar with. We turned and slowly walked up to the table shoulder to shoulder like a pair of aging gunslingers.

"Let me do the talkin'," Matt said, and I gave him a stern nod.

The four young women were noticeably flustered as we suddenly stood before them.

"You gals mind if we join you?" Matt said.

"I guess it's okay!" said the tanned, dark-haired girl as her friends looked at each other and giggled.

Grabbing a couple of chairs from another table, Matt squeezed in between the dark-haired girl and a busty blonde, both wearing jeans and halter tops, while I sat next to a cute, chubby girl in a black jumpsuit and another sexily dressed blonde. They were University of Oklahoma students who liked coming into town every now and then to see "the freak show," as Cindy, the tanned, dark-haired girl, referred to it.

I sat quietly and listened to Matt go on and on about his love for Michael Jordan, ice-cold beer, Florida beaches, and water sports—all of which was seriously interfering with my high. Fortunately, there was a sudden lull in his monologue, allowing me to turn to the cute, chubby girl, Melanie, and ask her if she wanted to dance.

"Sure!" she replied, and we rushed off to the dance floor together.

Once they saw me in action, the other three girls abandoned Matt as well and lined up directly behind Melanie to get a piece of me, taking me on one at a time and then quadruple-teaming me. Matt finally decided to join in and he and I managed to keep them all thoroughly entertained with our crazy dance moves. All of a sudden, we were Laurel and Hardy as we danced to "Cotton Eye Joe" by Rednex, instinctively grabbing each other's hand, doing a gentle back kick, and swinging around. Then I grabbed his other hand, back kicked with the other leg, and swung around in the opposite direction. It left the girls in stitches. Glancing toward the upstairs balcony, I saw Barbie staring down at me with an amused look on her face, which prompted me to dance even more crazily, my legs flying back and forth and all over the place like I was one of those Ukrainian Cossack dancers. Cindy put my skills to the test by placing her margarita directly under my bouncing feet. Much to everyone's amazement, including mine, my shoes never touched the glass and not a single drop was spilt. Sadly, it all came to an abrupt end just moments later. The music ceased, the lights came on, and everyone stood still, sighs and moans abounding.

"And that's the name of that tune!" the DJ said. "Go home, you crazy kids! Drive safe!"

"You're so adorable... like a big ol' teddy bear!" Melanie said to me as she reached up and gently squeezed my cheeks. "You're really sweatin' though. Do you feel overheated?"

"No," I replied, suddenly noticing Porsche and her fellow queens glaring at her just a few feet away.

"There's an after-party at Tony's house!" Matt shouted at the entire group. "Who's all comin'?"

"I am!" Cindy immediately exclaimed.

"Are you goin'?" I asked Melanie.

"Who's Tony?" she asked.

"Just some gay guy Matt knows," I replied.

"Am I goin' to a gay after-party?" she scoffed, looking at me as if I was insane. "I think not. This is as far as I go, I'm afraid."

I just smiled at her perplexedly.

"I'll see you around, sweetie," she said, and bopped me on the tip of my nose with her finger.

She walked up to her friends standing with Matt and started arguing with Cindy and the busty blonde—Megan, I think.

"Are you nuts?" she said to them. "You hardly know these guys! And I don't know a *damn* thing about this Tony character. How are you gonna get home?"

"I'm sure *they'll* take us!" Cindy said.

"We'll take 'em!" Matt concurred.

Melanie gave him a long, hard stare and then looked over at me with skeptical, mistrusting eyes. I guess I wasn't the adorable teddy bear anymore.

"Why don't you come with us?" Megan implored her. "It'll be fun!"

"No, thanks!" Melanie smirked. "I just hope you two know what you're doin'!"

She and the other blonde stormed off the dance floor together and headed for the exit. Suddenly remembering Barbie, I looked up to see if she was still there. The balcony was empty, and people were walking toward the stairs. I rushed over to the spiral staircase next to the exit and waited for her to come down but it was already too late, it appeared. I'd let her slip past me.

"Let's go, B!" Matt shouted as he and the girls stepped up to the crowd and slowly made their way to the green curtain. "You're holdin' up the show!"

"Yeah, I'm comin'!" I shouted back and went to join them.

Arriving at Tony's house, Matt barged through the front door without knocking and led Cindy and Megan to the back bedroom. I stayed in the living room and hid in my favorite spot next to the fish tank, since the room was already half-full and I was starting to come down a little. Over a dozen people stood around talking, and several couch potatoes were snorting lines off the coffee table like the night before. Barbie stepped out of her room, minus the hat, and walked right up to me.

"Twenty minutes ago you were hoggin' the dance floor," she remarked, "and now here you are lurking in the shadows! What gives?"

"I'm not lurking," I said, pretending to be offended. "Nor was I hogging."

She suddenly burst out laughing with that big, crazy cackle of hers. "I'm just fuckin' with you, man! You're okay!" She studied me very carefully and then nodded assuredly. "*You're* okay."

She immediately turned around, walked over to the coffee table, and knelt down in front of it, picking up a razor and preparing herself five or six lines. She grabbed a straw and snorted them up her nose in three seconds flat. Then she got up and left.

"You better not be standin' there when I come back!" she warned me before heading into the hall.

I was deeply frustrated as I watched her enter her bedroom and shut the door. *Enough of the meet cute already!* I thought. *How do I get to first base with this girl?*

Tony showed up late to his own party, walking through the front door with two intimidating-looking men he must've picked up at Saddle Tramps, both ruggedly handsome, extremely muscular, and dressed in black leather, like Tony. I noticed the large bag of coke in Tony's right hand—at least five ounces worth.

"B, where's Matt?" he asked me.

I pointed toward his bedroom.

"He got a girl with him?" he asked.

"Two, actually!" I replied.

"Figures," he smirked, and rushed down the hall while the other two headed for the coffee table.

Tony walked into his room and shut the door. Matt stepped out a few minutes later to check up on me.

"Tony's got plenty of pills on him if you need any more," he said. "Maybe you can offer Barbie one!"

I swiftly pulled out my wallet and thumbed through a slew of twenties. "Yeah, give me a couple."

"Could you get me one too?" he said.

I looked at him disapprovingly.

"What?" He shrugged. "You still owe me for that lap dance, remember? Besides, you make more money than *I* do... Mr. Twenty Bucks an Hour!"

"Eighteen fifty!" I corrected him, and begrudgingly forked over seventy-five bucks.

"I'll be right back!" he said, and walked off.

He returned with a little baggie and handed it to me.

"We're both gonna get laid tonight... I can feel it!" he said with a wink and took off again.

All right! I thought, forgetting that I was incapable of getting laid. That was an obstacle I'd have to deal with later. Right now, I needed to find a way to get into Barbie's bedroom. Just as I chewed up a pill, Porsche, Mo'Nique, and Kaneesha stepped through the front door.

"The Supremes, ladies and gentlemen!" a man shouted from the couch while a few people clapped and cheered.

"Please, no applause!" Porsche said. "You're makin' me all wet!"

"Woo!" the same man shouted.

"Yeah, baby!" shouted another.

"I meant with tears!" Porsche exclaimed. "Jeez, get your minds out of the gutter, you horndogs!"

She spotted me right away and walked up.

"Fancy meeting *you* here!" she said. "What happened to your lady friends?"

"They weren't my friends," I replied, at which point Cindy and Megan came bursting out of Tony's room, hopping mad.

"Speak of the devils!" Porsche sneered as they rushed up to me.

"What's up with your friend?" Cindy exclaimed.

"Huh?" I replied.

"He and that black guy locked themselves in the bathroom and they won't come out!" she said. "What the hell are they doin' in there?"

"It's a gay after-party, Cindy!" Megan scoffed. "What do you think they're doin'?"

They traded grimaces.

"We should've known better than to come here," Megan said.

"Is he gay?" Cindy asked me very sharply.

"Matt?" I replied. "Hell, no! At least I don't think so!"

"Well, *somethin's* goin' on!" Cindy said. "If they're just doin' coke, you'd think they'd let us come in and join 'em!" She paused for a moment and then asked, "Can you take us home? You'll have to drive all the way out to Norman."

"Man, I'm rollin' really hard right now!" I lied. "Can you wait for a little bit?"

"Never mind!" she huffed. "We'll call a cab. Where's the phone?"

"It's in there, hon!" Porsche sneered, and pointed to the kitchen and dining room entrance directly behind them.

"Come on, Meg," Cindy said. "This place is a total nightmare!"

"So long, cracker-bitches!" Porsche taunted, and waved at them as they stormed off to the kitchen. "Go back from whence you came!" She looked at me and shook her head. "I thought they'd never leave!"

"Porsche, come and sing for us!" someone shouted.

She smiled at me and rolled her eyes. "No rest for the wicked!" she said. She turned and walked over to Mo'Nique and Kaneesha, standing in the middle of the crowd. "Okay, what do you sons of bitches want to hear?" she exclaimed.

I turned my attention to the open door at the end of the hall, meanwhile, and slowly began to walk toward it filled with dread, yet strangely curious.

"Matt?" I said very meekly as I stepped through the doorway.

The room was empty, but I could hear voices in the adjoining bathroom over by the king size bed. I tiptoed toward it. The door opened very slightly, and I froze.

"I'll be out in a minute, girls!" Matt shouted through the crack. "Girls?"

"Shut the damn door and get back over here!" Tony said from within.

Matt promptly shut and locked the door. I resumed moving toward it. I could hear a lot of sniffing going on.

Then Tony said in a muffled voice, "Why don't you leave that shit alone for a minute?"

"I'm done," or "Okay," Matt said. I couldn't quite make it out.

"On your knees, bitch!" Tony exclaimed, and they both giggled.

The rest of their conversation was unintelligible 'til I stepped up to the door and put my ear to it.

"Bite down on it," I heard Tony say.

"I don't wanna hurt you," Matt said.

"Nah, it feels good," Tony said. "It hurts so good."

I heard more giggling as I stood there completely horrified. *This can't be!* I thought. *Matt loves strippers and orgies... and dancin' with two women at the same time! But I suppose he COULD be bisexual. No way! He must be doin' it for the drugs. Yeah, that's it! He's a coke whore!* I found it a little startling and utterly absurd that I preferred Matt the Coke Whore over Matt the Flaming Homosexual or even Matt Who Swings Both Ways. But it couldn't be helped. I quietly backed away from the door and let the two men finish their business.

The Bizarro Supremes were singing "You Keep Me Hangin' On" when I walked back into the living room— and they actually weren't half bad. *Why bother with the lip-syncing?* I wondered. I noticed Laura, the little blonde spitfire who licked my face, talking to a group of people in front of the window. She suddenly noticed me as well.

"Benny, baby!" she exclaimed. Her speech was slurred and she could barely keep her eyes open. "Come over here and give me a hug, you sexy thang!"

I reluctantly walked up to her and we hugged.

"What did you take?" I asked as we were still embraced.

"Just a couple of valiums," she replied. "Why? What did *you* take?"

"Ecstasy," I said.

"Good!" she said. "That means you're ready for me! Come over here and sit down!"

She grabbed my hand and dragged me toward the recliner, which was inconveniently empty once again.

"Not now, Laura!" I protested.

"Nope, shut it!" she exclaimed, placing her index finger over my lips. "You sat there with a drag queen in your lap for twenty whole minutes! Now you can sit there with me! And, I assure you, I am all woman!" We stepped up to the chair and she let go of me. "Sit down, big boy, and I'll tell your fortune!" she said, doing a very poor Mae West impression.

I sat down and then she hopped into my lap and proceeded to muss up my hair. I winced and scowled at her, which only made her laugh.

"Here, maybe this will bring me luck!" she said, and began rubbing my soft belly as if I was the almighty Buddha himself.

It was even more embarrassing and humiliating than the night before, which didn't seem possible. I was really beginning to hate that chair! Barbie came back into the room and knelt down in front of the coffee table to get her hourly fix. *It's now or never!* I thought as I watched her get back on her feet, quickly sliding out from under Laura and letting her fall to the cushion.

"Hey!" she shouted, and immediately laughed it off.

I caught up with Barbie before she made it to the hallway. "Barbie!" I exclaimed.

She stopped and turned around to face me. I took the baggie out of my lapel pocket, removed the remaining pill from it, and showed it to her.

"I got you one!" I said.

She looked at me like I was a complete imbecile and laughed. I was deeply humiliated for about a second. But then she showed me mercy by curbing her laughter and stepping in closer to accept my little gift. She snatched the pill out of my fingertips and took me by the other hand, leading me to her bedroom and opening the door. There was only one hippie sitting on her bed this time—the tall, lanky, bearded fellow with the horn-rimmed spectacles.

"Can you leave us alone for a while?" she said to him as we stepped inside.

He got up and walked out of the room without saying a word. She shut the door, walked over to her bed, and grabbed a wine glass from the nightstand.

"Just so you know... it doesn't make me horny," she said, holding the pill to her mouth. "It just makes me very talkative."

"I can't wait," I replied.

I took in my surroundings as she swallowed the pill and washed it down with her drink. There were lit candles all over the room—one on the nightstand, two on the writing table next to her window, and three on top of her dresser. The air reeked of burning wax and marijuana smoke. A black crucifix hung directly above her bed alongside a creepy black-and-white poster of Bela Lugosi, leering down at us in full Dracula attire. And on the wall directly across from him was a young Marlon Brando, looking all muscly and sweaty as Stanley Kowalski.

"You love Brando, too!" I said.

"Mmm-hmm!" she replied and nodded enthusiastically as she sat on the edge of the bed.

I walked up and sat down beside her. I was tempted to ask her why she had both Jesus Christ and Dracula hanging over her bed but decided to leave it alone.

"Can I ask you a question?" she said.

"Ask me anything," I replied.

"Why do you hang out with Matt?"

I shrugged and said, "We're not that close, really. He's just somebody I work with. Why?"

"It's just that you don't seem anything like him," she said. "Did he tell you that he came onto me the other night?"

"He did?" I replied. "I hope you told him to go fuck himself."

"Somethin' like that." She laughed. "I can't stand his type. He's a player. Only, I'm not sure which sex he prefers. Neither does he, I'd imagine." She took another sip of her drink. "What kind of work do you do?" she asked.

"Construction worker by day, writer by night," I said.

"Oh? What do you write?"

"Right now, I'm workin' on a screenplay."

"I'm a writer, too!" she said.

"Really?" I replied, only a little surprised.

"Well, I write poetry anyway," she said. "When I'm not tendin' bar at the T-Bone."

"A bartender, huh?" I said, very surprised.

"For now," she replied. "Since I can't make a nickel off my poems."

"Can I read them?" I asked.

She thought about it for a second. Then she got up, walked over to the writing table, and came back with a spiral notebook. She handed it to me before she sat back down. I opened it and began thumbing through it.

"Wow, there must be over a hundred poems in here!" I said, seeing almost every page filled with ink.

"A hundred and nineteen," she said.

She snatched the notebook out of my hands, flipped back to the first poem, and read it to me. Thematically, it was about an acid trip gone awry. Yet I was very impressed and even a little intimidated by her extensive vocabulary and strong command of the English language.

"Keep goin'!" I urged her after she was finished.

"Okay!" she said with a giddy smile.

She scooted to the middle of the bed to make herself more comfortable, crossed her legs lotus-style, turned the page, and read on. I scooted further onto the bed as well, lying down on my side and gazing up at her with my head resting on my hand. Her poems were dark and depressing, dealing with themes of loneliness, isolation, and death. But I was so enchanted by the sound of her voice that I hardly even noticed. After reading about a dozen of her finest compositions to me, she closed the notebook and set it down next to her.

"That's enough of that!" she said.

She reached over to the nightstand, grabbed a twenty-four-ounce Whitman's Sampler Assorted Chocolates box, and placed it in her lap. She then opened it to reveal a large bag of finely chopped cannabis, a stack of rolling papers, and a lighter.

"Uh-oh, what's this?" I joked as I watched her pour some grass into a paper and roll herself a joint.

"Have you ever smoked weed before?" she asked.

I shook my head.

"Then you're in for a treat!" she said.

"Won't it ruin your ecstasy high?" I fretted.

"I don't know," she shrugged. She looked at me sideways and added, "If you're tryin' to get in my pants, this is clearly the way to go!" Then she laughed at me, seeing that I was totally mortified. "Either this or coke," she said. "The latter makes my clit feel all tingly."

She laughed even harder, seeming to take great pleasure in making me blush. Sealing the joint with a lick of her tongue, she promptly stuck it between her lips, lit it up, and smoked it. She handed it over to me, and I took my very first puff of the whacky tobacky with only minimal coughing. It didn't do much for me euphoria-wise, since I was already high on X. But putting something in my mouth that just came out of hers was somewhat pleasurable and exciting. Before long, we were lying flat on our backs and passing the doobie back and forth like Cheech and Chong.

She became a real chatterbox, as promised. She talked about growing up in a trailer house with her boozing, pot-smoking Irish-American parents, Dermot and Keara Delaney, and her two younger siblings. She talked about being molested at age eleven by her boozing, perverted uncle, who happened to live next door, and her father becoming so furious once he caught wind of it that he attempted to castrate his brother with a shotgun—only to miss and blow his hand off instead. And she talked about leaving the nest when she was seventeen and shacking up with a meth head, who became so paranoid on the stuff that he wouldn't leave the house, boarding up the front door and all the windows to keep the boogeyman out. He began to see *her* as the enemy as well and became physically abusive toward her 'til she'd finally had enough and left him for his brother—another decent man suddenly turned bad by substance abuse. Alcohol was *his* poison, and she was his punching bag.

"I left *his* sorry ass, too!" she said as I stared up at the ceiling, completely aghast.

She'd lived such a hard life for someone so young. It made my life seem like a cakewalk in comparison. For once, I felt like an over-privileged, spoiled rich kid. At least now I understood why she preferred gay men. Before Tony came along, every single man in her life was weak and ill-tempered, and they all tried to victimize her—except maybe her father.

"I'm the oldest child in *my* family!" I suddenly blurted out, just to lighten the mood a little. "My brother's a big-shot lawyer in Hollywood. And my sister's married and has three kids."

"So tell me about your love life, Benjamin," she said while gently kicking my foot.

"My love life?" I gulped.

"I told you about *my* stupid ex-boyfriends," she said. "How many relationships have *you* had?"

I wanted to lie to her and say dozens. But I said, "One," which was also a lie.

"Her name was Robyn," I said. "I met her in college... English Lit."

I did in fact meet a girl named Robyn in English Lit and became deeply infatuated. It just wasn't much of a relationship.

"We weren't together for very long," I said. "She landed a publishin' gig and flew off to New York after graduation. I would've gone with her, but she gave me the brush-off with the old 'life is a journey' speech. 'We met, had a few laughs... but now it's time to say good-bye and go our separate ways because we're all on a journey. *Your* life is here, and my life is out there, somewhere.' Condescending bitch! How can my life be a journey if I'm expected to stay here and rot while she's conquering Manhattan?"

"You *are* on a journey!" Barbie said. "But yours is through the people you meet. You and I are on a journey right now... and who knows where it'll lead?"

"So far, so good?" I asked.

"You're still here." She shrugged. "You haven't walked out on me yet."

"Never gonna happen," I assured her.

"You went to college, huh?" she said.

"Mmm-hmm," I replied. "You?"

"Are you kiddin'?" She laughed. "I was lucky to make it out of high school alive. I was a lot skinnier and kinda geeky-lookin'. People made fun of me. The boys told me I looked like Martina Navratilova. When they really wanted to be mean, they just said I looked like a man."

"I was made fun of in school," I admitted. "They used to call me space cadet. You don't look anything like Martina Navratilova, by the way... or a man!" Maybe it was the ecstasy or the pot, or maybe it was her painful and humiliating admission, but something possessed me to come clean about my little one-sided college romance.

"I lied!" I blurted out.

"What?" she replied, and looked at me curiously.

"That girl I met in college," I said. "She wasn't my girlfriend. Hell, we weren't even friends! I was more like her stalker." There was an awkward pause. "Okay, we were friendly at first," I said, "whenever I gathered up the nerve to talk to her. But then I had to go and fall in love with her! And that's when things got a little hairy."

As I spoke, the old memories came back to haunt me. I saw myself at twenty-one with a patchy beard and an *Eraserhead* t-shirt, chasing Robyn all over the OU campus, standing outside her dorm at night and attending classes I wasn't enrolled in—all just to be near her. But I didn't want to bore or disgust Barbie with all that.

"It got to where Robyn was afraid to come anywhere near me," I sufficed to say. "It was her roommate who gave me the 'life is a journey' speech, hopin' I wouldn't chase her all the way to New York. I thought about it. But I decided that it was easier just to give up." I paused just long enough to let out a big, heavy sigh of disappointment. "So, to answer your question truthfully," I said, "I've been in zero relationships. I've never even been close to a woman."

Barbie looked at me with a surprised expression.

"I never finished college, either," I continued. "When I gave up on her, I gave up on everything. I dropped out with only a few semesters to go. And now I'm thirty years old and I make eighteen bucks an hour, working for my dad. It's pretty good money for a workin' stiff, but I could've done so much more with my life."

"You're a virgin?" she exclaimed.

"Possibly the world's oldest one at that," I nodded. "Pretty pathetic, huh?"

"No, it all fits!" she replied. "It's you... pure, untainted! The world hasn't got to you yet. Or, maybe you're too strong to let it get to you. Promise me you won't ever change, Benjamin!"

"Okay," I said, though utterly clueless.

"Are you gonna let me read your screenplay?" she asked.

"Sure," I said. "But I ain't done with it yet."

"I'll read whatever you've got." She shrugged. "And maybe you can come hear me sing?"

"You're a singer too?" I gasped.

She nodded and said, "I'm in a rock band!"

"Wow... a real Renaissance woman over here!" I joked.

"Shhhh!" she whispered. "You hear that?"

"What?" I whispered back.

She looked toward the door and listened very carefully. "There's someone out there!" she said.

She reached over the nightstand and placed her joint in the ashtray. Then she crawled out of bed and tiptoed over to the door, gently turning the knob and suddenly jerking it open. We were shocked to discover Tony and Matt standing on the other side of it, trying to eavesdrop on us, with Laura snickering directly behind them.

"What the hell are you doin'?" Barbie shouted at them.

Tony grinned and pointed at Matt. "He put me up to it!"

"Go away, jerk-offs!" Barbie exclaimed, and slammed the door in their faces. She looked at me, and we both shook our heads.

"Can you believe those two?" she said.

"Disgraceful!" I replied.

She walked up, laid back down beside me, and we talked the rest of the night away. I was amazed to discover how much we had in common. We opened up to each other about our food addictions, she being bulimic throughout her teens and me being a notorious overeater practically my whole life. And we discussed our mutual desire to become rich and famous, me as a Hollywood scriptwriter and she as the next Chrissie Hynde.

"I just hope I make it before I'm thirty!" she said, which made feel bad since I was already there.

"If I don't make it by the time I'm thirty-five, I'm checkin' out!" I foolishly replied.

She also declared her love for Cole Porter and George and Ira Gershwin tunes, even though she was currently in a rock and roll band. And she sang me a few verses of "Someone to Watch Over Me." Her singing voice was even more soothing and hypnotic than her speaking voice—and her pheromones a thousand times more intoxicating than a hundred pills at that precise moment. Never in my life had I been so comfortable around a woman. Being with her was the easiest and most natural thing in the world! Last night, I felt certain that I'd found a home and something to live for. Tonight, at long last, I had my soulmate!

CHAPTER FIVE

Barbie and I talked for nearly five hours straight—more talking than I'd done in years! Suddenly, I heard birds chirping outside and saw sunlight filtering through the mini blinds as we lay there silent and completely exhausted. *Ah, morning!* I contentedly thought to myself. *Wait, it's Monday! Aren't I supposed to be at the shop at seven thirty for a safety meeting? Hell, yes!*

"Shit! What time is it?" I gasped, quickly rising up from the mattress.

Barbie looked at the clock on the nightstand. "It's seven fifteen. Why?"

"I gotta go!" I said, jumping out of bed and hurrying to the door. I opened it, then turned around to see the curious look on her face. "I really enjoyed talking to you," I said. "Hope we can do it again sometime."

Swiftly stepping out of the room and closing the door, I darted through the hallway and opened the door to Tony's bedroom. Tony and Matt were passed out on opposite sides of the bed, both fully clothed. A mirror full of coke lay between them, and empty beer bottles were scattered all over the floor. I rushed up to the bed, grabbed Matt's arm, and shook it.

"Matt, wake up!" I exclaimed. "Matt!"

I kept shaking and hollering 'til he finally opened his eyes and looked up at me half-startled.

"What's goin' on?" he muttered with a sour morning face.

"You need to get up!" I frantically replied. "We're gonna be late for work!"

"Fuck it, man... it ain't happenin'," he groaned. "I took two valiums and a Tylenol." He yawned and said, "We'll just have to call in sick."

"Both of us call in sick?" I exclaimed. "How's that gonna look?"

"Okay, *you* go... and *I'll* call in sick," he said, and closed his eyes.

"You can't afford to take any more sick days!" I reminded him and jabbed him in the shoulder repeatedly, trying to keep him conscious. "Hey, you listenin' to me? Don't you dare go back to sleep! You wanna get fired?"

"All right, I'm gettin' up!" he groaned, shoving my hand away. "Stop pokin' me!"

He bitterly crawled out of bed and followed me out the door, barely awake and staggering through the hall like a zombie.

"We can still make it if we hurry!" I declared as I reached the front door and jerked it open.

I stepped out into the daylight and made a mad dash for the car parked next to the curb, swiftly getting inside and starting it up.

"Come on, Matt... get the lead out," I muttered, watching him stumble across the lawn.

He opened the door and flopped into the passenger seat.

"Shut the door!" I snapped at him.

"Don't yell at me!" he snapped back, finally reaching over to shut it while I put the car in drive and peeled away. "Just take me home," he said as he slumped down farther into the seat and closed his eyes.

"I'm goin' to work!" I said with dogged determination, speeding through the residential maze at forty miles an hour.

I made a left turn onto Northwest Twenty-third Street and raced toward the interstate. Then I shot onto the on-ramp and recklessly merged into oncoming traffic, nearly getting rear-ended by a large dump trunk. The driver swerved into the next lane, honking his horn.

"Why don't you slow the fuck down before you get us both killed?" Matt suggested while trying to sleep.

"We've got six minutes to get to work!" I pointed out to him, looking at the clock on the dash.

"So we'll be a few minutes late," he said.

"I've never been late in my entire life!" I replied and stepped on the gas, the theme to *Raiders of the Lost Ark* playing in my head.

Fortunately, my father's warehouse was less than five miles away and right off the interstate. I tore into the parking lot with a minute to spare. All the parking spaces in front of the rectangular building were full, so I had to create one, parking within ten feet of the main entrance. My father stood in the doorway, chatting with Homer, Tim, and a few others.

"Hey, we're here!" I said to Matt, who was unresponsive and appeared to be out cold. I nudged him in the shoulder. "Matt, wake up!" I shouted in vain.

I looked out my window and saw everyone staring at us. My father motioned for me to come join them and then pointed at his wristwatch. *Oh, God... this isn't good!"* I thought and shook Matt really hard in a state of panic.

"Wake up, goddamn it!" I exclaimed. "It's seven thirty!"

He didn't stir in the slightest, and his eyes remained closed. I looked out my window again and saw Dad and half the crew walking toward us.

"Oh, fuck... they're comin' over!" I frantically replied. "Damn you, Matt! Wake up, you worthless piece of shit! You weasel! You're a weak, little man!" I could see that it was useless. I might as well have been yelling at a corpse. "God, what did I do?" I whined. "Why didn't I just leave your sorry ass behind?"

The car was now completely surrounded. Sean pressed his face against the passenger window and looked inside while my father leaned over and tapped *my* window. I sighed and then stepped out to face the music.

"What's goin' on, Benji?" my father said, dressed like one of the crew in a white t-shirt and blue jeans. "What's wrong with Matt? Is he sick?"

I just stood there utterly speechless.

"Passed out drunk is more like it!" Sean answered for me.

"Yeah, he's totally shitfaced!" said the Kid as the others laughed and joked amongst themselves.

"All right, that's enough!" my father shouted over them. "Let's go inside and get started!"

He led us to the metal door that was standing wide open, stood in front of it, and watched us file in one after the other, eyeing me very sharply as I stepped through last. The rest of the crew was waiting for us in the break room. We all sat down at a long table and listened to our employer discuss the company's future while drinking coffee and consuming the doughnuts he provided for us. I didn't partake of the doughnuts this time around. I was too busy thinking about the ass-chewing I'd most likely receive after the meeting was over. Dad sat at the head of the table and gave his usual spiel.

"Guys, I've been biddin' like crazy!" he said. "We've got at least four jobs to start in October, which means we're really gonna have to buckle down on this one. We need to have all the walls up by Friday!"

Please don't say overtime! I kept repeating in my head.

"We'll probably have to put in some overtime," Dad continued. "I'm thinkin' ten-hour workdays for the entire week... maybe a full day on Saturday."

Nearly everyone at the table nodded agreeably because they loved being paid time-and-a-half more than they hated their jobs. But the way I saw it, eight-hour workdays were excruciating enough, especially on very little sleep. Tacking on two more hours and throwing Saturday into the mix just seemed cruel! Dad rambled on for nearly half an hour, discussing our upcoming jobs in more detail and then addressing the heat issue.

"Make sure you guys drink plenty of water," he said. "I know how hot it gets in that old building."

"You could bake a cake in there!" Homer quipped, sitting to the left of him.

"Sure nuff!" Tim concurred, sitting to my father's right.

"Well, take little two-minute breaks if you have to," Dad said. "I can't afford to lose any of you to a heat stroke." He shrugged and said, "I guess that's it. Any questions?"

Everyone was silent.

"Comments?"

Sean raised his hand at the other end of the table and said, "Yeah, I have one! Since Matt ain't carryin' his load today, I think he owes us all a lunch at the Red Dog!"

He garnered a few laughs and plenty of enthusiastic nods while I sat perfectly still and pretended to be invisible.

"You just worry about yourself, Sean!" Dad chided him. "Anyone else?"

Everyone clammed up again.

"Alrighty then!" he said, slapping the table and quickly getting to his feet. "Let's go to work, gentlemen!"

We all stood up and headed for the door.

"Benji!" he shouted as I attempted to sneak away in the crowd.

Shit! I thought, turning back around and walking back to the table.

"Why don't you take Matt home before you go to the jobsite?" he said. "He's gotta problem with alcohol, does he?"

"I guess," I replied.

"Drugs, too... I bet!" He nodded sternly. "Were you with him last night?"

"No!" I replied, vehemently shaking my head. "He asked me to pick him up this morning because his bike's in the shop. He seemed okay 'til we pulled in here! He just passed out, all the sudden."

"Don't offer him any more rides!" he demanded. "In fact, you probably shouldn't associate with him at all. I know you're just tryin' to help, but he's a lost cause. That's the problem with you, son... you're just too softhearted. You let people like that take advantage of you!"

"Are you gonna fire him?" I boldly inquired.

"I don't have much of a choice, do I?" he said. "He's callin' in sick all of the time... and, when he *does* show up, he's usually an hour late! He and Sean were two of my best workers, but they seem to have gone down the wrong path lately. It might be a good thing to split 'em up—"

"Can't you give him one more chance?" I pleaded.

"*I've* given him so many chances, Benji!" he exclaimed angrily. He immediately calmed himself. "Have him call me tonight." He sighed. "I'll have a long talk with him."

I nodded and hurriedly walked away before he changed his mind. Matt was still sprawled out in the passenger seat when I hopped into the car and drove off. He stirred suddenly and opened his eyes.

"*Now* he wakes up!" I sneered. "You were fakin' it the whole time, weren't you?"

"Huh?" he replied, as if he had no idea what I was talking about. "Where the hell are we goin'?"

"I'm takin' you home," I said sharply. "Then I'm goin' to work."

"You should've just let me call in sick—"

"Dad wants you to call him tonight!" I swiftly interjected. "I just saved your ass... so you'd better not blow it!"

"Did you tell him we were both partyin' all night?" he asked.

My silence gave him his answer.

"You didn't, did you?" He laughed. "You motherfucker! So your old man has no idea who the real party monster is! Goin' straight to work from an after-party all tweaked up on X... that's pretty awesome, bro!"

"Yeah, well, I haven't even started yet," I grumbled. "And he's makin' us work ten-hour days this week!"

"Ten hours?" he said with a grimace, then shrugged. "Eh, I'm sure you can handle it. You're a machine!"

"We never should've gone out in the first place," I said. "It was Sunday night."

"Then you wouldn't have hit it off with Barbie," he said.

"That's not the point!" I exclaimed. "I can't let that shit interfere with my day job!"

"Your priorities are so out of whack, dude!" he scoffed. "Do you really love your job that much... or are you just afraid of disappointin' the old man? It must be a bitch tryin' to live up to his expectations twenty-four seven!"

"I suppose you couldn't care less what *your* old man thinks of *you,*" I sneered.

"I never knew him," he replied. "He skipped out on me and my mom before I was born. The bitch probably *drove* him away by naggin' him to death and puttin' him down all the time... like she's been doin' to me my whole life. I was a hell of a basketball player back in high school... probably could've gone pro! But she never gave me any encouragement—flat-out told me I was no good, in fact. The sad thing is, I started to believe her. I kept missin' practice and started hangin' out with the stoners. That's how I met Sean." He looked out his window and shook his head. "Yep, I really could've been somethin'," he muttered, "if I had a couple of parents who actually gave a damn. Consider yourself lucky!"

"If she's as bad as you say she is, why don't you move out?" I asked curiously.

"I can't afford my own place right now," he said. "I don't make twenty bucks an hour, like some people I know!"

"Eighteen fifty!"

"Whatever."

Matt was given one more chance on condition that he joined Alcoholics Anonymous. My dad picked him up at his house and drove him to his first meeting that very same night. He even sat with him through the whole thing and drove him home afterward.

"It was awkward as shit!" Matt told me over the phone when he got back. "I gotta get fucked-up tonight so I can forget it ever happened. Do you wanna go?"

I said yes, even though I was probably setting myself up for another hellacious day at work with little or no sleep. It was worth it just for the chance to see Barbie again. She wasn't at the club, nor did Matt find any ecstasy there. We *did* happen to run into Simone and Desiree, however. We danced with them for a while. Then we all sat at the bar and tossed down beers and tequila shots. I was surprisingly jovial even without the pills. And the girls seemed to love my dry wit.

After Heaven shut down for the night, Matt and I followed them to their high-rise apartment in Edmond. It was very spacious and stylish, filled with odd-looking furniture and erotic art. The living room walls were covered with paintings and still photographs of gorgeous, bare-assed women—and gorgeous bare-assed men. And in the middle of the room next to the Rubik's Cube coffee table was a giant, three-foot-long rocking balls and penis sculpture, just like the one in *A Clockwork Orange.* Matt and I walked straight up to the big white schlong the moment we stepped through the door. After studying it for about a minute, Matt felt the tip of it and gave it a gentle push, both of us giggling like little boys as we watched it rock back and forth on the hardwood floor.

"Have a seat!" Simone said to us, stepping in from the kitchen with two rum and Cokes.

We sat down next to each other in matching lime-green bean bag chairs and she handed us our drinks. She went back into the kitchen to fix two more while Desiree stood in front of the entertainment center, thumbing through their CD collection.

"Rum and Coke, Dez?" Simone shouted from the kitchen.

"Yes, please!" Desiree shouted back. "Ah, here we go."

She slipped a disc into the CD player and a very sexy, sensual Portishead song began to play. Simone returned from the kitchen just as she stepped away from the stereo and they met in front of the coffee table. Simone handed Desiree her drink, then grabbed her buttocks and began ravaging her lips. In the heat of passion, they let their drinks fall to the floor and fiercely dug their claws into each other. I felt bamboozled! I assumed we'd all sit down, have a few drinks, another pleasant conversation, and I'd make them all laugh some more. But, apparently, chat-time was over, and there was no more need for the court jester now that the sextivities had officially begun.

Matt looked at me and laughed. "What's the matter? Haven't you ever seen a lick down before?"

"Is that what this is?" I replied.

Simone summoned Matt over with her forefinger as the two remained in blissful lip-lock.

"The plot thickens!" he said to me, waggling his eyebrows. "Hold my drink, will ya?"

He handed me his glass, lifted himself up from the chair, and went to join them, grabbing onto both of them and kissing Simone's neck. *Well, this is embarrassing!* I thought. *I guess I'm supposed to just sit here and watch?*

"B, jump on in here and gitcha some of this!" Matt shouted.

"I'm good!" I gulped.

Suddenly, the doorbell buzzed, and buzzed, and buzzed, making the situation even more unbearable.

"Do you want me to get that?" I muttered finally, at which point Desiree tore away from the group and headed for the door.

I turned around in the chair just as she answered it and saw some tall, goofy-looking character with a cheesy perm and a thick, dark mustache standing in the doorway. He looked like he was stuck in the eighties, a Tom Selleck wannabe, wearing flip-flops, gray slacks, and a blue silk shirt unbuttoned to the navel to expose the fur on his chest. He had a bottle of Chardonnay in one hand.

"Steve!" Desiree exclaimed, swiftly grabbing his other hand and pulling him inside.

"Who is it?" Simone shouted while Matt was busy sucking on her tits.

"It's Steve from upstairs!" Desiree answered.

"Well, get him over here!"

"I heard y'all playin' your music down here," he said to Desiree in a deep, monotone voice, "and was wonderin' if you could use some company. I brought the wine!"

She promptly shut the door, threw her arms around him, and they kissed. *Now I get it!* I thought. *I'm in a bad porno flick!* Switching back to Matt and Simone, I watched her grab his crotch and smile approvingly.

"I think it's time to move this party into the bedroom," she said to him, and he nodded. "Dez, we're takin' it to the bedroom!"

She took Matt by the arm and dragged him toward the hallway in back. Desiree and Steve immediately followed suit, walking right past me like I was a piece of furniture—a bean bag on top of a bean bag. I heard them slam a door shut and, shortly after, the girls were moaning and screaming with pleasure. *I'll give 'em an hour,* I thought, and continued to sit quietly, my discomfort soon giving way to boredom. Nearly *two* hours went by before I finally gathered up the nerve to go check on them. Things had quieted down considerably by then, though I'd occasionally hear somebody talking or giggling. I slowly walked down the hall, stepped up to the closed door, and knocked very faintly.

"Matt," I muttered. There was no response, so I knocked and spoke louder. "Matt!"

"What?" Matt shouted in a muffled voice.

"It's gettin' pretty late!" I shouted back. "Are you about ready to go?"

"Open the door, will ya? I can barely hear you!"

I opened the door slightly and spoke through the crack. "I said it's gettin' late—"

"What time is it?"

I looked at my wristwatch. "It is now four twenty-two!"

"Why don't you go on without me?" he shouted. "I'll have Simone drive me home!"

"You've gotta be at work at eight!" I felt inclined to remind him.

"Go home, B!" he shouted, sounding a little irritated. "Get all rested up so you'll be ready to tackle them walls!"

Then he grunted like a caveman, followed by lots of giggling. There was even a deep, monotone giggle in the bunch. *Fuck y'all!* I thought, immediately shutting the door and walking away.

I managed about two hours of sleep when I got home. I drove up to the jobsite at a quarter 'til eight and sat in the parking lot, waiting to see if Matt would show. Sean pulled up beside me in his Suburban and stared down at me through his window, making me feel uncomfortable. Homer pulled up on the other side of me in his old, beat-up pickup truck, then more trucks pulled into the parking lot one after the other. But still no Matt. The clock on the dash now read 7:56 a.m. *Oh well, I tried,* I thought, watching my coworkers hop out of their vehicles and straggle toward the building. *It's not my fault he's a dumbass!* I got out of the car just as Sean stepped out of *his* vehicle and we walked up to the building entrance together.

"Did you go out last night?" he asked.

"Uh-huh," I replied.

"Where's Matt? Did you leave him there this time?"

"Uh-huh."

"He ain't gonna make it, is he?"

"Huh-uh."

"Then I guess he's fucked," Sean said, shaking his head.

As we walked up to the door, a yellow corvette came roaring into the parking lot and stopped just a few yards behind us. Matt reached over the passenger seat, kissed Simone on the lips, and swiftly got out of the car, Sean and me looking on in disbelief. He seemed in good spirits and looked surprisingly clean and refreshed for someone who'd been orgying all night. And it was all just to show me up! *Well played, sir!* He waved good-bye to Simone as she peeled off and turned around to see us gawking at him.

"Why are you guys just standin' there?" he asked. "You're gonna be late!" He walked straight in between us and beat us to the door. "Let's get to work!" he exclaimed as he opened it and stepped inside.

We went out again on Thursday night. There was no sign of Barbie at the club or at Tony's afterward. I was beginning to worry that I'd scared her off somehow.

"There's no tellin' where that girl is," Tony said. "Probably out partyin' with her bandmates."

He offered me a pill as a consolation, but I refused it. Drugs were just a joy enhancer. I liked to take my misery straight.

"Okay, B." He nodded. "Just holler if you need anything."

He darted off to his bedroom and shut the door, probably to get away from Matt since we brought Simone and Desiree with us. It was obvious that he had feelings for the guy. And to see Matt sitting on his couch between two girls was pretty upsetting, I'd imagine.

"Benjamin, why don't you come sit with us?" Desiree exclaimed, seeing me standing alone in my favorite spot.

I walked over to the couch and sat down next to her. All three of them were busy snorting lines off the coffee table.

"You should try this, B!" Matt said. "It's good for the soul!"

"No, thanks," I sighed.

"What's up with you?" he asked.

"Nothin'," I replied.

"Bullshit... *something's* wrong!" he exclaimed as he continued eyeballing me.

"Would you like me to get you a beer, sweetie?" Simone asked me.

"Simone, leave him alone!" Matt snapped at her.

He quickly wiped her scowl away by leaning in and kissing her on the lips. I noticed people giving the pair dirty looks as they stood around talking. Just minutes later, Barbie stepped through the front door in her purple sweater and blue jeans. She walked right up and sat down next to me without saying a word. It was so quick and unexpected that I, too, was without words. We just sat there very quietly and traded warm glances while watching everybody try to outtalk each other and make drunken asses of themselves. I kept thinking that

I should say something, but she looked so content with that permanent crinkly eyed smile of hers. I didn't want to blow it. *Wow! I guess she really is my girl!* I thought, suddenly feeling like a king. I finally broke the silence about five minutes later by asking her how her night went. She gave me the so-so gesture, and we laughed.

"Mine, too," I said.

She suddenly leaned in closer and whispered, "Let's go to *my* room."

I swiftly jumped up from the couch and followed her into the bedroom. She turned on the lights and shut the door. Then we walked up to the bed, sat down, and she revealed to me the darker side of her nature by professing her fascination with the occult and people like Anton LaVey and Aleister Crowley. She grew so excited as she spoke that she got up, walked over to the little bookshelf next to her writing table, and pulled out several of her favorite books. We crawled into the middle of the bed together, sitting across from each other in the lotus position, and she began reading to me from Aleister Crowley's *Snowdrops from a Curate's Garden.* Admittedly, it was a little creepy, listening to her read the sick, perverted fantasies of the most infamous, black-hearted magician who ever lived while Bela Lugosi stared down at me with those wicked, hypnotic eyes. Yet, I enjoyed every minute of it.

Next, she read a few pages of the *Rosicrucian Manuscripts* to me, being into theology and having a fascination for ancient secret societies. Then she read several paragraphs from Timothy Leary's *The Psychedelic Experience,* being into LSD. I'd never even heard the term "Rosicrucian" before and knew very little about Timothy Leary, for that matter. Then again, I wasn't the voracious reader that she was. The last time I read a book from cover to cover was in college. And the only one I remembered fondly was Emily Bronte's *Wuthering Heights,* which I considered to be the greatest love story ever written. I just had to accept the fact that Barbie was smarter than I was and could teach me a thing or two, even though she was nine years younger and never had a lick of college. Finally, she showed me a book of Wiccan spells.

"So you really *are* into witchcraft!" I said, a bit taken aback.

"Of course!" she laughed. "Don't worry, Benjamin... I'm not gonna turn you into a newt!"

She told me a little bit about Wiccan philosophy, then set the book down with the others, grabbed a deck of tarot cards from the nightstand, and spread them out between us. *Man, this girl's really out there!* I thought as I watched the cards fall to the mattress one by one. *It's kinda sexy, though. No, scratch that. It's very sexy!* Just as she was about to read me my fortune, we heard a loud commotion in the hallway. We quickly jumped out of the bed, opened the door, and peeked outside.

"Here he comes!" Porsche kept shouting, running down the hall in a blue dress.

Tony burst out of his room behind her, wearing nothing but a red jockstrap, a gun belt with a holstered pistol on each hip, a pair of cowboy boots, and a white Stetson hat. The crowd cheered them both on as they entered the living room.

"Come on!" Barbie said to me with an excited grin.

We hurried into the living room and stood in the very back next to the fish tank, watching Tony and Porsche make their way through the crowd. She removed a jazz CD from the disc player and replaced it with another. The title song from the musical film *Oklahoma!* began to play and everyone clapped along to it in a mocking fashion as Tony lip-synced to Gordon MacRae's voice and he and Porsche danced bowlegged like a couple of cowpokes. Once the chorus took over, he whipped out his toy six-guns and waved them around while shaking his moneymaker and occasionally twerking his guests.

"He does this whenever he's hammered!" Barbie shouted at me over the music.

I laughed excitedly and started clapping with the crowd. *What a wonderful farce!* I thought. It was the perfect sendup of the place we were all unfortunate enough to call home—the reddest of red states! Matt jumped up from the couch as soon as the song ended and gave Tony a big hug.

"What a guy!" he cheerfully declared. "I love this guy!"

Judging by the ecstatic look on Tony's face, it was the exact response he was hoping for. But Matt pulled away just seconds later and was back on the couch, letting Simone have her way with him. Infuriated, Tony grabbed the first man he could get his hands on and kissed him long and hard, at which point his boyfriend, Neil, made a surprise appearance, walking through the front door with a young man in his teens. Both were scantily clad in black leather. From what Matt told me earlier, Tony and Neil had an open relationship and usually partied separately so they could bang other people. Thus, it probably wasn't too surprising for Neil to find Tony on another man's lips. But the moment he saw Matt kissing Simone he went totally ballistic, storming over to the couch and kicking Matt's foot to get his attention.

"Why don't you get a hotel room?" he snarled.

Matt simply smirked at him and went back to sucking face. Neil kicked his foot again. Matt looked at him with a puzzled expression.

"I'm serious!" Neil exclaimed. "Y'all need to leave! This is a gay party!"

Matt quickly stood up and got right in his face. "What's your problem, dude?"

"I'm tired of you dissin' Tony," Neil exclaimed, "flaunting these tootsies in front of him—gettin' him all upset! Are you deliberately trying to hurt the guy, or are you just plain stupid?"

"Leave him alone, Neil!" Tony butted in.

"Damn it, T," Neil replied, frustrated. "Can't you see what he's doin'? He ain't even one of us! He's just usin' you for the drugs... because he's a goddamn coke whore!"

Matt furiously lunged at him and they tore through the room throwing punches at each other, knocking people and furniture over. Barbie and I scooted closer together and kept tight against the wall, instinctively grabbing hands. I'd never seen such a violent, testosterone-fueled brawl—at least not in real life! I watched with trepidation as Neil took Matt to the floor and punched him in the face repeatedly. Tony rushed in and pulled Neil off of Matt, only for his partner to suddenly turn on him and smack him in the jaw.

"Oh, man!" Neil regretfully exclaimed as Tony clasped his hand over the wound. "Are you all right? Here, let me look at it!"

He moved in closer and reached up to touch Tony's face. Tony angrily slapped his hand away. Neil stepped back and didn't say another word. Simone and Desiree had already run to Matt's side and were helping him off the floor.

"I'll do whatever you say, Tony," he said after he got to his feet. His speech was slurred now that his face was battered and bruised. "If you want me to leave, I'll leave. But your boyfriend's full of shit! While he's out there fuckin' every man in sight, I've been right here with you!" He hesitated for a moment and said, "I love you, man."

"I know," Tony said. But then he noticed the multitude of confused, angry stares directed toward Matt—as if *he* was responsible for sucking the life out of the party. "Just go home, Matt," he said, noticeably conflicted.

"Let's go, girls," Matt sighed, and they all headed for the door. "Wait, where's Big B?" He turned, looked around the room, and immediately spotted me trying to blend in with the wall. "Come on, B!" he shouted.

I looked at Barbie. She seemed curious to see my next move.

"I drove," I shrugged, noticing the sudden look of disappointment in her eyes.

Sadly, I pulled away from her and followed my friends toward the door. I drove off into the night just moments later, listening to the girls fuss over Matt in the back seat.

"You poor thing!" Desiree said. "Does it hurt?"

"Nah, it feels good!" Matt groaned and slurred. "I need some Tylenol... Ibuprofen... anything!"

"Do you have any aspirin in here?" Simone hastily shouted at me, as if it was a matter of life and death.

"No," I answered very curtly.

"You'll have to wait 'til we get home, hon," Simone said to Matt.

"What was up with that dude?" Desiree asked, her tone full of disgust.

"I don't know!" Simone answered, equally disgusted.

"He's just jealous!" Matt said. "He knows Tony would rather be with me... if he could!"

I sneered at him through the rearview mirror. *You arrogant prick!* I thought. *Boy, did I ever hitch my wagon to the wrong horse! Five minutes ago, I was on cloud nine! Now I'm just the fuckin' driver... again!* It was all on me, of course. Had I behaved like a boss instead of my usual wimpy self, I would've thrown Matt the keys and let him drive himself home while I spent the night with Barbie.

"Woulda, coulda, shoulda," I muttered to myself, filled with regret. "Story of my life."

CHAPTER SIX

I woke up depressed the next day. All I could think about was that look of sheer disappointment on Barbie's face when I abandoned her; this as opposed to her beautiful, contented smile before disaster struck. Who knows what would've happened if I'd stayed with her all night—perhaps a first kiss? It was pure torture to think about what might've been. After ten hours of unrelenting hell in the sweatbox I came home, opened a bag of chips and a bottle of Pepsi, and sat down in front of the TV, thinking that I'd blown it big time. Whether I actually *did* blow it or not remained to be seen.

I went to take a piss and as I stood over the toilet doing my business, I noticed the bathroom scale looking up at me. And it began to speak.

"Hey, when you're through with that," it said, sounding just like Michael Keaton's Batman, "why don't you get on up here and let's see what you weigh?"

I tried to ignore it and look away, but I couldn't. It was a talking scale after all—and not the phony kind with the prerecorded voice.

"Climb aboard, sailor!" it goaded me. "It's been two whole months!"

"Go to hell!" I said.

"What, are you chicken?" it said. "Afraid to face the music? Get up here, you pussy!" Seeing that I was stubborn, it tried a softer approach. "You know, you might've even lost a few pounds," it said slyly. "They say ecstasy's very slimming."

"You might be right!" I replied, swiftly pulling up my pants, bending down, and dragging the scale away from the wall. I stepped onto it and stared down at the digital screen in anticipation. "Huh?" I gasped as "300" flashed before my eyes.

"Gotcha, lard-ass!" said the damn contraption with a sinister laugh. "Three bills... count 'em!"

It's gotta be a mistake! I thought, stepping off and back on several times. But I kept gaining a pound or two more!

"Give it a rest, pal!" it said to me finally. "You're only makin' it worse!"

I kicked it back to the wall and stormed out of the bathroom. *How can this be?* I thought. *I was two eighty just two months ago! At this rate, I'll be four hundred pounds by Christmas! I'll be one of those guys who's too big for his house! They'll have to lift me out with a crane! God, what was I thinking? I don't even deserve love! Who wants a man who won't take care of himself?* I realized that I had to make a choice, food or Barbie. Lots of hugs and kisses and sweet nothings or a big bucket of fried chicken, an extra helping of mashed potatoes with gravy, and a brownie fudge sundae with a cherry on top. It was a no-brainer!

I took the corn chips and Pepsi back into the kitchen and poured them into the sink. Then I reached into the cupboard, pulled out the Twinkies, Ding Dongs, powdered donuts, potato chips, Snickers bars, and Reese's Peanut Butter Cups, and poured them out as well, turning on the faucet full blast along with the garbage disposal. The latter had never seen so much action! Usually, my colossal stomach did its job. *No more junk food,* I said to myself. *Only fresh fruit and vegetables from now on... baked fish and skinless chicken.* I was determined never to be a disappointment to Barbie again. I'd be her boy toy, in fact.

That night, I drove to the shop in sweats and sneakers and worked out inside the building, jogging through a maze of shelves, workbenches, and heavy machinery for over an hour. The following evening I bought a stationary bike, took it home and put it together in front the TV, so I could lose weight while watching my favorite shows. The night after that, I traded in the clown car for a brand-new metallic gray Buick Regal sedan—the limited sport edition. It had comfy gray leather seats and a digital dashboard that resembled the control panel of the Millennium Falcon when all lit up at night. Plus, there was enough room inside to fit a thousand clowns. Matt was so proud of his new ride that he affectionately nicknamed it "the Party Mobile." *His* contribution to the cause was a brand-new pager, which he carried on his belt at all times so he could keep in constant contact with Tony—or whoever was supplying the drugs for the evening. He and Tony were closer than ever since being beaten to a pulp. And, at least for a very short while, he stopped using women as a buffer. Most of the time, it was just the two of them consuming mass quantities of drugs and doing God knows whatever else behind closed doors. Neither seemed terribly concerned that Neil could come bursting into the house at any given second.

I was always somewhere close by. I partied at least four nights a week and ingested anywhere from three to five pills a night. Struggling to get to work on time and make it through the day became a regular thing. And a burgeoning drug habit on top of a monthly car payment caused my checking account to dwindle down fairly rapidly. But I didn't care. I was happy just to finally have a life.

Everyone was impressed with my new car and my weight loss. I lost twenty-seven pounds in four weeks! But the one person I wanted to impress the most was never around, and I took it personally. The one night she *was* at home her bedroom door was shut, and there was a piece of notebook paper taped to the middle of it with the words "Keep Out!" written in red crayon. I stood by her door for what seemed like hours, angry and frustrated, contemplating going in. *That's it, I'm doing it!* I thought, just as Matt stepped in from the living room and caught me placing my hand on the doorknob.

"What are you doin'?" he whispered harshly.

"I have to see her!" I whispered back.

"No, you don't!" he said. "That's the X talkin'!"

I scoffed at the notion and slowly turned the knob. He got right up in my face and tried to talk some sense into me.

"Don't do it, man!" he said, still whisper-shouting. "You're just gonna blow it! Tony said she was really tired when she came home! She had to work a double!"

I reluctantly let go of the knob.

"Come on, big'n," he said, nodding toward the living room. "It's stag night."

I turned and followed him down the hall.

Two nights later I was staring into a dark, empty room again, feeling that all was lost. I overheard Tony talking to Matt in the living room.

"Where the hell's B?" Tony asked.

"Shit, I don't know," Matt said. "Probably in Barbie's room, sniffin' panties."

Hey, that's not a bad idea! I thought as I listened to them laugh. *Why didn't I think of that? It'd be so easy! And it's the next best thing to her actually being here!* Slowly moving away from the wall, I sneaked into her room and tiptoed over to the walk-in closet, the light from the hall guiding my way. I quietly slid open the door and smiled greedily as I looked down at a laundry basket full of dirty clothes. I felt like a leprechaun staring at his pot of gold! I got down on my knees and started digging through blue jeans, bras, and fishnet sweaters 'til I came across a pair of light-blue panties. *Mmm, nice!* I thought, grabbing them with both hands and giving them a thorough examination. I focused on the gusset, which had covered her flower, lifted it to my nose, and gave it a quick whiff. Not surprisingly, it smelled like a fresh batch of strawberries! Suddenly, I heard people talking right outside the bedroom door. I frantically threw the undergarment back into the basket and dropped flat on the floor, watching Matt and Tony walk past. As soon as I heard Tony's door slam shut, I sprang to my feet and scrambled out of the room. I headed for the living room couch and sat down next to Rog and Skippy, waiting in vain for Barbie to come walking through the front door. Matt came back into the room and sat down on the other side of me.

"Hey, man... we need to talk," he said with a surprisingly sober expression. "You need to forget about Barbie. Can't you see what she's doin' to you? A girl like that will bring you nothin' but heartache!"

I subtly rolled my eyes. The last thing I needed was a lecture from *him*—of all people.

"I hate to break it to ya, big'n," he continued, "but if it's love you're lookin' for... one, you've come to the wrong place and, two, you can do a hell of a lot better than Barbie. If you ask me, love's a total crock anyway."

"Weren't you in love with a girl?" I sneered.

"Yeah, I was," he said grimly. "'Til I caught her sleepin' with another man and she tore my heart out. It opened my eyes... made me see the light! True love between a man and a woman doesn't exist. Somebody's always fakin' it."

"Matt's right!" Roger said. "Happily ever after only happens in the movies. If you wanna be happy in real life, find someone you enjoy havin' sex with... and stick with him! I mean *her*... sorry."

He and Skippy laughed. Noticing Tony walk into the room, I angrily stood up and shoved through the male-dominated crowd to get to him.

"Hey, T... got any pills on you?" I asked.

"Does Dolly Parton sleep on her back?" he joked. "How many do you need?"

"Six!" I boldly replied.

"You sure about that?" he asked.

"Yep!" I said, adamantly nodding my head.

"Now you're talkin', doll face!" Roger shouted.

"Somebody's gonna have fun tonight!" Skippy added.

Tony reached into his pants pocket and pulled out a baggie full of pills, removing a few and then handing me the bag. I slipped it into the inner pocket of my sports jacket, forked over a hundred and fifty dollars, and rushed to the front door.

"Wait! Where you goin'?" Matt shouted as I opened it. "I could use a couple of those!"

"Somewhere where there's not so many men!" I replied, and walked out.

I took out two pills and chewed them up while driving into the Inferno parking lot. I swiftly got out of the car, walked inside, paid the cashier, and went straight for the dance floor, which was fairly packed for three o'clock in the morning on a weekday. I stepped into the middle of the crowd and danced to some bass-pounding techno rap song. It was total bliss once I started to get off. I came down an hour and a half later. But, thankfully, I had my small stockpile of goodies to get me right back up there again. As I continued dancing, I reached into my lapel and pulled out the baggie. *What the fuck?* I thought, staring down at a wet, empty bag in disbelief. It appeared that I'd left it open slightly, allowing the sweat that covered my body and my clothes to infiltrate it and melt its contents into a fine, powdery liquid. I desperately scraped the bottom of the bag and licked the residue off my finger. Then I stuck the whole baggie in my mouth, chewed it up, and swallowed it. But my efforts were futile. I crashed hard and began dancing angry, angry at the world for being such a shithole—and angry at Barbie for leaving me all alone in it! Over to my left, I noticed a group of black girls laughing at me as they danced. After I looked away, of them even had the nerve to sneak up from behind and dry hump me in the rear end. I wasn't sure if she was making fun of me or just being overly friendly but I assumed it was the former. Furiously putting my weight into her I pushed her all the way back to her friends—my enormous back serving as a bulldozer.

"Asshole!" she bitterly shouted and flipped me off as I pulled away.

I simply smiled and danced over to my corner, realizing that I'd made several enemies. Yet I soon discovered that I'd turned the whole room against me. Everyone was giving me dirty looks, both on and off the dance floor. They must've thought I was some poser or show off—a John Travolta wannabe. And I was beginning to agree with them, especially as the floor became less crowded and it was just me and a few other showboaters dancing like there was no tomorrow. Suddenly, my heart wasn't in it anymore. I was about to call it quits when I happened to look toward the sidelines and saw crazy Laura sitting alone at one of the tables in a sexy dress, staring right back at me with sad, lonely eyes. It caught me completely off guard and caused me to stand perfectly still. Maybe she was a kindred spirit after all, I thought as I exited the dance floor and walked up to her table. She appeared pleasantly surprised.

"Wanna get the fuck out of here?" I asked her very bluntly.

"Hell, yeah!" she grinned, quickly getting up from the chair, grabbing her purse, and accompanying me toward the exit.

I realized I'd made a mistake the moment we stepped into the car and drove off. She suddenly turned into an insufferable toddler, playing with all the knobs and buttons in front of her, rolling the windows up and down, switching the music to some obnoxious hip hop station, and turning the volume up full blast. I casually reached over and turned it back down.

"God, I love this car!" she said excitedly. "How much horsepower she got under the hood?"

"Hell if I know." I shrugged.

"V-six or V-eight?"

"You got me."

"Why don't you pull over and let *me* drive?" she said.

I smiled and shook my head.

"Why not?" she said. "You got somethin' against women drivers? I betcha I could really make this baby fly!"

"That's what I'm afraid of," I said. "It's not even paid for yet!"

"Party pooper!" She sulked. But she instantly grew excited again. "Oh, I know... let's go to Porsche's! She's havin' a huge after-party!"

"I don't think so," I said.

"Where ya takin' us, then?"

"Tony's!"

"Tony's is boring!" she sighed. "We can always go to Tony's." She looked at me and grinned. "Are you afraid of drag queens?"

"No!" I laughed.

"You are, aren't you?" she laughed. "Come on, it'll be fun! P-p-p-p-please... please, please, please, please, please—"

"What's the address?" I said, just to shut her up.

"Yes!" she exclaimed victoriously and gave me directions.

We headed downtown and drove through a posh neighborhood filled with old, expensive houses, finally coming upon a three-story monstrosity with a slew of cars parked in front of it. We parked along the street, got out, and tromped through the yard to get to the front door. Laura banged on it repeatedly 'til a pint-sized drag queen in a dark wig and a red miniskirt answered.

Two larger drag queens stood behind her, gawking at us. *I've gotta bad feelin' about this,* I thought.

"Laura!" the little drag queen said.

"Jasmine!" Laura said, and stepped up to hug her.

"Who the hell is it?" Porsche shouted from the next room.

"It's Laura, the crazy bitch!" Laura shouted back at her.

"Well, get your ass in here!"

I followed Laura inside and stepped into a huge, luxurious living room full of drag queens—as if we'd just walked in on a crossdressers convention. Porsche was slouched down in the middle of the sofa sharing a crack pipe with her fellow Supremes, Mo'Nique and Kaneesha, all three draped in white ermine fur stoles. Everyone else hovered around them like they were the belles of the ball while *Disco Hits of the '70s* played loudly on the audio system.

"Benjamin!" Porsche exclaimed, swiftly getting up and walking over to greet me.

She grabbed my hands and just stood there taking me in as five or six other transvestites gathered around us, staring me up and down like I was eye candy.

"Who's your friend?" asked a hulking, three-hundred-pound Ethel Merman look-alike. I remembered her from the floor show.

"This here's Benjamin!" Porsche answered. "Isn't he a doll?"

"Yes, he is!" Ethel Merman agreed, and gently extended her hand to me. "Call me Daphne."

I shook her hand and cringed as she proceeded to run her fingers through my hair.

"I love your hair," she said. "So thick and curly. A woman would kill for hair like this!"

"And what about those eyes?" Porsche said.

"Mmm, yes... so dark and mysterious!" said a busty, dark-haired Bettie Page impersonator. "Do you know who he looks like? Richard Gere!"

"He *does* look like Richard Gere!" Daphne exclaimed.

"Maybe a plump Richard Gere!" Laura remarked, before everyone got too carried away.

"You mean a husky Richard Gere!" Porsche corrected her.

"A *burly* Richard Gere!" Daphne said as she felt my flabby bicep.

"I honestly don't see it," Laura said, shaking her head skeptically.

I started to feel a little nervous, meanwhile, afraid that I was about to be gangbanged by the cast of *The Crying Game*. Yet there was a part of me that enjoyed the attention. It was nice to be treated like a piece of meat for a change. And imagine how flattered I was to discover that I had a group of fanboys—or fangirls, rather! To make the experience even more enjoyable, I tried to pretend that these were real women lusting after me.

"Come sit down with me, hon!" Porsche said, and dragged me over to the sofa.

I plopped down between her and the other two divas while the rest of the group huddled around us except for Laura, who found an empty chair clear across the room—away from all the hoopla. She seemed more perplexed than I was by the sudden star treatment. While we passed the crack pipe around, she removed her house key and a baggie full of cocaine from her purse and kept herself entertained by doing key bumps. My first hit of crack was amazing. The euphoria was so intense that it even put ecstasy to shame! But the feeling only lasted for about a minute, and the subsequent hits weren't nearly as potent. So ecstasy was still king in my book. Porsche grabbed a half-empty bottle of scotch from the coffee table and shared that with me as well. The more I drank from it, the easier it was to imagine that I was surrounded by beautiful women, rather than a bunch of ugly, delusional men in wigs. I started a conversation by asking Porsche how she managed to acquire such a big, beautiful home. She said that she owned a hair salon somewhere on the gay strip, and business was doing well.

"So if you're lookin' for a sugar mama, here I be!" she joked, and slapped me on the leg.

Then Kaneesha, sitting against my other leg, brought up the fact that I looked a little nervous.

"Don't worry!" she laughed. "Most of us aren't even gay... or bi, for that matter."

"What are you, then?" I asked curiously.

"Straight!" she said.

"I have no sex drive whatsoever," Mo'Nique said, seated next to her. "So I guess that makes me asexual."

"Same here," said Jasmine, the pint-sized drag queen sitting on the arm of the sofa. "I felt like I was put on this earth strictly to entertain folks."

"Wow," I muttered, my mind completely blown.

"Better keep an eye on me, though," Porsche warned me.

"Ditto," Daphne said, winking at me from a nearby recliner. "What about you, Benjamin... gay or straight?"

She and about a dozen others waited for my answer in anticipation.

"He's straight," Porsche sighed. "But I'm workin' on him."

"Do you gotta girlfriend?" asked the Bettie Page look-alike, smoking a joint on the floor in front of me.

"No," I answered. "Well, kind of." I hesitated for a moment, then proceeded to profess my love for Barbie Delaney.

Only Porsche seemed to know who I was talking about. "Well, you couldn't have chosen a more elusive creature."

"Tell me about it," I said.

I told them all about that glorious night inside her bedroom and how she'd been avoiding me ever since. Surprisingly, they all appeared very interested and concerned.

"Ahhh, he really loves her," Jasmine said to the entire group.

"It sounds like she has feelings for you, too," Kaneesha said to me. "How old is she?"

"Twenty-one," I replied.

"And you're what?" she asked.

"Thirty."

"Ah, I never would've guessed."

"Well, there's your problem right there," Daphne said. "She's too young for you! You need a more mature woman... someone such as myself—"

"Daphne's right," Bettie Page said. "She may have feelings for you, but at *her* age she's probably not ready for a serious relationship. Sadly, you're both just victims of bad timing."

"Maybe it's not as bad as all that," Porsche said. "Maybe she's an old-fashioned girl at heart... and she's waitin' for you to pop the question."

"Marriage?" I said.

"No, silly," she laughed. "Ask the girl out! Was you ever plannin' on doin' that?"

"Yeah, at some point," I said. "I'm takin' it slow."

"That's probably why she's never at home," she said. "Why buy a cow when you can get the milk for free?"

"Are you sure we're not talkin' about marriage?" I asked suspiciously.

"It's called playin' hard to get," she said, bopping me on the head, "and it's all part of the dating game." She shrugged and added, "It's either that or she's just not that into you."

"Yeah, that's what I'm afraid of," I sighed. "What if I ask her out and she says no... she just wants to be friends?"

"Then it's time for Plan B," Porsche replied.

"Plan B?" I said curiously. "What's Plan B?"

"Let's just take it one step at a time," she said.

"Boy, this is some party," Laura interjected from across the room, snorting up the last few bumps of cocaine. "I'm so glad we came."

"Did you say somethin', deary?" Porsche shouted at her.

"Nope, just talkin' to myself!" she exclaimed.

Things got a little hazy after that. The scotch began to sneak up on me and I became something of a flirt. Then, all of a sudden, I got up and made a complete ass of myself, dancing around the room to Gloria Gaynor's "I Will Survive," constantly bumping into furniture and falling into people's laps. Daphne decided to take full advantage of the situation, rushing up in front of me and dancing extremely close. Jasmine and Bettie Page joined in and they each took turns brushing their manginas up against me. Before I knew it, I was dry humping and French kissing Daphne, all the while thinking, *Wow! I'm kissing Ethel Merman!* Laura quickly stepped in and pulled me off of her.

"All right, you guys... that's enough!" she exclaimed, just as Porsche walked over to the stereo and turned it down.

"Daphne, you should be ashamed of yourself," Porsche scolded her with just a hint of a smile.

"What did *I* do?" Daphne exclaimed, also with a sly, little smile.

"Let's go, naughty boy... time to take you home," Laura said to me, immediately grabbing my arm and dragging me away.

"Bye, Benjamin!" several drag queens shouted all at once.

"Y'all come back now, you hear?" Daphne said.

"Benjamin, wait!" Porsche exclaimed.

She grabbed something from an end table and caught up with us before we reached the entryway.

"Here's my phone number," she said, handing me her business card. "Call me this weekend and keep me abreast of the Barbie situation. I can help."

"You know, you look really beautiful in this light," I said, reaching up to caress her cheek.

She swiftly jerked her head away and laughed. "Get out of here, you vixen."

Laura huffed and resumed pulling me toward the door. Opening it, she yanked me out onto the front porch and continued dragging me down the driveway.

"What's your fuckin' hurry?" I protested. "I was havin' fun in there!"

"I did you a favor," she said. "You'll be thanking me in the morning, trust me." She finally let go of me when we reached the sidewalk. "Give me your keys," she demanded. "I'm driving." She immediately cut me off as I started to squawk. "Eh! Eh! Don't argue with me! You're in no condition to drive."

She held out her hand and I begrudgingly placed my keys in it, which turned out to be a huge mistake. She was in no better shape to drive than I was! Wired to the gills on coke, she turned the main thoroughfare into a racetrack, pushing the accelerator to the floor, dodging cars left and right by constantly switching lanes. It sobered me up really quick, for we were either headed for the morgue or the county jail.

"Man, look at us!" she shouted excitedly. "We're really flyin'! I told you I was a good driver."

"You might want to slow it down a bit!" I exclaimed.

"You're not enjoying this?" she asked, looking surprised.

"No."

"Well, that's too bad, 'cause I'm just gettin' started!" she said, and laughed like a maniac.

"I'm serious," I said more firmly. "You need to slow down."

She responded by running through a red light. I was furious.

"Damn it, Laura!" I exclaimed. "Slow down and pull over... now."

"No way, Benny baby!" she laughed. "I'm the king of the road!"

Desperate to end her reign, I grabbed her purse sitting between my feet, rolled down my window, and stuck it outside, smiling at her the whole time. She gave me a quick glance and her eyes nearly popped out of her head.

"You wouldn't," she said. "Don't you dare, you fucker! I've got a whole eight-ball in there!"

"I guess you'd better pull over then, huh?" I said.

With a heavy sigh, she eased up on the gas and pulled over to the side of the road. I quickly reached over, turned off the engine, and pulled the key out of the ignition.

"All right, get out," I said as I opened the car door.

We both stepped out and switched places. Then I started up the car and got back on the road.

"Jeez, you really *are* a party pooper," she sulked.

"Yep, that's me," I replied.

I drove her back to her old AMC Eagle station wagon in the Inferno parking lot and followed her to her apartment at her request. I guess she wasn't quite ready to be alone just yet—and neither was I.

Her place was even smaller than mine, replete with old, beat-up furniture and smelling of cat piss. She had a big, pug-nosed Persian cat named Mr. Peepers. The damn thing kept glaring at me as he lay on top of the TV set next to the aluminum foiled rabbit ears. Laura gave me a beer to nurse. Then she sat down next to me in the loveseat and we talked for a bit. I asked her about her sexual preference, and she said that she was open to anything—whatever the hell that meant. I was also surprised to learn that she was a huge David Bowie fan, as was I. But she also loved John Stamos, *Melrose Place*, 2Pac, and NASCAR, all of which I despised. Thus, my mind began to wander as she spoke, and I wondered what Barbie was doing at that very moment. I preferred to be with *her*. I looked over at the grandfather clock in the corner of the room and saw that it was nearly six o'clock.

"Guess I'd better go," I said. "I've gotta be at work at eight."

"Why don't you sleep here?" she said.

"On the loveseat?" I asked.

"No, in my bed... with me," she said.

I suddenly felt very uneasy. *Here I go again,* I thought, *havin' to weasel my way out of sex!*

"I know," she groaned, "you're savin' yourself for the right girl."

"How did you know that?" I asked, completely stunned.

"Matt told me," she said.

"You know that I'm a—"

"Yep! He told everyone."

"That motherfucker," I scowled.

"I'm not askin' you to fuck me, Benny," she said with a laugh. "Did I say anything about sex? I just thought it'd be fun to cuddle for a while. You're very cuddly."

A few minutes later we were in her bedroom, stripping down to our undies and hopping into bed together. She nestled against my body, rested her head on my bare chest, and we talked about our favorite movies 'til she fell asleep. I just lay there very quietly and listened to her snore. It felt good to have an actual woman sleeping on my chest. If only it was the right woman. I'm pretty sure Laura didn't see *me* as a potential love interest either. I was just her giant teddy bear that she could take to after-parties and snuggle up to at the end of the night. Fun and cuddly doth not a great lover make!

It wasn't until I arrived at work a couple of hours later that I realized I'd forgotten about Matt and felt completely responsible when he failed to show up, being his ride and personal motivation coach. He finally came roaring into the parking lot on his Harley forty-five minutes late. But, luckily for him, my father wasn't around to see it, and none of the crew bothered to rat him out. So he got away with it this time.

We were tearing down high walls inside an old warehouse, with the overhead doors raised all the way up to let in the cool autumn breeze. Oh, how I loved the fall! At the end of the workday I went home, took a quick shower, put on some clean clothes, and headed off to the T-Bone Bar and Grill, where Barbie worked practically every evening. Porsche was right. If I was interested in a girl I should ask her out, like most boys do! The worst thing she could do was no. I'd probably get over it in thirty years—forty tops!

I walked into the restaurant scared but determined, like a man on a mission. Fortunately, I managed to get there just before the Friday night rush. There were only a handful of customers sitting in the booths, and the bar was totally empty. I walked up to the middle bar stool and sat down. Barbie suddenly stepped in from the kitchen, wearing her uniform—a blue shirt with the T-Bone emblem printed on it and her nametag. She was noticeably taken aback when she saw me.

"Benjamin, what are *you* doin' here?" she said as she walked up to me.

"I needed to see you," I replied. "It's been a while."

"I've been extremely busy lately," she said. "Workin' doubles, practicin' with the band… I'm usually too tired to party."

"That's okay," I said. "I'm gettin' sick of that whole scene anyway. I was hopin' we could start doin' stuff together... you know, regular stuff... like regular people—"

"What are you saying, Benjamin?" she said, looking a little uneasy.

"I'm tryin' to ask you out." I blushed.

She stood speechless.

"I thought we could go somewhere nice," I said, "like Steak and Ale or the Olive Garden. Then we could see a movie... or go bowling. I'd love to take you bowling."

"I don't bowl," she said very sharply, which threw me off a little bit.

"Neither do I," I said. "So it'll be a new experience for both of us—"

"I'm not like regular people, Benjamin," she said, "nor do I want to be! I'm a night owl and I love to party! This is who I am. So take it or leave it."

"I'll take it," I muttered, embarrassed, and took a moment to recollect myself. "It doesn't necessarily have to be like a date date. We could like order takeout, maybe go see a Metallica concert afterward. It doesn't matter. I like you... a lot... and I just wanna spend more time with you... but away from Tony's and the club—"

"Benjamin, we're friends," she said. "You wouldn't want me any other way, believe me."

Now *I* was rendered speechless, for those were the exact words I didn't want to hear. It hurt me very deeply to learn that I was strictly friend material in her eyes.

"Can I get you somethin' to drink?" she asked.

"I'll take a scotch on the rocks," I muttered, and started digging through my pants pocket.

"No, it's on the house," she said. "Any particular brand?"

"Surprise me."

She stepped away to fix my drink and came back moments later, setting it down in front of me.

"Thanks," I said, quickly grabbing it and chugging it down. I looked up at her as I put down the empty glass and forced a smile. "Friends, huh?" I said.

"Friends." She nodded and smiled back at me.

"It doesn't feel like friends," I boldly threw into the conversation. "I hardly ever see you anymore. We're more like casual acquaintances."

"You're right," she said. "I haven't been much of a friend to you. I'll do better, I promise. I want us to be friends forever."

A man stepped up to the bar and she went to take his order. She came back with her eyes all lit up, as if she'd just thought of something.

"My band's playin' at the Horny Toad next weekend," she said. "You should come."

"Sure, *I'll* be there," I replied.

"Great!" she exclaimed. "We've been rehearsin' for it for weeks! That's why I'm never at home. We're usually playin' 'til like five or six in the morning."

She leaned into the bar and looked directly into my eyes as she continued speaking. She said that she was sick of singing cover songs and she'd begun writing her own material.

"You should turn your poems into songs," I suggested to her.

"Hey, you might have somethin' there!" she laughed.

Maybe friendship *wasn't* such a bad thing, I thought. There we were, sharing our thoughts and feelings, staring deeply into each other's souls. It was about as intimate as *I* could ever hope for in my current condition. Our conversation came to an abrupt end when two of her hippie friends came waltzing into the establishment and stood at the end of the bar. It was the lanky fellow with the horn-rimmed glasses, Brian, I think, and some other long-haired, scraggly looking character that I hadn't had the pleasure of meeting yet.

"Hey, guys!" Barbie exclaimed and rushed over to talk to them.

She seemed much more relaxed and talkative in their company, so much so that she never bothered to return. I suddenly felt like an outsider, watching the three of them converse and joke around like old marine buddies. They were showing me what true friendship was all about, and it made me extremely jealous—just as a friend! *Fuck this friendship business!* I thought. *I'll never be any good at it!* I put up with being ignored for a good five minutes before I finally jumped up from the stool and waved good-bye to her.

She waved back and shouted, "Later, dude!"

Before I managed to take off, I felt someone sneak up behind me and give my shoulders a firm squeeze. I turned around and saw that it was Matt.

"What's goin' on?" I said.

"I came to see the chef," he said, referring to Tony, who was working back in the kitchen. "He gets off in an hour. What about you?"

"Barbie," I said, and pointed at her as she continued talking. "I asked her out."

"Oh, yeah?" he gasped, unable to conceal his disapproval. "What did she say?"

"She said she doesn't bowl," I replied. "See you around."

I walked off and left him standing there with a puzzled expression.

CHAPTER SEVEN

I called Porsche on the phone Saturday morning to tell her that Plan A was a bust. I should've listened to my gut, I told her, let Barbie get to know me better before I laid all my cards on the table. It was too much too soon!

"At least now you know where you stand with her," Porsche argued. "Stop your frettin'... friends is good! Friends I can work with."

She then told me to come over right away so we could contemplate our next move. I pulled into her driveway soon after, parking next to her candy apple red Lamborghini convertible. Suddenly, *my* car looked like a piece of shit sitting directly beside hers. Porsche stepped out of the house before I reached the front door, dressed less glamorous but more sexy than usual in cut-off denim shorts, pink leggings, a cut-off sleeveless t-shirt, and dark sunglasses. She shut the door, made sure it was locked, and met me in front of the porch steps.

"Come on, baby... let's go for a ride," she said.

"Where are we goin'?" I asked as I turned and followed her down the driveway.

"Shopping."

"Shopping?" I scoffed.

"Don't scoff," she said. "It's very therapeutic! It always cheers *me* up when I'm feelin' down."

"But I don't need anything," I said as I walked up to the passenger door of her little hot rod.

"Yes, you do," she assured me. "Get in."

We got into the car; she backed out of the driveway and took off like a bullet. It felt good riding with the top down on a gorgeous sunny day.

"Okay, Plan B," Porsche said. "Be a friend to her, Benjamin... if that's what she needs. Be her *best* friend, in fact! Whenever she needs someone to talk to or a shoulder to cry on, you be that guy. Don't give up on her just because she isn't ready! I mean, if she's truly the one. Many a great romance began with friendship. And people *do* change, you know! We're all born into this world bein' selfish, ungrateful little pricks... gradually becoming more compassionate and giving as we get older. At least some of us! Just be patient... give her time. She'll come around."

"You really think people change all that much?" I asked.

"Yes, I do," she replied. "But, obviously, I'm not as cynical as you, Mr. Poopy Pants."

She reached over, turned the stereo dial to a sports station, and turned up the volume.

"I didn't know you were into sports," I said.

"Honey, I am a basketball fanatic," she replied. "Nuttin against college ball, but I swear I'll give up drinkin' and convert to Christianity if we ever get an NBA team here."

"You look like you might've played a little ball yourself," I said.

She laughed and said, "Size doesn't always mean anything! I've never been athletically inclined. What about you? Were you a sports god in your prime?"

"Not hardly," I laughed. "But I *was* on the high school football team."

"Let me guess," she said. "Offensive tackle?"

"Defensive nose guard," I replied. "I wasn't that good, though. I kept the bench warm, mostly. But I was a force to reckon with out on the practice field... and the coaches loved me for it! I always gave the first-stringers hell, made 'em look bad... which ultimately made 'em better players. It gained the respect of my teammates, but that was about it. No one else gives a shit about football practice," I sighed and added, "Nope, my only claim to fame was bein' friends with the high school quarterback... Ritchie Dickerson. He was my arch nemesis from kindergarten all the way up to middle school, always makin' fun of me and callin' me names. One time, he spilled his lunch tray all over me and pretended like it was an accident! But, when I joined the high school football team and he saw what a badass I was, we became really good friends. I went from a nobody to Mr. Popular's sidekick! Then I lost track of him after graduation and became a nobody again." I hesitated for a moment, then boldly pressed on. There was something I had to get off my chest before our friendship went any further. "Sometimes we'd hang out in Queer—I mean Gay Tow—the gay strip."

She smiled and said, "You can call it Queer Town if you want to. *I* do! What the hell were you two scalawags doin' *there?*"

"It was us and about half the football team, actually," I said. "Usually, we stood outside Club H and waited for an unsuspecting customer to come out. Then we'd drag him to the back of the building and beat the crap out of him." I regretfully shook my head. "The things I did just to fit in! That shit still haunts me."

"Those poor saps you bullied are probably still haunted, too," she said. "You're lucky *I* wasn't there! I would've gone full Chuck Norris on your asses—put *y'all* out of commission for the entire season."

I chuckled and said, "No doubt."

"I don't care about your past," she said. "You think *you* were a problem child? I tried to burn the house down and fry my parents in their sleep! They finally disowned me after that... sent me to live with my grandma. The main thing is you learned from your mistakes and grew into the man you are today. And the fact that that shit still haunts you is a good thing! It means you have a conscience... unlike a lot of people I know."

I realized that we were headed for Gay Town the second she got off the interstate and turned onto Pennsylvania Avenue. We soon drove past Club H and its vast, empty parking lot, then the Inferno, then a half-dozen quaint little shops stacked together in a row, including an antique shop, a flower shop, and Porsche's hair salon. She pointed it out to me as we whizzed past it. She made a right turn at the corner and we drove past the infamous leather bar, Saddle Tramps, and the even more infamous Paradise Inn—the old three-story hotel known to many as the sex palace of the homosexual community. She made another right turn at the next corner and parked in front of a big and tall shop called "Just for Bears."

"What are we doin' *here?*" I asked as she shut off the engine and opened her door.

"I'm buyin' you a new suit," she said. "You're startin' to wear out that black one."

"That's all right," I said, vehemently shaking my head. "I don't wanna put you out."

"You're not putting me out," she said. "I'm loaded, remember? You want to look your best for you know who... don't you? Get your ass out of this fuckin' car and let me help you."

I reluctantly got out and followed her to the entrance. She turned and flashed me a giddy smile before opening the door.

"Don't worry, this'll be fun!" she said. "I'll pretend like I'm Norma Desmond, here to buy my man some nice duds. And you're the William Holden character... the poor, miserable, out-of-work screenwriter."

"That isn't too much of stretch," I grumbled, walking in behind her.

"Philip, how's it goin'?" she said to the male salesclerk in front of the counter, as if they were old friends.

"Peachy," he said, and gave me a sidelong glance. "I can see *you're* doin' well, Miss Thang."

He was a walking cliché with the effeminate voice, gold earring dangling from one ear, ponytail in back while balding in front, and his belted blazer.

"My man here needs a suit," Porsche said.

"Yes, he most certainly does," Philip replied, turning his nose up at my old jeans and flannel shirt. "Follow me."

He led us to the back of the store and I tried on one suit after another. Porsche kept saying no to everything. One suit was too flashy, another too boring. And Philip was constantly agreeing with her, which made him the worst salesperson ever. Honestly, I thought they all looked good on me. But nobody wanted to hear *my* opinion on the matter. I was just the model! Porsche said to pretend that we were in *Sunset Boulevard,* but it felt more like Alfred Hitchcock's *Vertigo* to me. And I was Kim Novak, being made over by a crazed, almost maniacal Jimmy Stewart! Finally, about thirty minutes later, I stepped out of the changing room in an olive green double-breasted ensemble—plus my holey white socks—and neither of them shook their heads this time, which was a good sign. They just stood there eyeballing me for one whole, excruciating minute.

"Perfect," Porsche said.

"Mmm-hmm," Philip agreed. "It really brings out the eyes. Will that be cash or charge?"

"Don't rush me, Phil," she said. "Now we need a dress shirt, maybe some shoes.... Oh, and a decent pair of socks."

She walked up and looked at me with adoring eyes.

"So this is the one?" I asked, elated that she'd actually found something she liked.

"See for yourself," she said, pointing at the mirror on the dressing room wall behind me.

I turned around and stared at my reflection, totally amazed at how sharp I looked. It put my black ensemble to shame—though Johnny Cash would probably disagree. Porsche sidled up to me and gazed into the mirror as well.

"Look at you," she said. "You're a prince! Forgive me for sayin' it, but Barbie's a fool! I'd be all over you if I was her. Whenever you get fed up with the opposite sex, let me know... will you?"

I tried out my new look at Tony's house that very same night. And, luckily, Barbie just happened to be there. She stepped up to me as soon as I walked in, looking totally amazed.

"Benjamin, you look handsome," she said.

Thank you, Porsche! I thought. I couldn't have hoped for a better response. I immediately reciprocated by telling her she was beautiful.

"I'm not beautiful," she replied.

"You are to me," I said.

We sat in the living room and talked for a while. Then I finally got to take her for a spin in my new car. She didn't seem all that impressed with it, probably because she wasn't as materialistic as I was. It was just a car, after all, something to get you from A to B. She never mentioned my weight loss either, which struck me as kind of odd. We're talking a whopping forty-eight pounds so far! But, then again, why would she? I had a problem with my physical appearance—she didn't. It probably didn't matter to her if I was a four-hundred-pound gorilla or a ninety-pound weakling. She only saw my inner beauty. This was pure speculation, of course. I hadn't a single clue what was going on inside her head. Yet I could tell that she was making a conscious effort to be a better friend to me. She continued to stay away from the club, but I could count on her being at home more often than not. Most of the time, we'd lock ourselves in her bedroom and smoke weed all night. I was actually beginning to grow fond of the stuff, but only if she was smoking it with me. Sometimes we'd sneak into the living room just to look at all the party animals. It was often more entertaining than the local zoo!

There were still nights when she was mysteriously absent, in which case I'd cling to Laura, or she'd cling to me—one or the other. All I knew for sure was that she was loads of fun when I was high, and not so much when I started to come down. Unlike Barbie, who never wanted to go anywhere, Laura liked to bounce from one club or after-party to the next. She loved to be seen, and I loved being seen with her. It made me feel like a real ladies' man. Consequently, a rumor spread like wildfire throughout the gay community that we were fuck buddies, and I neither confirmed nor denied it. Sick of being the odd man out in an overly sexual environment, I was more than happy to acquire the reputation of a dirty dog. I was the Rhett Butler of the gays!

One Tuesday night, Laura talked me into doing an eight-ball with her. Though the prospect of becoming a cokehead didn't sound too appealing, I'd always been fascinated with the white powder—ever since I saw *The French Connection* as a kid. We ditched Matt and Tony at the club and went to *her* place, where she promptly ordered the drug over the phone and had it delivered to her door like it was a pepperoni pizza. Our delivery boy was a big, scary Mexican dude named Jorge, wearing a black Starter jacket, sweatpants, and a gold chain around his neck. Yet, despite his thuggish appearance, he was warm and friendly toward Laura, and vice versa. And the transaction went very smoothly. He handed her a big ball of coke wrapped in aluminum foil; she handed him my hundred and twenty dollars, and he left. She tore away the aluminum foil to reveal a big plastic bag full of nose candy, swiftly removing the twist tie, pouring a third of the contents onto the dinner table, and spreading it out with a debit card. Then she cut a straw in half, stuck it in her nostril, and immediately went to town on the stuff, saving the last few lines for me.

"You're up, big boy," she said, and handed me the straw.

I stepped up to the table, bent down with the straw in my nose, and took my first snort of coke. It hit me hard and fast, a huge rush of euphoria followed by tons of energy—more than I knew what to do with! Soon, we were both pacing the floor like caged lions. Yet I felt more like King Kong.

"I'm King Kong!" I said to Laura with a crazy laugh.

"And I'm Godzilla!" she exclaimed. "Look out, Tokyo! Here I come!"

We only did about half the bag before we were out the door and headed for the party mobile. I gladly let her drive this time and even kept telling her to "punch it" when she was already going over eighty miles an hour. She parked in front of Saddle Tramps and double dog dared me to go inside with her. *How bad can it be?* I thought, blindly following her into the joint. As one would expect, the place was crawling with men; scantily clad men turning the dance floor into an orgy pit, go-go boys dancing for dollars in nothing but G-strings, and big, tough-looking biker types in black leather, some of them making eyes at me and licking their chops as if I was a big, juicy steak! It was a massive assault on the senses and I felt myself getting shorter by the minute, from King Kong to a pet monkey!

I tried to keep a safe distance from it all, even though the room was small and cramped, gravitating to the back wall and holding on tight. I noticed Laura standing at the bar with two behemoth bikers. One of them was fondling her breast as she spoke to him, which made me laugh and shake my head. Her taste in men was a puzzlement to me—first the scary drug dealer, now these two goons! She finally looked at me, and I timidly summoned her over with my forefinger. She put the bikers on hold and walked to the back of the room.

"What's up?" she shouted over Jimi Hendrix's "Purple Haze."

"Can we go now?" I bluntly exclaimed. "I hate this place!"

She simply laughed at me like I was a wuss or something, but I didn't care. I just wanted out!

She shrugged and said, "Might as well! They're about to shut down anyway."

We scrambled out the door and headed off to the next adventure. One of her gay friends was throwing an after-party at the Paradise Inn, so she drove us about thirty yards and parked in back of the building. There was a horde of people standing outside a first-floor hotel room. We worked our way through them to get to the door and stepped into an even larger crowd. I'd never seen so many people crammed into a three-hundred-square-foot room. I could hardly move—or breathe, for that matter, especially with a thick haze of marijuana smoke polluting the air. While Laura began mingling with a group of friends, I decided to turn back and head for the door. It felt good to get out of there and breathe in the fresh air.

I wandered to the front of the complex and went inside, curious to see if the hotel lived up to its name. All I saw was an old lobby in dire need of a makeover. And the place was infested with hookers, tweakers, and creeps—all on the prowl. Stepping into the main hallway, I saw a discotheque and a piano bar right next door to each other. Both had already shut down for the night. But the little gift shop across the way was open twenty-four hours—if ever you were in need of dildos, lube, or gay porn. I walked toward the exit at the end of the hall, stepped out into the courtyard, and stood at the edge of a beautifully lit swimming pool. I was standing in the very core of the building, surrounded by all three floors and over a hundred rooms. The blinds were raised and the lights shined brightly in most of the windows, allowing me to view a myriad of peep shows all at once. All I can say is, there was a whole lot of sex and drug consumption going on in Paradise that morning! There was a young man and woman shooting up heroin in one window and a fat guy jacking off in another, plus a plethora of guy-on-guy action and girl-on-girl action. *Now I'm in "Rear Window"!* I thought. *The cops would have a field day in this place!* Yet, from the looks of it, the police pretty much stayed clear of Gay Town and let its inhabitants do as they damn well pleased. Maybe the hotel manager was screwing the chief of police. I don't know. But, whatever the case, I decided that the Paradise Inn wasn't for me, and moseyed on out of there to find Laura. I went right back into that little hellhole and managed to tear her away from her friends. Then we drove off to her apartment for a little nightcap. She finished the rest of the eight-ball; I drank a Screwdriver.

"You sure you don't want any of this?" she asked as she stood over the table with her straw.

"Yep," I said. "I gotta be leavin' soon."

"Don't be a bird brain," she said. "You know you can sleep here with *me.*"

She flashed her big, blue eyes at me and gave me a come-hither look, causing the warning siren to go off in my head.

I calmly got up from the loveseat, shook my head, and said, "Nah... it's easier just to go home, so I can get up and put on some clean—"

"I want to have sex with you!" she blurted out.

"I can't!" *I* blurted out.

"Why not?" she argued. "Everyone thinks we did it already! Let's make it official!" She walked up to me and grabbed my hands. "It won't take long, I promise," she assured me. "Just a little quickie... one for the road...

and none of that foreplay crap! Wham-bam-thank-you-ma'am."

"I really need to go," I insisted, and jerked away from her.

"God, you're such a goody-two-shoes," she laughed. "Your reputation's tarnished! People don't think you're a virgin anymore." She grabbed ahold of me again. "So come to bed with me, you manwhore."

"I'm sorry," I said, jerking away from her once more. "I'll see you later." I turned and walked hurriedly to the door.

"I take it back!" she furiously exclaimed. "You're not a goody-two-shoes, you're a chicken shit! Just go home and jack off, why don't you?"

More hostile words and profanity spewed from her lips as I slipped out and closed the door. I jumped into the car and quickly sped off, angry at myself and my ailment. I would've been okay with Laura being my first—as long as Barbie was my last! But, as usual, my flaccid penis had the last laugh, once again reminding me that I'd never be able to bang either of them!

On Thursday night, I was up to my old tricks, dancing alone on a crowded floor, rolling and sweating my ass off. Over to my right was Porsche, dancing with a handsome young man. And to my left was Matt, Simone, and Desiree, dancing in threes. I suddenly noticed Tony and Neil step onto the dance floor, the former in black leather and the latter in brown leather. Tony smiled and winked at me as they broke into dance and I smiled back, thinking, *Good, the gang's all here... well, almost!* When I looked straight ahead again, I was surprised to see Barbie standing before me, looking like an angel in a sexy red miniskirt. I stopped dancing and just stood there gawking at her in total awe. She laughed and began swinging her hips and snapping her fingers to the music. I followed her lead, then suddenly we both let go and were giving it our all to KC and the

Sunshine Band's "Keep It Comin' Love," which instantly became my favorite song of all time. It was amazing! I'd never seen her dance before! And to see her become so animated, so free-spirited, and just allow herself to be silly and have fun with a cheesy yet uplifting song from the seventies was a glorious sight to behold. Maybe she didn't bowl, but she sure could dance!

"Okay, friends and lovers," said the omnipotent DJ over his microphone, "let's keep on sweatin' to the oldies," and he started playing "Everlasting Love," by Carl Carlton.

As Barbie and I continued feeding off each other's energy and making each other laugh, I made the mistake of looking toward the crowd in front of the dance floor. Laura was standing right there in front of everyone and staring at me with a long face—no doubt trying to make me feel guilty. I *did* feel bad for her, but she knew I had a thing for Barbie. We just chose not to talk about it. Barbie saw me looking at her and immediately regained my attention by turning around and pressing her back up against my chest while bumping and grinding. Boy, did that feel good! I believe she actually brought some life back into my little pecker! She then looked straight at Laura and the two women glared at each other 'til Laura, defeated, turned and walked away. It was the subtlest cat fight I'd ever seen! And to think that they were fighting over me made it even more surreal!

Barbie and I danced all the way to closing time, making it the single greatest moment of my entire life. The first all-nighter inside her bedroom was now a close second. I met her at Tony's afterward and we went to her room to smoke a joint. As we lay in bed together, passing it back and forth, she inquired about my sex life.

"So, I hear you popped your cherry," she said nonchalantly, as if it didn't matter to her one way or the other.

I hesitated to respond. *I have to be careful here!* I thought. Did she prefer me to be pure and untainted or experienced and worldly? Would it please her to know that I was saving myself for her—or would it scare her off? I decided to go with the truth.

"Nope, still a virgin," I said. "I have no idea how that rumor got started... but there wasn't any fuckin' goin' on. We just partied together, that's all."

She just shook her head as I grabbed the joint from her and took another hit. Thankfully, nothing more was said on the matter.

CHAPTER EIGHT

I drove straight to the warehouse from the after-party with Matt as my copilot, both of us still rolling from the night before. Consuming twelve pills between us in one night would do that. My pretty white shirt, olive green slacks, and shiny black dress shoes now served as my work clothes. That day, we were tearing out a high wall together, working thirty feet in the air on a scissor lift that my father had just rented. It was old and very wobbly when it was thirty feet off the ground. And the platform we were both standing on was only four feet wide from guardrail to guardrail and eight feet long, so there was very little room to work or move around. We stood side by side, pulling sheetrock off the wall and tossing it in the pile behind us—the entire platform rocking fiercely back and forth the whole time. I would've been scared for my life had I not been feeling such an incredible buzz, not only from the ecstasy but from lingering memories of the past seven hours.

"Do you think this thing could tip over?" I asked Matt as I peeked over the guardrail and stared at the concrete far down below.

"Probably," he said, and we both giggled as we worked, tearing through the wall in front of us like we tore up the dance floor. Who knew the construction biz could be so fun and exciting?

"We should save a couple of pills for work," I said, which was most definitely the drugs talking. "Sure would make the day go by a lot faster."

Matt laughed at the thought and pretended to be stoned out of his gourd. "Man, this wall is so beautiful," he said as he ran his fingers over it. Then he caressed his cheek with his hammer. "I love this hammer! I love my crappy job."

We giggled some more, just as Sean walked in and looked up at us with envy.

"You guys better get to work!" he shouted. "The boss just drove up."

We flat-out ignored him and kept on giggling.

"Okay... just thought I'd warn you!" he bitterly exclaimed, and walked off.

After he was gone, I said, "We'd better get to work! The boss is here."

We started hammering through sheetrock and yanking it off the wall like a couple of madmen. I yanked on one piece so hard that I fell backward when it broke off, hitting the guardrail behind me, which was only thirty-nine inches tall and barely reached my lower back. If I hadn't regained my balance in that final second, I probably would've gone over the top!

"Jeez, I thought you was a goner!" Matt gasped.

"Yeah, me too," I said, and we both knelt down to recover from the shock.

Of course, that was the very instant my father walked into the room.

"Let's get busy, fellas!" he shouted. "It's not break time yet!"

We immediately got up and went back to work while he continued looking up at us suspiciously.

That evening, I received a phone call from Sean, which seemed a little odd since he'd never called before and we hardly ever spoke at work anymore. I'm not even sure how he got ahold of my number.

"Hey, Big B... what's up?" he said.

"Hey," I replied.

"You gettin' ready to go out?"

"Nope, we're takin' the night off."

"Does Matt still talk about Miami?" he asked bluntly.

"Not lately," I replied. "Why?"

"Remember when he said he caught Miriam cheatin' on him and nearly killed the guy?" he said.

"Yeah."

"It's all bullshit," he said. "Don't you think the cops would've caught up with him by now?"

"Haven't really thought about it."

"When he came back, I let him stay with me for a couple of weeks," he said. "It was a disaster! He kept callin' her long-distance and runnin' up my phone bill. I had no idea it was goin' on 'til I got the damn thing in the mail. It pissed me off, big time! You know how he is with other people's money. He just don't give a shit."

"I hear ya," I laughed.

"I thought I had a couple of lovebirds on my hands," he said, "tryin' to send me to the poorhouse! But that wasn't the case at all! Miriam called *me* up one night and begged me to tell him to quit callin' her! She didn't want anything to do with him."

"Really?" I replied.

"The way she tells it," he said, "*she* walked in on *him* and caught him suckin' a man's dick... some guy he met at the bar or a drug dealer, I suppose! She threw him out of the house—told him she never wanted to see him again. But he hung around and stalked the shit out of her... 'til she finally got her *new* boyfriend to knock some sense into him. He's a linebacker for the Miami Dolphins."

"Ouch," I replied.

"You ain't a-kiddin'," he said. "I guess that's when he realized it was hopeless and hightailed it back here." After a brief pause he snapped, "Don't you dare say anything to *him* about this!"

"No, of course not," I replied.

"He doesn't know that I know," he said. "I can't believe it... my best friend, a guy I've known since kindergarten, is a fuckin' switch-hitter! He could be a *total* queer for all we know."

"No way," I said. "He's always got a girl or two with him when we're at the club."

"It's just a front!" he exclaimed. "Who's that dead actor? Rock Gibson, Dash Riprock—"

"Rock Hudson," I said.

"Yeah, that guy!" he exclaimed. "I heard somewhere that he married a straight bitch to hide his perversion from the general public. No one had a clue that he was queer, 'til he got AIDS."

"Well, there's no doubt in my mind that Matt digs the ladies," I said. "And, as far as the dick sucking's concerned, he was probably just doin' it for the drugs."

"So you're sayin' he's a coke whore?" Sean snapped. "Is that supposed to make me feel better?"

"I'm just guessin' here," I said in my own defense.

"There's not too many straight guys who'd be willin' to suck another man's cock for some blow," he argued. "They'd have to have a little faggot in 'em to begin with."

"Oh, I don't know," I said. "I'm sure there's plenty of addicts out there that'd do just about anything to get their fix... faggot or otherwise."

"Which one are you?" he asked sharply.

"Huh?"

"Gay or straight?"

"Straight, of course," I hastily replied.

"So, why do you hang out at Club H?" he said. "We know Matt's excuse."

"I just like the people there!" I exclaimed, a bit rattled by his line of questioning. "Tony, Porsche, Rog and Skippy... they're like family."

"You've already got a family," he said, "a very well-to-do one! Most people would kill to have a family like yours."

"I don't really fit in there," I said. "I'm like the black sheep... adopted at birth. My parents could've avoided me altogether if they'd just been patient and waited a year or two. They ended up havin' two perfectly fine children... a boy and a girl... born of their blood."

"But now you're right where you belong," he said with a hint of sarcasm in his voice.

"Yep!" I said.

"In queer town... with *those* misfits."

"Yep."

"Rog and Skippy."

"Uh-huh."

"I hate to break it to you, Big B," he said, "but those people aren't your friends! You just share a mutual interest in designer drugs."

"Sorry, but you're wrong," I said. "If you'd just come out and party with us, you'd see that they're really nice folks."

"Party with the gays?" he scoffed.

"Why not?" I said.

"Seriously?" he huffed. "Do we really need to go there?"

"Let's do it."

"Okay," he said. "There's only two things I can't stand in this world... niggers and queers! Oh, and spics... three things."

"Might as well throw the Jews in there—"

"And Jews!"

"What, is it just that they're different?"

"It goes much deeper than that!" he exclaimed. "Niggers... killers, thieves, and junkies, for the most part! Spics... also criminally inclined! Plus, they're comin' over here illegally and takin' our jobs! Jews... they killed Jesus! Nuff said! Queers... nasty, filthy degenerates! All they think about is sex."

"You're Italian, aren't you?" I continued needling him.

"What of it?" he said. "Italian-Americans built this country! My father was a construction worker, like me. *His* father was a bricklayer! And my great-grandfather also did somethin' with his hands, though I'm not sure what."

"What about the Mafia?" I said.

"Huh?"

"The Italian Mafia... one the most criminally inclined organizations in America, feared throughout the land."

"You know what, Big B?" he said. "I'm not havin' this conversation with you. We're obviously not seein' eye to eye here. Talk to you later, man." *Click.*

"I think he's comin' around," I said to myself and laughed as I hung up the kitchen phone.

I saw a whole lot of Laura in the weeks that followed. I thought she'd given up on me, but no such luck. We kept bumping into each other at the club just as the drugs were kicking in and she'd have me drive her somewhere while I was inebriated, usually to places that clashed with my high, like a jazz club full of hipsters or some underground establishment swarming with angry grunge rockers. Afterward, we'd finish the night off at *her* place, snorting lots of cocaine. It was all a deliberate ploy to keep me away from Tony's house, and I was always too fucked-up to do anything about it—or even care. I'd wake up the next day furious at myself for letting her sabotage my love life.

It'd been twelve days since I saw Barbie last, thanks to her. I had to ask myself if it was worth spending time with a woman I wasn't romantically attached to. And the answer was a resounding, "Hell, no!" Whenever I was with her, I felt even more alone than I would've been at home by myself, raiding the refrigerator, staring at the TV, or whittling away at my screenplay. At least at home there wasn't someone talking in my ear constantly and I could watch whatever I wanted to on the boob tube. It was my loner mentality shining through. Sure, I could use a mate, but I could do without friends in my life. Bottom line, I had to get rid of Laura somehow!

That opportunity finally presented itself on a weeknight in October when she called me and begged me to come over. I was in no mood to party so early in the evening, having just got off work. But I knew she'd have plenty of coke lying around the house to re-energize me, so I went. I knocked on her door and a big, burly black man answered, nearly twice my size and almost completely naked except for a pair of white briefs.

"I-i-s Laura here?" I stammered nervously, caught completely off guard.

"Yeah, man," he said in a deep voice and let me in.

I followed him into the living room and found her sitting in the middle of the floor with three other men, playing cards in their undergarments—strip poker, I presumed. Two of the men appeared to be skinheads with their shaven heads and multiple tattoos on their hard, thin bodies. The third man was also covered with tattoos but was short, stocky, had a Mohawk, and looked Samoan. I had a strong hunch that they'd all spent some time in the joint. *Where in the hell does Laura find these guys?* I had to ask myself once again. *She* sat at the head of the circle with her breasts exposed and holding a set of cards in front of her. All she had on were her panties.

"Big B, you made it," she said, noticing me standing in front of the entrance in a state of shock. "Come grab a seat."

I stepped a bit farther into the room while the big black man rushed right in and rejoined the group. *No, I'm not doing this!* I thought, suddenly turning around and heading for the door.

"Wait! Come back, Big B!" Laura laughed. "Where ya goin'?"

"Come back, Big B!" the big black man and little Samoan shouted together mockingly.

"Yeah, man... don't be rude!" one of the skinheads exclaimed very sharply.

I turned and walked back into the room before they all got up to tackle me and sat down on the loveseat directly behind them. Mr. Peepers was lying next to me, giving me the stink eye.

"No, sit here by me... so I can teach you how to play," Laura said, patting the carpet.

I firmly shook my head and said, "Y'all go ahead and finish your game. I'll just watch."

"Okay, but you're playin' the next one," she warned me.

It was bad enough having to sit there and continually look down at their half-naked bodies, but pretending to enjoy their crude sense of humor was pure torture. I felt like I was at work.

"Hurry up and bet, will ya?" Skinhead Number One snapped at Skinhead Number Two. "I gotta get home and bang the shit out of the old lady."

I wasn't even sure if that was a joke. But everyone else thought it was mildly amusing.

Then the black guy asked the Samoan guy if he'd ever licked a man's balls before.

"No, but I ate your mama's pussy last weekend," the latter responded. "I call it Tuna Helper Fridays."

Both skinheads laughed hysterically as if it was the funniest thing they'd ever heard. And I was almost appalled to see Laura cackling right along with them, pretending to be one of the guys. I'm surprised she wasn't wearing a dealer's visor and chomping on a cigar. Just when I thought she couldn't be any less attractive to me, she laid down a full house to the Samoan's royal flush.

"You lose again, girl," Skinhead Number One said to her with a fiendish grin. "Go ahead and take them panties off."

"Take 'em off! Take 'em off!" all four men started chanting while pounding their fists against the floor.

She swiftly stood up, slid her pink panties down to her feet, and stepped out of them, kicking them aside. Catcalling and wolf whistling ensued and she appeared to be enjoying every second of it, simply holding out her arms and circling around twice—so we could soak it all in. *Crazy bitch probably lost on purpose!* I thought, suddenly feeling sick to my stomach. I sensed a gangbang in her immediate future, and I wasn't about to stick around for it! I got up and stormed out of the room. She immediately came running after me in her birthday suit and grabbed onto my shirt sleeve. I plodded onward, dragging her with me.

"Damn it, stop!" she exclaimed. "What the fuck's the matter with you?"

"You invited me over here just to embarrass me, didn't you?" I snapped. "You always seem to get a big kick out of that."

"No, I just wanted the guys to meet you," she said. "I told 'em you were a barrel of laughs! But not tonight, apparently. If I knew you was gonna be an old sourpuss—" She finally let go of me as I reached the door. "I think you're overreacting!" she shouted desperately.

"Am I?" I scoffed, pulling the door open. "You're standin' there naked, Laura."

"So what?" she said with a laugh. "I like bein' naked! Please don't walk out on me again, Benjamin! Don't you know how much that hurts?"

"Sorry, but it's not gonna work," I said, quickly stepping out. We were done—at least for the time being.

It was back to just me and Matt the following night. Before entering the club, we stepped up to the payphone and he called my dad to tell him how his AA meeting went. Luckily for Matt, Dad only attended the first one with him. But he was still required to call in and give Pops a full report every Monday and Wednesday night after the bogus meeting was over. Usually, he made the call from that very payphone next to the club entrance. It was just his way of saying, "Fuck you, boss."

"Yes, sir, you're absolutely right... it *is* the devil's brew," he said over the phone as I stood just a couple feet away, rolling my eyes at him. "Thank God I'm not a slave to it anymore! I feel like a new man! Yes, sir... I will! You too, sir! Bye-bye, now."

"You're fuckin' Eddie Haskell, you know that?" I sneered at him as he hung up the phone. "You're lucky he doesn't make us piss in a cup every morning."

"So are *you*," he retorted.

We went inside, bought some pills, met some chicks, and eventually hit the dance floor. But all I could think about was going to Tony's place afterward, so I could see Barbie's face and stare into her beautiful green eyes. Thank God, the night flew by as usual. The lights came on just as I was coming down, and the DJ urged us all to head for the exit.

As I was walking off the dance floor, I noticed Sean standing alone at the bar, looking all dapper in a blue double-breasted suit. Matt and I were also dressed to kill, him in his gray sports jacket, ripped jeans, and baseball cap and me in my olive green suit. I walked straight up to Sean and gave him a big bear hug, making him noticeably uncomfortable. I couldn't help myself. I was so happy and surprised to see him.

"Have you been here all night?" I asked as I let go of him.

"Just got here," he said, shaking his head. "I left Shenanigans a little early."

Matt stepped up to the bar with Simone and looked at Sean with a straight face.

"How's Shenanigans?" he asked.

"It's still there," Sean said, and the two men just kept nodding at each other—forever, it seemed.

Finally, Porsche, Kaneesha, and Mo'Nique walked up to break the unbearable silence, all in their gold sequin dresses. Those three were always in character!

"There you are," Porsche said to me. "I've been lookin' for you all night!"

"I was out there the whole time," I shrugged.

"So was I!" she said.

She bent down to hug me and kiss my cheek while Sean looked on in horror and disgust—probably afraid that he'd lost *me* to the dark side as well.

"Don't *I* get a hug?" Kaneesha asked after Porsche was finished with me.

"Of course," I said, throwing my arms around her and receiving another peck on the cheek.

I hugged Mo'Nique next and then introduced them all to Sean, who suddenly looked very tense as they greeted him with hellos and complimented him on his good looks. Being ogled by three large black men in drag must've been a total nightmare for him.

"Well, we'd best be on our way," Porsche said. "Nice to meet you, Sean! Maybe I'll see you at Tony's later."

She winked at him while Kaneesha and Mo'Nique waved and blew him a kiss, respectively. Then the three of them scurried away, bringing the tension right back into the room. My workmates were too proud to even look at each other.

"We'd better get goin' too," Matt said, taking Simone by the hand and walking off without saying good-bye.

"You're going to the after-party, aren't you?" I shouted at him.

"Yep!" he shouted back.

I urged Sean to come along, but he said he'd rather go home. And I could understand why. Matt sure as hell didn't make it any easier for him. There was just no getting these two kids back together, it seemed. Sean and I walked out into the parking lot together and went our separate ways.

Things were even more awkward at Tony's house, at least for me. Barbie wasn't there, but Laura was. And, much like Matt and Sean, we couldn't even look at each other. Whenever we *did* happen to exchange glances, it was very unsettling. I usually tried to stay clear of Tony's bedroom, afraid of what I might find in there. But, this time, I rushed down the hall and walked right in since the door was already half-open. Tony, Matt, and Simone were lying face-up on the bed, fully clothed and sharing a mirror full of coke.

I walked up to Tony lying on the end and said to him flat-out, "I'm gonna need a lot more pills."

"You got it, B," he replied, swiftly getting out of the bed and fixing me right up.

I took a couple of hits, stuffed the rest in my pants pocket, and headed back to the living room, which was growing more crowded by the second. I could hear Laura joking around with Rog and Skippy on the couch, so I took a sharp turn into the dining room, sat down at the table, and waited for the pills to do their stuff. Sitting directly across from me was a handsome young man I'd seen and talked to once before. Only now he looked very ill, gaunt and pale-skinned, with lesions on his face and neck. *AIDS!* I thought.

He looked at me and said, "How's it goin'?"

"Fine," I replied. "And you?"

"I'm still here," he said with a little sigh.

His handsome young partner stepped into the room with a baggie of coke and sat down next to him.

"Okay, we're all set," he said, pouring it all on the table and spreading it out for him. He handed him a rolled-up dollar bill, patted him on the back, and said, "There you go, buddy! It's all yours."

The sickly man quickly hunched over the table and sucked up the lines one by one. It was actually quite sad, seeing a dying man desperately clinging to the carnal pleasures in life. I had to get up and leave the room.

I stepped into the living room and began mingling with the crowd. I'd become such a permanent fixture in the gay party scene that everyone knew me by name and I was constantly greeted with hugs and kisses as I wandered from one group to the next. I felt like the token straight guy!

As I stood with a group of lesbians, I noticed Sean walk through the front door. He must've followed me from the club and was sitting in his vehicle the whole time, debating whether to come in or not. *The poor guy's a glutton for punishment!* I thought as I looked at him in shock and awe. I said good-bye to the lesbians and went right to work, heading straight for the kitchen and grabbing a beer from the fridge. When I went back into the living room, I found Sean standing between the fish tank and the door—in case he needed to flee at any given second.

"I'm glad you came," I said while handing him the bottle of beer.

"Thanks, man," he said and gulped it down.

I swiftly removed the baggie from my pants pocket, took out a pill and said, "Here, this might help, too."

"Gee, I don't know," he replied, which I took as a maybe.

"You'll love it, trust me," I said, raising my eyebrows up and down and smiling fiendishly like I was Satan.

He let out a huge laugh and said, "Ah, Big B... I don't know what I'm gonna do with you." He took the pill from my hand, put it in his mouth, and swallowed it, swiftly washing it down with his beer. "I hope you didn't just kill me," he said.

"I'll go tell Matt that you're here," I said, and started to walk off.

"No, don't!" he exclaimed, immediately grabbing my arm. "Stop fussin' over me, will ya? Go do your thing and let me stand here for a while."

"All right," I said, and went to mingle some more.

As I was busy talking to a guy, I glanced over at Laura and she looked at me. Neither of us were able to look away this time 'til she suddenly jumped up from the couch and stormed into the hallway. If she was trying to make me feel guilty again, she'd succeeded. Who was *I* to tell her it wasn't going to work? We weren't even in a serious relationship, just party buddies, I think. Sean was still glued to the wall, meanwhile, looking extremely uncomfortable. He reminded me of myself when *I* was the rookie. Ten minutes later, I noticed he was gone. *Damn it, Sean!* I thought, disappointedly shaking my head. *If you'd just stuck it out for a few more minutes!* But then I looked over toward the couch and there he was, snorting coke off the coffee table with Rog and Skippy while they discussed cinema—*Léon: The Professional*, in particular—which both he and Roger adored, from the sound of it. Every now and then, someone would walk up to the couch to shake Sean's hand and say that they were glad to finally meet him. I'm pretty sure everyone in the room knew about his and Matt's situation by now. And they were all doing their damnedest to make him feel at home. It made me very proud!

Porsche finally arrived at three in the morning. She squeezed in next to Sean and immediately struck up a conversation with him, discussing everything from OJ Simpson's slow-speed car chase to Anna Nicole Smith's marriage to some old, rich guy on his last legs—all while consuming lots of blow. Mo'Nique and Kaneesha showed up thirty minutes later with a karaoke machine and took the party in a whole 'nother direction. They hooked the thing up to the television and then everyone gathered around to watch one inebriated, tone-deaf asshole after another butcher perfectly good songs. There seemed to be no end to the cruelty! People who should never be allowed to sing in public were fighting over the microphone, determined to humiliate themselves no matter what!

Then, all of a sudden, Porsche, who stood directly across from me with Sean by her side, shouted, "Let Benjamin go next!"

"Yeah, Big B... show us what you got!" Sean shouted with a sly grin.

"Big B! Big B! Big B!" chanted the rest of the crowd.

Being fully inebriated myself, I boldly stepped up to the machine, selected a song from the playlist, picked up the mic, and sang "Fooled Around and Fell in Love," which pretty much summed up my mental state at the time. The lyrics kept flashing before me on the TV screen in case I'd forgotten a line or two. I wasn't no Mickey Thomas of the Elvin Bishop Group, but I at least managed to sing in tune. And, for that alone, I received tremendous applause and left people begging for more. I was more interested in payback, however, swiftly walking up to Sean and sticking the microphone in his face.

"Huh-uh," he said, and fiercely shook his head while Porsche kept nudging him in the shoulder and egged him on and the crowd began chanting *his* name in unison.

He suddenly burst out laughing and said, "All right, you guys! You asked for it," jerking the microphone out of my hand and stepping up to the plate. He picked out a song, put the mic to his lips and belted out, "Come on, come on, come on, now touch me, babe!" in a silky baritone voice, causing everyone's jaw to drop to the floor, including mine. *Jim Morrison's in the house!* I thought. Tony, Matt, Simone, and Laura came rushing down the hall and stood in the back of the room, all with amazed looks on their faces. Obviously, Matt wasn't aware that his former best friend had such a powerful singing voice. And Laura looked so impressed that it gave me an idea. When Sean was finished singing, everyone cheered and applauded louder than ever, which made me a little jealous, to be perfectly honest.

"Sing us another one!" someone shouted.

"Encore! Encore!" shouted someone else.

"Really... y'all want another one?" Sean giddily exclaimed with a newfound confidence in his crooning abilities.

Oh, my God... I've just created a monster! I thought. *Now he's gonna give up construction and sing in hotels!*

"Yeah, let's hear it!" Porsche shouted.

"All right, here it goes," Sean said and turned to Kaneesha standing next to the control panel.

"Play it for 'em, darlin'," he said. "Play 'Danke Schoen.'"

She punched in the appropriate number and the cassette began to play. First came that familiar bassline. Then Sean started snapping his fingers and jumped right in.

"Danke schoen, darling, danke schoen!" he sang with the same silky smooth baritone voice. "Thank you for all the joy and pain!"

People immediately clapped along, including Matt, who'd worked his way to the front of the crowd and had a huge smile on his face. Sean's voice began to waver as he noticed him for the first time. He stopped singing about halfway through the song, dropped the mic, and slowly walked up to him. Kaneesha shut off the music and everyone stood silently as the two men stared each other down. It looked like they were about to go for their pistols—if they'd happened to be wearing any! Then Sean stepped in closer, threw his arms around Matt, and they hugged it out.

"Awwww," said the entire crowd in unison and applauded once more.

Those standing closest to the two patted them on the back while Porsche rushed right in, gave Sean a hug, and then a quick peck on the lips. He appeared a little confused at first but quickly shrugged it off and returned the favor, attacking her lips long and hard. *Uh-oh, time to make my move!* I thought, swiftly walking up to him and tapping him on the shoulder. He pulled away from Porsche and turned around.

"You were right, Big B!" he exclaimed excitedly. "I love these guys!" He leaned in closer and nodded his head toward Porsche, still standing behind him. "She's really man, right?" he said in a low voice.

"Yes," I said very clearly and sharply, so there wouldn't be any more confusion on the matter.

He simply nodded, looking a bit disappointed.

"Come on, there's someone I want you to meet," I said, grabbing his arm and dragging him over to Laura. "Laura, this is Sean," I said. "Sean, this is Laura."

They smiled and shook hands. I'm sure she was very glad to meet *him* because he was a handsome stud, much better-looking than me, unfortunately. And he was glad to meet *her* because she was a female. *Okay, my work's all done here!* I thought, and left them to their own devices. I noticed Porsche glaring at me from a distance and shaking her head. I simply shrugged at her and kept on walking. I flopped down on the empty couch and just sat there, enjoying the fruits of my labor. Sean and Matt were back together. Sean and Laura were getting to know each other. I was two for two! Just when I thought I couldn't be more satisfied, Barbie stepped through the entrance and stood there smiling at me for thirty whole seconds before she walked into the room and sat down next to me.

"Would you put your arm around me?" she asked. "I'm not coming on to you. I'm just cold."

Thank you, faulty heater! I thought, and put my arm around her as I should've done in the first place, without her having to ask. She then rested her head on my shoulder and we sat in perfect silence and contentment, tuning out all the noise around us. It was just another fond memory to look back on and wonder what the hell went wrong!

CHAPTER NINE

November 19, 1994—Saturday Night—With Laura out of the way, I was finally able to go to the Horny Toad to hear Barbie sing. It was a seedy little bar on the east side of town, commonly referred to as "the hippie bar." She was already on stage with her band when I walked in. The tables were all full, so I sat down at the bar and ordered a peach piña colada. Looking around me, I could see that I was sorely overdressed. It was strictly a holey jeans and t-shirt crowd, and here I was in my favorite dancin' suit. But I wanted to look my best for Barbie.

After I paid for my drink, I swiveled around on the bar stool to get a good look at her and the band. I instantly recognized Brian and his scraggly young friend, who was with him at the T-Bone many weeks ago. He was on bass guitar while Brian stood behind the keyboards, wearing shades in place of his regular glasses. There was yet another long-haired hippie plucking the lead guitar and a fat Indian banging on the drums. I suddenly recalled seeing them all in Barbie's bedroom, smoking weed, when I first met her.

She stood at the front of the stage, screaming into the mic and dressed like a rock star in Iron Fist heels, skinny jeans, and a ripped halter top that showed off her cleavage and navel. I wasn't sure I liked the look. It certainly wasn't the same girl who gently sang Cole Porter to me in private. The song was dark and brooding, "Doll Parts," by Courtney Love and her Seattle grunge band, Hole. And her voice was so powerful and electrifying that Janis Joplin would've been envious.

The audience was completely captivated by her, which made me extremely jealous. *Stop looking at her that way, people!* I kept thinking to myself. *She's mine!* But it was useless. They all adored her and she obviously loved being adored. As much as *I* wanted to be adored, never in a million years would I have the courage to stand in front of hundreds of strangers and sing my heart out—not without a shitload of pills and piña coladas! I wished I'd never seen this side of her. She wasn't like me at all! I was probably kidding myself, thinking I could make it as a screenwriter. But she had the potential to actually go places with that amazing voice of hers. I had an eerie feeling that I was going to lose her to the world—if I hadn't already.

She finished the song to rousing applause and whistles and went straight into another Hole favorite, "Miss World." Then she sang Sound Garden's "Black Hole Sun" and "Spoonman," finally ending the set with a couple of Nirvana songs. It was grunge night at the Horny Toad!

"Thank you!" she said as the audience cheered and applauded her. "We are Rude Awakening... and *we* are out of here!"

I watched them make their exit, then turned back around to face the burly female bartender while another band took the stage. Five minutes later, I felt someone poke me in the back.

"Hey, buddy... you're on my stool," he said to me in a deep voice.

I swiveled around and saw that it was Barbie, pretending to be a man. She laughed and said, "Gotcha!"

"Hey, girl... you were awesome!" I said.

"Oh, thanks," she said. "Do you want to come sit with us?"

Who's us? I wondered. I was hoping it'd just be me and her.

"Come sit with us," she insisted. "We won't bite."

"All right," I said.

I got up and followed her to the front row of tables. Her bandmates and their girlfriends, or groupies, were seated at two tables scooted together right in front of the stage.

"Hey, guys... this is Benjamin!" Barbie shouted.

The music was so loud that I could barely hear her.

"Hey, man... I'm Zack!" the lead guitarist shouted at me. "Have a seat!"

I sat down at the end of the table next to Barbie, with Brian seated directly to her left. He was the only male band member who didn't have a girl practically sitting in his lap. They all sat very quietly and looked up at the stage, watching the band play "Free Bird." I nudged Barbie in the shoulder to get her attention.

"They're pretty good, aren't they?" I shouted as she turned to look at me.

She sternly shook her head and then laughed. Suddenly, Brian grabbed her arm to get her attention. He whispered something in her ear and she laughed hysterically. *What the hell's so funny?* I thought. *Is he a comedian now?* We spent the rest of the night vying for her attention. The band ended their set with "Break on Through (to the Other Side)" by the Doors, and the crowd went wild.

"Yeah! It's about fuckin' time!" Zack shouted.

The whole group got up and danced around the tables, except for me. I remained seated and let Barbie enjoy the moment without me. I watched her dance with Zack, then the bass guitarist, then Brian. Finally, the lights came on and Merle Haggard's "Okie from Muskogee" played over the PA system. I guess that's how the nights always ended there at the Horny Toad. I continued to sit patiently and watched Barbie talk to all her fans gathered around her. But eventually I grew tired of waiting, got up, and left. She caught up with me as I walked out the door and shouted my name. I turned around to face her.

"You were just gonna leave without sayin' good-bye?" she said.

"Well, you were busy talkin' to people," I said. "I didn't want to get in the way."

"You're a real piece of work, you know that?" She laughed. "We're all goin' to Skunk's house now. You're comin', right?"

"Which one is he?" I asked.

"The drummer," she replied.

"Oh," I said. "Yeah, sure... I'll come."

"Good," she said. "You can ride with us in the van."

She pointed toward an old black van sitting in back of the parking lot. The side door was open and the bass guitarist was making out with a giggling teenage groupie on the floor of the vehicle.

"I'll just follow you," I said.

"You sure?" she asked. "It's way out in the boonies. You might get lost."

"Don't worry," I said. "I'll be right on your tail the whole time."

Moments later, her bandmates and their lady friends loaded their equipment into the van and drove off, heading into the woods on an empty dirt road. I was practically riding their bumper with my headlights shining on them. Zack and his girlfriend were behind *me* on his motorbike. I had no idea where we were or how I'd get home later without the motorcade. Getting lost in the woods was one of my greatest fears, which was why I usually avoided them.

We drove through a long, dark maze of trees and bushes 'til we came upon an old, dilapidated two-story house with rotted siding. We parked in front of it and stepped out of our vehicles.

"Well, here we are," Barbie said, walking up to me. "This is where we usually practice. There's no one around for miles, so we can play as loud as we want! Oh, and before we go in I guess I should warn you... the place is haunted."

"Great," I replied.

She laughed and led me to the door. We all walked inside and she showed me the den. The room was dank and dark, even after she turned on the lamp, and it was filled with dusty, old furniture. It instantly reminded me of the Norman Bates house.

Skunk came into the room and turned the stereo on almost full blast while Barbie took me into the kitchen and pulled a couple of beers out of the fridge. Then we all gathered in the dining room and sat down at a long table. Barbie and I sat at one end, Brian at the other, and his male counterparts sat in between with their girlfriends in their laps.

"This house has a history, you know," Skunk said to me. "The previous owner killed his wife right here in this very room."

"Really?" I replied.

"Yeah," he said with a forceful nod and wide-eyed stare. "In the winter of sixty-three."

I had a strong hunch that he was just trying to scare me. But I played along.

"He blew her head off with a shotgun," he continued. "Then he hanged himself from the ceiling fan." He pointed at the rusty, old fan directly above us.

Now I knew he was full of shit! I couldn't imagine anyone hanging themselves from that flimsy, little thing—and certainly not with a table in the way!

"*That* ceiling fan?" I gasped.

"One and the same," he said. "I still see him hanging there from time to time."

"He must be a midget," I said to Barbie in a low voice.

She suddenly burst out laughing.

"Okay, *don't* believe me," Skunk shrugged. "You think I would've bought this place if it *wasn't* haunted?"

He looked at the pretty brunette in his lap and they kissed. Zack and the bass guitarist started making out with *their* women as well. Barbie and I stood up and scooted our chairs back against the wall to distance ourselves from the lot. I wasn't quite bold enough to reach in and plant a big wet one her, but I at least managed to put my arm around her without her having to ask. Though she seemed okay with it, Brian obviously wasn't. He kept glaring at me from the other end of the table while the smoke from his doobie poured out of his nostrils. Actually, he was creeping me out more than the house and all of its supposed history. Suddenly, "Linger" by the Cranberries began playing in the other room.

"Oh, I love this song," exclaimed the pretty blonde in Zack's lap. I believe her name was Rhonda.

They both got up and started slow dancing. Then the other two couples did the same. *Now what do I do?* I thought, contemplating whether or not I should ask Barbie to dance.

Finally, she smiled at me and said, "Come on, let's show 'em how it's done," and we quickly got up to join them.

I grabbed hold of her hand, placed my other palm on the small of her back, then we moved our feet ever so slightly, dancing so close that I could feel her breasts brushing against my chest. *This is way better than disco dancing!* I thought. At least I didn't have to worry about my cock making a surprise appearance! I noticed Brian glaring even harder as he sat alone at the table. But I didn't feel the least bit sorry for him. He should've brought an extra groupie.

We all split up after the song ended. Barbie and I went upstairs with Zack and Rhonda and stepped out onto the deck to get some fresh air, sitting alongside each other in reclining lawn chairs and staring over the balcony. The crickets were chirping away and I could hear a coyote yipping and howling off in the distance. But, other than that, it was a quiet, peaceful night, and there was romance in the air; 'til Brian stepped outside and snagged the empty chair next to Barbie, pinning her between us so we could fight over her again. He lit up another joint and shared it with her—and her with me.

Rhonda suddenly looked over at Barbie and asked her how the past life regression therapy was going. I'd almost forgotten that Barbie was into all that reincarnation nonsense.

"It's all right," she answered. "Turns out I was a peasant girl livin' in France durin' the Renaissance." She sighed and added, "I guess some things never change."

"Who do you want to be in the *next* life?" I asked her, just to make conversation.

"A man," she swiftly replied. "With a very large penis."

God, me too! I thought.

"How 'bout you?" she asked.

"Honestly?" I replied. "I hope reincarnation's a load of crap... because I'd probably come back as a mosquito or something."

"It *is* crap," Brian suddenly blurted out in his grim, monotone voice. "When you're dead, you're dead... just worm meat... or a pile of ashes. That's all we amount to in the end."

"Excuse me while I go slit my wrists," Zack said to Rhonda, causing her to laugh hysterically.

"All I'm sayin'," Brian grumbled, "is that we should enjoy this—whatever the hell this is—for as long as it lasts! It only comes around once."

"You can't bring up reincarnation around this guy," Barbie said to me while gently punching Brian in the arm. "His mama dropped him on his head one too many times. And now he's utterly convinced that human beings have no souls." She scowled at me playfully. "But what's your excuse?"

"Hey, I've got an open mind," I said. "Maybe reincarnation *does* exist! But only a moron would suggest that we don't have souls."

She promptly shoved the joint in my mouth to shut me up. I took a long puff, handed it back to her, and just lay there very quietly, staring up at the stars. The stuff was so relaxing that I could barely keep my eyes open.

"Don't you go to sleep on me," Barbie said.

"I won't," I assured her.

Yet I *did* doze off for only a few minutes, I believe, and when I woke up she was gone... and so was Brian. Rhonda was now on top of Zack in his chair, and the two were making out. I got up, tiptoed to the sliding glass door, and quietly stepped back inside. As I headed toward the stairs, I heard voices at the other end of the house, followed by Barbie's crazy, distinct laugh. So I turned and walked farther into the dimly lit parlor, entering a long, dark hallway. The light was on in the last room to the right. I slowly crept up to the door, peeked around the jamb, and found them sitting in the middle of the bed, facing each other. Barbie had a belt wrapped tightly around her bicep, and the other end of it was clenched between Brian's teeth as he poked a needle into the crook of her arm and shot her full of heroin. He swiftly removed the belt and syringe from her arm and watched her drop to the pillow with a smug look on his face. I'd never seen her more content—or smile so lovingly. He immediately lay on top of her, and they kissed. I was completely devastated. *How could she choose the grim reaper over me?* I wanted to storm into the room and give them a piece of my mind. But I held in my anger and simply turned and walked away, rushing downstairs and storming out of the house. Skunk was playing a harmonica for his girlfriend on the porch swing.

"Leavin' already?" he asked me as I shot past him and made a beeline for the car. "Have a good night!"

I jumped into the vehicle and tore out of there, bawling my eyes out. Reaching into the glove compartment, I pulled out my Carpenters CD, slid it into the machine, and played "Good-bye to Love" in a continuous loop. As I cried, it suddenly occurred to me that I had no idea where I was going or what direction I was headed in, which left me emotionally confused—the pain of a broken heart clashing with my fear of being lost in the woods. Thank God I had a full tank of gas!

After driving around in circles for nearly an hour, I finally stumbled upon a paved road and an actual street sign and hurried home to lick my wounds.

The next day I just wanted to sleep. But I made the foolish mistake of leaving the phone on the hook, and the damn thing woke me up at twelve in the afternoon while I was dreaming of a better life. I tried to ignore it and go back to sleep, but it just kept on ringing.

"Goddamn it," I growled, finally reaching over the nightstand and grabbing it.

It was Porsche, who was now in the habit of calling me every day and twice on Sundays, just to see how my love life was going.

Only, this time, she called to chew me out for standing between her and Sean the other night.

"You don't think I'm good enough for your friends?" she chided me.

"No," I mumbled into the phone, still barely awake. "It's more like they're not good enough for *you.* Can we talk about this later? I had a rough night and I just wanna go back to sleep."

"What happened?" she asked sharply.

I reluctantly told her the whole story, thinking that I'd at least gain her sympathy. But no such luck.

"So now you're just gonna give up?" she said.

"What else can I do?" I replied. "Obviously, she'd rather be with *him.* So, screw it."

"That's your foolish pride talkin'!" she snapped. "I wouldn't go there if I was you... unless you wanna be alone and bitter, like you are now. Let's just put things in perspective here. The guy's the keyboardist in her band, right?"

"Uh-huh."

"Then I seriously doubt that he's the love of her life," she said. "It's just a sex thing... that's all. We gals need to get laid every once in a while! So, forget about him. He's nothin'! Your biggest threat is the heroin. And, to be perfectly honest, I don't think you can beat it... not right now anyway. You just gotta stay the course—continue being her friend. Be nice! Don't confront her about last night... or she's liable to push you away even more. In fact, you should forget it ever happened."

"Okay," I numbly replied.

"Go back to sleep now, my dear," she said, "and dream of white unicorns and rainbow lollipops." *Click.*

The following night, I did exactly what she told me not to do. I drove up to the T-Bone and confronted Barbie about her heroin addiction. Yet I did it in my own subtle way, and Brian's name was never mentioned. First, I tried to persuade her to run away with me and leave the whole damn party scene behind. She thought I was joking, of course. And maybe I was.

"We can go wherever you want... the East Coast, West Coast," I said full of enthusiasm—and possibly shit. "Or, we could go overseas! I hear Paris is nice! It really doesn't matter as long as I'm with you."

She shook her head skeptically as she stood behind the bar, preparing my drink. "I can just see myself gallivantin' all over the country with you," she said. "What are we gonna live on?"

I simply shrugged and said, "Love."

She burst out laughing while setting my margarita before me. "You just keep dreamin', Benjamin! That's what you're good at."

I could see that she wasn't about to take me seriously, so I cut right to the chase and bluntly asked her what heroin was like. She seemed a bit rattled by the question, as if she suddenly realized that I'd caught her in the act. Or, maybe she knew it all along—and thus was afraid to ask me why I left so abruptly.

"What's heroin like?" she repeated, after a moment's pause.

"Yeah," I said. "What's all the hoopla about? Why do you enjoy it so much?"

"Best feeling in the world." She shrugged.

"Even better than sex?" I asked.

"Oh, yeah," she nodded. "Sex is good... if you can find a partner who knows how to do it right. But very few men have been able to satisfy me. Heroin never lets me down."

"Would you ever give it up?" I quickly blurted out.

She looked at me harshly. "Tony says you're up to six pills a night," she said. "Why so many?"

"Best feeling in the world," I said with a slight laugh. I gave it more thought and added, "It brings out the romantic in me. I felt dead inside before the X came along."

"Would *you* give it up?" she asked.

"In a heartbeat," I confidently replied. "I mean, if *you* will. The X brought me back to life... but so did you. And I'd choose you over a stinkin' pill any day. You're the only drug *I* need."

She looked at me admiringly, encouraging me to complete the sales pitch.

"So what do you say?" I asked. "Are you willin' to quit cold turkey with me?"

"Sure," she scoffed. "And then we can run off to France together."

I huffed in frustration and said, "Okay... if you're not gonna stop, will you at least let me do it with you?"

"Heroin?" she replied, and then sternly shook her head. "Huh-uh."

"Why not?" I exclaimed. "Damn it, Barbie... if you don't want to run away with me, that's fine! But if we're gonna stay here in this shithole, you've gotta let me in." I took a moment to regain my composure and said, "Fuck Paris. I just want to be with you."

Her intent stare suggested to me that she was seriously considering my proposal. Then something caught her attention directly behind me and her eyes suddenly lit up.

"Hey, guys!" she exclaimed as Brian, Skunk, and Zack stepped up to the bar and sat down next to me.

"Oh, good... the band's here," I said, pretending to be happy to see them.

CHAPTER TEN

November 21, 1994—I drove to my parents' house shortly after work to celebrate my thirty-first birthday. I used to love birthday parties—when I was three years old! Now they were just painful reminders of how swiftly time flies. My childhood and adolescence seemed to go on forever. Yet my twenties were a blur, just one birthday after another in quick succession. And it seemed like only yesterday when I was celebrating my thirtieth birthday—a sure indicator that my thirties were going to be a blur as well. Turning thirty was painful enough. But now at thirty-one, I could clearly see that I was going to be a cranky, old codger before long. And what had I accomplished in those thirty-one years? Nothing! Not a damn thing! To make matters worse, I was about to enter an enormous house full of family members and extended family members who would undoubtedly embarrass and humiliate the shit out of me for growing older. A slew of them were gathered together in my parents' living room when I stepped through the front door.

"There's the birthday boy!" Uncle Al shouted, followed with cheers and applause. He walked up to me and shook my hand. "Thirty-one, huh?" he exclaimed, shaking his head. "You'll be forty before you know it."

I've got to get out of here! I thought while sporting a big, phony smile. A whole other slew of people were sitting outside by the pool, taking full advantage of an unseasonably warm November evening. I quickly made my way to the sliding glass door and stepped out to join them. My father was flipping steaks on the grill in his chef's hat and "Don't Forget to Tip the Cook" apron.

"Benji, how do you want your steak?" he exclaimed.

"I don't care," I said.

"Well-done, medium, medium-rare, or raw?" he persisted.

"Medium's fine," I answered.

"One medium, coming up!" he exclaimed, sticking a slab of raw meat on the fire with his pearl-handled tongs.

I walked up to the pool and pulled up a chair next to my mother, Carol, and my sister, Jennifer, who were busy thumbing through the family album in their bathing suits. Both were thin and attractive, one barely fifty, the other just a year younger than me. Seated to my right was my thin, attractive, younger brother, David, and his beautiful, blonde, pregnant wife. They'd just flown in from LA for my birthday and Thanksgiving, respectively. My Uncle Hugh, Aunt Lucille, and a couple of cousins filled the rest of the chairs. Everyone wished me a happy birthday. Then we all sat quietly and watched my brother-in-law and three young nephews play volleyball inside the pool. Every now and then I'd catch someone giving me a strange look, which was why I hated family get-togethers. Obviously, they were as uncomfortable around me as I was around them. I was the weirdo of the family, the one who never talked and was always alone—no wife, kids, girlfriend, or even a personality to speak of. I'm pretty sure they all thought I was gay. I wished I could've surprised them for once by bringing Barbie to the party. Then I wouldn't have felt so alienated, and probably would've been more sociable.

My mother suddenly looked over at me and said, "Ben, don't you wanna swim?"

"I didn't bring my trunks with me, Mom," I replied.

"You can go in your tighty whities," said my sister, seated closest to me. "Or, do you wear boxers?"

I simply glared at her.

She gasped. "Are you freeballin'?"

"Why don't you go sit on the edge of the pool and get your feet wet?" my mother continued fussing over me.

"I'm fine, Mom!" I snapped at her.

"Oh, look... here you are," my sister said to me seconds later, pointing at a picture in the family album. She showed it to my mom and they both had a good laugh, after which she stuck the book in *my* face and showed it to me. "Back when you were kinda cute," she joked.

It was a picture of me as a five-year-old kid, standing in the kitchen with a stunned look on my face and an ear of corn dangling from my mouth. I guess the shock of being caught on camera caused my shorts to fall down, and my hands were busy trying to pull them back up.

"Fuck off," I said to Jennifer, and shoved the book away.

"What's your fuckin' problem?" she exclaimed.

"All right, you two... knock it off," my mother quickly intervened. "And enough with the filthy language."

That damn scrapbook and constant reminiscences of the past were two more reasons I hated family get-togethers. The last thing I needed was to be reminded of my humiliating, life-long obsession with food. Growing up under my parents' roof, I was prone to sneaking into the kitchen late at night to steal food from the refrigerator. The flashbacks continued to haunt me, like the night I gobbled down half a pan of leftover lasagna with my bare hands, my face covered with ricotta cheese and tomato sauce. It was just as good cold, I remembered. My father jokingly labeled me "the Food Bandit" while my mother had far worse names for me. Maybe if she hadn't been such an incredible cook!

One year she made my father a three-layer, Italian cream cake for his birthday and left it sitting in the refrigerator overnight. Big mistake! When she stepped into the kitchen the next morning, there were little cream-colored crumbs all over the floor. She frantically pulled the cake out of the refrigerator, removed the plastic cover, and was completely mortified. Someone had massacred her beautiful cake!

"Benjamin Michael Oldman!" she furiously shouted.

I slowly crept into the kitchen in my pajamas, looking guilty as hell. I think I was ten or eleven at the time—old enough to know better. But I couldn't help myself. I was in love with food. And, the kitchen was usually closed to anyone under five feet five inches tall. Mom wouldn't even let us have snacks!

"Did you do this?" she asked, pointing at the butchered cake on the counter.

"Uh-huh," I mumbled, and then she really let me have it.

"How could you?" she exclaimed. "That cake was for your father! Only a selfish little pig would do such a thing!"

Now I realized that she was just speaking out of anger and frustration. She wouldn't normally be so hurtful. But, back then, those words devastated me and would stick with me for the rest of my life. Whenever I looked at myself in the mirror, all I saw was a pig, which was why I usually avoided them. I hated going to Mom and Dad's for the very same reason. That grand, old, two-story house was just a reminder of who I was—and what I was trying to run away from.

"Steak's on!" my father shouted as he placed the last one on the silver platter.

"I'll go round everyone up," my mother said, getting up from the lawn chair and heading for the house.

"Guys, get out of the pool and dry off!" Jennifer shouted at her husband and kids. "Time to eat!"

We all sat at a long picnic table in the middle of the backyard and ate T-bone steak, baked potatoes, corn on the cob, dinner rolls, and my mom's famous guacamole salad. Then, after we filled our bellies, cleared the table, and helped Mom with the dishes, we moved to the living room and everyone watched me open my presents. They were mostly gag gifts. I got an ear and nose hair trimmer from Uncle Al, a box of Grecian Formula from Uncle Herb and Aunt Lucille, and twenty-four bottles of Ensure from Cousin Frank. But I also received plenty of birthday cards full of money and a five-hundred-dollar check from my parents. So I came out ahead.

Next, I blew out the thirty-one candles on my birthday cake, everyone sang "Happy Birthday" to me, and we gorged on cake and ice cream. It was actually kind of fun. And I was holding up fairly well in the hot seat—or on the couch, rather—until Jennifer brought out the scrapbook again and showed everyone my naked baby photos, literally making me the butt of the joke. To add to my humiliation, my father began telling the same, old story that he told every year on my birthday—the story of me as a two-week-old infant.

"He was barely a six-pounder when Carol and I adopted him," he said with a proud smile, as if it was the happiest day of his life.

I never understood how my parents could love me so much from the get-go, since I wasn't blood-related. I doubt that *I* could love a perfect stranger so easily, unless that perfect stranger happened to be Barbie.

"He was so tiny," my father continued, "that I could hold him in the palm of my hand! And, boy, was he quick! I'd set him down and he'd scuttle across the floor like a little mouse."

That part of the story had always sounded a bit dubious to me. Who was I, Tom Thumb?

"And now look at him," my father thankfully concluded as everyone gawked at me. "I can't even pick him up with *two* hands."

All my kinfolk exploded into laughter while I sat there sweating bullets. I couldn't wait to get home!

Having a birthday on the twenty-first of November meant that I was forced to endure two family get-togethers almost back-to-back. A cold front blew in on Thanksgiving, so we ate inside at a long table and had turkey with all the trimmings. At least this time the focus wasn't on me.

After a second helping of my mom's delicious cornbread dressing and a large slice of pumpkin pie with loads of whipped cream on top, I sneaked out of there without raising any eyebrows and hurried home to watch my Dallas Cowboys annihilate the Green Bay Packers. Matt called me during half-time just to let me know how much *he* hated Thanksgiving.

"I've got to get out of here before I kill someone," he frantically exclaimed in a whisper. "Everyone showed up for this one... my two grandmas, all my aunts and uncles, even my dickhead brother! There's about a hundred people crammed into this shitty, little house... and they're all startin' to get on my nerves." He paused for a second to calm down. "So do you wanna go out tonight?"

"The club ain't even open on Thanksgiving!" I naively exclaimed.

"Yeah, it is," he assured me. "Thanksgiving and Christmas are their biggest nights! I just called Tony. He said he'll be there."

Ecstasy on Thanksgiving... hmm, I thought. "All right, I'm in," I said.

I didn't have to pick him up at his house anymore, now that the whole gang was back together again. Sean did the honors. We met at the club at eight o'clock and walked in together in our party suits. Sure enough, the place was chock-full of people—all Thanksgiving-haters, no doubt. It was just another typical Thursday night at Club H!

We went to join Tony, who was seated at a table with Neil, and he immediately informed me that Barbie was spending the holiday with her family at the trailer park. *Oh well, I guess it's just me and the guys tonight,* I thought. But, actually, it was just me and the pills. I bought four from Tony for a hundred bucks. And, as I sat waiting for two of them to kick in, I noticed Porsche, Kaneesha, and six other drag queens tearing up the dance floor. I was out there with them just five minutes later. Then, all of a sudden, Matt, Sean, Tony, and even Neil joined in, creating one enormous circle. *Now this is what Thanksgiving's all about,* I thought, filled with elation. *Spending quality time with family and friends!* My faceless DJ friend seemed none too happy, though.

"All right, people," he grumbled into the microphone while the music kept on playing. "They pay me to work the holidays, but what's your fuckin' excuse? You should be at home drinkin' eggnog with your folks... not out here trippin' the light fantastic." He laughed and said, "I'm just fuckin' wit ya! Party on, kids."

The celebration continued at Porsche's house later. Everyone showed up, except for Barbie and Laura. Matt and Sean were flirting with a bunch of drag queens inside her massive living room. And I was in the dining room with Rog and Skippy, smoking a crack pipe while we discussed our favorite movie musicals. Roger's was *Singing in the Rain,* bar none. Skip's were *Oliver!* and *My Fair Lady.* And mine were *West Side Story* and *The Sound of Music,* the latter of which was a bit too schmaltzy for their tastes.

"What can I say?" I shrugged. "Guess I'm just a sucker for a good, old-fashioned love story set to Rodgers and Hammerstein."

"Poor B... you're just a hopeless romantic," Rog joked, though it was no joke.

As we spoke, I couldn't help but notice the unsightly, red lesion on his neck, just above the shirt collar.

Though I tried to ignore it as best I could, the whole time I was thinking, *Oh no, not Roger... my fellow cinephile with the biting wit and sweet, lovable Steve Martin face!*

The next time I saw him was at Tony and Barbie's house a couple of weekends later. He and Skip were sitting alone on the couch, which seemed odd. It was usually a very popular piece of furniture, especially when there were drugs on the coffee table. And everyone loved Rog and Skippy! They were like the perfect gay couple! But, that night, people preferred to stand and were keeping a safe distance from them for some reason. When I stepped up to say hi, I could see exactly why their friends were ignoring them. Roger's illness had progressed considerably. He now had lesions on both sides of his face, and the one on his neck was much bigger. Plus, he was very pale and looked thirty pounds lighter.

"How ya doin', guys?" I said.

They both smiled and nodded as I sat down next to Roger. I wasn't sure what to say next, so I simply blurted out the first thing that popped into my head.

"So... have you seen any good movies lately?"

Skippy looked over at me as if I'd just committed a huge faux pas. But Roger suddenly broke out laughing.

"Oh, Big B... you kill me," he said. "That's what I like about you! You're not afraid to be yourself... and you say whatever's on your mind." He looked around the room. "Most of these people won't even talk to me," he said. "They act like I'm already dead. If they think I'm just gonna go away and hide in some dark, little room, they might as well forget it! I'm stayin' right here... and I'm gonna keep on partyin'." And with that he leaned over, put the straw to his nostril, and snorted three big lines. "What else is there?" He shrugged. "Work, dreams, ambition... it don't mean nothin' in the end! It's all bullshit! I'm just happy to be alive. We'll all be leavin' soon."

I just sat there in total awe of him, starting to grasp the whole party 'til you drop thing. *Look at Roger,* I thought, *going out like a boss!*

December 25—I went to my parents' house for more turkey and dressing. But, again, I didn't stay long. It was another eat and run. I spent the rest of the day at home, waiting for Matt to call. Yet the phone wasn't ringing, which was surprising and a bit of a bummer. I really wanted to see Barbie and wish her a merry Christmas. Plus, I was bored, a little depressed, and didn't feel much like writing. *Why isn't he calling?* I wondered. *This is the one night we should be partying! It's Jesus's birthday, for his sake!* Night fell, yet no friend in sight. I decided to suit up anyway and go it alone.

The Club H parking lot was packed when I got there. But all I had was crappy three-two beer from the local truck stop, and I wasn't about to go in there on my own without the proper lubricant. I drove right on past and went straight to Tony and Barbie's house to see if they were there. They were home all right! The light was on in the living room and her Crown Victoria was parked in the driveway. Otherwise, it was empty, which was a first. Normally, there were six cars crammed in the driveway and at least twenty more parked in the street. But it appeared that Tony was taking a night off for once, and I didn't want to barge in on them uninvited. So I just sat there against the curb and stared into the window, even though I couldn't see anything through those damn curtains. *I wonder what the hell they're doin' in there,* I thought. *Watching "It's a Wonderful Life..." or a porno flick, perhaps? Is there any chance Tony could be bisexual? God, I hope not! There's no way I could compete with him in the looks department! He's a black Adonis!* The only thing I knew for certain was that it was the worst Christmas ever. It was usually the most magical time of the year, with all the pretty lights, the carolers, and such. But this one really sucked balls! I felt no love, no peace on earth, no goodwill toward men. There wasn't even snow on the ground! And I didn't see one nativity scene on the block, nothing to make me think that this was unlike any other lonely, miserable night of the week.

December 31—It was Saturday night, New Year's Eve, and the gang was out in full force. I found myself dancing with this very hot chick just as the clock was about to strike twelve. Even more surprising, it seemed that she was really into me. I would've been ecstatic if I hadn't been in love with someone else. This girl could've been Miss Oklahoma for all I knew, with those big, blue eyes and long, lustrous blond locks. Yet I was utterly miserable. I didn't even bother to remember her name, though she'd just told it to me before she asked me to dance. *What is it again... Ella, Elsa, Eleanor?* I asked myself as we danced. Her gay friend and his lover, dancing alongside us, seemed to be fancying me as well. It appeared that I'd just made three new friends.

"It's exactly one minute 'til twelve, folks," the DJ said after the song ended. "How 'bout a moment of silence as we say good-bye to 1994?"

Everyone stood very still and quiet, so quiet that I heard Ester, Edna, or whoever, whisper to her friend, "He got me all wet."

She sounded amused when she said it, so it probably wasn't out of malice or disgust. Yet I chose to be deeply humiliated. *I thought they were really diggin' my fancy footwork!* I said to myself in sheer horror. *They were just humoring me the whole time while I showered them with flop sweat! I knew somethin' was up when she asked me to dance. She just felt sorry for me after watching me dance by myself the entire night!*

I furiously turned to Eliza and shouted, "Forgive me, Your Highness! I didn't mean to sweat all over you!"

Then I stormed off the floor and headed for the restroom in back, leaving them in total confusion, no doubt. Those poor innocent people... I was probably doing them a huge favor! Stepping into the empty restroom, I walked up to the counter and looked at myself in the mirror. I could hear everyone counting down the final seconds through the restroom door. *So here we are again,* I thought. *Another New Year's countdown... with no one to kiss at the end of it. I blame Barbie for this. When is she gonna wake up and realize that we were meant to be so much more than just friends?* It didn't help that I knew exactly what she was doing—and who she was doing it with. 1995 was already shaping up to be a rotten year!

CHAPTER ELEVEN

Business had already slowed down to a crawl during that winter season. Those of us who weren't laid off spent most of the time cleaning up the shop. Then came spring and, all of a sudden, we were swamped, having four jobs to start all at once. Dad brought the entire crew back and split us up in threes. He sent me downtown to work with the two old-timers, Tim and Homer. I wasn't sure why, but I suspected he was trying to keep me away from Matt. We were simply having way too much fun working together. It's not that I minded working with the geriatric set. I enjoyed listening to Homer's tall tales during break time. Most of them were quite fanciful, even though he swore to God that they were true. But once we slapped the tool belts back on, he and Tim were all business, and both were far less tolerant of my ineptitude than the younger guys. Homer was constantly jumping on me over the littlest things, such as holding my tape measure on the wrong mark or screwing a metal stud in backward. Then he'd add some assholish remark like *"How* long have you been workin' here?"

"Too damn long," I'd retort, causing him to laugh and shake his head at me.

As aggravating as it was, the old man had a point. I'd been in the business for nine years straight since leaving college and still knew next to nothing about framing walls. Construction work just wasn't my thing. It was like trying to teach Oscar Wilde how to dig a ditch or hang wallpaper. I know it's sacrilege to compare myself to the great one, but it was exactly how I felt at the time. And to think my dad once offered me a supervisor position! He even offered to buy me a brand-new pickup truck so I could drive from jobsite to jobsite, looking like a big shot. Knowing that I lacked the know-how, confidence, or swagger to pull off such a brazen deceit, I turned him down flat. I told him that I'd rather work in the trenches with the grunts. Well, maybe I didn't use those exact words. It meant I was in for a much harder life, but at least there were few responsibilities. I could just show up every morning, work to my heart's content, and make lots of money without a care in the world—and in total anonymity. I was just another cog in the machine. This clashed with my desire to be somebody, of course. But I had to pay the rent.

We were building a new office on the fourth floor and west end of the old YMCA building. The room came equipped with a window overlooking a huge parking lot in front of two small buildings. And directly across the street was the Alfred P. Murrah Federal Building—a slick-looking, rectangular, nine-story building with a glass facade.

April 19, 1995—Wednesday, 9:00 AM—I'd been working with Homer for only an hour and was already fed up with him, bossing me around, treating me like a complete imbecile. *Who does he think he is?* I thought. *Someone should remind him that I'm the boss's son!* At the moment, he was mad at me for cutting a metal stud a half-inch too short. I was cutting them to length with my tin snips and handing them to him to screw into the bottom track.

"This one's trash," he grumbled, and handed the thing back to me. "You just wasted a perfectly good stud."

"Why don't you cut 'em, then?" I furiously exclaimed, and threw it on the floor.

Both he and Tim looked at me strangely. They'd never seen me lose my cool before. *Uh-oh, how am I gonna get out of this one?* I immediately thought to myself, embarrassed and ashamed for letting my petty feelings get the better of me. Then the devil stepped in to save me. All of a sudden, there was a massive explosion the likes of which I'd never experienced before. It was so loud that it rang my eardrums. The floor shook violently, all the windows shattered, and the dropped ceiling collapsed on top of us. We impulsively threw down our tools and hunkered down, thinking that we were under attack. Seconds later, there was an eerie silence, followed by hundreds of car alarms going off simultaneously outside the building.

"What the hell was that?" Tim exclaimed.

We got up, rushed over to the window, and stood utterly speechless as we stared through the gaping hole in the glass. Two minutes ago, it was a beautiful spring morning. Now cars were on fire across the way, others crushed beyond recognition. Plumes of thick, black smoke filled the entire parking lot, rising three hundred feet into the air. And the two buildings directly behind it were severely damaged. But the real horror show was on the other side of the smoke-filled street—at ground zero. The glass face of the federal building was completely ripped away and lay in an enormous pile of rubble on top of a giant crater. I never thought I'd see destruction of this magnitude—at least not in real life. And here it was just a hundred yards in front of me. *Did somebody just declare war on us?* I wondered. *Who did we piss off now?* Without saying a word, Tim and Homer quickly removed their tool belts and headed for the exit.

"You comin', Ben?" Tim shouted.

"Nah, we should probably stay here," I said, "and let the police handle it."

"Bullshit!" Homer exclaimed before they stepped through the door. "Get your ass out here!"

I huffed, unbuckled my tool belt, threw it on the floor, and rushed after them just as the emergency alarm sounded and a calm, female voice came over the loudspeakers.

"This building must be evacuated. Please proceed to the nearest exit in an orderly fashion."

Suddenly, a horde of pencil pushers scurried out of their offices and cubicles and raced me to the lobby. There was already a crowd standing in front of the elevator once I got there. Yet there was no sign of Tim and Homer, so I took the stairs and caught up with them before they reached the second floor.

"What do you think it was?" Tim asked Homer. "A gas leak, maybe?"

"That wasn't no gas leak," Homer scoffed. "More like a bomb."

"Terrorists?"

"Yep."

Terrorists in Oklahoma? I thought. *No way!*

We exited the stairwell and followed the crowd into the main lobby. As we inched our way to the double doors, my father's voice blasted through the two-way radio.

"Eagle One to Eagle Two!"

Tim jerked it off his belt and put it to his lips. "This is Eagle Two."

"You guys all right?" my father asked.

"Yeah, we're fine," Tim answered. "There was an explosion—"

"Yeah, I know," Dad interrupted him. "I heard it all the way over here at the shop. I'm lookin' at the smoke right now, in fact. And it's all over the news. They think it was terrorists!"

"Roger that," Tim said. "They're makin' us evacuate the building. So we're headin' over there to check it out... see if we can help."

"Y'all be careful," Dad said. "Well, I better go now, the guys just showed up. We're gonna load up the truck right quick, then we'll be headed out there shortly. Give us... oh... about twelve minutes, I'd say. Over and out."

"What the hell's he gonna do?" Homer scoffed.

"Really," I agreed.

We stepped out of the building and ran across the street, with several others running alongside us, tromping over chunks of brick and broken glass. The debris was scattered for miles and even polluted the murky-brown sky, gobs of paper hovering through the filthy air like a kettle of vultures. A very distinct, pungent odor also permeated the air. It smelled like ammonia and burnt plastic. And building and car alarms continued to wail, along with the loud, screeching sirens of emergency vehicles entering the scene from the opposite direction. It wasn't downtown Oklahoma City anymore. I felt like I was in war-torn Bosnia or Rwanda. The heat grew more intense as we drew nearer to the bombsite. Though I couldn't see the ravaged building through the smoke, I could already see dozens of injured victims lying in the middle of Fifth Street, and dozens of people walking around in a daze, their faces covered with blood and soot. Finally coming to a standstill in front of the building, I saw more injured victims lying helplessly on top of the enormous rubble pile, many screaming for help.

While the basement and first floor of the building were buried beneath the pile, the rooms of the other eight floors were left completely exposed by the blast. It was as if I was looking into a giant doll house, only a doll house from hell with all the debris, twisted metal, and rebar hanging down. I could've sworn that I heard people screaming from inside the building as well, probably trapped under layers of walls, steel beams, and concrete flooring. It was too horrifying to even imagine!

Thank God the fire department was on the case. A fire truck sat with its back to the building, and three brave firefighters were entering the deathtrap from an aerial ladder sticking through a fifth-floor opening. Tim and Homer rushed toward the pile to help the wounded, meanwhile. They climbed about a quarter of the way up and knelt down beside a woman lying flat on her back and crying hysterically. They tried to lift her up by the shoulders, but whenever they tugged and pulled she let out a terrible scream. Homer suddenly turned around and looked at me.

"Damn it, Benjamin... get your ass up here and help!" he scowled.

I couldn't believe he was still barking out orders at me. We weren't even on the jobsite! But this time I probably deserved it. They were up there trying to save people while I stood impotent and in a state of shock, like everyone around me. I immediately snapped out of it and went to join them. It wasn't an easy climb. The pile was very steep and there were lots of holes, jagged rocks, and twisted metal to avoid.

The first unusual thing I noticed as I began my ascent was a woman's red shoe partially buried in the rocks—a harbinger of things to come. When I finally reached Tim and Homer, I could see what the poor woman was crying about. Her clothes were ripped to shreds, and there were shards of glass all over her body, one protruding from her left eye and two in her neck—near the jugular. She also had a large gash on her forehead and blood was trickling down into her other eye, rendering her blind. Homer lay next to her with his arm around her, doing his best to calm her down.

"Oh God, it hurts!" she screamed.

"I know, dear," he said. "But we have to move you. It isn't safe here! My name's Homer, by the way... and these other two gentlemen with me are Tim and Benjamin. We're gonna lift you up very gently now and carry you on out of here, so the paramedics can take you to the hospital and get you patched up. Okay?"

"Okay," she muttered repeatedly, suddenly more calm and cooperative.

Wow, I said to myself. *Who would've thought that Homer, a man who liked to cuss, spit tobacco, tell kinky stories, and torment the hell out of me, was actually a people person?*

"Grab her feet!" he barked at me.

I quickly bent down and grabbed her ankles while he and Tim picked her up by the shoulders, and we slowly carried her down the steep slope. Why I was the one walking backward, I'll never know. But, luckily, I managed to make it to the bottom without tripping all over myself. A couple of paramedics took over at that point, swiftly lifting her onto a gurney and wheeling her toward one of the ambulances.

Just as my colleagues and I were heading back to the pile, my father came bursting onto the scene with the whole crew behind him. There was Matt and Sean, of course, the Kid, Ron the Biker, Billy the Ex-con, Russell, who used to work at the tire plant before it went bust, and some new guy—the redshirt. They looked like they were ready for war, wearing hard hats, goggles, dust masks, gloves, and knee pads. Some were even carrying shovels and pickaxes, as if they were planning to dig up a few bodies. It seemed disrespectful, in a way. Not far behind *them* were about fifty more volunteers and first responders. And several more squad cars and ambulances came roaring up Fifth Street, making it appear as if my father had brought an entire army with him. He walked up to us wearing only a hard hat, gloves, and his old work clothes and carrying an armload of protective gear.

"Here, Benji... put these on," he demanded, handing *me* a hard hat and a brand-new pair of work gloves, followed with goggles, knee pads, and a dust mask. Then he handed Tim and Homer the exact same items. "We had to park a couple blocks away because of all the debris," he explained to us as we put on the gear. "Otherwise we would've been here sooner." He looked up at the building and shook his head in disgust. "My God, what's this world comin' to?" he muttered to himself, and then turned to the rest of the crew and said, "All right, men... looks like we've got our work cut out for us here. Let's get started!"

We swiftly darted off and followed him up the mountain of rubble alongside EMTs, paramedics, police officers, and anyone else willing to lend a hand. Most of the wounded had been extracted from the top of the pile, so we began digging underneath, working in large groups. We had three EMTs, a female police officer, and even an off-duty nurse searching with us. I still remember the nurse quite vividly—petite, long, red hair, beautiful blue eyes, in her late thirties, maybe, wearing blue jeans and a white long-sleeve sweater with the American Flag and "God Bless America" printed on it. She must've caught me glancing at her at least a hundred times during the search, which was a little awkward. But it couldn't be helped. She intrigued me somehow. I even took off those silly goggles and that damn dust mask so she could get a good look at *me.* At one point, I overheard her introduce herself to the female cop. She said her name was Regina and that she'd come all the way from Midwest City after watching the news and learning that there was a daycare center in the building. This was certainly news to *me!*

"Twenty-one children unaccounted for!" she bitterly exclaimed, seeming bound and determined to find them all.

As was his custom, my father immediately tried to take charge of the entire group, telling us where to dig and such, but *she* was the heart and soul of the whole operation. It was her dogged determination and keen eyesight that led us to our first victim. She miraculously spotted a tiny sliver of human flesh sticking through the rubble, swiftly dropping to her knees and clawing around it with her bare hands. Me, my dad, Tim, and

Homer joined in with our thick, heavy-duty leather gloves and feverishly pulled away rock, brick, glass, and gunk 'til an entire arm was exposed—and then a shoulder. The female cop—Joan, I think—the three EMTs, and the rest of the Oldman clan had already dropped down beside us and were working on the lower half of the body—"body" being the key word. I was quite certain that we were digging up a corpse. Little by little, we exposed the back of a man's head, his bare shoulders, his upper and lower back, and a large concrete slab covering his legs—four feet wide and twelve inches thick. It might as well have been a boulder!

"Uh-oh, that can't be good," my father remarked as he looked over at it. We continued digging all the way down to the man's face and chest, after which he looked at Regina and Homer and said, "You two think you can pull him out of here while we lift that monstrosity off of him?"

They both nodded.

"Super!" he exclaimed, and turned to me and Tim. "Let's go, guys."

The three of us got up and walked over to join Matt, Sean, the Kid, Ron, and even Joan the Cop, who was big enough to take us *all* on. Standing just a couple of inches apart, we bent down and put our mitts under the huge chunk of rock.

"Okay, everyone... on three!" my dad exclaimed. "One, two, three!"

We grunted and strained, lifting it up just high enough to let Homer and Regina pull the man free.

"We're good," my father grunted. "Let it drop."

We quickly let go of the damn thing and collectively breathed a sigh of relief. Yet, our effort was in vain, as we soon discovered. The man's legs were crushed. And, when we turned him over, we saw that he wasn't breathing. *Just as I thought... a fucking corpse!* I said to myself as four unlucky coworkers picked up the body and carried it down to the street. It was a devastating blow to all of us, especially when we looked around and saw other groups freeing survivors left and right. Only, Regina looked more frustrated than devastated.

"Come on, let's keep searchin'!" she said, trying to pep us up. "There's plenty of people buried alive under here! I just know it!"

She turned around and led us farther up the pile. Joan warned her not to get too close to the building, since she wasn't wearing any protection. Yet we continued to climb, and she took us right to our next victim with that X-Ray vision and bloodhound nose of hers. This time we knew the poor soul was alive. He or she had two fingers sticking up from the debris and appeared to be waving at us. We quickly swarmed around the digits, dropped down, and dug. Gradually, brick by brick, glass shard by glass shard, we exposed the entire hand with all its fingers intact and wiggling frantically... then an arm... then a man's face. He wiggled and pushed with all his might as my father grabbed his hand and pulled. Then, all of a sudden, he burst up from the rubble, gasping for breath. We all clapped and laughed excitedly, as if we'd just brought a brand-new bouncing baby boy into the world! But he was actually a slight, middle-aged man with cuts and bruises all over his face, covered from head to toe in gray dust. Homer and I helped him to his feet after he'd caught his breath.

"Thank you, thank you," he kept muttering to me, his fingernails digging into my arm as if he was afraid to let go.

Joan the Cop got right up in his face and said, "Sir, are you all right?"

He just looked at her, obviously confused and disoriented.

"What is your name, sir?" she asked him.

"B-B-Bill," he stuttered. "My name is Bill."

"Hey, Bill!" we all said to him almost simultaneously in total elation.

My father had Homer and me help him down to the medical tent that had just been set up directly across the street. The whole group was staring up at the building when we returned, watching the firefighters pull a heavyset woman out of the fifth-floor opening and help her onto the ladder. Apparently, she'd lost her dress in the explosion. All she had on was a slip covered with soot. Everyone on the rubble pile and on the street down below applauded and cheered as they slowly began their descent down the ladder—everyone except for Regina, who was still deeply frustrated.

She caught me gawking at her and said, "We're running out of time!" She then looked at the second floor of the building, which was no more than twenty feet away, and asked, "Do you think they could still be in there?"

"Who?" I asked curiously.

"The children."

I didn't have an answer for her, so I stood silent. Then, suddenly, as if on cue, we heard a woman scream for help somewhere inside the building. Regina looked at me and gasped.

"The firemen are in there," I said. "They'll get her out."

Our group began to disintegrate after that. Dad, Joan, and the three EMTs continued working together while Tim and Homer branched out on their own, as did Matt and Sean, who simply wandered from one group to the next to catch a glimpse of a body or body part that'd just been discovered—proving to me once again that neither of them had a conscience. I stuck with Regina, of course. We went to help a policeman and two female EMTs, trying to save an infant buried under a thick layer of rocks and cement dust. Though initially ecstatic that we'd finally found one of the children, Regina nearly fainted when we pulled the baby girl out and saw that she'd been smothered to death. She and I just stood there helpless, our faces and hands covered with dust as we watched the policeman carry the infant down to the tent to be placed in a body bag. Regina crouched and stared pensively at all the chaos on the street. She then looked up and caught me gawking at her again.

"I'm sorry, I didn't catch your name earlier," she said.

"Benjamin," I replied.

"I'm Regina," she said with a bittersweet smile. "Nice to meet you, Benjamin. Too bad it had to be like this."

"You're tellin' me," I said with a slight chuckle. "I didn't think I'd be—"

"Shhh," she interrupted me. "Do you hear that?"

"What?"

She quickly rose to her feet and turned toward the building. I assumed she heard someone screaming again, but I honestly couldn't hear anything at that precise moment.

"I'm going in there," she said.

"That's probably not a good idea," I replied, just as she rushed off.

"Wait, I'm coming with you!" I shouted, and rushed after her, climbing all the way to the top of the heap and standing within inches of the remaining structure.

I suddenly felt very uneasy. The building kept making cracking and popping noises, as if it could collapse at any given second. And, every so often, I'd hear falling debris come crashing down close by. Holding onto the building, we walked out to the very edge of the rubble pile. From there, it was a three-foot jump to get to the nearest second-floor opening—and a forty-foot drop to the pavement down below. Regina took a bit of a running start and made the jump with ease. *I* failed to realize the significance of the running start and came within an inch or two of falling to my death, both feet barely hitting concrete. *Jeez, that was close!* I thought, looking over the jagged edge of the building. I immediately shook it off and went looking for Regina, who'd taken off without me.

"Is anyone here?" I heard her shouting.

The building continued cracking and popping. Plus, there was the steady groan of support beams buckling under all the stress. I felt like I was on a sinking ship! Walking was extremely difficult. Every inch of the floor was covered with ceiling tile, ceiling grid, and broken glass—the same beautiful glass that had decorated the whole north side of the building.

"Regina, where are you?" I shouted, walking through the dark, dismal remains of a hallway. The place would've been pitch-black if it wasn't for the daylight shining in.

"How's it goin' up there, Briggs?" said a loud, staticky, male voice blasting through a walkie-talkie.

It scared the hell out of me!

"It's a real mess here, Chief," a man answered. "We're talkin' multiple bodies."

I slowly pressed on, following the sound of his voice. He was very close, just beyond the large pile of wall and ceiling debris up ahead.

"Do I need to send you more help?" said the voice on the walkie-talkie.

"No... we've pretty much got it covered," the man answered.

"Roger that."

I crept up to the pile, hunkered down, and peered out from behind it. Though it was dark, I could plainly see a team of firefighters and EMTs leaning over a stack of dead bodies, stuffing them into body bags and loading them onto gurneys. Most of the bags were small—the only way I could tell that these were children being loaded up and wheeled away. It was just a terrible, bloody mess.

Regina must never see this! I thought, looking on in horror. *I've gotta go find her and persuade her to leave somehow!* I immediately got up and turned around, only to discover her standing right behind me in plain sight, seeing exactly what I'd seen and noticeably distraught. I grabbed her arm and tried to pull her away.

"Let's go," I said to her in a low voice. "There's nothin' we can do here."

Yet she wouldn't budge.

"Please, Regina," I implored her, and then nodded toward the daylight. "There's people out *there* that need our help."

"Hey, you two... what are you doin' in here?" a man shouted at us in a strong, authoritative voice.

I turned to see that it was the firefighter with his walkie-talkie in hand.

"This building isn't safe!" he exclaimed. "Are you hurt?"

"We were just leavin'!" I replied. "C'mon, Regina."

She reluctantly turned around and headed back with me. "They're all dead," she said very solemnly.

"Maybe not," I said, assuming that she was referring to the children. "We've found plenty of survivors, so far."

"No... they're all dead," she said with absolute certainty. "What kind of monster would do such a thing?"

"I don't know," I sighed.

Walking up to the concrete edge, she took a running start and jumped back onto the rubble pile. I hesitated, recalling what happened the first time, and then made the mistake of looking down. Most people would consider it an easy jump—just three measly feet! But, in my defense, it was at an extreme angle from one surface to the next. And, for a person who was afraid of heights, those three measly feet seemed more like a mile when facing a forty-foot drop.

"You're thinkin' about it too much!" she shouted, standing next the building. "Just do it!"

Yeah, you pussy! I thought. *Are you gonna let a girl show you up?*

"You gotta jump, Benjamin!" she shouted with a slight laugh. "It's the only way out!"

Good point, I thought, and quickly jumped across. Once again, my feet barely touched the edge of the pile, and I desperately reached out to her as I was sliding down. She swiftly grabbed my hand and pulled me to safety.

"Good job," she said, and patted me on the back while I stood there with my head between my knees, trying to catch my breath.

As we started to walk away from the building, something hit her on the back of the head.

"Ow!" she cried out, hunching over and grabbing the wound. "What was that?"

I looked directly behind her and spotted a piece of concrete on top of other pieces of concrete. Only, this one had a speck of blood on its visage, and it was about the size and shape of a baseball. If it'd fallen all the way from the top of the building, which I assumed it did... well, I didn't want to think about it. I was just amazed that she was still standing.

"Here, let me see it," I said, attempting to get behind her to assess the damage.

She quickly turned to face me and said, "No, I'm fine! Let's just go."

She was staggering a little bit as we headed down the slope, suggesting to me that she *wasn't* fine. We rejoined my father's group and started working next to several new faces, including an extremely desperate-looking man who was hastily picking through the debris as if he'd lost his car keys down there somewhere.

"Hi, I'm Regina," she said, and extended her hand to him.

He shook it and said his name was Del. "I'm lookin' for my wife," he added bluntly.

"Oh, no!" Regina gasped.

He tossed aside a piece of sheet metal and dug into his jean pocket. "Here, I've got a picture of her," he said, pulling out his wallet and nervously flipping it open to show us a picture of him and the young woman together. "Her name's Susan," he said.

"She's adorable," Regina said. She hesitated for a moment, then added, "We were just inside the building, lookin' for survivors! You think, maybe—"

"No, she wouldn't be in *there,*" he said assuredly. He pointed toward the building. "See that huge chunk that's missin'?" he said. "That's where she was. Her office was on the third floor, right next to the window. She was standin' there wavin' at me when I dropped her off this morning. And now she's in here somewhere." He immediately put his wallet away and went back to work. "I don't want her to be dead!" he exclaimed. "But it kills me even more to think that she might be buried alive under all this mess!" Regina and I went right back to work as well, dead set on helping him find his wife. Deep down, I thought it very unlikely that we'd find any more survivors. But it felt good just being part of something and sharing a common goal. Joan came over to help and kept feeding us disapproving looks.

"I saw you two go in there," she said to Regina finally. "What did you see?"

"Nothin'," Regina bitterly replied. "You were right. We should've stayed down here."

"A rock fell and hit her on the head," I suddenly blurted out. I felt that someone else should know.

"Jesus, Regina," Joan chided her. "You need to go down to the tent and get it checked out."

"I'm fine, *really,*" Regina persisted. "It's just a little sore is all."

"Still, I think you should have a doctor look at it," Joan said. "A head injury's nothin' to mess around with! But, why am I tellin' *you* this? *You're* the nurse."

As we continued working side by side, pulling away debris, Regina glanced and smiled at me. Then a look of consternation swept over her face and she fell onto Joan, who was also working next to her, collapsing in her arms. Joan had an EMT grab her ankles and they carried her down the slope completely unconscious. I had a terrible feeling she wasn't going to make it. And, I knew I'd never see her again regardless. She was just passing through, just like everyone else in my life who wasn't related. But she'd forever haunt my memory. *Why didn't I offer her my hard hat?* I angrily asked myself while I watched her being loaded into an ambulance. *And why is it just now occurring to me that I'm even wearin' the damn thing?* Now she'd probably die, thanks to my stupidity and complete lack of chivalry!

"Hey, B... come look at this!" Matt shouted at me, standing with Sean just ten feet away.

They said nothing when I approached, their faces covered with goggles and dust masks. They simply pointed at the severed hand lying in front of them. It was big and hairy, with a gold wedding band on the ring finger. Obviously, the fuckers were just trying to get a reaction out of me! I even caught them exchanging glances, probably grinning from ear to ear underneath those dust masks! But I was so desensitized by then that the only reaction I could muster was utter contempt for my two sidekicks.

"What's wrong with you guys?" I said to them, just as my father sneaked up from behind.

"What are y'all standin' around for?" he barked at us. "Don't forget you're still on the clock."

"They found somethin'," I said, and pointed at the severed appendage.

He looked down at it and grimaced. "What a rotten deal," he said. "The poor guy." Then he waved at an EMT working nearby. "We found a hand over here!" he shouted. "What do you want us to do with it?"

As I stood there laughing on the inside, cranes, bulldozers, military trucks, TV news vans, and several more squad cars arrived on the scene, sirens blazing. The police officers stepped out of their vehicles and began closing off Fifth Street with sawhorse blockades and yellow tape while one of them walked up to the pile with a bullhorn and put it to his lips.

"I need everyone to climb down from the rubble!" he said to all sixty or seventy of us, as if we had no business being up there in the first place.

We just looked at him like he was crazy.

"Come down from there, please!" he said. "We have reason to suspect that there's a second bomb in the building... and we have to clear the area."

Suddenly, everyone came barreling down the slope all at once, and many kept on running for another mile or so. Armed soldiers escorted the rest of us to a checkpoint nearly three blocks away. As we walked, a horde of news reporters and cameramen rushed in and surrounded us, sticking their cameras and microphones in our faces and trying to outshout each other.

"No comment!" I kept saying to them like some big-shot celebrity.

The bomb threat turned out to be bogus. Most of us felt that it was just a ploy to remove us from the area. When rescue efforts recommenced forty-five minutes later, the bombsite was deemed too dangerous for civilians to reenter. Only professional rescue workers were allowed back in. Del and my father were furious, and immediately laid into the armed guard standing over the barricade.

"Do you know how many people we saved this morning?" my father was quick to point out to him while

Del argued that he had every right and even an obligation to search for his missing wife.

"I'm sorry, but I have my orders," said the guard, turning a deaf ear.

My father rushed over to the mayor and a couple of other suits who'd just arrived on the scene and gave *them* a piece of his mind. He actually went to high school with the mayor and considered him a dear friend. But they wouldn't let us back in either. They admired my father's spunk and gung-ho attitude, however, and put him in charge of materials and supplies. Me and the crew loaded up in back of the big truck and he drove us from one lumberyard to the next to purchase wood for shoring, tools for digging and cutting, head protection, eye and face protection, lung protection—everything the rescue workers would need in the coming days and weeks. We spared no expense, since the government was footing the bill.

Many other Oklahomans who weren't involved in the rescue effort found other ways to contribute as well. Restaurant owners gave the first responders free meals, clothing store owners brought in truckloads of visibility jackets, safety vests, and work boots. And hundreds lined up to give blood. It was a flood of community support like never before!

Later that afternoon, my father went back to the lumberyard and bought about two hundred sheets of plywood so we could board up all the broken windows in the YMCA building. It was also in shambles, even though it wasn't hit directly—broken glass and piles of debris everywhere. But our main concern was to cover the windows and scoop up the broken glass in every office and on every floor. Meanwhile, construction crews from all over the state were busy boarding up windows in the surrounding buildings. From what *I* heard, there were over three hundred damaged buildings in all—and God knows how many broken windows!

It was dark outside and we were completely exhausted by the time we reached the eighth and final floor. Dad had already gone home for the evening. After we nailed and screwed up the last sheet of plywood, we sat down and rested awhile. It was the longest day ever—and also the worst. But, some good came out of it. For once, I felt like I belonged, both to the community at large and to the human race. It gave me a buzz just thinking about it! Matt and Sean were lying on the floor, staring grimly at the ceiling. Maybe they had consciences after all. The Kid was sprawled out in the office chair. And *I* was seated on the edge of the desk between Tim and Homer, both unusually quiet—no dirty jokes or complaining about the ex-wife. We were all too tired to talk. But then Homer surprised me with a sudden pat on the shoulder.

"You did good today, Kiddo," he said. "I'm proud of you."

Wow! I thought. *Not even my dad would say something like that to me. Am I like the son he never had?* And here I thought he despised me! I was just this inept kid who could never hold a job on a construction site if my dad didn't happen to own the business.

I watched the nightmare unfold all over again when I got home that night. Not only were we the top story on CNN and the few other cable news channels, we were the evening's entertainment on all four major networks, replacing hit shows like *Roseanne* and *Ellen*. I learned that Regina's last name was Henderson. She was thirty-eight years old and lived in Midwest City with her husband and four children—two from a previous marriage. Currently, she was in a coma at St. Anthony Hospital, just eight blocks from the bombsite. *Come on, Regina... wake up!* I kept thinking to myself.

Of the twenty-one children that were in the daycare that morning, fourteen were confirmed dead, thus far, along with over a hundred adults. Yet, miraculously, six children survived and were in intensive care. And now, more than twelve hours since the blast, a fifteen-year-old girl had just been rescued from the basement of the building, which was at the very bottom of that enormous pile. I wouldn't have thought it possible. *Wait 'til Regina hears about it!* I thought. It was determined that a truck bomb caused the explosion, but the perpetrators were still unknown.

Matt called around ten o'clock. "Man, this day really sucked," he groused. "I could really use a pick-me-up. How 'bout you?"

"Yeah, sure," I numbly replied.

It sounded like a good idea at the time. But, even after a couple of pills, I couldn't escape the horrific images forever embedded in my brain. As I was getting down with Porsche on the dance floor, I kept seeing bloodied corpses, severed limbs, dead babies, innocent people crying in pain or walking about like total zombies. Plus, I kept thinking about Regina, hanging on for dear life in a hospital bed. *How can anyone be dancin' with so much tragedy around them?* I had to ask myself, feeling like such a fool—a dancing fool! *Will things ever be the same? Is this the end of fun?*

I went to the after-party later, but only because I really needed to see Barbie, hoping we could comfort each other through all this mess. Her bedroom door was shut when I arrived. But, seeing that World War III had just broken out in our own backyard, I took it upon myself to barge right in without knocking. I probably should've known that Brian would be with her. They were sitting up in the bed together, sharing a joint.

"Benjamin!" Barbie exclaimed with a spaced-out grin. Clearly, she was on something much stronger than the weed.

"Ever heard of knockin', dude?" Brian sneered at me.

"Leave him alone," Barbie said, gently slapping him on the arm. "He can come in whenever he wants." She then looked at *me*. "You can come in whenever you want, Benjamin," she said. "You don't even have to knock."

I angrily walked out on them and shut the door. Seeing the two of them together was the last thing I needed, though it seemed a fitting end to such a shitty day. Heading down the hall, I bumped into Skippy, who was stepping out of the dining room with a beer in his hand.

"Hey, Skip," I said. "Where's your *better* half?"

"Roger's gone," he bluntly replied. "He passed away on Saturday."

"Fuck!" I blurted out, too flabbergasted to say anything more.

"Yep, he's gone," he said with a solemn nod, and walked off.

He grabbed a seat at the end of the couch and buried his face in his beer. Matt and Sean sat next to him, chatting with the two lesbians on the other end and telling them about all the gory things they saw that day, only the severed hand was now a severed head. Everyone in the room was listening in very closely as if it was news from the front—everyone except for me. I tried to tune them out as best I could, wishing that they'd just shut up about it. They made it all sound so trivial in their current state—and in our current surroundings.

Suddenly, a group of people walked in from Tony's bedroom, including the man himself—plus Neil, Porsche, and Laura. I had no idea what they'd been smoking or injecting back there, but they all appeared more exuberant than usual, especially Neil, who was usually antagonistic. Strangely, he hugged me and gave me a big smack on the lips as he stepped into the room. I wasn't sure how to take it. On the one hand, it was good to know that he actually liked me, or at least found me mildly attractive. On the other hand, he was a guy! Tony and Porsche hugged me next while Laura and I just looked at each other for what seemed like an eternity.

"Come here, you big galoot," she said finally and stepped toward me.

I met her halfway, and we embraced. Neil stepped up to the coffee table, meanwhile, and looked down at Matt. *Uh-oh!* I thought.

"What the hell y'all talkin' about?" Neil said to him.

"They pulled a bunch of people out of the rubble this morning," Tony interceded. "You're lookin' at a couple of heroes."

"Benjamin, too!" Porsche exclaimed.

"Tell him how many you saved," Tony said to Matt.

"I don't know," Matt replied. "I lost count." He turned to Sean. "How many would you say... ten, twelve?"

"More like twenty," Sean answered.

"Twenty or more," Matt said to Neil, and shrugged.

Neil just kept staring at him. Then, all of a sudden, he saluted him, after which he grabbed an empty beer bottle from the coffee table, held it up, and exclaimed, "Here's to all the poor souls who lost their lives today! Thank God, I wasn't one of them."

"Hear, hear!" and "Amen!" people shouted back while Porsche rushed over to the CD player to put something else on.

The title song from *Oklahoma!* burst through the stereo speakers and everyone began clapping and singing along to it. Tony and Porsche joined forces and broke into their little bowlegged dance and do-si-do routine. It was such a blatant show of disrespect, and I had no desire to be part of it. No wonder we considered ourselves outcasts! We were all so full of hate! I walked out the front door and headed home just as they started playing and singing along to REM's "It's the End of the World as We know It (And I Feel Fine)."

CHAPTER TWELVE

Since the attack, I'd become somewhat of a TV news junkie. In the following days, I was shocked to learn that the terrorists were three of America's own—one a decorated war veteran! I also learned more than I cared to about the Michigan Militia, the anti-government, extremist group that the three men were associated with. Their beef was with the federal government, not us! We were just a bunch of dumb Oakies whose lives didn't mean shit to them. It wasn't the first time people living elsewhere in the country had turned their noses up at us. We were like the Rodney Dangerfield of the fifty states—"flyover country," as East and West coasters often referred to us. In movies, for instance, we were often portrayed as the backward hayseed, whether the character was a big, clumsy oaf, a pretty farm girl, a boozy old broad, or a rich oil tycoon. Basically, we were comic relief, silly little people with silly little lives, a bunch of nobodies going absolutely nowhere. Might as well bomb the hell out of us! But I digress.

On Sunday night came the tragic news that Regina had passed away in the hospital, just four days after being admitted. She was now the one hundred and sixty-eighth and final victim of the attack. It seemed very odd to me that in her mad, desperate attempt to save the children she wound up being one of the dead. It was a damn shame, too! She was a good, warm-hearted soul and I found her quite fascinating. She was Barbie's polar opposite—a slightly older woman who was completely down-to-earth and actually cared about people. Yet it wasn't like I'd have a chance with her, had she lived. She already had a family of her own.

How do people do it? I wondered. *How do couples get together and manage to stay together?* It seemed damn near impossible since we were all on different timelines. Regina had been married twice and had four children; I still had a long way to go in both those endeavors. Her life had just ended; I'd continue to trudge on. Barbie was in her early twenties and still had a lot of growing up to do; I was in my thirties and was ready to settle down. Being born nine years apart made us almost incompatible. But then you had oddballs like my parents, born almost four years apart, and yet they'd been happily married for over thirty years. *How the hell did they manage that? Just an old-school thing, I guess. They were a product of the silent generation. Knowing my luck, my perfect soul mate probably died over a hundred years ago—or hasn't even been born yet. She could be one year old and barely able to walk. Or, she could be ninety-one years old and barely able to walk. The bottom line: It's all fucked!*

As much as they pissed me off on that terrible day, I wasn't through with my gay friends any more than I was through with Barbie. I needed them more than ever, in fact. I didn't want to be left alone to think about that horrific event. The problem was that our group kept getting smaller. People were either dying of AIDS or moving away to more exciting and gay-friendly places like San Francisco, Los Angeles, or fucking New York City! Plus, Matt and Tony's relationship was on the skids again, which made my future in Gay Town uncertain. It all began with Matt's constant bickering about having to live with his mother and Tony offering him a simple solution. I was right there with them when that conversation went down.

"Why don't you just move into the spare bedroom?" Tony said, extremely excited about the prospect. "Better yet, we could share *my* bedroom."

Matt felt it necessary to remind him that he wasn't queer, which caused Tony, Porsche, Skippy, and practically everyone else in the room to burst out laughing. I assumed they all had reason to suspect otherwise.

Tony wasn't about to let it go this time. He kept pressuring Matt, not only to move in with him but to finally come out and admit to himself and the entire world that he was indeed a queer. Matt rebelled by bringing girls over to the house again, usually in pairs. And, before long, he and Tony were back to avoiding each other and partying in separate rooms. Neil started coming around more often during the fallout, no doubt to comfort Tony and drill it into his head that Matt was no good and was just using him for the drugs. When Matt and I showed up to party one August morning, Tony's front door was locked for once. Matt banged on it repeatedly 'til Neil answered, opening it just enough to stick his head out.

"Well... are you gonna let us in?" Matt scowled.

"Tony says you're not welcome here anymore," Neil sternly replied.

"Bullshit," Matt said. "Let me talk to him."

"He doesn't want to see you," Neil said, and shut the door.

Matt banged on it again, but no one answered. It appeared he'd been cut off, which meant that I'd been cut off as well by association... no more drugs, no more after-parties. That Friday we hung out at Saddle Tramps, hoping to find another connection. But no dealer would take our money. Apparently, the news had spread that we were a couple of drug whores from Straight Town, pretending to have gay love just to score some dope. And all because Matt refused to be gay! I for one was deeply offended. I wasn't no drug whore, and I sure as hell wasn't no phony. My love for Barbie was genuine! And I'd come to love Tony, Porsche, Laura, Skippy, and the late Roger almost as much as I loved ecstasy. Matt paged Simone and Desiree, and we were able to get party favors through them at least. But all they had was coke, crystal meth, and crank—no ecstasy. I'd heard a lot of bad things about crystal—that it kept you up for days, rotted your teeth out, and made you look like the Crypt Keeper in a matter of weeks. And crank was just a lower form of meth, supposedly made of kitchen and bath cleaners. That didn't sound too appealing to me either. So I partied on coke, hard liquor, and beer that night, all poor substitutes for the love drug. Instead of being an extremely charming and likeable social butterfly, I was a boorish, loudmouthed, coked-up drunk!

On the following night, Matt went off on his own, searching for E, while I stood waiting for him in front of the Club H dance floor. He just looked at me very grimly and shook his head when he returned.

"Guess we'll have to settle for booze again," I sighed.

"No fuckin' way!" he exclaimed. "We need our mojo... and Tony's got the goods."

I nodded in agreement and joked, "We'll just have to make him an offer he can't refuse."

He looked at me with a puzzled expression.

"It's from *The Godfather*," I said. "Never mind."

We immediately left the club and drove to Tony's house on an ecstasy mission. Yet there were ulterior motives that neither of us dared to speak of. I wanted to make sure that Barbie and I were still friends. And I'm pretty sure Matt wanted Tony's friendship back. He'd pushed him way too far, and now it was time to make amends.

The street and driveway were packed with cars as always, and we could hear the music blaring inside the living room. But, once again, the door was locked. Matt kept pounding and pounding on it 'til finally, someone answered. It was a young lesbian this time.

"What?" she huffed as she stuck her nose through the door.

"Have Tony come to the door," Matt demanded. "I need to talk to him."

She turned and shouted, "Tony! Is Tony here?"

"Shut the damn door!" a male voice shouted from within. It was definitely Neil.

"Sorry, man," she said to Matt, and quickly shut the door.

Matt furiously pounded on it some more. Then he turned, jumped into the flowerbed, and pounded on the living room window. He soon gave up and, as he was climbing out, three or four revelers came to the window and peeked through the curtains. They pressed their faces against the glass and started taunting us.

"Yoo-hoo! Hey, there... sweeties! I hear you knockin', but you can't come in!"

"You motherfuckers," Matt growled at them and then turned to me. "Let's go to the back."

I followed him toward the back of the house. He opened the gate to the stockade fence and we stepped into the backyard, slowly creeping up to Tony's bedroom window. The lights were on inside the room and I could see silhouettes of people moving about through the thin curtains. Matt moved in closer and put his nose against the windowpane to get a better look.

"Can you see anything?" I asked.

"Yeah, he's in there," he said, and banged on the glass.

Suddenly, the curtain was pulled back and Tony's face appeared. Matt jumped back and laughed.

"There he is!" he exclaimed. "Let us in, bitch!"

Tony let go of the curtain and walked away. Seconds later, the back door opened on the opposite end of the house and he stepped out on the porch.

"What do you think you're doin', Matt?" he said as we walked a little closer to him.

"We came to party!" Matt exclaimed. "Are you gonna let us in, or what?"

"I don't think so," Tony said.

"Why not?" Matt said. "Look, I brought Big B with me... the one-man party machine!" He slapped me on the back.

"Damn it, Matt... don't you get it?" Tony snapped. "I can't do this anymore! You know how I feel about you... and you obviously don't feel the same! So screw it! Just let it be."

He turned to go back inside.

"Can you help us out, at least?" Matt shouted, bringing him to a halt. "We need some pills!"

Tony glared at him and exclaimed, "Get the fuck out of my backyard before I call the cops!"

I'd never seen the man so angry. He quickly stepped into the house and slammed the door shut.

"I guess that means we're not gettin' any X," Matt sighed. Then, frustrated, he added, "Why can't we all just have a good time? Why do we have to let feelings get in the way?"

Suddenly bold and determined, I said, "I'm going in."

"Yeah, good idea," Matt said excitedly. "He'll let *you* buy some!"

I swiftly headed for the back door.

"Get us ten!" Matt exclaimed. "No, twelve!"

I knocked, and Tony answered.

"He sent you up here for the pills, didn't he?" he scowled.

"No, it's not about that," I swiftly replied. "I just wanna talk to Barbie."

He just looked at me and sighed in exasperation.

"Please, Tony," I begged him. "Will you let me see her?"

"She's in her bedroom," he said, opening the door a little farther to let me in.

"Thank you," I said, hurriedly walking through the kitchen, dining room, and crowded hallway.

Her door was open this time, so I walked in. The first two things I noticed were the syringe and bent spoon lying on her nightstand. They seemed to be mocking me. She sat in the middle of the bed with her tarot cards spread out in front of her and a small group of twenty-somethings seated around her, all looking stoned out of their gourds. There was even a young couple passed out on the floor.

"Hello, Benjamin," Barbie said to me with disappointment in her voice. "I'm a little upset with you right now. I don't like how you're treatin' Tony."

"How *I'm* treating him?" I exclaimed. "That has nothing to do with *me!* That's between him and Matt."

"You're always with him," she scoffed, "Mr. Six Pills a Night."

"I'm not usin' Tony for the drugs, if that's what you're implying!" I exclaimed. "If anything, I'm using the drugs to get to *you!*"

"Oooh, that's really deep, man," said one of her doped-up, female hippie friends sitting on the edge of the bed.

"Is there any chance we could talk alone somewhere?" I asked Barbie.

"No," she said flat-out.

"Don't do this to me, Barbie," I begged her.

"What?" she numbly replied.

"Push me away like this," I said. "I'm not Matt, and you know it! I'll tell you what... why don't I just join y'all?" I rushed up to the bed and squeezed in between two of her friends. "There... now what were we talkin' about?"

They all just looked at me with dazed expressions.

"Better yet, go ahead and juice me up," I said, getting up to remove my sports jacket. I sat back down, frantically rolled up my shirt sleeve, and placed my arm in Barbie's lap. "I'm ready," I said. "Pick a vein, any vein."

She remained very still and averted her eyes from me, which made me all the more desperate.

"Come on, let me have it!" I continued egging her on. "I wanna be hip."

"Stop it, Benjamin," she said very calmly, yet appearing embarrassed.

"What, am I messin' with your high?" I snapped.

"No, but you're gettin' way too serious," she replied. "Just go away, will you?" She suddenly looked me straight in the eye. "We're friends."

Those last two words hit me like a bullet, just like before. Yet, if there was any truth to them, at least our friendship was still intact. So I got what I came for. I got up and walked out the door, feeling a little embarrassed myself. Matt was waiting for me inside the car.

"Did you get it?" he asked the moment I opened the door.

"Nope," I said as I sat down behind the steering wheel and shut the door.

"No?" he exclaimed. "You were in there for like ten minutes! What the hell was you doin', then?"

"I was talkin' to Barbie!" I shouted back at him.

"Oh." He sighed. "How did that go?"

"I'm not sure," I said, completely befuddled.

"Well, is it over?" he asked. "You're actin' like it's over."

"If it's not, it probably should be," I said. "I'm not gettin' anywhere with her. And I don't think I ever will."

"Maybe it's for the best," he said. "I told you the girl was nuts. Tony thinks she might be bipolar. Plus, her uncle molested her as a child. So there's that." He reached over to pat me on the shoulder. "But you did all could," he said. "Gave it your best shot. And, for that, I'm proud of you, bro."

"She was the only girl I could ever talk to," I lamented. "Most of 'em are so unapproachable. It's probably the closest I'll ever come to finding love."

"Don't say that—"

"Well, it's true," I said. "Not only did God make me fat, he made me incredibly shy... especially around women. And that's a pretty lethal combination."

"Do you think it's easy for *me* to meet women?" Matt exclaimed. "You think you're the only one with problems? Take a look at this!"

He took off his Dallas Cowboys baseball cap for the first time ever and leaned over to show me his receding hairline and the shiny bald spot on his crown.

"Jesus!" I gasped.

"Oh, come on! he exclaimed. "It's not *that* bad... is it?"

"No, of course not," I said. "It just kinda caught me by surprise. I've never seen you without the hat."

"No one has," he said. "I'd give my friggin' left nut to have thick, wavy hair like yours."

And I'd give anything for a left nut, I thought, *except maybe my right arm... or my other nut!*

"Let's trade," I jokingly said to him. "My hair for your body! What do you say?"

"I don't know if I want to go that far," he said, and we laughed.

Then I took another long look at his hairline. "You know, it's really not that bad. It's just receding a little. And we'll all have a bald spot... eventually."

"Okay, that's enough of that," he said, and threw the cap back on.

"Ever thought about shavin' it all off?" I asked. "À la Bruce Willis?"

"I'm goin' with what I've got for as long as I've got it," he said.

"Yeah but, why hide it?"

"For the same reason your wearin' that heavy sports jacket in the middle of summer," he said. "I'm not ready to be the bald guy, just yet." He paused for a moment, then added, "That's what I loved about Miriam. She saw me with my hat off all the time and didn't care. She loved me for me. I never should've fucked that up. She was the best thing that ever happened to me."

All right, here's your chance! I said to myself. *Let's get to the bottom of this once and for all!*

"I thought *she* was the one who fucked up," I said very tactfully.

"No, man... it was me."

"She caught you with another woman?"

"Not exactly," he said, considering whether he should elaborate or not. "All right, I might as well let you in on another secret. You've probably heard the rumors by now."

"I haven't heard nothin'," I said.

"Yeah, right," he laughed. "She caught me with a man! I'm bisexual."

I looked at him with my mouth agape, pretending to be shocked.

"It's just sex, when it comes to guys," he said. "I'm not about to fall in love with a man... not in this life! And that's what's drivin' Tony nuts. I love the guy, I really do. But I won't allow myself to be *in love* with him. I'll never cross that line." He looked at me with a stern face. "Don't you dare tell Sean any of this."

"I won't," I assured him.

I thought for sure that confession time was over, especially after *that* huge revelation. But he went on to tell me about his fear of being alone, meaning that he was monophobic, which would explain why he was living in his mother's basement.

"That's another thing I like about you," he said, "besides the hair. You're all alone in the world, yet you seem to be okay with it."

"I'm not *that* okay with it," I replied.

"But you seem to be handling it pretty well," he said. "I couldn't live by myself. I have to have people around me at all times. It's a hell of a lot worse than being shy... as far as *I'm* concerned."

I not only felt compelled but obligated to reveal *my* awful secret at that point.

"I'm impotent!" I suddenly blurted out.

He looked absolutely horrified, as if I'd just told him that I was dying from cancer.

"You mean, you can't have sex?" he said.

"Yep," I sighed.

"It doesn't work at all?" he said, staring down at my lap.

"Well, I can piss through it," I replied. "But, yeah... that's about it."

"Wow," he said. "You can't even jack off?"

"I try," I answered. "Every once in a while, I'll achieve an orgasm—"

"Okay, we don't need to go there," he grimaced. "Sorry I brought it up."

"It mostly just lays there like a wet noodle," I said, bitterly looking at my crotch. "I can't even pleasure *myself* with it... when I feel like it."

"So that's why you're a virgin," he said.

"Yeah, that, and the shyness thing," I replied. "I've got a whole mess of problems."

"Jesus, what keeps you goin'?" he said. "I mean, what's there to live for?"

"Lots of things!" I exclaimed. "I still love bein' with women... talkin' to them, makin' them laugh! And there's food, of course... my writing... ecstasy helps! Hell, I just enjoy breathing! It feels good to wake up in the morning and think 'Hey, look at me. I'm still here!'"

He reached over and grabbed my shoulder. "No offense, big'n," he said, "but if my pecker ever stopped workin', I'd probably have to shoot myself."

"None taken," I sneered, quickly starting up the engine and peeling away.

***

Matt and I separated for a while after that night. He started hanging out with Simone and Desiree and developed a taste for crystal meth as well as coke. Sean had grown tired of the gay scene—and Laura too, I suppose. I guess she proved to be too crazy for him, as she was for me. He went back to Shenanigans, ditzy blondes, the Macarena, and early morning breakfast buffets, which pretty much left me out in the cold. Having become something of a monophobe myself, I had to get used to going out alone.

The following Saturday night, I sat at the bar with my back turned from the dance floor and played the town drunk, chugging down screwdrivers while staring at my miserable reflection in the mirror behind all the liquor bottles. Though not a huge fan of orange juice, I'd finally graduated from drinks that tasted good to drinks that got me hammered the quickest. And, for me, vodka and OJ were just the ticket!

Sitting two bar stools down from me was a man I remembered seeing at an after party—the John Waters look-alike with the slight build, thin, graying hair, and pencil mustache. We kept each other company as we drank. He told me about his younger boyfriend, Philip, who'd just left him for another man. And I told *him* about the love of *my* life, who insisted on keeping our relationship platonic.

"I want to be her knight in shining armor," I said to him in a slurred voice, "ridin' in on my white horse to save her from a lifetime of loneliness and heartache. But she doesn't even see me as an older brother! I'm more like a... pen pal."

"No! That's awful!" he frowned. "You've gotta remember, though, women are like a whole 'nother species. It's their job to make us miserable... one of the reasons I'm glad to be gay! Most men, on the other hand... and I say most... are simple, loyal creatures... much like my Labrador retriever. Do you see where I'm goin' with this?"

"No," I said dimly.

"All I'm sayin' is," he slurred, "maybe you should forget about women and find yourself a good man. You're in the right place for it. Look, they're all around you!"

"I think you may be onto something!" I exclaimed, as if he'd just come up with the perfect solution. But then I let out a heavy sigh and said, "Oh, wait a minute. I'm straight."

"That sucks!"

"Doesn't it, though?"

"The whole goddamn world is straight," he grumbled. "Just think... if you were gay, you could have any guy in this joint."

"You think so?" I gasped.

"I *know* so," he said. "You're what we commonly refer to as a bear."

"Is that good?"

"You bet your sweet tushy it is!" he exclaimed. "We love bears! I'm hopin' to take one home with me tonight, in fact! I love to feed the bears... and rub their giant tummies."

"I'm a bear!" I said with an excited grin.

"Yes, you are," he concurred. "A big, hairy one."

"Urrrrh," I growled, and he growled back.

We sat there for nearly a whole minute trying to out-growl each other. Then, all of a sudden, I heard someone clearing their throat and turned to see Porsche sitting next to me.

"Guess what, Porsche?" I exclaimed. "I'm a bear!"

"I know," she said, smiling affectionately. "Why are you sittin' here alone? Where's your sidekick?"

"Off doin' his own thing." I shrugged. "We were banned from Tony's house—"

"Yeah, I heard," she said. "Tony has no beef with you. If you were to show up at his house by yourself, I'm sure he'd let you in. It's just that you and Matt are always together... and Tony wants him out of his life."

I simply smiled at her and hung my head. She suddenly stood up, grabbed her cocktail and purse from the bar, and said, "Come with me."

Intrigued, I got up and followed her through the crowd. We climbed up the narrow staircase, walked past the upstairs bar that was also crowded, and headed for the door in back of the room. She opened it and we stepped into a short hallway.

"Where are you taking me?" I asked.

"You'll see," she said.

She opened a second door and we entered a small room with a rack full of dresses on one end and a set of makeup tables and mirrors on the other.

"It's a dressing room," I said.

"Mmm-hmm," she replied.

She set her purse down on the middle table, along with her cocktail, pulled a blue sequin dress off the rack, and stepped behind the dressing screen in the corner, swiftly changing out of her blouse and blue jeans.

"So this is where you get ready for your floor shows," I quickly deduced.

"Yep," she replied. "I didn't want to get all gussied up tonight... but now it appears I must." She stepped out wearing the flashy, low-cut dress. "What do you think?" she asked, extending her arms and twirling around.

"Amazing... as always," I said.

"Thank you, dear." She winked. She sashayed over to the table and flopped down in the swivel chair. "Don't be shy, hon," she said. "Come sit with me."

Walking up to an adjoining table, I sat down next to her and watched her put on her ruby-red lipstick and then apply gold glitter eyeshadow to her eyelids.

"This is what you brought me back here for?" I asked.

"Oh, here," she said, digging into her purse and taking out a key.

She unlocked a drawer beneath the tabletop and pulled it open to reveal a mini gold mine of pills and bags full of white powder. I was shocked, though I tried not to show it. I never imagined that she'd be running her own little pharmaceutical business from inside the club. It was either that or she had one hell of a drug addiction. She removed a couple of pills from the drawer and handed them to me.

"Go ahead, take 'em," she said.

I stuck them in my mouth and swallowed them, and she gave me her drink to wash them down with.

"The next time you need stimulants or depressants of any kind," she said, "you just come to me, sweetie. You don't need to go through Tony or Matt anymore."

Yay! I've got my own connection now! I thought.

Once her look was complete, we went back downstairs and met Kaneesha and Mo'Nique on the dance floor. Even before the pills had a chance to wear off, she tossed another one into my mouth in mid-dance—as if I was her trained baby seal. She wasn't about to let me come down. It was total bliss!

We went to her house afterward, and all of her friends showed up. It was Drag Queen City, once again! There, in the privacy of her own home, ecstasy was served by the shitload in candy dishes and came in many different shapes and colors. Porsche came walking up with such a dish as I lay sprawled out on the sofa, looking down on me with a heavenly smile. I could've sworn she was wearing a halo!

"Try the orange tulips," she said as she held the dish in front of my face. "They're exquisite!"

I snatched an orange pill from the pile, popped it in my mouth and chewed it right up, grinning like the proverbial kid in a... well, you know! Jasmine, the little, pint-sized drag queen, sat down next to me and talked, and talked, and talked—mostly about the OJ trial. Daphne, the three-hundred-pound Ethel Merman look-alike, kept her distance, meanwhile, and gave me sly, come-hither stares all night. I came to know each and every one of those lovely ladies by name, just as I'd come to know all of Tony's friends before they started dropping off the planet. I felt that I'd found a new home and a new family. I even let the gals in on my awful secret, since the proverbial cat was already out of the... well, you know! I told them about the impotency *and* the diabetes. They just looked at me and shook their heads in pity.

"You might be straight," Porsche said, "but you're in the same boat as the rest of us. We're all just a bunch of ragtag misfits."

I eventually nodded off right there on the sofa and woke up at noon, after everyone was long gone. Porsche walked into the room looking surprisingly refreshed, unlike myself, dressed very casually in jeans and a halter top.

"God, you look like a mess," she said, alluding to the dark circles under my eyes, my pale skin, and disheveled hair.

I looked exactly how one was supposed to look after a night of carousing.

"We need to do somethin' about that bird's nest," she said resolutely while giving me the once-over.

She swiftly grabbed her keys and purse, locked up the house, and took me for a spin in the Lamborghini, driving us all the way back to Gay Town, which looked more like a ghost town on a Sunday afternoon. We parked in front of her beauty salon. She opened the place up and we went inside. Then she threw a cape over my suit and had me lie back in a chair with my head over the sink, her extra-large falsies dangling in my face as she leaned over to turn on the water.

"Why so tense?" she said, sensing my sudden wariness. She laughed and said, "Don't worry! My intentions are completely honorable. I'm just gonna shampoo your hair and give you a trim. You'll love it, I promise."

She sprayed my hair wet, rubbed shampoo all over it, and massaged my entire scalp while gently humming something to me the whole time. I believe it was "Lovin' You" by Minnie Riperton.

"Almost done here," she said, seeing me tense up again.

She stuck my head under a dryer when she was finished, then dragged me over to her booth and sat me down in the chair.

"Now watch me work my magic," she said as she stood over me with a pair of scissors and a comb and began snipping away.

After a moment of awkward silence, she asked, "Have you told Barbie about your ED problem?"

"What's the point?" I grumbled. "It's not a sexual relationship."

She bopped me on the head with her comb. "Good friends can become great lovers, remember?" she scolded me.

"Yeah," I replied.

"Fuck buddies seldom do," she said. "It's just two naked people havin' sex—tryin' to get off. Anyone can be your partner... no names, faces, or personalities required." She paused for a second, then added, "I've never cared much for intercourse myself... I mean, with a man. That's *anal* intercourse, you know."

"Yeah," I answered, appalled, wondering how we got on the subject.

"But it doesn't matter," she said. "I've found that there's plenty of other ways to satisfy your man... or woman. I'll make you a list when we get home." She looked at me and winked. "You've got so much love in you, Benjamin," she said. "Men like that are hard to come by these days. Don't sweat the small stuff." She swung me around in the chair and faced me toward the mirror. "There, you see?" she said. "All done."

I was blown away. Just a few snips here and there and voila! I was a new man, very stylish and clean-cut! I looked and felt like a movie star.

"Does mama know her stuff or what?" she said.

"Mama knows her stuff!" I enthusiastically replied.

She laughed, bent down, and kissed me on the cheek. Then she went straight for the lips, giving me a quick peck and jumping back in horror. It happened so fast that I wasn't sure how to react. I wasn't upset or disgusted, but *she* certainly was.

"Please forgive me, Benjamin," she pleaded. "I didn't mean to betray your trust. You're straight... and you're in love! I should respect that."

"No, it's okay... really," I said, and licked her taste off my lips, hoping it would make her feel better. "Actually, it wasn't that bad."

"Would you like another?" she asked.

"Not at this time, thank you," I replied.

CHAPTER THIRTEEN

When I wasn't partying with Porsche, I was at the T-Bone, keeping Barbie company while she tended bar. It was the only way I could see her now that I was banned from Tony's soirées. We talked, joked around a bit, and made each other laugh—just like old times. But, all the while, I kept thinking, *This is what hell must be like,* because all I wanted to do was reach over the bar and kiss her beautiful lips. I felt like I was stuck in a romantic comedy and I'd been typecast as the gay friend. My only reason for being was to provide moral support, give her sage advice, and keep her entertained. And the script was a billion pages long! There seemed to be no end to it! But then I received a phone call that had the potential to change everything. It was Matt, calling to fill me in on the latest gossip.

"Neil has AIDS and he's in pretty bad shape," he said nonchalantly. "The fucker tested positive for HIV over a year ago and chose not to tell anybody about it. You'd think Tony would be pissed! He could be infected too, for all we know. But, nope! He plans on movin' in with the guy and bein' his full-time wet nurse." He let out an exasperated sigh. "*Soooo,* he's quittin' his job, the drugs, the partyin'... and he's sellin' the house."

"What's Barbie gonna do?" I asked.

"Find another place to stay, I guess," he said. "She's got 'til the end of the month."

I wouldn't wish AIDS on anybody, not even Neil. It was such a vile, relentless disease, and I'd witnessed its destruction firsthand. But his misfortune was my window of opportunity. And I jumped through it headfirst! I sat patiently at the bar the following night and waited for my cue. Luckily, Barbie seemed quite distressed over the situation.

"I don't know what *I'm* gonna do," she said while fixing me a screwdriver. "I'm not gonna move back into my parents' double-wide! That much I *can* tell you! Skunk said I could stay with *him* and *his* girlfriend. But I probably wouldn't get *any* sleep with that damn ghost in the house! That leaves Brian, Zack, and Jeremy... the bass player. They share a rent-house in Nichols Hills." She laughed to herself. "Between the three of them, can you imagine how much hair's left in the shower?"

"You can come live with *me!*" I suddenly blurted out.

She laughed.

"I'm serious," I said. "It's just a one-bedroom, but it's plenty big enough for two people! *And* I've got a sofa bed."

"I don't wanna put you out," she said.

"Put me out?" I laughed. "What are you talkin' about?"

"I know how much you value your privacy," she said, "with your writing and all."

"Eh, screw that," I said. "I'm tired of livin' alone. It's boring as hell! It'd be nice to have someone else around for a change."

"Nothin's gonna happen, you know," she said. "I mean, if we were to do this."

"Huh?" I replied, pretending like I had no idea what she was talking about. "I'm just helpin' out a friend! That's what friends do, right... help each other out? You need a place to stay. I need someone to keep me company. Problem solved!"

"I guess we could try it out for a while," she said, "'til I can afford my own place."

"Sure, why not?" I said. "Let's give it a trial run."

"I'm payin' half the rent, though," she said.

"You bet your ass you are!" I exclaimed, making her laugh.

Matt was a little upset when I told him the news over the phone, since I'd never let him stay over at my place for even one night. And I sure as hell wouldn't let him move in with me—if he'd asked.

"I guess I'm not pretty enough for you," he grumbled, which was true.

Porsche was happy for me, however, and even threw me a party on a Saturday afternoon to celebrate my victory. Although it felt more like a going away party, the way she kept looking at me with that melancholy smile of hers. I think she realized that she'd be seeing far less of me from now on. As I stood talking with several of our drag queen friends, she walked up to me and kissed me on the forehead.

"I don't know how you did it," she said, "but you did! You got her to move in with you. Congratulations."

"Thanks, Porsche," I smiled.

"Just don't blow it," she warned me. "Oh, and it's Michael... Mike."

"Mike?"

"Michael Jerome Whitney," she said. "That's my real name. And I'm thirty-seven years old." She suddenly appeared regretful. "I don't know why I just told you that. Must be the E."

September 28, 1995—Christmas came early that year! On a quiet Thursday evening, Barbie came to my door with all of her belongings packed in one large suitcase. I let her in and giddily showed her to the bedroom.

"This is *your* room now!" I cheerfully exclaimed as I led her inside.

She looked at me and sighed. "I don't wanna take your room from you—"

"Nope, I insist!" I exclaimed, and sat down on the edge of *her* queen-size bed, with a brand-new floral bedspread and designer sheets. "It's pretty comfy! Come sit down on it."

She walked up and sat down next to me. *"Very* nice," she said. "Are you sure you wanna do this? I'd be just as comfortable sleepin' on—"

"The couch is mine!" I exclaimed, feigning excitement and making her laugh again. "I haven't unfolded it before! Can't wait to try it out."

By the next day, she'd made the room her own. She totally witchified it, in fact! Bela Lugosi hung over the bed while a young, chiseled Marlon Brando hung on the opposite wall. And there were scented, colored candles spread out all over the place—two on the nightstand, two in the windowsill, three on the dresser, and four on the writing desk, which was now *her* writing desk. The word processor was also hers. Someone might as well have been using it!

At first, it felt kind of odd to come home from work and find her sitting on the couch, watching TV—but odd in a good way. It was like coming home to the wife after a hard day's work, except that dinner wasn't waiting for me on the table. I never saw her cook anything—or eat anything, for that matter. All the canned goods, fresh vegetables, meats, fruits, and dairy products I bought just before her arrival were hardly ever touched. The refrigerator and cupboards remained full for weeks. *Is this girl even human?* I wondered. I was able to sit and visit with her for about twenty minutes whenever I got home. Then she had to go get ready for work. She'd leave around 5:00 p.m. and come home very late—anywhere from one to four in the morning. Obviously, she wasn't coming home directly from work. I'd be in bed by then, so she usually let herself in with the spare key that I had made especially for her. *My* partying days were pretty much over—or so I thought. There just didn't seem much point in going out anymore when the one person I wanted to be with was right there at home. The only problem was that we barely managed to see much of each other. I was always coming when she was going. Or, I'd wake up at the crack of dawn to get ready for work and she'd be fast asleep. She might've slept all day, for all I knew. There were a few surprise encounters, though. One morning, I accidentally bumped into her while stepping out of the bathroom.

"I need to pee-pee," she said, looking so adorable with that oversized t-shirt draping over her panties, groggy-faced, and her hair all a mess. It made me miss morning wood!

A couple of mornings later, around 3:00 a.m., she brought the entire band home with her.

"Shhh! He's sleeping," I heard her whisper as they tiptoed inside and gently shut the door.

I lay very still in my sofa bed and pretended to be unconscious, listening to them shushing each other while they inched their way past me. They started giggling once they reached the hallway. Then, all of a sudden, the bedroom door slammed shut and there was more shouting, cursing, and cackling than I'd ever heard before inside my little Shangri-La! It wasn't long before the neighbors began banging on the walls. *Oh, fuck!* I thought, worried that I'd have to get up and go tell them to hold down the noise. Yet I waited it out. Within an hour or so, things got deathly quiet. Now I was worried that I'd have to get up and go see if they were still alive! But I fell asleep and was woken by the alarm clock on the end table at seven o'clock sharp. The moment I opened my eyes I noticed Brian, Zack, and Jeremy sitting at the dining room table, wolfing down my Apple Jacks and Cap'n Crunch. Seeing them help themselves to *my* cereal, *my* bowls, and *my* utensils was a tad infuriating at first. But then I thought, *Oh, well... at least someone's enjoyin' all that food I bought!*

Unfortunately, it became a regular thing for Barbie to invite her bandmates over and raise a ruckus, at least once a week and every weekend—including Sunday night. So I decided to throw a little after-party of my own. I figured, *What the hell? If you can't beat* 'em, *join* 'em! And maybe it would get them out of the bedroom for once! I bought two cases of beer and invited Matt and Sean over on a Saturday night. We were all crammed together on the living room sofa, tossing back Molson Ice and watching Riddick Bowe knock out Evander Holyfield in the eighth round. Meanwhile, Barbie and the band were in the bedroom, doing *their* thing. I was pleased to discover that, after a few drinks, *my* friends were even rowdier than hers, which led to the neighbors banging on the walls again.

"Hold it down in there!" a woman shouted on the other side of the dining room wall.

"Eh, shut up!" Matt shouted back at her in his cranky, old neighbor voice. Hearing laughter in the bedroom, he turned to me and said, "Are you gonna invite your girlfriend in here, or am *I* gonna have to do it?"

"She's not my girlfriend," I replied. "And you do it."

"Hell, *I'll* do it," Sean said, swiftly getting up and heading down the hall. He knocked on the door and shouted, "Are y'all decent?"

I heard him open the door and a conversation followed. He came walking back into the room about a minute later.

"They're comin'," he said. And, in a whisper he added, "I think they were shootin' up! There's all kinds of drug paraphernalia back there." He smiled at me as he sat down. "You better hope the po-po don't come pay you a visit."

"Fuck 'em," Matt sneered. "They can't come in without a search warrant."

"Here comes your girlfriend," Sean smirked, just as the five of them stepped into the room.

I quickly scooted over and made room for Barbie at the end of the sofa while Brian sat down on the arm of it, turning me and him into a pair of bookends again.

Zack and Jeremy plopped down in the recliner over in the corner, then Skunk planted his large ass on *its* arm. I'm surprised they didn't break it! I would've offered them all a beer, but they'd already helped themselves to it, except for Barbie. She loathed the taste of it even more than *I* did. *All right! Now we're talking!* I thought. *All of us together in one room!* But then I remembered that Barbie and Matt were bitter rivals and should never be in the same room whenever they were inebriated—or even when they weren't inebriated.

She noticed him sitting on the other side of me and said, "I'm surprised to see *you* here, boyo! Shouldn't you be out chasin' tail... or suckin' somebody's penis?"

It seemed a little harsh. But, judging by the spaced-out look in her eyes and the slurred voice, it was most definitely the heroin talking. At least the guys in the recliner had a good laugh over it. I felt certain that Matt was about to jump up and punch one of them in the face and then there'd be a huge brawl between the construction workers and the cover band. But he kept his cool and remained a perfect gentleman, even as the barbs continued to fly.

"Which do you prefer?" she asked him. "Muff or cock? C'mon, man! Time to get off the fence and choose a side!"

"Barbie, that's enough," I finally intervened, since Matt was either too offended or too considerate of my feelings for her to spit out a witty retort.

She glared at me and then looked away in disgust.

"I guess I'm out of here," Matt huffed, and started to get up.

"No, stay!" I exclaimed, and grabbed his thigh.

"Yeah, stay," Barbie said. "We're goin' back to the bedroom. C'mon, guys."

She and her bandmates got up and quickly left the room.

"That went well," Sean remarked. He smiled at me and added, "Your girlfriend's kinda feisty! I like that."

He got up to leave a few minutes later.

"I hate to leave you guys," he said, "but it's about time for my late-night booty call."

"Go on, git," Matt growled at him as he opened the front door and walked out. Then Matt looked at me and resentfully shook his head. "That fucker can't even go one night without the pussy," he said. "It was supposed to be stag night! You know, just us guys and your girlfriend, perhaps... if she hadn't been such a... never mind."

He stayed with me and kept slamming down beers into the morning hours, getting so drunk that I could hardly tell what he was saying.

"Let's go to the girls' apartment and get some blow," he mumbled.

By "girls" I assumed he was referring to Simone and Desiree.

"I'm not drivin' clear out to Edmond just for *that* shit," I protested.

"I need it to sober up!" he exclaimed.

"It's five thirty in the morning!" I shouted back. "We're likely to get pulled over!"

"You're not even drunk! You've been sippin' on that same beer all night."

"This is my eighth one!

"Oh, hell... where's your keys?" he grumbled. "I'll drive." He slowly got to his feet and stumbled toward the door. "Better yet, I'll take the Harley."

"Oh, all right," I sighed. I quickly got up and grabbed my keys from the end table.

It looked like he was about to fall asleep in the passenger seat as we drove away from the apartment complex.

"You're gonna have to tell me how to get there," I said to him sharply. "I forgot."

"Just get on the highway," he numbly replied with his eyes half-closed. When we were about to reach the interstate two minutes later, he said, "You know what? Fuck Edmond! Hurry up and switch lanes, here! Then get on the other ramp and head east."

"Where the fuck are we goin'?" I asked.

"Just do it," he whined.

I got on the eastbound interstate, turned south onto I-35 at his urging, and drove all the way to Norman, Oklahoma, fearfully watching for cops the whole time. Though I wasn't as wasted as Matt, I was far from sober.

"Get off here," he said.

I exited the highway as instructed and swerved down a country road for another mile or so, with the sun slowly creeping up on us. Finally, he had me turn onto someone's property and pull up beside a closed iron gate. Quickly getting out of the car, we climbed a wooden fence next to the left gate pillar and pulled ourselves up and over it like agile teenagers. We were clearly on another mission, but I had no idea what we were after this time. Matt seemed to know exactly where we were, where we were going, and what sort of mischief we were up to, so I followed him unto the breach like a loyal, obedient soldier. Walking just a few feet from the gravel road leading from the gate, using the trees for cover, we came upon a big, beautiful glass house sitting directly in front of a big, beautiful, green lake. We swiftly ran across the road and tried to get as close to it as we could without being spotted, dropping behind a large oak tree and some bushes less than twenty yards away.

"Who lives *here?*" I whispered.

"Neil," Matt answered.

"Really?" I said. "What the hell does he do for a livin'?"

"He *was* in the floral business," he answered. "His partners just bought him out."

"He acquired all of this from sellin' flowers?" I said, a bit too loudly.

"Yes," he whispered. "Keep it down!"

"Damn! I'm in the wrong business," I whispered back.

A man suddenly stepped out onto the porch in his pajamas and sat down at a little, round table, lighting a cigarette as he stared toward the lake. I had no idea who he was. He looked very frail and was completely bald.

"Who the hell is that?" I whispered.

"Neil," Matt replied.

"Are you fuckin' kiddin' me?"

I couldn't believe it! All his tanned muscles and gorgeous, wavy blond hair were gone. And he appeared to have aged forty years since I last saw him.

"Here he comes," Matt whispered as we watched Tony step outside in boxers and an undershirt.

He walked up behind Neil, bent down, and put his arms around him. Neil turned his head and they kissed.

"It kills me to see him wastin' away like that," Matt said, looking deeply frustrated.

"I thought you hated him," I replied.

"I was talkin' about Tony!" he snapped at me.

"Do you do this every morning?" I asked him concernedly.

"What?"

"This!"

"Not *every* morning," he replied.

Wow! Matt's become a full-blown stalker! I thought. That he chose to travel all the way out to the country to spy on Tony instead of rushing after his early morning fix was proof enough for me that he actually loved the dude.

Tony sat down next to Neil, bummed a cigarette from him, and lit it up. Then they both got up a few minutes later, stepped off the porch, and walked out to the end of a wooden dock to watch a gaggle of geese paddle to shore. The two men embraced and started kissing again.

"All right, I've seen enough," Matt said in disgust.

We quickly sprang to our feet and scurried away, keeping low to the ground. We were so tired by the time we got back to the apartment that we immediately pulled out the bed, crawled in together, and went right to sleep. We were practically spooning each other when I woke up that afternoon. *What the fuck went wrong?* I thought. *This should've been Barbie lying here next to me!*

The heroin had brought out a whole new side of her. I felt like I was living with Dr. Jekyll and Mr. Hyde. And the vile substance continued to put a wall between us. When she wasn't at work, she was locked away in the bedroom, being so quiet that I was afraid she might've OD'd on the stuff. One night I knocked on the door and asked her if she was all right.

"Yeah, just reading a book!" she exclaimed.

At other times when I knocked and asked her the same question, she'd answer with, "Yeah, I'm tryin' to write this damn song," or, "Yeah, just got a headache."

That was the extent of our conversation night after night. We were like perfect strangers living under the same roof. And it was all thanks to the smack! It was the one thing keeping us apart, and the one thing that could bring us closer together, as I'd known all along. My worst enemy had the potential to be my greatest ally. So, with that in mind, I pleaded to her once more to let me in, both literally and figuratively.

"Barbie, would you let me in?" I exclaimed, urgently pounding on the door. "We need to talk."

"Can it wait?" she shouted. "I'm kinda busy right now!"

"No, it can't," I firmly replied. "It's important."

She unlocked the door and opened it. Then she walked over to the bed and lay down, dazed and numb as always. I hadn't seen the inside of the room for quite some time. The cluttered nightstand looked just like the one in her previous room. There was the candy box full of marijuana, an open package of cotton balls, three unused syringes, a bent spoon, and the main attraction—a large baggie of brown powder.

"What's wrong?" she asked.

"I can't take this anymore!" I blurted out.

"What are you talkin' about?" She bristled. "I've been a pretty good roommate, haven't I? I try to stay out of your hair, pay half the rent, buy my own food—"

"I want you in my hair!" I exclaimed. "I want our friendship back, goddamn it!"

"We're still friends," she said.

I solemnly shook my head. "We don't even talk anymore."

"Okay." She shrugged. "Let's talk."

"Maybe later," I said. I grabbed the bag of powder from the nightstand and held it in front of her. "Right now, I'd rather do this."

"No," she said, shaking her head.

"Why not?" I argued. "The bag's half-full... there's plenty of needles—"

"You're a good man!" she exclaimed. "I don't want to be responsible for turnin' you to the dark side."

"I'm already on the dark side!" I fired back at her.

She laughed to herself and said, "Ecstasy ain't nothin' like heroin."

"Why don't you let *me* be the judge of that?" I replied.

It got her to thinking. "All right," she said with a shrug and a sigh. "It's your apartment... your decision." She clapped a couple of times and held out her hands. "Toss it to me," she said. "Then take off your socks and shoes and come lay down beside me."

I tossed her the baggie and removed my shoes and socks while she leaned over the nightstand and began fixing me up, pouring some heroin into the spoon. She then dipped a syringe into a cup of water, sucked up about fifty units' worth, and squirted it into the spoon, lightly stirring the mixture together with the needle 'til the powder was completely dissolved. Next, she tore a cotton ball in two, rolled one of them into a tinier ball, and dropped it into the solution, sticking the needle into the cotton and drawing up all the liquid. The cotton was used to filter out the insoluble, little particles and brown specks that could kill me faster than a blood clot. The things I did for love! I had already crawled in next to her by the time she was finished, sitting up with my back against the headboard, staring down at my bare feet.

"Why am I barefooted?" I asked her curiously.

"I don't want to leave any track marks on your arm," she said as she crawled to the other end of the bed with the syringe and a box of alcohol swabs and sat over my feet. "You think your dad would ever check your feet?"

"No," I laughed.

She spotted a vein on the top of my right foot, rubbed a swab over it, and stuck me with the needle, swiftly pushing down on the plunger. My feet were a little numb from the diabetes, so I hardly even felt it. I was doubtful that I'd feel anything at all, in fact, since she chose to inject me in the lower extremities—or the Land of the Dead, as I often referred to it.

She crawled back up beside me and we sat very patiently for nearly an entire minute, waiting for the fireworks to go off, though it began to appear that the drug was totally wasted on me. *Great! Now what?* I thought. *After all my whining and makin' such a big production over the whole thing, should I at least pretend like I'm getting off?* But then it hit me... intense euphoria, that extremely warm, fuzzy feeling as if I was being wrapped in God's enormous blanket, no worries or inhibitions—everything the ecstasy had to offer and more! Finally, there was a drug to give the pills a run for their money, I realized as I sank down to the pillow. Yet, whereas the E made me content to be out in public, the H made me content to be alone—or alone with Barbie, anyway. As long as *she* was in the room, it was my new drug of choice!

We shot up again the following night, only we did it together this time—or five minutes apart, to be exact. She injected herself in the ankle and me in the other foot. It took a minute for the drug to travel up my bloodstream, just like before. But, once the rush swept over me, it was impossible to hold back my affection for her. I just lay there ogling her as she sat up next to me. She smiled at me and reached down to caress my cheek. Then, much to my amazement, she pulled off her t-shirt and removed her bra, giving me something else to ogle over—her big, voluptuous breasts!

"Well, are you just gonna lay there and stare at me?" she said with a sly grin.

I immediately got up from the pillow, rushed in, and attacked her lips while she slid her hand down my jeans and grabbed ahold of my cock. *Uh-oh!* I thought as we continued kissing. Our eyes popped open simultaneously and I noticed her puzzled expression. She jerked her hand out of my pants. I jerked away from her lips.

"It's not you, it's me," I blushed, forced to come clean. "I can't get hard."

"Jeez, that must be awful," she said concernedly.

"Eh, what can you do?" I shrugged.

"How do I pleasure you?" she asked.

"Believe me, you are," I assured her. "How do I pleasure *you?*"

She thought about it for a second and said, "Suck on my tits!"

I gladly obliged, moving down to her chest and wrapping my lips around her left nipple. I nibbled and sucked for a good three minutes, causing her to breathe more and more heavily. Then I stopped and looked up at her.

"What about..." I said, nodding toward her crotch.

"Yeah, go ahead," she replied.

She swiftly unbuttoned her jeans and pulled them down to her knees along with her panties while I slowly worked my way down there with my lips. She began to pant and moan the moment my tongue touched her vagina. *Well, you can't be more intimate than this!* I thought with a mouth full of bush. *Is this really me givin' a woman oral pleasure? No way! It's gotta be a dream!* I'm sure the heroin rush helped shape my opinion. But, for me, oral sex was the only way to go, because I enjoyed giving more than receiving—especially when I was giving it to Barbie! Soon, I had her in full climax mode. She was panting and moaning violently and her back kept slamming against the headboard.

"Yes!" she repeatedly screamed with delight and laughed as the warm, sweet juice flowed out of her and drenched my tongue.

Her body suddenly went limp and she reached down to pat me on the shoulder as if to tap me out. I quickly rolled off of her and wiped my mouth with my shirt sleeve.

"Okay, now it's your turn," she said, calmly catching her breath.

"Huh?" I replied, completely thrown for a loop.

"I showed you mine," she said. "Now you show me yours."

"You don't want to see mine," I laughed, hoping she was kidding.

"Yes, I do," she said. "Get up and take it all off."

"Okay," I sighed. I reluctantly got up, walked to the other side of the bed, and stood directly before her. "But, I've gotta warn you," I said, "I'm a lot more appealing with my clothes *on.*" I slowly unbuttoned my shirt and took it off, then pulled off my jeans and underwear and kicked them aside. I probably couldn't have done it without the heroin. "I haven't lost all the weight yet," I said as I stood there completely naked. "I've got about forty pounds to go... maybe fifty."

She quickly hopped out of bed without saying a word, placed her hand on my chest, and gently ran her fingers through my chest hair. I winced as she felt my right man boob, then cringed as she leaned in and covered my nipple with her lips. For a second, I thought she was going to suck on it like I did hers—a little tit for tat! But she merely gave it a gentle kiss and ventured downward, slowly moving her hand down my hideously scarred beer belly. I suddenly felt very uneasy and instinctively grabbed her hand before it reached my cock.

"I told you, it doesn't work!" I snapped at her.

"Shhhh," she softly replied, placing her other hand over my lips. "You *do* get orgasms, though?"

"Well, yeah... sometimes."

With a nod and a smile, she tore her hand away from mine and went right back to work, grabbing my penis and gently massaging it—in hopes of resuscitating the little fucker. *C'mon, buddy, be a good friend for once and help her out a little bit!* I pleaded to him mentally. And I think he listened, for once. I could feel him moving and stiffening up ever so slightly. *Come on, keep going!* I said to him. *You can do it! I believe in you!* But, alas, she only managed to give me a semi. Or, she gave me a semi! It was the glass half-empty/half-full sort of thing. At least my prick got hard enough for her to get down on her knees and suck on it a little bit. I orgasmed within seconds and the thing exploded like Mount Vesuvius, causing her to laugh hysterically, her face all covered with jizz! I swiftly picked my shirt up off the floor and tried to hand it to her in place of a towel.

"Sorry about that," I blushed.

"Some things can't be helped, Benjamin," she said as she continued laughing.

I lay in bed half-naked with her for a while as we started to come down. But then I got up and headed for the sofa, fearing that I'd overstayed my welcome.

CHAPTER FOURTEEN

Now, whenever Barbie's friends came over, I'd stay up and party with them in the living room, doing heroin, coke, crystal, crank—whatever was on the menu that night. They usually stayed over 'til three or four o'clock the following afternoon—or even later. Needless to say, the place was in constant shambles. And my "career" suffered as well, for I started coming in late, exhausted, and not fully sober. I was more than *two hours* late one morning and my father just happened to be there. I told him that my tire blew out on the highway and I had to go buy a new one because I was afraid to drive too far on my little donut spare. I think he bought it, thankfully.

Another morning, I was so wasted I had to call in sick, which was also a first. It soon became a regular thing, however, yet I was never confronted on the issue. Matt showed up five minutes late on a Friday since I wasn't there to look after him anymore. My dad happened to be on the jobsite on that day as well and fired him on the spot. Matt called me up later that evening, sounding a little distraught—and quite drunk.

"What the fuck am I gonna do, man?" he groaned. "I can't lose this job! Can you see me in some burger joint, wearin' a nametag and a silly hat?"

"Frankly, no," I replied.

"I'd do it if the money was right," he said, "but not for no five bucks an hour! That's just addin' insult to injury. Someone needs to talk some sense into your old man. He can't afford to lose *me*. I'm the best damn sheetrocker there is! No one hangs it faster than me."

"Well, he *did* say he'd fire you if you ever showed up late again," I said on my father's behalf.

"It was five minutes!" he exclaimed. "You came in two hours late the other day! Sometimes you don't even show up at all!"

"I was sick!" I replied, sticking to my story.

"I see what's goin' on here," Matt said. "He's had it in for me since day one... because he thinks I'm a bad influence on you. He thinks *I'm* the reason you've been fuckin' up lately. But, hell... we don't even hang out together anymore!"

"You're probably right," I said. "But what can you do about it?"

"Help me out, here," he beseeched me. "You're his son! Talk to him. Tell him we haven't been partyin' together... that you're your own man. Stand up to the motherfucker for once and call him out on his bullshit."

"I'll see what I can do," I sighed.

On Sunday evening, I quietly stepped into my parents' house and crept up to my father's office at the end of the hall. He was sitting at his desk, doing paperwork.

"Hey, Dad," I said nervously.

"Just a second," he replied, raising his hand to stop me while he continued writing something. A few awkward minutes later, he put down his pen.

"Okay, shoot," he said to me, sitting back in the chair and putting his hands behind his head. "What's goin' on, Benji? Is this about Matt?"

"Yeah," I replied.

"He's used up all his chances," he said firmly. "He's done."

I could already tell by the angry look in his eyes that I'd made a foolish mistake.

"You should forget about Matt and worry about yourself," he said. "I don't know what the heck you're doin' at night, but this comin' in late... or not comin' in at all... it ends now! I probably don't tell you this often enough, but you're the best worker I've got, Benji. You've always given me a hundred percent and, except for this last month or so, you've never missed a day. I could always count on you to set an example for the other guys... and that's how it should be. You're my son!" He leaned in and pointed a stern finger at me. "Straighten up."

I simply nodded, then quickly turned and got the hell out of there. It was stupid of me to think I could save Matt when I was in hot water myself—and even more stupid to think that I could actually talk some sense into the old man. All I said was, "Yeah."

After I got off work the next day, I drove to Matt's house to tell him the bad news. He wouldn't let me come in for some reason. Maybe he was ashamed of his house—or his mom. He stepped outside and we talked in the driveway.

"It's a no-go," I said to him right off the bat. "Sorry, man... I tried! There's just no talking to him once he's made his mind up."

"That's all right... fuck it," Matt replied. "I've got other plans now anyway."

"Really?" I said.

"Yeah," he said. "My mom's got over ten thousand dollars saved up... and she's gonna let me borrow some of it so I can start my own business."

"What kind of business?" I asked curiously.

"Construction, what else?" He shrugged, then excitedly slapped my shoulder. "Ain't that somethin'? I'm gonna be a commercial contractor, like your pops! We'll probably be biddin' on the same jobs! It might be a little touch and go at first. But I'm gonna git me a van and I'll be workin' out of *it* for a while... and Mexicans work fairly cheap. Mark my words, your old man's done! I'm gonna outbid the shit out of him—run the fucker right out of business."

"Wow, that's some plan you've got there," I said, almost in a state of shock. "I mean, in a diabolical sort of way. Who do you think you are, Goldfinger?"

"What can I say?" He shrugged. "Payback's a bitch."

"Yeah, but this is my father you're talkin' about," I argued. "My family, my livelihood—"

"Don't worry, bro." He smiled. "You can come work for *me.*"

***

Skunk and the boys dropped by the apartment on Tuesday night with a bag full of primo crystal, and I ingested enough of the stuff to keep me up for days. I got so paranoid that I thought the DEA was going to come pounding on my door at any second. I kept staring through the peephole and peeking through the mini blinds on my living room window, checking for flashing lights. Barbie and company thought I was hilarious. They knew a tenderfoot when they saw one. Fishing for more laughs, Skunk tried to talk me into taking a hit of acid with him. *Oh, what the hell?* I thought, since I'd never taken it before and it was the last drug on my to-do list. I grabbed the tiny piece of blotter paper from him and placed it under my tongue as instructed. Then, about thirty minutes later, I began hallucinating like a son of a bitch! My little apartment became a carnival funhouse. I could actually see the walls and ceiling closing in on me, as if I was living in a giant trash compactor. Barbie grew a pair of horns and a dark goatee as we were talking on the sofa. And, at one point, I made the mistake of looking at *myself* in the bathroom mirror. My face was lime green, and I had big, pointy ears like some alien creature on *Star Trek*. It wasn't much of a funhouse as far as *I* was concerned—tweaking, tripping, hallucinating, extremely paranoid and claustrophobic.... For the first time on my little drug quest, I just wanted to come down and be normal again.

Seven o'clock came all too soon, and I was still wide awake and tripping. Yet I wasn't about to call in sick after the ass-chewing I'd received over the weekend. I'd just have to clock in and tough it out as always. *You're the Machine!* I kept telling myself. *Be the Machine!* But the moment I entered the jobsite about fifty minutes later, I was more like the Zombie—tired, sluggish, and pretty much brain-dead. Sean must've known I was on something. I noticed him, the Kid, and Ron the Biker laughing at me as I walked up to the gang box to strap on my tool belt. Or maybe it was three gorillas laughing at me. Their faces kept switching back and forth with every glance.

Tim and Homer tried to carry on a friendly conversation with me before we got started, but I couldn't understand a single word they were saying. I think they were speaking Japanese. *This is fucked!* I thought as I stood there nodding at them and looking stupid. *I'm never gonna pull this off!*

I began the morning by helping Tim hang sheetrock, as I'd been doing all week. He did all the cutting, hauling, and hoisting the sheets into place. I simply screwed them to the wall with a screw gun. It was the easiest job in the world when I had all my faculties and was able to concentrate. But being dead on my feet created a bit of a challenge, apparently. I thought everything was going smoothly 'til Tim inspected my work after we'd hung several sheets and saw that eight screws out of every ten had missed the studs by an inch or more. Trying not to explode, he immediately snatched the screw gun out of my hand.

"Here, I'll do this," he said. "Why don't you go sweep the floor or somethin'?"

It felt like the walk of shame, wandering off to fetch a broom while everyone else was busy putting up walls or hanging sheetrock. Though I continued to amuse the hell out of Sean, others seemed shocked and even saddened by my behavior, especially Homer.

I grabbed a broom leaning against the wall and pushed it up and down the floor, still moving at a snail's pace—a damn near vegetable in motion! I also felt very nauseous. I wasn't sure if it was from the LSD, the crystal meth, an empty stomach, or all three. Plus, the hallucinations started to kick in again. Now the entire crew was dressed in gorilla suits! I thought I was in a *Planet of the Apes* sequel! And the pile of sawdust in front of my broom suddenly turned into a pile of brown scorpions. As if that weren't enough, the walls began closing in on me, the enormous office space growing smaller by the second. It was too much all at once. I suddenly felt very dizzy and even more nauseous.

"Fuckin' acid," I mumbled to myself, blaming it all on the LSD.

And, with that, I hunched over with broom still in hand and puked all over the floor.

"Are you all right over there, Ben?" Tim shouted at me from a distance. "You should probably go home if you're not feelin' well!"

"I'm fine," I groaned. "I'm just gonna clean this up."

I walked over to the gang box and came back with a trash can and a large roll of paper towels, swiftly getting down on my hands and knees to clean up my own vomit. All of a sudden, I felt so dizzy that my head started spinning and I had to lay down. Next thing I knew, I was sprawled out flat on my back in a pool of vomit with everyone staring down at me in complete dismay and disgust. I felt a lot better, though!

"Are you gonna be okay, son?" Homer asked concernedly, at which point I simply burst out laughing.

I finally saw the hilarity of the whole situation. Yet I was the only one laughing this time.

"What the hell are you on?" Homer snapped at me.

"Crystal meth, acid—"

"Damn, boy!" Ron the Biker exclaimed. "Even *I* wouldn't mix those two together! You tryin' to kill yourself?"

Tim and Homer bent down and helped me to my feet.

"You'd better get the hell out of here," Homer said. "Your father's on his way with a load of materials... and you don't want *him* to see you like this."

"Don't worry, we'll cover for you," Tim sighed. "I'll tell him you're sick and you were pukin' all over the place."

"Hell, we'll just show it to him," Sean added.

"Thanks, guys," I humbly replied. "I owe you one."

"Just watch yourself from now on," Homer said as I turned and walked away with yesterday's dinner all over my back. "You're better than this."

I went home, slept all day, and woke up feeling normal again, just as the band arrived for Round Two. I did some crystal meth, a little coke, shared a joint with Barbie and Brian, and a bottle of Jack Daniel's with Zack. But I said no to Skunk when he offered me another hit of acid. That stuff was a total nightmare! Yet, even without the LSD, 7:00 a.m. came in a flash and I found myself in the same predicament as the morning before—sleep deprived and too fucked-up to work.

I stayed home this time and tried to figure out how I was going to get out of the enormous hole I kept digging myself into while snorting a mountain of cocaine from the coffee table—Tony Montana style. I needed to stay awake to think. Barbie was there to keep me company, since it was her day off; although she'd occasionally sneak off to the bedroom, probably to shoot up behind my back. She told me her dealer had run out of smack, but I knew how greedy people could be with the stuff— or any drug, for that matter.

The phone suddenly rang at three o'clock in the afternoon. No doubt, it was my father, wondering why I wasn't at work. *What am I gonna tell him?* I wondered as

I sat there and let it ring. *I've been gone for two days now!* I realized I'd have to face the music at some point, but I needed to come up with a really good whopper first. The phone rang again at four o'clock, then five, then six.... It was stressing me out so much that I finally had to unplug the damn thing.

Around midnight, Barbie's friends showed up for the third and final round and brought plenty more crystal meth with them to keep the party rolling. By sunrise, I realized that I was about to reach an all-time low—three missed days in a row without calling in sick. But I was too fucked-up to care anymore. I was stuck in Fantasyland, where there were no consequences for my actions, and no one on the outside could ever reach me. While most people were going to work, I lay in bed with Barbie. She was singing me a couple of songs she'd just written—and they were actually pretty good! I could hear Skunk and the boys laughing very loudly in the living room. Last time I checked, they were getting baked to an old *Road Runner* cartoon.

After Barbie was finished singing to me, we lay there silently for a while. Just before 9:00 a.m., there was a sudden knock on the front door, and one of the guys answered it before I managed to crawl out of bed.

"Am I at the right apartment?" I heard my father say as I stood at the bedroom door. "What's goin' on here? Where's Benjamin?"

Damn! I thought, then quickly stepped out of the room and walked down the hall, coming to a dead stop when I saw him standing in the entryway and staring right at me with a look of betrayal in his eyes. He simply shook his head at me, turned around, and walked out. I swiftly ran after him, rushing out into the breezeway and bolting down the stairs. I caught up with him on the sidewalk.

"Dad, what are you doin' here?" I said to him sharply, as if he had no right to come check up on me.

He stopped, turned around, and got right in my face. "What am I doin' here?" he scoffed. "I haven't heard from you in days! And you won't answer your damn phone! Your mom and I were worried sick! We thought you'd gone missing or somethin'! What's going on with you, Benji? Why are there a bunch of deadbeats on your couch, smokin' hooch?"

"They're just friends," I said.

"What about you?" he asked. "Are you high right now? Don't lie to me!"

"Maybe a little," I said.

"Jesus, son!" he furiously exclaimed. "Where's your head? Don't you know you could get serious jail time for that? It's called Possession of an Illegal Substance!" He took two steps back and looked away from me before his anger got the better of him, rubbing his scalp in frustration. "I just don't understand you," he said. "I pay for your college education and you blow *that* all to hell—"

"I didn't belong there!" I immediately exclaimed. It wasn't the first time he'd thrown it in my face. "I'm not college material."

"It took you five years to figure that out?" he retorted. "It was like pourin' cash down the drain! All my hard-earned money... wasted." He shrugged. "I thought, oh well, I'll just have him come work for me. I'll make him a supervisor, so he'll be able to run the company someday... when I'm gone. But you didn't want anything to do with that, either! You said you'd rather be a laborer! Now, don't get me wrong... I love my crew. I think they're a great bunch of guys. But most of 'em are barely scrapin' by, even though I pay 'em good money. Tim's got an ex-wife and three young'uns bleedin' him dry. After he pays alimony and child support, he ain't got nothin' left hardly! He's havin' to work side jobs to make ends meet. Homer, too." He laughed to himself. "That old fucker chopped his finger off with a Skilsaw!

And he lives in a shack! Are you sure that's the life you want for yourself? Their parents were dirt poor. Lucky for you, *we're* not! You could have anything you want... if you'd just apply yourself and finish what you started. But I guess you'd prefer livin' here in this little cracker box of an apartment... associatin' with stoners and junkies. Meanwhile, your little brother's in California, makin' over a hundred grand a year! He's got a nice house, beautiful wife, a baby on the way—"

"Why do you always gotta bring *him* up?" I finally fired back at him. "I'm not my brother!"

"No, *you're* not," he agreed. "You're smarter... and kinder! But you keep makin' these poor decisions with your life and it's buggin' the hell out of me." He pointed toward my living room window. "Who the hell are those people?" he exclaimed. "Why are you hangin' out with scum?"

"Maybe because I don't see 'em as scum," I muttered. "They're really nice people, actually."

"Well, they're gonna end up in jail... or prison," he said. "*Or,* they're gonna OD on somethin'! I'd hate to see that happen to *you.*" He began to step away. "Don't come to work on Monday," he said. "You need time to decide whether or not you want to be part of the Oldman team. I won't have a junkie workin' for me."

Wait, did he really just call me a junkie? I thought, watching him storm toward the parking lot. *Tough love, I guess.*

He looked at me one last time before he climbed into his white van and shouted, "You should stop by the house more often! Your mother's dyin' to see you!"

He jumped in and quickly drove off. I always wished I could've said more whenever I watched him peel away angry like that. I wish I could've told him the reason why I never finished college, never moved away, never got married, never did anything spectacular with my life... or the reason why I ate and drank too much, did drugs, and "hung out with scum," as he put it. It all stemmed from extreme shyness and low self-esteem. But how do you explain something like that to your old man? I wasn't about to tell him that I had ED, either!

Walking back to the stairwell, I noticed Barbie standing in the breezeway, just outside the door. She must've overheard everything.

"I guess I should've warned you," she said as I climbed up the stairs. "I'm trouble. I'll go pack my things."

She turned to go inside.

"No! Wait!" I exclaimed. I raced her to the door and grabbed her arm in the doorway. "You're fine," I said. "Everything's fine."

"Yeah, right," she scoffed. "I'm not gonna stand between you and your family, Benjamin! You need to patch things up with your dad. Tell him everything's *my* fault."

"Fuck *him*!" I carelessly exclaimed. *"You're* my family."

"No, I'm not!" she angrily snapped at me and jerked away from my grip. "I'm not your wife, either."

"I know that!" I laughed.

"Look, it was fun," she said. "I always enjoyed playin' house when I was a kid. But playtime's over. I'm movin' in with the guys."

She hurried inside, packed her clothes, candles, posters, and notebook full of poems and songs back into the suitcase, loaded it into the black van, and took off with her bandmates. After seven weeks of total chaos and contentment, I had the place all to myself again. It was so quiet and peaceful that I just wanted to hang myself.

On Tuesday of the following week, I went back to work. I got there on time, kept my mouth shut, and did the job. It was a little awkward at first. But, by morning break, I was joking around with the guys as if nothing ever happened. I was back to being the quiet, easygoing, and always dependable workhorse that they all knew and loved. Between jokes, Homer shook my hand and said, "Welcome back."

A couple of nights later, Porsche and friends threw me a coming home party. She cheerfully threw her arms around me as soon as I walked through her door and exclaimed, "Welcome back, sugar!"

Toward the end of the night, when everyone was either coming down or passed out, she sat me down at the dining room table and we had a little heart-to-heart.

"I'm afraid I've got some bad news," she said. "Well, bad news for *me* anyway. I went to get tested the other day... like I do every three months or so... and it didn't go too well this time. I'm HIV-positive."

"Oh, God! Not you, too!" I suddenly cried out.

She ended up having to console *me*. "It's okay," she said very calmly and put her hand over mine. "I plan on stickin' around for a very long time. I'm not goin' down without a fight, anyways. Who knows? Maybe I'll be the first horny old broad to beat this damn thing."

Though angry and pessimistic, I gave her a courtesy laugh.

CHAPTER FIFTEEN

March 1996—The band split up for some reason or another, and Barbie quit her job at the T-Bone to be a full-time singer at Mama Jo's Chicken and Blues, a little restaurant and pub in Midwest City known for showcasing blues musicians from all over the state—and for its chicken and waffles. I liked to eat *mine* at the bar while listening to Barbie sing the blues.

She covered everyone from Billie Holiday to Janis Joplin, with a small horn section backing her up—and Brian accompanying her on piano, of course. There was just no getting rid of the guy! When I tried to have a conversation with her between sets, he'd always pop up and drag her away from me. Usually, he'd take her to the dressing room backstage, most likely to shoot her up with dope. She was a totally different person whenever she came back out, and I didn't seem to exist to her anymore. I'm sure everyone knew she was on something the moment she took the stage again, the sleepy eyes and slurred voice being a dead giveaway.

It became progressively more noticeable night after night. But what really frustrated me was that she mostly sang tender love songs and sad ballads about lost love, and I could actually see and hear her pain as she sang them. It was such a big slap in the face, especially when she sang "The Man I Love," an old George and Ira Gershwin tune made popular by the wonderful Ella Fitzgerald. The whole time she was singing it, I sat there in the dark, thinking, *I'm right here, dammit! I should be the man you love! Why can't you see it? What the hell's wrong with me?* It was almost as if she actually *was* aware of my presence and was doing her best to alienate me and shit all over my dreams.

What happened directly after her set confirmed my suspicion. As she walked off the stage and sashayed toward me in her sexy blue dress, a young, good-looking stoner type standing at the other end of the bar grabbed her arm and pulled her in. I was ready to pounce! But she didn't seem the least bit insulted by his cheekiness. In fact, she began flirting with him. Perhaps she knew the guy. She suddenly moved in closer to him. He put a hand on her waist, the other on her tush, and they kissed. The longer the embrace, the angrier and more jealous I became.

I furiously stood up, flung my cocktail glass to the floor, and shouted, "You fuckin' bitch!"

It immediately got her attention, along with everyone else's.

The surly, black bartender grabbed his bat beneath the bar and exclaimed, "Get the fuck outta here!"

I glared at her for a couple seconds longer, noting the fearful look in her eyes. Then I quickly stormed out of the place and laid low for a while, haunted by that last look she gave me—the look of abject terror. It was the same expression Robyn had on *her* face when I was stalking her. After that fiasco, I swore I'd never put myself through such suffering and humiliation ever again. I wasn't just done with women, but with the whole human race!

And now, more than ten years later, I was right back where I'd started, obsessing over a girl who obviously didn't feel the same, following her around like a puppy dog and throwing temper-tantrums at the drop of the hat. *How did it all come to this?* I wondered. One minute I'm on top of world, for I'd finally met "the one." The next minute I'm in full stalker mode, trying to recapture that feeling again.

After a two-week layoff, I returned to Mama Jo's with a strengthened resolve. I was determined more than ever to fight for her, declare my love for her a million times if I had to! And I brought reinforcements with me this time; a six-hundred-dollar diamond heart necklace. I wasn't sure why I hadn't thought of it before. I enjoyed buying her expensive things. Surely, no one else cared about her *that* much, at least not anyone in Mama Jo's. All they wanted from her was sex! It was up to me to save her from them—and from herself.

With that in mind, I buttoned my sports jacket, checked my hair in the bar window, and boldly stepped inside, finding the last empty barstool to plop down on. The crowd was wild and rambunctious, a typical Friday night, and a blues rock band played loudly on stage. I turned to watch them and noticed Barbie coming out of the dressing room in a stunning black V-neck sequin dress. She froze when she saw me and then proceeded with caution.

"What can I get you?" asked the husky-voiced bartender.

I swiveled back around and was embarrassed to see that it was the same black guy from the other night—the one who was about to bash my head in with a baseball bat. He looked like Chuck Berry, only meaner, with a graying pompadour and wearing a flashy, red silk shirt.

"Oh, it's you," he sneered. "Give me one good reason why I shouldn't eighty-six your ass."

"It's all right, Hank!" Barbie exclaimed, suddenly walking up beside me. "He'll be cool." She looked at me and smiled. "Won't you?"

"Yeah," I said to Hank the Bartender. "I'm really sorry about the other night. I'm willin' to pay for any damages."

He rolled his eyes at me and said, "What you wanna drink?"

"Vodka and orange juice, please," I replied.

Barbie and I looked at each other and giggled silently as he went to prepare my drink.

"Better watch yourself," she said. "You don't wanna get on his bad side."

"I think I already have," I said.

"Well then, I suggest you don't break any more glasses! His wife owns the joint."

"Mama Jo?"

"The one and only," she said. "What got into you the other night? Why did you freak out on me like that?"

"I don't know," I blushed. "I saw you kissin' that guy and I just...." I shrugged. "Okay, I'll admit it! I was jealous."

"You shouldn't have been jealous of him," she replied. "He's nothin'."

"Did you go home with him?" I asked curiously.

"Well, yeah," she said. "But I spent most of the night throwin' up in his toilet."

"You didn't go to bed with him?"

"I did, actually." She grinned. "But we didn't do anything... hardly."

I just kept looking at her 'til she started laughing.

"What?" she exclaimed. "I can't help it! I'm an Aries."

"So you're blamin' it all on your astrological sign?" I said, completely dumbfounded.

She nodded resolutely. "Just like you couldn't help blowin' up like you did... and scarin' the hell out of everybody! You're a Scorpio."

"I blew up like that because I love you," I said. "And it hurts to see you kissin' someone else. I blame it all on love, not the fuckin' month I was born in."

"I get it," she sighed. "You don't believe in astrology."

Hank the Bartender came back and slammed my drink down in front of me, somehow easing the tension in the room. It seemed like the perfect time to surprise her with my gift.

"I got you somethin'," I said, reaching into my breast pocket and removing a tiny box from inside.

"Oh, Benjamin... don't be buyin' me shit," she whined.

Yet I undauntedly placed it directly in front of her.

"Open it," I said.

She slowly removed the lid and was met with a shiny diamond necklace.

"Holy shit!" she exclaimed, taking it out of the box to examine it more closely. "This must've cost you a fortune!"

"I gotta admit, it wasn't cheap," I said with a sheepish grin.

She gave me a mild slap on the shoulder. "What am I gonna do with you?" she scolded.

"Don't worry," I said. "It's not like I'm expectin' anything in return. I don't even expect you to wear it! It's just a little somethin' to remind you that someone out there loves you. I love you, Barbie...." I paused suddenly, having absolutely no idea what her middle name was. "We've known each other for almost two years now," I said, "and I don't even know your middle name."

"It's Sue," she replied.

"Really?" I said in amazement. "That's my mother's middle name!" Then I continued where I left off. "I love you, Barbie Sue Delaney," I said in a loud voice, so all the drunks could hear. "Hell, I ain't afraid to say it! I'd shout it from the mountaintops... if there *were* any mountaintops! I love you, girl!"

She laughed and exclaimed, "You're too much!" Then she stepped in to kiss me on the forehead. "Thank you for the necklace," she said softly. "Of course I'll wear it. Help me put it on, will ya?"

She handed it over and turned her back to me. I put it around her neck and gently hooked the chain together.

"How does it look?" she said, swiftly turning back around.

"Beautiful," I gasped in awe, though it wasn't the damn necklace I was referring to. Then I spontaneously burst into song while she stood close. "I love you, Barbie Sue, with a love so rare and true," I began, changing the lyrics to "Peggy Sue" ever so slightly—and singing more like Elvis than Buddy Holly. "Oh, Barbie, my Barbie Sue-u-u! Well, I love you, girl, and I want you, Barbie Sue."

She slowly backed off without uttering a single word, yet smiling affectionately.

"You didn't like that one?" I shouted in jest as I watched her turn and walk away. "I've got others!"

She sashayed over to Brian, who was sitting alone at a table, drinking a Heineken and giving me the evil eye. She sat down across from him and they talked a bit. Then they got up, headed for the hallway in back, and stepped into that confounded dressing room. When they returned to do their set, she was so smacked-out that Brian had to help her up onto the stage and practically carried her up to the microphone, just so she could embarrass herself. She strained and mumbled through every song and kept forgetting the lyrics. Her last song was "Someone to Watch Over Me," which technically wasn't the blues. But *her* rendition was pretty bluesy. And she at least managed to make it all the way through that one without a hitch. I was instantly reminded of the night she sang it just for me.

She finished the number to minimal applause and then hobbled offstage while Stevie Ray Vaughan took over on the jukebox. I was hoping she'd come over to sit with me for a while, but she'd forgotten all about me again. Instead, she walked up to a group of scruffy-looking bikers who'd summoned her to their table. She sat down on the youngest and handsomest biker's lap and began flirting with him. Bad move!

While she was getting juiced-up backstage, I was busy slamming down screwdrivers one after the other—under

Hank the Bartender's watchful eye. I was a ticking time bomb waiting to go off! The moment I saw the two kissing, I sprang to my feet and dashed over to the table. Only one of the leathery-faced behemoths noticed me approach. The other two were deep in conversation, and Barbie was still sucking face.

"I love you, Barbie!" I exclaimed in a moderately loud voice.

Yet no one seemed to hear me except for that one biker, who was staring right at me in disbelief.

"I love you, Barbie!" I exclaimed even louder, which quickly got everyone's attention.

"Please, just go away... will you, Benjamin?" Barbie pleaded.

"Not unless you come with me," I said.

"Why can't you get it through your thick head?" she exclaimed, frustrated. "We're friends! That's all we'll ever be."

"No, there's something there," I said. "And you know it!"

"What's your problem, friend?" asked the biker whose lap she was sitting on. "Can't you see you're upsettin' the lady? Why don't you go back over there and calm down?"

"Why don't you mind your own fuckin' business?" I retorted, causing his buddies to jump out of their chairs and stare me down like three angry bulls.

"Hey, cupcake," snarled the hairiest and meanest-looking one of the bunch. "You lookin' to get hurt? Take a hike!"

Barbie quickly intervened, jumping off the younger man's lap and walking up to me.

"Go home, Benjamin," she said very gently. "You don't belong here."

"Neither do *you*," I replied.

"Yes, I do," she said, appearing ashamed.

Now that I had her inside my space, I went for broke, swiftly grabbing her arms and reaching in to kiss her. My tongue barely touched the inside of her mouth before she turned her head—the ultimate rejection! Suddenly, I felt somebody digging their claws into my shoulder and turned to see Hank the Bartender foaming at the mouth, his trusty bat at his side.

"All right, asshole!" he exclaimed. "I've had just about enough of you! Let's go!"

I felt I had nothing to lose at that point, so I turned to Barbie and attempted to kiss her once more. She gave me her cheek again and struggled to break free, prompting her biker friends to come to her rescue. They managed to tear her away from me and then drove me back toward the exit. I tried to resist as best I could, but there was just no holding back a horde of angry bikers! I kept losing ground.

"I still love you, Barbie!" I shouted at her as she stood helpless. "This don't change nothin'!"

"Pipe down, lover boy," Mean and Hairy growled at me.

Hank the Bartender tried to keep his customers at ease, meanwhile.

"Don't worry, folks!" he exclaimed. "We're just takin' out the trash!"

They shoved me out the door and took me into the alleyway. Appropriately enough, a thunderstorm was brewing and it started to rain. Once they got me away from the building and the general public, Hank finally stepped in and punched me in the gut with the end of his bat, hitting me so hard that it knocked the wind out of me. They all let go of me and I fell to the ground, gasping for breath.

Mean and Hairy bent down over me and said, "Breathe, son... breathe," which actually seemed to help.

When my diaphragm was working properly again, Hank stepped in once more and stuck his bat in my face.

"You've got some nerve," he said, "to come into my establishment... not once, but twice... and harass the hell out of *my* customers! You think you're a badass? Sheeeit! You're just some over-privileged white kid who can't hold his liquor."

"Fuck you," I sneered at him.

It probably wasn't the wisest thing to say at that point, but vodka's a hell of a drink!

"That's it," Mean and Hairy shrugged. "To the dumpster, boys!"

"Wait! What are you doin'?" I frantically exclaimed as they lifted me by the arms and dragged me over to a little five-foot-tall dumpster. "Come on, guys! Can't we talk about this?"

But it was useless. They were dead set on humiliating me to the fullest and were already laughing about it, in fact, imagining how stupid I was going to look covered in refuse. As we reached the front of the trash bin, two bikers grabbed my ankles and they all lifted me completely off the ground, preparing to toss me in like a bag of garbage.

"Okay, gentlemen... on three!" Hank shouted.

"Don't you dare throw him in there, you fuckin' vultures!" Barbie shouted, suddenly coming to my rescue. She ran up to Young and Handsome, who was holding me by the ankle, and hit him in the arm repeatedly. "Let go of him!" she demanded.

All four of them looked at her like she was crazy—and who could blame them? They thought they were doing her a favor. They let go of me and let me drop. Then she jumped in front of me and kept swinging her fists at them 'til they backed off. Suddenly, a bolt of lightning lit up the night sky, followed by a roaring thunder and a heavier rain.

"Let's get out of this shit!" Mean and Hairy exclaimed, and they all headed back to the bar, except for Hank.

I scooted up against the dumpster and Barbie knelt down beside me, placing her hand on my shoulder.

"You got off easy this time, white bread," Hank scowled at me, his hair and clothes already soaking wet. "I better not catch your honkey-ass 'round here ever again." He pointed the bat at me one last time. "Consider yourself warned." He looked at Barbie and added, "You're on in twenty minutes, girl! Go in and dry off."

"You're not going back in there, are you?" I asked her as he turned to walk away.

"Of course!" she shouted through the rain, with squinty eyes. "I'm on the clock! You're goin' home now, I hope. They'll probably hang you the next time they see you. Believe me, I know their type."

"How can you stand to be around people like that?" I asked, which turned her off instantly.

"I'll see you around, man," she sighed, quickly getting up and running for shelter.

I couldn't just get up and leave after that! It almost ended beautifully, with her saving my life and then fussing over me. But then I had to go and offend the hell out of her.

"How can you stand to be around people like that?" I kept mocking myself in my dumb guy voice as I sat there getting soaked.

It sounded like something my father would say—or some over-privileged white kid. Maybe I was a chip off the ol' block after all, even though adopted. The thought of it both terrified me and made me extremely proud. But there was one thing I knew for sure. I wasn't going to win Barbie over with a holier-than-thou attitude, telling her who she should or shouldn't hang out with. It certainly wasn't winning my father any points with *me!*

It stopped raining for about an hour, then started up again. I was still sitting by the dumpster. She looked more fucked-up than ever when I watched her come out after closing time. She was staggering around like a drunk and holding onto some strange, little man very tightly—or he was holding onto *her* tightly. I expected her to walk out with the young and handsome biker or someone equally young and handsome. But who the hell was this guy? He had to be in his fifties! Plus, he was wearing oversized eyeglasses and had a ridiculous comb-over! Was she going home with pedophiles now?

After they passed me by, I came out into the open and followed them. He took her to his SUV at the far end of the parking lot, pushed her up against the side door, and then looked around to see if anyone was watching. Luckily, I was hiding behind a car just a couple of spaces down. She laughed excitedly at first, but then appeared a little uneasy as he leaned in to kiss her.

"Wait... what are you doin'?" she said.

That's it! I thought, stepping out and rushing in to save her.

I grabbed ahold of that poor little guy and beat him senseless—glasses and all! I wasn't even sure if he deserved it or not. I just couldn't allow her to go home with him. I was also angry and frustrated over the ass-kicking I'd received earlier and was simply paying it forward. I must've hit him in the face at least ten times before Barbie suddenly turned on *me.*

"Stop it!" she screamed furiously, using my shoulder as a punching bag and forcing me to let go of him. She continued punching me in the chest and the midsection, which was already sore. "Why won't you go away?" she screamed.

"I love you!" I said, trying to grab her arms.

"Stop saying that!" she exclaimed. "You don't even know me!"

"Like hell, I don't!" I furiously replied, finally managing to secure her wrists. "Goddamn it! Why don't you want me? I know I'm not perfect, but I'm workin' on it! I'm gonna start takin' testosterone injections and lose the rest of the weight! I've lost over fifty pounds already! I lost it for you!"

"That was a mistake!" she exclaimed, completely repulsed, trying to jerk away from me with all her might. "Let go of me!"

She kicked me in the ankles repeatedly and stomped on my foot. Then, as a last resort, she threw up on my slacks and shoes, causing me to let go of her immediately. Afterward, she hunched over and blew chunks all over the asphalt. I took it upon myself to hold her hair back for her. When she was finished puking, she dropped to her knees and looked as though she was about to pass out.

"We need to get you home," I said, bending down to pick her up.

I hurriedly walked her out of there and left my victim lying facedown on the pavement. He could've been dead for all I knew. She must've been too sick to put up a fight, thank God! Had she been kicking and screaming *or* completely passed out, I would've looked even more suspicious, dragging her to my car. I strapped her in the passenger seat, jumped in, and quickly drove off. She kept slipping in and out of consciousness as we drove onto the expressway. At one point she woke up, looked at me, and gasped, which immediately turned into a look of sheer disappointment.

"Oh, it's you," she muttered. "Take me to my house, will ya?"

"I don't know where you live," I said.

"Nichols Hills," she said.

"Where in Nichols Hills?"

There was no answer. She appeared to have nodded off again.

"I'm takin' you to my apartment," I said resolutely.

She was still unconscious when we got there. I had to unbuckle her, scoop her up in my arms, and cradle-carry her up the stairs. I somehow managed to unlock the door, open it, and get her inside without dropping her. Then I took her into the bedroom and laid her down on the bed. I showered and changed into something more casual as she slept, laying down beside her with the light on afterward so I could keep a close eye on her. She woke up suddenly and turned on her side to face me.

"What am I doin' here, Benjamin?" she asked, looking at me strangely.

I wasn't sure how to answer that, so I simply blurted out, "You're sick. I'm takin' care of you."

"I'm *not* sick," she argued. Yet she suddenly appeared extremely nauseous. "Oh, wait... yeah, I am," she said, quickly crawling out of bed and rushing to the bathroom.

I listened to her hurl into the toilet bowl for almost fifteen minutes—intermittently, of course. Then she returned and lay back down.

"I've got puke all over my dress," she groaned. "I smell like puke.... Doesn't it turn you off?"

"Huh-uh," I answered. "You can take a shower if you want."

"Wouldn't you rather bathe me?" she said with a sinister smile. "I'm surprised you haven't done it already."

I simply smiled back, which seemed to really piss her off.

"Why are you always starin' at me?" she snapped.

"I don't know," I muttered, still gazing into her eyes.

"Well, stop it," she said. "It's makin' me uncomfortable."

I continued staring, prompting her to reach over and wave her hand in front of my eyes.

"Yoo-hoo!" she taunted me. "Are you in there? Why don't you make yourself useful and give me a blowjob? That *is* your specialty, isn't it? You sure as hell got me off... another satisfied customer! You're the king of the pussy-eaters! Muff diver extraordinaire."

She laughed maniacally while I lay there on the verge of tears. It wasn't just that my feelings were hurt. She wasn't the same person I'd met two years ago. And that special bond we shared was now totally nonexistent. *Did we actually spend hours talkin' to each other in her bedroom—or was it just a dream?*

She managed to sleep it off for a few hours. *I* couldn't get to sleep at all, as much as I tried. I just lay there and watched *her* sleep. *If only she could stay like this,* I thought. She looked so peaceful. I was glad to see that she was Dr. Jekyll again when she woke up later that morning. She even smiled at me.

"I can't fight you anymore," she said.

"Huh?" I replied.

"You win."

"I don't understand."

"You want me to say the words?" she said.

I continued looking at her cluelessly.

"All right," she said. "I love you."

Thinking that she was joking, I gave her a chuckle. But when I realized that she was completely serious, I swiftly got up from the pillow and sat against the headboard. She did the same.

"Really?" I gasped. "You love me?"

"Isn't it obvious?" she said.

"No, not really," I replied in earnest. "Wow! You actually love me."

"For what it's worth." She nodded.

"It's worth everything!" I joyfully exclaimed.

But, as I sat there in a state of true ecstasy, she totally blindsided me.

"Brian and I are leavin' in June," she said bluntly. "We just need to save up a little more money, then we're goin' to New York."

New York! I thought. *Why did she have to mention that place?*

But all I said was, "Why?"

"We're suffocatin' here," she said. "We need to branch out—go someplace where our music will be appreciated... where there's people like us... you know, artists, musicians. We've been talkin' about it for a long time... even before you and I met."

Hesitantly, I started to ask, "Are you and him..."

"God, no," she laughed. "Don't be silly! He's just a friend! But we have the same goal. We both want to be in a real rock 'n' roll band and play our own music. We wanna be rock stars! And it's never gonna happen here. I don't want to be stuck here frontin' cover bands or singin' George Gershwin tunes for the rest of my life."

"Let me go with you!" I blurted out, excited at the thought.

"No, Benjamin," she objected strongly.

"Why not?" I frowned. "And please don't tell me my place is here."

"I'd never say that," she said. "Honestly, I don't know where you belong. But it probably isn't in Oklahoma. And it definitely isn't with me. The way I am right now, we wouldn't last three months. Hell, we barely lasted two, livin' as roommates!"

She didn't actually say it, but I could hear what she was thinking next. *Please let me go, Benjamin!* Yet it was way too much to ask. She was the only female on the planet who'd ever seen me naked—other than my mom. And, as an added bonus, she seemed to be okay with what she saw. For someone like me, that level of intimacy was hard to come by.

I drove her home shortly after that. It was painful to imagine that in two months she'd be completely out of the picture—and I'd have to forget about her. I couldn't see myself chasing her all over Manhattan, which was my only other option. I'd just have to get over her, like I did Robyn. It'd probably take years. And there was no way I could do it while she was still around.

Zack and Jeremy moved out of the rent house in Nichols Hills. Now Barbie and Brian had the place all to themselves. *Lucky son of a bitch!* I thought as I watched her get out of my car and walk up the driveway. *If I'd settled for being friends, maybe I could've been bangin' her every night—or givin' her oral pleasure, rather!*

Now that I knew exactly where she lived, that's where I usually ended up after a night of carousing, parking directly across the street with a twelve pack of Molson Ice in the copilot's seat. Just being within a fifty-foot radius of her was better than being alone. And there was always the slight chance that I'd catch a glimpse of her through the window. It was usually after 3:00 a.m., and most of time the lights were on, so I just assumed she was in there. The beer was warm and tasted like piss, as always. But, as distressed as I was, I needed to be a belligerent drunk—and nothing made me angrier than a twelve pack of Molson!

The closer it came to her desertion, the more bitter and frustrated I became. One drunken night, instead of camping out in front of her house, I felt compelled to go home and write her a good-bye letter. It was the first and only letter I'd attempted to write to her—and the first time I'd sat in front of the word processor in over a year. Fueled by rage, beer, and hard liquor, the words poured out of me like raw sewage from a busted drain pipe. It was that nasty! And yet, it was probably the best damn thing I'd ever written, which wasn't saying much.

Dear Barbie, it began. *How can you say that you love me and then, in the next breath, tell me that you're leaving? If you truly loved me, it seems only natural that you'd want to stay here and be with me. So, either you're lying to me or you don't know what love is. And I suspect that it's a little of both. It seems that you've been playing me for a sucker since the very beginning. You tricked me into thinking that you were like me—the sensitive, artistic type—and that we were kindred spirits. Then you made me fall in love with you, seducing me with your music and poetry, only to bail out on me afterward by becoming cold and distant. Thanks for making me go it alone, by the way. That's all I needed at this time in my life—more unrequited love! You were a rare find when we first met; very beautiful, yet congenial and easy to talk to. Now you're evasive, unapproachable, and a total disappointment—much like everyone else in this world.*

I typed on and on in a similar vein for nearly five whole pages, ending with—*If you deliberately set out to destroy me, then I'm sorry to disappoint you. Sure, I'm a little more skeptical now and less trusting of people. But it won't stop me from looking for someone more deserving of my affection. I still believe in love. You tried to make me feel ashamed and embarrassed for chasing after you. But I'm neither! And I'll never apologize for it. Loving you brought out the best in me! Never have I shined so brightly than in these past twenty-one months. I do agree with you on one thing, though. I probably don't belong here in Oklahoma. That's why I'm leaving for Hollywood in the fall, to be with fellow screenwriters and learn from them. So I guess this definitely means good-bye. I'm sure it'll be a relief to know that I won't be following you all the way to New York. Good-bye, my beautiful, green-eyed girl! Sorry, I just had to throw that in one last time.*

Sincerely, B

P.S. I lied when I said that I lost the weight for you. It was mainly for health reasons. I have type 2 diabetes, you see. I don't know why I didn't tell you. I guess I didn't want you to think that I could keel over at any time. But, if I had lost the weight strictly for you, would that be such a bad thing? You gave me a reason to live and be healthy again, and I wanted to look and feel my best for you. I wanted to be your prince!

The part about moving to California was just a bluff, of course. I doubt I was courageous enough to actually pull *that* one off. And everything in the postscript was a flat-out lie. I *did* lose the weight just for her. I was basically just blowing off steam while trying to get my creative juices flowing once again. I never knew that writing angry letters could be so cathartic!

I printed the entire thing and reread it, and it was even more petty and vindictive than I realized—the handiwork of a true Scorpio! Recently, I'd gone to the local library to read up on astrology, so I knew a thing or two about us Scorpios. We were determined, emotional, intuitive, passionate, exciting, and magnetic. Yet we could also be jealous, resentful, compulsive, obsessive, secretive, and obstinate. Aries, on the other hand, were adventurous, energetic, pioneering, courageous, enthusiastic, confident, dynamic, and quick-witted. Yet *they* could also be selfish, quick-tempered, impulsive, impatient, foolhardy, and dare-devilish. That was Barbie, all right. Maybe astrology wasn't a bunch of bullshit after all!

I even went as far as to fold up the four-and-a-half-page letter, stuff it into an envelope, and seal it. But I wasn't sure that I'd actually send it to her—not until the following night, when I got even more shit-faced. This time, I drove up to her house while she was still at work, sneaked up to her front porch, and placed it in her mailbox.

I have no idea if she actually read it or what she thought about it if she did. We never saw each other again. Thanks to Tony, I knew the exact time of her flight and what airline she'd be flying with. But there was no way I was going to show up at the airport with all her friends and wish her a fond farewell—especially after that damned letter! I burned *all* my bridges with *that* foolish stunt! Then again, I was pretty certain it was over.

***

June 3, 1996—No one hated Mondays more than me. Yet this one was especially gloomy, even though it was a beautiful, sunny evening. I stood outside the barrier fence of Will Rogers World Airport, hundreds of yards away, and watched Barbie's plane take off with Peter, Paul and Mary's "Leaving on a Jet Plane" playing in my head. I'd already spent weeks crying over her. Now I was simply numb.

Later that night, Porsche tried to console me on her sofa. It was one of those rare occasions when we had her house all to ourselves.

"You know what they say," she said. "If you love someone and it's truly meant to be, let them go and they'll come back to you someday... or something to that effect. I'm paraphrasing."

"Who's they?" I asked skeptically.

"Who do you think?" she said, rolling her eyes at me. "Beautiful, shiny, happy people... like yours truly."

"Yeah, that's what I thought," I sighed.

"Here, let me show you a magic trick," she said, pretending to pull an ecstasy pill from my ear and offering it to me with a clever smile.

Why not? I thought, and took it. Thus began the darkest chapter of my life—my self-destructive phase. Drugs and alcohol were no longer social enhancers. Fuck society! I used them solely as a means of escape— and to kill the pain.

CHAPTER SIXTEEN

While *my* life had turned to shit, things were looking up for ol' Matty Matt—at least from what he told me over the phone. He used the money his mother loaned him to buy a van, a portable table saw, and lots of hand tools. And he'd already hired his first Mexican, having landed a small job not too far from *our* jobsite. But, even more surprising, he'd finally moved out of his mother's basement and was renting a house. Stranger still, Simone was living with him. Apparently, she and Desiree had a falling out over some girl, so Matt now had a live-in girlfriend! He then proceeded to tell me that Sean had gotten back together with Domino the Stripper and she'd recently moved in with *him*. In fact, they were going to Vegas to get married in a couple of weeks. *Well, how 'bout that?* I thought. *I stop hangin' out with 'em for five minutes and all of a sudden, they've both got wild chicks of their own. Only, they managed to tame theirs, at least enough to get 'em to move in with them, not as roommates but as lovers, and in Sean's case—husband and wife!*

I wandered into Club H over the weekend, found Laura standing alone at the bar, and bought her a few drinks. And, just like that, we were back together again. We left the club completely soused and drove all over town looking for her dealer, then an after-party, while doing key bumps with her house key. It seemed we were always driving around in search of something. She was just another restless soul, constantly bored and unable to stay in one spot for too long.

Sometimes I'd let her drive since she loved the car so much—if she begged me enough, that is. She must've fancied herself as Shirley Muldowney or A. J. Foyt. Besides flying down the interstate at warp speed, she enjoyed driving into an empty parking lot at four in the morning and doing a couple of donuts before speeding off. It was good for a cheap thrill and a quick laugh. My poor car, aka the party-mobile, had just been paid off and already looked like it'd seen one too many parties, with crud and beer stains all over the floor and inside all the cracks and crevices. And that new car smell was replaced with a musty vodka-and-mildew odor. Just outside my door, the side view mirror had been torn off somehow and was left dangling on its cord. I had no idea how it happened, nor could I explain the large gash in the middle of the door. Mr. Hyde could probably tell you.

As dangerous as it was to drive around with one less mirror, there was no way I could get it fixed. Buying eight balls and pills every other night drained my bank account down to zilch. I was basically living from paycheck to paycheck. There were times when I had to write a bad check or hock the little TV to make it through the week. I even asked Dad if he'd pay me in advance on one occasion. He begrudgingly agreed to it, but not without a lecture and a mild ass-chewing.

"Damn it, Benji!" he snapped at me while sitting at his desk. "Where's all your money goin'? You should have over a hundred thousand dollars saved up, as much as I'm payin' you! What do you plan to retire on? Don't you even care about your future?" Seeing that I had no answers for him, he angrily grabbed his checkbook and wrote me out a check. "You'd better not make a habit of this," he said. "I don't do it for the other employees... and just because you're my son doesn't give you special privileges."

He promptly signed it and handed it to me.

"Thanks," I said, slowly turning around and trudging out of his office.

Vowing that I'd never do that again, I went to my bank the following week and took out a five-thousand-dollar loan. I used my banged-up car as collateral. That money lasted about six months. Then I was back to writing hot checks; 'til the bank got fed up and closed my account. So I was making monthly payments for money I no longer had and to a bank I was no longer associated with. But I'm getting way ahead of myself here! While I still had five thousand dollars at my disposal, I started hanging out with Matt again—when Laura or Porsche weren't available.

Matt had a pretty nice place for a little two-bedroom rent house. It was definitely a step up from his mother's rent house. And, from what he was telling me, his business was booming. So now all he had was a massive drug habit to overcome. Having Simone in the house wasn't helping matters much. I could sense that she didn't want me around. She probably wanted to be alone with him so they could get high together. And me being there gave him an excuse to go out and flirt with other women. God forbid that I'd have to go out by myself!

She made a huge fuss as we were leaving the house one night and swore to him that she wouldn't be there when he returned. But I guess he knew better. Neither of us had much luck meeting anyone at the club. And, since it was his night out without the ol' ball and chain, we decided to buy an eight ball, rent a cheap hotel, and hire a couple of hookers. It sounded like a blast, and I was so fucked-up that I completely forgot about my curse. I suppose Matt did as well. It was only after we called the massage parlor that I realized what I was getting myself into.

Within fifteen minutes, two attractive twenty-somethings arrived at our hotel room and we handled the money situation first. I told the little Asian hottie who had her eye on *me* that I only wanted a blow job, since that wasn't a total disaster when Barbie gave me one. She took me into the little bathroom in the corner while Matt and his blonde playmate jumped in bed, and we proceeded to take off all our clothes. Well, at least I did. She only took off her top, along with her bra, and let me squeeze her breasts. Then she got down on her knees and went to work on Mr. Grumpy as I stood against the sink, silently praying.

"Houston, we have a problem!" she said right off the bat, seeing that it was completely flaccid.

She started rubbing on it very gently, growing more and more frustrated by the second 'til finally she was yanking and pulling as hard as she could. I felt like I was being milked!

She stopped, looked up at me and said, "It doesn't seem to be cooperating."

"That's okay," I sighed. "Let's just forget about it."

"No, no... I can do this!" she exclaimed, full of spunk and determination. "Maybe it'd help if you laid down on the floor."

I reluctantly laid down before her, my bare back against the cold, linoleum floor, and she got down on top of me, putting her lips on my cock and trying to blow it up like a balloon. She did this for five minutes straight, to no avail. And it had now escalated to the most humiliating experience of my life.

"All right, get off!" I exclaimed. "It doesn't work."

She slid off me, and I quickly got off the floor.

"Geeze, I'm really sorry," she said. "I did my best."

"I know," I said. "It's not your fault."

I grabbed my clothes from the countertop and my black sports jacket from the shower rod and quickly stepped out, putting them on in the dark. I could hear Matt and the blonde hooker moaning over on the bed, which humiliated me all the more. *Why the hell can't I be like other boys?* I wondered as I furiously stormed out of there. It was a real Pinocchio moment!

I went to the Inferno, rushed out onto the floor, and started dancing. The coke and ecstasy had worn off by then, so I didn't have my bubble to protect me. I could see and hear all the negative shit I was oblivious to whenever I was rolling; people giving me dirty looks, others snickering or flat-out laughing at me like I was a clown!

I even overheard a young, shirtless man say to his partner, "That fat ham thinks he's John Travolta," as they were dancing beside me.

I got so angry that I broke into my war dance, sweeping across the dance floor like a guided missile— all steely-eyed and light-footed. It was me against the world!

I literally danced everyone off their feet and had the dance floor all to myself by the time 6:30 rolled around. The room was completely empty, it appeared, except for me, a couple of bouncers, and the young DJ in his booth. Suddenly, the strobe lights were shut off and the fluorescent lights came on, stripping the club of all its mystery and menace. It was just a big, empty warehouse!

"Time to go home, dude," the DJ said into the microphone as the song ended. "It's almost seven in the morning."

I came to a complete standstill, gave him a slight nod, and slowly walked off the floor. I stepped outside, shielding my eyes from the morning sunlight. I felt like a fucking vampire! The Gay Strip was a ghost town, once again. A dirty, disheveled homeless man came walking toward me as I crossed the deserted street and stepped up to my Buick parked in front of an old tire shop.

"Hey, can you help me out?" the man said in a gruff voice.

I swiftly unlocked the car, jumped inside, and locked it before he reached the door. He gently tapped on the window.

"Hey, what your problem?" he asked. "Help me out, man!"

I immediately started the engine, put the car in reverse, and tore out of there.

***

January 3, 1997—I was at my lowest point mentally and financially, writing bad checks and hocking home appliances for pills and eight balls while Barbie controlled my subconscious.

After snorting coke all night, Laura and I arrived at Club H just before closing and scurried up and down the joint looking for ecstasy. The drug was getting harder to come by now that more kids were dying from it and John Q. Public had deemed it a scourge to humanity. I'm sure the police were already aware that Club H was a drug haven, along with all the surrounding bars. But only now had they decided to do something about it. The word on the street was that there were undercover cops all over the strip. Hence, most drug dealers began to shy away from the clubs while their customers and my friends were getting busted left and right and being forced to rat on them.

Laura could spot an undercover cop a mile off, having been a club regular and a fixture in the gay community for so long. She knew an interloper when she saw one. I, on the other hand, was a tad reckless and naïve in the current climate, seeing how trusting I was of people. She had a full-time job trying to keep me out of trouble. While she was busy talking to some guy who usually had what we needed, I was getting chummy with a pretty girl in front of the dance floor. She walked right up to me and told me I was cute, which should've been a red flag. Then she said that she'd like to party with me, and she wanted to know if I could get us some E.

"We're workin' on that right now," I assured her and took her to meet Laura, who'd just completed the transaction. "Laura, this is Sumner," I said. "She wants to party with us." I bent down and spoke into her ear. "And she's lookin' for some X," I whispered.

Laura scowled at me and said to the girl, "Excuse us for a minute," quickly pulling me away. "You fuckin' idiot!" she exclaimed. "Can't you see she's five-0?"

"*She's* five-0?" I said doubtfully. "No way! She's practically a teenager!"

She laughed and said, "Don't you ever watch *21 Jump Street*?"

"Fuck, no!" I replied.

"Okay, *The Mod Squad* then!" she snapped. "The fuckers recruit 'em straight outta high school!" She grabbed my arm again and started dragging me toward the exit. "We need to go," she said. "I'm packin'."

As we were walking to the car, she pulled a baggie out of her purse and handed me two pills.

"Oh, good... Mitsubishis!" I exclaimed, looking down at the little green pills with the famous car logo imprinted on them.

Mitsubishis were the latest thing, supposedly heroin-laced and, by all accounts, quite potent. I couldn't wait to try them! I chewed them both up before we even stepped into the car, as did Laura, and they began working their magic on me the moment I peeled out of the parking lot; butterflies in the stomach, tingly fingers, sweaty palms.... I sensed that something really big was about to happen!

"Have you done these before?" I asked her excitedly.

"Yeah, man," she said. "We're gonna have a blast, I guarantee it."

She told me the address of an after-party and switched the radio dial to an alternative rock station, turning the volume all the way up. As much as I hated Chumbawamba and their new "Tubthumping" song, it sounded great at the moment. Laura and I looked at each other and grinned, just as the chorus chanted: "I get knocked down, but I get up again!" Obviously, we were getting off at the same time.

I turned onto a residential street and stepped on the gas, attempting to get to our destination before that first huge wave *really* hit me. We were going seventy miles an hour without even realizing it, both of us laughing excitedly, whizzing past cars parked against the curb like they were obstacles in a video game. I was dangerously close to sideswiping one or all of them. And the steering wheel kept inching in even closer, I having lost all control of it. Yet I felt too good to care. We were still laughing when I plowed into the front end of an El Camino and sent it flying off the curb. I drove on with my door and front fender smashed in, my two left tires gone, a busted front axle and Laura thrown on top of me, since neither of us were wearing our seatbelts. But we only got about another three yards or so before the car completely shut down on us.

"Man, are you all right?" I said to Laura, who was sitting in my lap with her back against the window.

She was a little dazed and shaken up, just as I was. But there were no noticeable scrapes or bruises on her, oddly enough.

"Yeah, I think so," she answered. Then, with a nervous laugh, she added, "Dude, that was awesome! I mean, I'm sorry about your car and all.... You're fully insured, right?"

"Yeah," I replied. "We'd better get out of here before the thing explodes."

"That only happens in the movies!" she laughed.

My door was jammed and wouldn't open, so she got off me, grabbed her purse, and we crawled out on the passenger side. The front end of both vehicles were crushed beyond recognition, the El Camino now resting on the front lawn, spewing antifreeze.

"Oh, my God... your beautiful car!" Laura exclaimed.

I shrugged and said, "It's a piece of shit, now."

As we stood over the wreckage, an old woman stepped out of her house directly across the street and shouted, "You stay right there! The police are on their way! I'm tired of you kids barrelin' through here like it's the Indy 500!"

She immediately went back inside while more lights came on in the surrounding houses and dogs kept barking without end.

"I can't be here when the cops come," Laura said. "I'm *already* on probation for drug possession."

"Really?" I said, shocked that she'd keep something like that from me.

"Yep," she replied, "and I'm really rollin' right now! They tend to notice those things."

"You should go, then," I said.

"Come with me!" she urged, while taking several steps back. "You don't wanna waste your high at the police station!"

I shook my head and said, "It'll just make things worse when they catch up with me later. But there's no sense in both of us goin' down."

"I hate to leave you like this," she said, stepping back even farther.

"Get out of here, you crazy kid!" I exclaimed, forcing a smile.

She quickly turned around and took off down the street, just as the portly, Hispanic man whose car I'd crashed into came rushing out of his house in his bathrobe. He took one look at his car and began cussing me out in Spanish.

"I'm sorry!" I shouted back at him while foreign obscenities continued to fly. "I'll make it up to you! I promise!"

Finally, I heard a siren roaring in the near distance and, seconds later, a police car pulled up to the scene, its headlights and siren lights flashing in my eyes. A gruff-looking, middle-aged police officer and his young female partner stepped out of the car and split up. She went to calm the angry man. I got the old guy. First, he asked me if I was okay. I assured him that I was, and then explained to him what happened. I told him that I took my eyes off the road for a split-second to pick up a CD case that'd fallen next to my feet.

"I might've been speedin' a little," I added, to make the story sound more believable.

But I think my appearance and demeanor were telling him a different story. I was sweating profusely, for one thing. Plus, I was very tense and alert, and my pupils were probably the size of M&Ms.

"Have you been drinking, son?" he asked me flat-out.

"Maybe one or two beers," I replied, which was also a lie.

Along with all the coke I'd inhaled at Laura's house, I'd had at least ten screwdrivers. The female police officer stepped up to me after speaking with several of the neighbors standing nearby.

"Was there a girl inside the car with you?" she asked.

"A girl?" I chuckled.

"Someone said they saw a girl get out of the car."

"There was no girl... just me."

They both looked at me as if they knew I was lying. Then they asked me to take the field sobriety test. I refused. I also refused to blow into a breathalyzer, much to their annoyance. Matt had told me at least a dozen times that I should always refuse the SFST, breathalyzer, or any type of drug test if I happened to get pulled over while intoxicated. The police would most likely confiscate my license and throw me in jail for twenty-four hours, he explained to me. But, with a decent lawyer in my corner, it was the one sure way to beat a DUI rap. I trusted Matt's advice, for once. And, as a result, the police took away my license, handcuffed me, threw me in the back of their car, and hauled me off to jail. It was all so new and strange to me. If it wasn't for the ecstasy keeping me all warm and cozy, I probably would've been shitting my pants!

At the police station, the fuzz gave me a charge sheet and placed me in a holding cell. I was charged with suspicion of DUI, fined a thousand dollars, and my court date was in three weeks. Twenty minutes later they processed me, fingerprinted me, took my mugshot, confiscated my sports jacket, belt, shoelaces, everything in my pockets, and patted me down for the second time. They treated their customers like cattle, with all their pushing and prodding. I figured they'd have me strip everything off and put on a jumpsuit. But, nope! They escorted me through the jail hall in my dress clothes and shiny, black shoes without the laces, uncuffed me, and threw me into an enormous cell with about sixty other inmates. *So this is where the party's at!* I thought. They all looked at me like they wanted to kill me. It must've been the fancy clothes. They were probably thinking, *What a pansy-ass!* I walked to the back of the cell very gingerly, being careful not to bump into anyone, and sat down in the corner.

I noticed a payphone on the wall close by, but there was no one I needed to call. I wasn't about to ask my dad to come bail me out. The less he knew about my incarceration, the better. I'd just have to stick it out on my own. It'd all be over in twenty-four hours. Quite a few people were still staring me down, especially the big, bald black guy leaning against the bars. I knew it was just a matter of time before he came over to say hello, so I bowed my head, shut my eyes, and pretended to go to sleep. It was the closest I could come to being invisible. *Now if only I could really get some shut-eye!*

There was nothing worse than coming down in a jail cell. Suddenly, there I was, sitting on a cold floor inside a dark enclosure without my bubble, my blanket, with a bunch of mean, scary Neanderthals staring down at me, wishing to do me harm of some sort. Fear and anxiety took hold of me again, a thousand worries hitting me all at once. *How am I gonna get to work on Monday without a car? How am I gonna pay for a new one? Where do I find a really good lawyer who ain't too expensive?* It was all so overwhelming that I started to feel a little sick, right about the time a new drunken customer was brought into the corridor. He was kicking and swearing so hard that it took four guards to deliver him to us. They removed his handcuffs, tossed him inside, and swiftly slammed the door shut. He was *our* problem now. This guy was a different kind of scary; not huge and imposing but short, thin, and wiry, with wild hair, a scraggly beard, and little, beady Charles Manson eyes. He even talked like Charles Manson.

"I want my lawyer, you fuckin' pigs!" he furiously exclaimed through the bars and pounded his fists against them.

When the guards were finally gone, he turned around and scanned the entire room, looking for someone to pick on, no doubt. Strangely enough, he chose the largest man in the cell—the bald, black dude who'd had his eye on *me.*

He got right up in the big man's face and said, "What you lookin' at, nigger?"

I thought there was going to be a tussle. But Big Black just glared at him, which was something he excelled at.

Little Man threw his hands up in Big Black's face and shouted, "Boo!"

Then he looked for someone else to taunt. Again, I knew it was just a matter of time before I became a target. I was the elephant in the room, the leopard with spots, the wounded gazelle!

Thankfully, a guard stepped back into the corridor about a minute later and shouted, "Benjamin Oldman!"

Oh, great... that's me! I thought, quickly getting up and rushing toward the front.

"You're outta here," he said to me through the bars, unlocking the cell door and sliding it open.

"I'm with *him*," said the little, scary man, trying to step out behind me.

"Back off, Hindley," said the guard, shoving him back inside and slamming the door in his face.

That couldn't have been twenty-four hours! I thought as I was being escorted through the long corridor. *I wonder who bailed me out?* We stepped through a metal door, entered the main lobby, and there stood Porsche in a pink miniskirt, yellow pumps, and a rainbow Afro wig. I'd never seen her look quite so colorful!

"There you are... finally!" she exclaimed. "Can you believe I've been here since four o'clock, tryin' to bail you out? And now it's a quarter 'til seven!"

"You shouldn't have bothered at all," I said.

"You know, you're probably right," she retorted. "But it's a done deal! Let's go."

We walked over to the property clerk's office and I got all my belongings back, immediately throwing on my sports jacket so I'd feel like somebody again. Then I put on my belt to hold my pants up and re-laced my shoes to keep *them* from slipping off. The cops were looking at me differently as we headed for the exit. They probably thought I was Porsche's pimp! We walked out of the building and passed through a group of young street toughs sitting on the steps—presumably the newly released.

"Hey, beautiful!" one of them shouted at Porsche while the others catcalled her.

"Cool it, heathens," she turned around and chided them.

But I'm pretty sure she was enjoying every second of it, the way she was strutting and shaking her ass for them. We hopped into her Lamborghini convertible parked against the curb and took off.

"Thanks for bailing me out," I said to her.

"What are friends for?" she replied.

"I'm gonna pay you back, you know."

"Don't worry about that."

"How did you know I was in jail?" I then asked her curiously.

"Laura crashed my after-party and told us the whole story," she said. "Fuckin' bitch! I can't believe she left you holdin' the bag."

"I told her to leave," I said. "There was no need to drag *her* through all that shit! *I* was drivin'."

"Where to now?" she asked.

"Take me home... please," I eagerly replied and gave her the address.

I talked her into coming upstairs with me when we got there.

"So this is it," I said as she stepped through the door behind me and looked all around. "My little man cave."

"*Little* bein' the key word," she remarked. "I'm sorry, but it just isn't you."

"What do you mean?" I said, a bit offended. "I kinda like it! It's pretty cozy."

After I shut the door, I flopped down on the sofa, grabbed the remote from the coffee table, and turned on the TV, hoping she'd come join me. But she just stood there, turning her nose up at the place.

"You should be livin' like a prince," she said.

"But I'm *not* a prince," I replied, flipping through the channels with the remote. "What kind of prince gets strung out on coke and ecstasy, wrecks his car at two in the morning, and spends the rest of the night in jail?"

"Good point," she said, walking over and sitting down beside me.

"All in all, I think I lucked out," I said. "I could've killed someone."

"Yeah, well… thank God you didn't," she replied, patting me on the thigh. "Let's just count our blessings, shall we?"

I suddenly stopped flipping once I got to the classic movie channel. They were showing one of my favorites, *Casablanca*. And luckily, it'd just started.

"Oh, this is a good one!" Porsche exclaimed, and we sat there silently and watched it all the way through, occasionally trading warm glances.

I accepted her offer to loan me another thousand to add to the thousand-dollar bail bond. And that evening, I bought a '79, lemon-yellow Volkswagen Rabbit from a private seller. It was just an old rust bucket, but I didn't care. Even if it only lasted a few weeks on the road, at least it'd buy me some time before the check came in for my newly deceased Buick, assuming it was totaled. For the moment, I was happy just to have something to drive to work on Monday morning. I'd done a pretty good job of keeping my drug habit away from the workplace since the Barbie-as-roommate fiasco. And, thankfully, I wasn't about to take two steps back.

My coworkers were a bit puzzled, however, when they saw that I'd traded in my slick, sporty Buick Regal sedan for an old, beat-up clunker—and my dad even more so. I told him that I'd rather have the money in savings—for my future.

"A car's just somethin' to get you from A to B," I said.

After work, I went to the towing company where my car was impounded. It was dead all right! Its front end was mangled to the core, making it completely undriveable. My once beloved party-mobile was now the tragic victim of my folly. I could hardly stand to look at it.

"You didn't deserve this," I muttered ashamedly.

Porsche let me borrow yet another thousand to hire an attorney. I went to see a guy Matt had used to get him out of *his* DUI a few years back. According to Matt, he was the best in the business. He was your typical lawyer-type, extremely confident and reassuring, wearing spectacles, a gray beard, and a blue suit and tie. The old man even smoked a pipe as he sat across from me at a long conference table. He said he could reduce my DUI charge to reckless driving and that I probably wouldn't have to serve any more jail time, just a little community service, perhaps. He also commended me for not taking the breathalyzer or any drug tests.

"It'll make my job a little easier," he said. "So... any questions?"

"Do my parents have to know about any of this?" I blurted out.

He looked at me like I was a total dumbass and said, "Not if you don't want 'em to."

That was all I needed to hear. He was my man!

He did everything he said he would. He got me off with reckless driving and no jail time. I just had to receive counseling every other night of the week with a whole room full of bad drivers. In six weeks' time, I received a check from the insurance company for seven thousand dollars, enough to pay Porsche back with four thousand to spare. I could buy a slightly better car with it as it was intended for, but my Volkswagen Rabbit turned out to be a little gem. A month and two weeks in my possession and it was still running like a champ. I kind of enjoyed driving it, too. It was humbling, and I felt more down-to-earth than I had in the Buick.

I used the rest of the insurance money to pay off my bank loan. I was determined not to purchase any eight balls with it, which meant no more Laura. Porsche continued supplying me with the pills, however. And I'd occasionally buy a gram of crystal meth from Matt. I usually brought the shit home with me to consume in private. Alcoholics preferred to drink alone; junkies liked to get high alone—a scary thought, but true nonetheless. *Am I a junkie now?* I wondered.

I'd gotten so used to crystal meth that it no longer made me paranoid or suffer severe hallucinations. It was actually quite euphoric, though not as much as ecstasy. And it made me horny. I liked to get naked on the stuff, watch Skinemax, and try to jack off. Sometimes I'd even wander outside for a bit in my birthday suit. There was something very thrilling and liberating about getting naked in public. A shrink would probably say that I was expressing a strong desire to be intimate, being closed off and repressed for so long. And if I couldn't bare all for that special someone, then why not the world?

One morning, around 4:00 a.m., I decided to go for a drive in the buff. There wasn't a single soul out and about at that time—or so it appeared. As I got into my Rabbit and started it up, a security guard came walking up the sidewalk in front of me, shined his flashlight in my face, and stepped up to the car. *Oh, shit!* I thought, rolling down the window for him. I'm pretty sure he knew I was naked, even though he could only see my bare upper half. And I was quite certain he'd ask me to step out of the car so there'd be no doubt. Then he'd most likely call the real cops on his walkie-talkie to have them come haul me off to jail again—this time as a sex offender!

Instead, he grimaced slightly and said, "What are you doin'?"

"Just goin' to the 7-Eleven to get a six pack and some beef jerky," I bluntly replied.

"Oh, okay," he said, and just stood there with a confused look on his face as he watched me back out of the parking space.

I guess he didn't feel like dealing with a big, fat, naked guy for some reason or another. Maybe he was at the end of his shift. If he'd been one of those gung-ho rent-a-cops, my ass would've been grass for sure!

***

Several weekends later, I asked Matt and Simone to get me some heroin. I'd deliberately stayed away from it because it reminded me of Barbie. Now I was desperate for the stuff because it reminded me of Barbie. Matt and Simone stayed away from heroin as well. I think they were afraid of it. And yet they were into just about every other drug under the sun. I found that quite amusing, even though I understood why anyone with a little common sense would fear the smack. It was so easy to suffocate on it. But I was very lonely and depressed, and it was the only drug capable of bringing my girl back to me, at least in memories. And maybe it'd give me some comfort. Matt was reluctant to help me out. Simone wasn't. She was probably hoping I'd OD on the stuff so I wouldn't bother them anymore.

"If I get this shit for you, you'd better be fuckin' careful with it," Matt said to me very sharply. "It might end up killin' you... and then I wouldn't be able to live with myself."

It was one of the few times I realized how much he cared about me.

"It might take a couple days," he continued. "When we get it, we'll call you. In the meantime, you'll have to settle for this."

He threw a baggie full of crystal meth on the coffee table in front of me.

I went to pick up the H on the following weekend, took it straight home, and sat in bed with all the necessities gathered in front of me on the nightstand, including Barbie's picture that I stole from Tony's bedroom one night.

"Well, here goes nothin'," I said, wrapping a belt around my arm and injecting myself in the inner elbow.

Then I lay down and got off while staring at Barbie's face. Nothing, indeed! Sure, it felt good, but nowhere near as good as it felt the first time I tried it. It was missing the one key ingredient—Barbie in the flesh, lying there beside me. Without her, I was just jacking off! And, after the rush came and went, I felt even more empty and alone than I did before I shot up. Heroin was overrated. Self-gratification was overrated. It scared me to think that seventeen years from now, when I was fifty, I could still be doing this shit—maybe not heroin, but some other lethal drug. Perhaps I'd go back to my first drug of choice—food! *What's more pathetic than a fifty-year-old nobody pleasuring himself?* I thought. *Answer: A seventy-year-old nobody pleasuring himself. Then, the next thing you know, I'm dead and some smartass writes on my tombstone: Here lies Mr. Nobody, who wasted his entire life pleasuring himself. I can't let that happen! This all has to stop... now! To hell with drugs! To hell with people! People are hard. Tryin' to find someone to love me was hard—damn near impossible. I should've spent all that time and energy tryin' to perfect my creative skills, since I clearly belong in the world of fantasy. In that world, I had complete control; people looked up to me, and I always got the girl.*

The very next night I was back at my writing desk, back to the original dream of becoming a successful screenwriter. Time was *really* working against me now. At thirty-four, I'd never be an Orson Welles, but I still had a chance to make something of myself. Fifty was the cutoff. After fifty, it'd be too late. I couldn't even imagine being so old—and I didn't want to! Hopefully, by then, I'd have fame and fortune to compensate for my decrepitude.

"Gilroy and Hodges burst into the crack house with guns blazing," I began typing on page fifty-four. "All four henchmen are cut down in a hailstorm of bullets. Wolfgang flees into the kitchen and escapes through the back door." *That's it!* I thought with an excited grin. *Stick to the basic formula and I've gotta surefire hit... hundreds of millions worldwide! Gene Hackman gets his third Oscar... Nic Cage his second!*

CHAPTER SEVENTEEN

My story was yet another gritty New York crime drama involving a cynical, burned-out old cop and his young, idealistic partner and ending with one of the most thrilling climaxes ever, a bloody shootout between the cops and a vicious drug lord inside his secret lair. It all takes place somewhere in the Bronx—hence the title *Bloodbath in the Bronx*. Never mind the fact that I'd never been to the Bronx. I couldn't even locate it on the map! And I knew next to nothing about police work except for what I'd seen on TV or in the movies. My motto was: "Write what you *don't* know" and let your imagination take you to places you'd never been before. Oh, and to hell with research! All my research was done on TV with over a thousand other cop dramas to choose from.

After three straight weeks of sitting at home in front of the word processor, I was over a hundred pages into my little masterpiece and nearing the end. Porsche was the only person wondering where I was the whole time. She called me on a Wednesday night, begging me to come over. I told her I was busy, so she made a surprise visit and I took time out to watch an old movie with her. Movies were my passion again, but not the sappy musicals and love stories I'd adored so much. Roger was right about one thing—*Forrest Gump* was shit! I now preferred film noir, with its dark and twisted characters and stark black-and-white cinematography. Women were usually the antagonists, the femme fatales, out to destroy the hero. And very rarely was there ever a happy ending. That was reality, to me, and film noir was my comfort food, along with cheeseburgers, Mexican TV dinners, tater tots, potato chips, cake, apple pie, ice cream.... Yes, I piled the weight back on—in a matter of days, in fact.

Porsche continued calling every other night, inviting me to her after-party, but I always declined. It got to the point where she was actually furious with me.

"You can't keep shuttin' people out like this!" she shouted through the receiver one night. "It ain't healthy! And you were doin' so well! You were dancin', makin' lots of friends.... Now it seems you've reverted back to your old self... Benjamin the introvert, the misanthropic recluse! I was hopin' I'd never have to meet that guy. It makes me sad, really."

Now *I* was furious. Here I was, trying to stay out of trouble and better myself, and she saw me as sad and pathetic?

"You know what?" I said. "Fuck dancing... and fuck friends!"

"There's just no talkin' to you," she grumbled, and hung up.

She didn't give up on me, though. Since I wouldn't go to her after-parties, she brought the party to me one early Saturday morning—two thirty, to be exact. She and about fifteen other drag queens, including Kaneesha, Mo'Nique, Daphne, and Jasmine, showed up at my door and squeezed into my tiny living room. Good thing I was still up, typing away on my keyboard, or they would've caught me in my underwear! Kaneesha opened the bottle of wine and bag of pretzels she'd brought with her while I pulled out the blender and made us strawberry daiquiris. Then I put *Out of the Past* into the VCR and we watched Jane Greer dupe Robert Mitchum, often discussing the characters' wardrobe choices, throwing pretzels at the screen, and adding funny bits of dialogue here and there—*Mystery Science*

Theater style. I didn't realize how much I'd missed those gals!

***

November 21, 1998—I was deeply depressed. It was my birthday again, and I was expected to show up at my parents' house soon to celebrate it. Thirty-five freakin' years old! The way these damn birthdays kept piling up, I'd be forty in no time. But I already felt like I was seventy, so what the hell? To add to my misery, I'd just received another rejection letter from a Hollywood agent in the mail, my tenth one thus far. So now it was official—*Bloodbath in the Bronx* was an unwanted piece of garbage and I was a talentless hack. It appeared that I was destined to be a nobody despite my best efforts, a thought that laid heavily on my mind as I got all dressed up and headed off to the party.

The damn thing was just as I expected; aunts and uncles teasing me about nearing the forty mark, nieces and nephews looking totally bummed-out and wishing they were somewhere else, like me, and gag gifts galore! I was glad when it was all over. *Okay, I've got two choices here,* I thought while driving home, *either give up on my dream and go back to bein' a dancing fool and a drug addict or get to work on that second screenplay.* I immediately chose the latter. And I already had an idea for it. I'd simply turn the old cop into an ATF agent and make his idealistic younger partner a woman—a black woman. *Yeah, that's it,* I thought. *Attract black and female audiences all at once! And, instead of a drug lord as the villain, how 'bout a... gun dealer? ATF agents* chase *gun dealers... of course! Makes perfect sense! I should make him more sinister, though. Besides sellin' guns to teenagers, he... kills people... and not just any people... women! Perfect! He's a serial killer on the side! He murders women and children! Oh, and we've gotta change the setting. Instead of New York, let's make it... LA! Of course, it's gotta be LA. If it's not New York, it's*

LA! Boy, I'm really pumped, now! Let's go home and write this sucker!

***

May 3, 1999, 6:30 p.m.—I stood at the living room window, marveling at how quickly the sky turned dark and foreboding. The tornado sirens began to go off, just as the phone in the kitchen started ringing again. No doubt it was my parents, wanting me to come over and get in the storm shelter with them. I probably should've answered it thirty minutes ago, but it was too late to drive anywhere now. The storm was right over me, accompanied by a fierce, sixty-mile-per-hour wind, blowing large tree branches and loose debris across the open field. The weatherman on TV kept warning me to move away from the window, go downstairs, and get in the neighbor's closet since I lived in an upstairs apartment. But I didn't know my neighbors well enough to ask them to share their closet with me. I felt that I had no other choice but to stand there and watch my very first tornado come through. It seemed a little unfair that I hadn't seen one yet. It was one of the few perks of being born here! And at least I'd have *some* satisfaction before I died, getting to witness the awesome power of God in action. My screenplay, *Guns for Tots,* was another stinker, out-stinking the first one, in fact, with a grand total of nineteen rejection letters. And I couldn't come up with a single idea for a third script, so I guessed I'd have to find some other way to become famous. Maybe being sucked up by a tornado was my best bet. At least I'd make the papers.

All of a sudden I heard a mighty roar, not like a freight train, as everyone kept telling me, but more like the T-Rex in *Jurassic Park.* Then the huge, gray monstrosity showed its ugly face, plowing through the field at an alarming speed, snapping trees and telephone poles in half. It was far more frightening than the T-Rex—probably because it wasn't a CGI character in a movie. Yet it missed me by about a hundred feet!

"Hey, asshole... I'm over here!" I taunted the beast, and motioned it to come and get me.

But it turned in the opposite direction, tearing through a playground and a day care center just east of me. Luckily, the little house was shut down for the evening. The evil menace then shot through a creek bed and ripped up the large stockade fence concealing several rows of houses, continuing to chew up and spit out everything in its path—swing sets, Big Wheels, motorboats, shingles, sheet metal, bricks, aluminum siding, windows, etc. I felt very certain that people would lose their lives in this one. Why I was spared, I'll never know! It kept heading east and finally dissipated just before nightfall.

I got a feeling of déjà vu as I saw emergency vehicles rush to the scene and hundreds of people leave their apartments, heading toward ground zero. But this time I stayed put and watched it all from my recliner. The TV newsman gave me a damage report. It was an F5 tornado, the largest one ever to hit the Oklahoma City metro area, destroying nearly two thousand homes here on the south side of town and in Bridge Creek, Moore, Del City, Midwest City, and Chickasha. Nine people had been confirmed dead thus far; over a hundred were injured, and many were still missing. An elderly woman speaking to a reporter in front of her partially destroyed mobile home was lamenting the death of her twenty-nine-year-old son, who was killed in their bathtub somehow.

She laughed reminiscently and added, "He loved to eat."

That really got to me for some reason. Then, all of a sudden, my dad was on TV, pulling people out of the rubble and loading them up in his van to take them to the hospital. And Mom was right there with him!

Apparently, this was all happening live at a rest home not too far from them.

"Well, what do ya know?" I said with a laugh. "Stan the Man."

"This is how we do things here," my father said to the reporter sticking a microphone in his face. "We all band together and help each other out whenever disaster strikes."

"You tell 'em, Dad," I said, genuinely proud of the old man and wishing I could be more like him.

Driving away from the apartment to go to work the next morning, I noticed that the whole complex was still in one piece. Yet, less than a hundred yards up ahead, the day care center and an entire housing addition were completely decimated. There were already dozens of people standing in the rubble, digging around for their belongings and consoling one another. But for me, it was just another day—business as usual.

***

September 11, 2001—I'd finally come up with an idea for my third screenplay, a light-hearted romantic comedy about a young couple on their first date—aptly titled *First Date*. I was already on page twenty-four, and it was absolutely hilarious thus far—comedy gold! So I was pretty stoked driving into work on that fine Tuesday morning. I was working with Tim and Homer in an occupied suite, a law firm. As I sat waiting for them in the parking lot, there was a special news bulletin on the radio. A Boeing 767 had just crashed into the North Tower of the World Trade Center in Lower Manhattan, New York City. Then, about fifteen minutes later, as we were busy hanging sheetrock and listening to NPR, we heard that a second plane had crashed into the South Tower of the World Trade Center. That's when we started to worry. New York was under attack! And, as fate would have it, my parents just happened to be vacationing there that week. The future of the company was in jeopardy! The lawyers and their staff were kind enough to let us sit with them in their breakroom, and we all watched the tragedy unfold on television. It appeared that the people above the 99th floor of the North Tower were doomed, as were the people above the 85th floor of the South Tower. And I just hoped to God that Barbie wasn't working or eating breakfast there—or my parents, of course! We all gasped in horror when the South Tower suddenly collapsed and were utterly stupefied as we watched the North Tower fall just thirty minutes later. It was more devastating than the tragedy that had befallen us six years ago, even though I was watching it on the tube and it was almost fifteen hundred miles away. I always hated New York City for taking the two women I loved away from me. But now I felt sorry for the people there. They were victims, just like we were. They didn't deserve any of this! Although I didn't give two shits about Robyn anymore, I was deeply concerned for Barbie's safety. There was actually something there between us. It wasn't just imagined. And I felt there was a good chance that we'd be back together soon.

Needless to say, no one managed to get much work done that morning. Just before lunch, the head honcho called me into her office over the intercom and handed me her phone.

"Hello?" I said.

"Benjamin?" said a familiar female voice on the other end.

"Mom? Are you all right?"

"Yeah, we're fine," she said, though she sounded a little frantic. "Your dad's standin' right here! He says hi."

"Hi, Dad," I said.

"I guess you've heard the news," she said.

"Yeah," I replied.

"We were stayin' at the Hilton, right across the street from it," she said. "We saw people jumping off the towers from our window. It was so sickening that we finally decided to get the heck out of there. Thank God we didn't stick around to see those things collapse." She paused for a moment, and I heard Dad trying to calm her down. "But, anyway... we're safe," she said. "We're at another hotel in Brooklyn now."

"That's a relief!" I said.

"We're comin' back a little earlier than we planned," she said, "even if we have to drive. I always wanted to see Manhattan, but now I just wanna get out of here and come back home to you guys." I could hear Dad talking to her again. "Well, your father says I need to let you go now," she said. "I just didn't want you to worry about us."

"Thanks," I said.

"I love you," she said.

"Love you, too."

"I'll see you soon," she said. "Take care, now." *Click.*

Good! The parents are okay! I thought. *Now what about Barbie?* I could've just called her up to see how she was doing. But, instead of asking her if we could keep in touch, I chose to write that nasty, fake letter, telling her to go fuck herself!

I hurried home that afternoon and called the T-Bone, hoping Tony was working there again. Thank God, he was! The manager went to fetch him for me.

"Hello?" he said.

"Hey, Tony," I said.

"Who is this?"

"It's me, Benjamin."

"Who?"

It suddenly dawned on me that we hadn't seen or talked to each other in quite some time.

"Benjamin," I said to him once more. "B."

"Oh, hey, B," he said. "What's up?"

"Have you heard from Barbie?" I quickly blurted out.

"Barbie?" he said. "No, man! We didn't part on the best of terms. Sellin' that house was a spur of the moment deal. She took it kinda hard when I asked her to leave. Why are you askin'?"

"I was just worried about her."

"Oh, yeah... the planes," he said. "I wouldn't worry about it, B. I doubt if she was anywhere near those buildings. New York's a big place."

"Yeah, you're probably right," I said. "So, how's things with you?"

"Workin' the kitchen again," he sighed. "Livin' at Neil's place."

"Oh, really?" I said. "How's he doin'?"

"Neil's dead," he said curtly. "He died about four years ago... left the house to me."

Jesus, has it really been that long? I thought, completely taken aback. Then I mumbled, "I'm sorry."

"It's okay," he said. "It's been four years. I should get back to work."

"Oh, yeah... of course," I said. "Sorry to bug you."

"You're fine, B," he laughed.

"I'll talk to you later," I said.

"Right, B." *Click.*

***

December 16, 2001—A stray cat started hanging around the apartment building—a big, beautiful Calico cat with green eyes and a big, bushy tail. I made the mistake of feeding her a leftover crab cake before going to work one morning and, ever since, she'd come upstairs at night and sleep in the breezeway. When I stepped out every morning there she'd be, curled up next to my door. I was feeling a bit bored and lonely on this particular Sunday morning, so I decided to let her in and gave her a bowl of milk with some Cap'n Crunch sprinkled on top for flavor. It seemed like the next logical step. Since I failed at *human* relationships, might as well take in a cat! Besides, it was Christmas.

She was unusually friendly for a feral cat. After she was finished eating, she snuggled up next to me on the sofa and we watched a little TV together. Then she jumped off, walked over to the door, and just looked at me. I assumed she wanted to go back out, so I got up and did her the favor. And that pretty much summed up our relationship from that point forward. I'd let her come in to visit for a while and eat my food, and then she'd be on her merry way. She was a feral cat, after all, and enjoyed the great outdoors, which suited me just fine—no commitment for either of us.

The neighbors started to complain, though. She never strayed too far from the building, now that she'd found her meal ticket, and there were dead critters and cat poop everywhere. Sometimes she'd leave a dead bird or jackrabbit on my doormat as a gift, I suppose, and I was always quick to dispose of the body. Nevertheless, the old lady next door to me—a PETA fanatic, no doubt—confronted me one evening and said she was sick and tired of seeing mutilated birds in the breezeway. She even threatened to tell the manager.

"You should keep your cat indoors," she lectured me. "That way she can't hurt any other animals. And she might even get hurt herself, if she's not careful."

She glared at me as she spoke, as if she had something sinister in mind.

"But she's not my cat!" I argued.

"I've seen you lettin' her in and out of your apartment," she said. "She's your cat."

I became a little more committed after that. I named her Miss Kitty, put a collar around her neck, bought her real cat food—the wet *and* the dry kind, so she could have the best of both worlds—got her a litter box, took her to the vet to get her vaccinated, and only let her out in the evening when I was home from work—or late at night when everyone was in bed. I was usually up at two or three in the morning anyway, working on *First Date*.

As I was busy petting her on a Tuesday night, I noticed that she was a little more plump around the midsection and, in my naivety, I assumed that I was overfeeding her.

"Just dry cat food for *you* from now on, little missy," I said to her.

Two Saturday mornings later, I let her out at one o'clock and she never returned, which had me worried. Then about nine thirty that same morning, I heard a lot of squeaking and scratching outside my door and opened it to see Miss Kitty standing on my doormat with a squeaking, newborn kitten clenched between her teeth. She waltzed right in and headed straight for the bedroom, coming out seconds later with an empty mouth and going back outside, since I was standing there with the door wide open—in a state of shock. She went downstairs, crawled into the bushes in front of the building, and came back up with another squeaking baby between her teeth. This went on five more times— seven newborn kittens in all! And I had no idea who the father was—some horny old tomcat, I presumed. She deserved better!

She stashed the noisy little buggers in the corner of the walk-in closet that I always left open for her, finally crawling in there with them and letting them feed off of her. It was such an amazing thing to watch, a proud mother nursing her kittens. She looked perfectly content and was positively glowing as she suddenly gazed up at me with those big green eyes. But then anxiety slowly seeped in and I thought, *What the hell am I gonna do with eight cats?*

The first couple of weeks were a cinch. They just stayed in the closet the whole time and only Mama would come out every now and then just to eat and drink. Yet, on the third week they began walking, and most of them were adventurous enough to come out of the closet and get a lay of the land. I had to be careful where I stepped at all times. They liked to sneak up on me when I wasn't looking and surprise me. Often two or three of them would crawl underneath the covers late at night and rub up against my leg. And, coming home from work one afternoon, I found them all snuggled together on the edge of the bed next to the bedroom window—sunbathing, it appeared. They looked so adorable that I wanted to keep them.

By week four, however, they were chasing each other all over the apartment, eating out of their mother's food bowl and playing in her litter box. My cute little mogwai were becoming gremlins! I could just picture what my furniture would look like a few months from now when they were much bigger, what the litter box would look like, and what the place would smell like. They simply had to go! I put an ad in the paper that read, "Seven adorable, newborn kittens, free for the taking," and they went like hotcakes, all except for one—the runt of the litter. While the others were either Calicos or had beautiful orange fur, hers was gray with patches of gold and white here and there—the only thing she inherited from her mom. I decided to keep her, seeing that I didn't have much of a choice. At least Miss Kitty would have someone to play with. And I named her Lisa, rather than some stupid pet name like Fluffy, Button, Zippy, or Doo-Dah!

A year flew by and she was still just a tiny little thing—only half her mother's size. But she was very playful and energetic and she made me laugh, along with Miss Kitty. I felt less lonely with them around. Finally, at thirty-seven-years of age, I had a family of my own!

***

August 5, 2003—In my fifteen years at Oldman Construction, I'd never been hurt once. But, ever since Barbie went away, I'd become more reckless on the jobsite—just as I was in the party scene. I used to be afraid of heights. But now it didn't faze me one bit to stand on a wobbly scaffold, twenty feet in the air, or climb to the very top of a twelve-foot ladder. I just didn't give a shit.

On this fateful Wednesday afternoon I was doing just that, standing at the very top of a twelve-foot ladder, screwing a metal stud into the top track of a twenty-foot wall. My screw gun could barely reach it. Suddenly, I lost my balance and fell, trying to hang onto the stud the whole way down. It ended up slicing my fingers to the bone. I could see them dangling from my right hand and spouting blood all over the concrete as I lay there gasping for breath. I thought my lungs had collapsed or I was having a heart attack. I had no idea how either of those felt! My coworkers immediately came to my rescue. Homer picked up a rag and wrapped it tightly around my wounded hand.

"Breathe," he said to me very calmly. "Just breathe."

Soon, I was breathing normally again. Apparently, I only had the wind knocked out of me. Sean called for an ambulance on his cell phone, meanwhile. And Tim went to fetch me a chair. He came running back, helped me to my feet, and sat me down in it. I wished he'd just left me lying on the floor in an embryonic position. Now the pain below my right rib cage, where I fell, was even more intense.

"Ambulance is on its way," Sean said.

"Hang tight there, son... and try to relax," Homer said, knelt down beside me with his hand on my arm. "They should be here any minute."

I looked down and noticed that it was his *disfigured* hand on my arm, the one with the ring finger missing. *Oh, my God!* I thought. *My hand's gonna look worse than his!*

All of a sudden, my dad came rushing into the warehouse with the rest of the crew behind him. It was dress-up day for him again—a beige shirt and bowtie.

"Benji, you all right?" he asked as he stood over me.

"He fell off that twelve-foot ladder," Tim said, pointing to it on the floor. "He must've cut his hand on a stud. His fingers are in really bad shape."

"I just called for an ambulance," Sean said. "It's on its way."

"To heck with that!" my father snapped at him. "We're not waitin' here all day for those guys! The company can't afford it anyway! C'mon, son!" He grabbed me underneath the left arm and he and Homer lifted me to my feet as I winced in pain. "I'm takin' you to the hospital," he declared.

They loaded me up in the passenger seat of his van. Then he put it in gear and tore out of the parking lot. I'd always seen him driving like a maniac from a distance, but now I got to witness it up close. Only it was ten times worse, being an emergency situation, driving twenty miles over the speed limit, constantly switching lanes and honking his horn. Riding with Laura was less scary, and that was really saying something!

"Hang on, Benji... we're almost there," he said.

We pulled up to the emergency entrance in three minutes flat. Then he helped me out of the vehicle and took me inside, his arm wrapped tightly around my waist.

"My boy here needs help!" he said to the woman at the front desk. "He fell off a ladder and cut up his hand."

She asked me for my license and insurance ID card. I slowly pulled out my wallet with my good hand, took out my credentials, and handed them to her, still wincing in pain. She made a copy of them and gave them back to me. Then she handed me a form to fill out—about ten pages long. My dad and I went to sit down amongst the wounded. He pulled his pen out of his shirt pocket and began filling out the first page for me.

"It's always like this," he said to me, shaking his head. "A bunch of red tape. You just gotta grin and bear it, I suppose."

After we finished all the paperwork and handed it back to the lady, someone took us to a waiting room and we sat there for another twenty minutes. *If it was a head injury, I'd be dead already!* I thought. Dad even pointed that out to me.

"If it was a head injury, you'd be dead already," he said, shaking his head again.

We were finally taken into the examination room and the nurses checked my vitals and took X-rays of my chest and hand, after which the doctor came in to give me the diagnosis—three fractured ribs and tendons severed in all four fingers. They bandaged me up and then we were off to see the hand surgeon, who assured me that my fingers would be fine—much to my relief. I spent the night at my parents' house in my old bedroom, doped up on painkillers. The following morning, Mom and Dad took me back to the clinic to have my tendons repaired.

When I woke up from the surgery, my hand was wrapped up in a splint and my fingers wouldn't open all the way. They were permanently stuck at a sixty-five degree angle due to the massive scar tissue that had built up inside them.

"But with some physical therapy," the doctor said, "your hand should be able to function properly again... with only a minor disability."

Oh, good! I thought. *It looks like shit, but at least I'll be able to eat and wipe my ass with it again... in about six weeks... maybe! I make one bad decision at work, tryin' to please the old man, and suddenly I'm disfigured for life.*

***

May 11, 2007—I took off my shoes and socks to go to bed and noticed that my big toe on my left foot was slightly bigger than the one on my right foot and kind of red. I examined the toe more closely and saw that there was a hole in the back of it, about a quarter-inch wide. *Hmm, that's unusual,* I thought. I had no idea how it got there, but I assumed it happened at work somehow. The strange thing was that it didn't hurt at all.

I got a needle out of the desk drawer and stuck it in the hole. My eyes suddenly bugged out of my head like Jeff Goldblum's in *The Fly* as I watched it go in all the way—clear to the bone and beyond, it seemed. It was as if there wasn't any bone in there at all! Yet I wasn't alarmed enough to have it looked at, for some stupid reason. I didn't have time to go to the doctor, and seriously thought it would heal on its own. I didn't even have time to worry about it, so I didn't. There was work, which was really becoming a pain in the ass with all the overtime, and then there was my latest screenplay—the fifth one, to be exact.

Bloodbath in the Bronx and *Guns for Tots* were flat-out failures, as you might remember. I scratched *First Date* about three-quarters of the way through because I sucked at comedy. And *The Everyday Housewife,* a character-driven/fish-out-of-water story about an adventurous, young housewife who travels to—you guessed it—New York City, received only three rejection letters before I suddenly gave up on it.

This time, I knew I was trying to sell a piece of crap and I wasn't going to kid myself anymore, thinking it was a masterpiece. So, in a sense, I guess I'd really grown as a writer, having become more objective about my own work. With age and experience comes wisdom, as they say. *Demon in the Woods* was my foray into the horror genre. I'd written eighty pages thus far, and I was determined to finish it and get it out there. I wasn't about to let anything stop me, not even a hole in the bottom of my foot!

***

August 2007—*Demon in the Woods* was another flop. But at least I was getting some positive feedback in my rejection letters. Several agents told me that they liked the story but either they didn't represent horror or it was too cerebral for a horror flick—and therefore unmarketable. So my instincts were correct. I'd written a hell of a story! I just failed to realize that today's horror flicks were geared towards teenagers and twenty-somethings who merely wanted to be entertained. No one cared to see the next *Rosemary's Baby*. Or, maybe I was just kidding myself again. Whatever the case, it was five strikes and I was out. No more screenplays for me! I guessed I'd have to take up golf.

***

October 12, 2007—My left foot had been bugging me all week. It hurt just to walk on it by the end of the workday, and I couldn't wait to get home and take my shoes off. I also noticed that my toe was growing larger and redder. On that Friday afternoon, I went straight home and soaked my foot in a tub of warm water. I figured that if I just kept doing that all weekend, I'd be good to go by Monday morning.

That night I had a sudden relapse, after staying away from the drug scene for so long. It all started with a phone call from Matt. I hadn't seen him for ages, it seemed, but we still talked on the phone a lot. He was having trouble with Simone, who was now his wife, and he wanted me to come over so he could cry on my shoulder.

"Oh, all right," I said, even though I rarely ever went out at night anymore—especially on a Friday or Saturday night.

He was about twenty pounds heavier than the last time I saw him, with his little beer belly. He'd bought a larger house and was a bigshot commercial contractor now, like my dad. He boasted of having eight employees and three jobs going on at once. And he also had a family to support—two boys, ages five and three.

"Now if I can just get Simone to stick around and help out a little," he said as I sat there listening in the matching recliner. "I'm takin' care of these noisy little fuckers all by myself."

His children *were* awfully noisy, I observed. At the moment, they were fighting over a toy monster truck on the living room floor. Finally, Matt gave them an ultimatum.

"Either shut the fuck up or take it to the bedroom!" he shouted over them.

They immediately rushed off to their bedroom, fighting over the truck the entire way.

"And shut the goddamn door!" Matt exclaimed.

Then he proceeded to tell me more about his marital woes. Apparently, Simone was still heavy into the party scene and was using up their savings to buy drugs. Having cut up all her credit cards and transferred the money into a secret account, he now believed she was prostituting herself to get her fix. He used his stalking skills on her one night and caught her sleeping with a black man—a pimp and drug dealer, as he later discovered.

His life was a real soap opera, and by the time he was finished telling me all the gruesome details, we both needed a stiff drink. He didn't do much coke or ecstasy anymore. He was now into prescription painkillers like Lortab and OxyContin, whenever he could get them. Yet, after a few rum and Cokes, we agreed that we could use something stronger, both of us smiling as we agreed, as if we were ready to bring back old times. First, he dug through his wife's underwear drawer and found some leftover crank, which we shared. Then he called one of his young employees who pushed narcotics on the side, and had him bring over two grams of crystal meth. We spent the whole weekend doing the stuff without any sleep. Simone finally showed up on Sunday morning to join in on the fun and even had her black boyfriend bring us some more!

Of course, by the time Monday rolled around, I was dead tired and felt like I could sleep for a thousand years. On top of that, my foot was killing me—a sharp, throbbing pain like never before in my big toe. Yet I wasn't about to miss work. I hurried home to take a cold shower and was shocked to see how large the appendage had grown. It had swollen to twice its normal size—a Fred Flintstone toe! Plus, it was yellow—almost white—smelled like a dead monkey, and was oozing pus. I poured a whole bottle of hydrogen peroxide on it, slapped on a Band-Aid and a sock as best I could, and finished getting dressed for work. I barely made it through the entire workday, having to work with my shoes off during the final stretch. The pain was so unbearable that I went straight to the hospital from there and checked myself into the emergency room. The doctor and nurses winced when they took a gander at my toe.

"I've never seen one that big!" one nurse gasped.

"You're probably gonna lose it," another one warned me.

"Yep, it's a goner," said the doctor himself.

They winced even more when they tested my blood sugar and saw that it was over five hundred.

"Don't you check it regularly?" the doctor asked.

I had to admit to him that I didn't. I'd stopped testing over a year ago because it was always high and there was nothing I could do about it except worry or even panic—and end up OD'ing on glipizide. My parents showed up around that time and caught me sprawled out on the examination table in one of those skimpy hospital gowns, my bulging, discolored, Fred Flintstone toe exposed to the entire world.

"Oh, dear!" My mother grimaced.

"God, son... you should've told us!" My father grimaced.

It was all so embarrassing, to say the least! After a few X-rays of my colossal toe, the doctor came back and informed me that the infection was most likely from an ingrown toenail and it was so severe that it ate right through the skin and went straight to the bone, much like the acid blood in *Alien*—or acid in general. He also told me that there wasn't much bone left and there was probably no saving the appendage. We gave it our best shot, though. I spent weeks sitting at home, pumping antibiotics into my arm intravenously while homecare nurses re-bandaged my foot every other day. But, in the end, the doctor was right. The toe had to go!

***

November 19, 2007—Just two days before my forty-fourth birthday, I was being wheeled into the operating room to have my left great toe amputated, looking up at all the fresh, young faces walking alongside me. Taking me into the room, they pushed my gurney up against the operating table and had me slide over. Then a young man in his mid-to-late twenties walked up to me and introduced himself as my anesthesiologist. He seemed so happy to assist me. They all did, in fact. And why shouldn't they be? They were young, highly successful, and made tons of money off poor, overweight, middle-aged slouches like me, who didn't take care of themselves and were losing body parts to diabetes or peripheral artery disease. *This whole ordeal has been so humiliating,* I thought as they were putting me under. *Just cut the damn thing off already!*

I refused to even look down at my feet when I woke up. But I had to at some point and, in my humble opinion, my foot looked much better with the hideous monster toe still attached to it! Now it seemed alien to me. *Well, I'm definitely a freak now,* I thought, *in body and soul! Will Barbie still love me... now that I'm a fat, balding, nine-toed, old man with hair growin' out of my ears like a fuckin' troll and a fuckin' claw for a hand?* And, if that weren't enough, I was walking with a slight limp. Hopefully, it was just temporary—'til my foot was completely healed. But, it appeared that my dancin' days were over for good.

Porsche came to see me the next day, as she had every Tuesday since the injury, and kept begging me to let her see it as we sat on the sofa together.

I finally gave in and said, "Promise me you won't make a face."

"I swear to God," she said, raising her right hand to heaven.

"Okay," I sighed, bending down to remove the hospital bootie. "But I gotta warn you, it isn't pretty."

I took off the bootie and hesitantly removed my sock to reveal a bandaged foot minus the big toe.

"It's not so bad," she said as she kept staring down at it. "I'd still do ya!" She nodded her head assuredly. "The face is all that matters anyway," she said. "Who cares about feet?"

"Oh, I don't know," I replied. "People with foot fetishes, maybe?"

"Well, that's not me... I assure you," she laughed. "Now go ahead and put your sock back on. That's the one good thing about feet... you can keep them dogs covered up."

I sneered at her and bent down to put on the sock.

***

November 21—And suddenly I'm forty-four, just six years away from the big 5-0—doomsday! Porsche was throwing me a party that night, around ten o'clock, despite my strong objections. It meant that I'd have to endure two birthday celebrations back-to-back. But she was very insistent when we discussed it the day before.

"I'm makin' a big cake for you and everything," she said. "So you'd best be there."

I got to her house just before everyone else did, wearing that damned bootie on my left foot in place of a shoe—another reason I didn't feel like celebrating. I kept ringing the doorbell and banging on her door, finally giving up and letting myself in since it was unlocked. I could hear the blender running in the kitchen.

"Porsche?" I shouted.

"I'm in here!" she shouted back.

I walked through the living room and came to an abrupt stop as I reached the dining room. There was a big banner hanging across the ceiling that read "Happy Birthday, Benjamin!" And in the middle of the dinner table was a big, triple-layer chocolate cake with the number forty-four on top. I knew Porsche loved to cook and celebrate birthdays, but this was too much!

"I told you not to go to all this trouble," I complained to her as she stepped out of the kitchen in an apron.

Then I noticed the glum look on her face and the newspaper clasped tightly to her chest.

"What you got there?" I asked curiously.

"There's somethin' you need to see," she said. "I should've told you about it yesterday, but you've been through so much already and I was hopin' to get you fucked up before I—"

"What's goin' on, Porsche?" I blurted out, suddenly very uneasy.

"I read the obituaries every day now," she continued, walking in closer. "Don't know why. I guess I don't want the grim reaper to think I'm afraid of hi—"

"Would you please tell me what this is about?" I exclaimed.

She slapped the newspaper down on the table and pointed to where she wanted me to read. "Right there."

I leaned over and saw Barbie's old high school picture.

"What the fuck?" I frantically replied. "Is this a joke?"

"I wish it was, baby," she said.

I read the words beneath her picture aloud. "Barbie Sue Delaney passed away Monday night, November the nineteenth, two thousand seven—" I looked up at Porsche in a state of utter confusion. "Monday?" I exclaimed. "That's the same night I got my toe chopped off... and right before my frickin' birthday!"

"Just a coincidence, sugar... that's all," she assured me.

I read further. "It says she died in her hometown of Midwest City, Oklahoma, at the age of thirty-five." I looked up at Porsche again, even more confused. "She was *here?*" I finished reading the rest of it to myself. "It doesn't say *how* she died," I said afterward.

"You know what *that* means," Porsche said.

"What?"

"Probably a suicide... or an overdose."

"No way," I said. "She *loved* life! She loved to laugh." Then I suddenly turned on Porsche, as if it was all her fault. "Remember what you said to me?" I exclaimed. "You said if you love someone let 'em go... and they'll come back to you someday."

"If it was meant to be," she said. "I'm sorry, but you and her weren't exactly a match made in heaven. She had *way* too many problems! And you deserved better."

"I don't want to hear this," I said, furiously walking away from the table.

"You *need* to hear it!" she exclaimed before I managed to leave the room. "Now that she's gone, maybe you'll move on—get on with your life. I hate to see what you're doin' to yourself. She didn't just break your heart. You let her destroy all the good in you. And now you're just a hard, bitter old man... a shut-in."

"She loved me, Porsche," I said. "She even said it to my face! That's why I hung on for so long. Do you know how rare that is for someone like me... to find someone who actually loves me?"

I turned back around and quickly stormed out of the room.

"She's not the only one who loves you, you know!" she shouted as I reached the door. "What about your cake?"

CHAPTER EIGHTEEN

At least I was off for a few more weeks, thanks to my big toe—or lack thereof. I just lay in bed all day, thinking about Barbie's passing. There were so many unanswered questions. What was she doing back home? When did she get here, and why didn't anyone tell me? How did she die? Was it suicide... or did she finally OD on something? *She was only thirty-five years old,* I thought. *Man, I wish I could've seen her at that age... if only I could've seen her just one more time. It seems like decades since I saw her last. She probably felt like I did when I turned thirty-five. It depressed the hell out of me. I felt so old, so alone! And now I'd do anything to be thirty-five again. She should've hung on. I mean, if she killed herself. It's a shame we didn't get a chance to grow old together. She left me here to rot all by myself!*

I also couldn't help but wonder if I was being punished for my actions, seeing how her death and my amputation fell on the same night. There was no doubt in my mind that all that meth in my system caused the infection to worsen. But was there a higher power involved as well? Was God punishing me for my drug lust by taking Barbie and toe away in one swipe? *Damn! If I could just take back that entire weekend. I was doin' so well! Just one phone call from Matt and everything goes to hell.*

I went to Barbie's funeral the day after Thanksgiving— Black Friday. I sat in back of the church incognito— shabby clothes, my old windbreaker, a floppy camouflage hat, and sunglasses. I wasn't sure if I was fooling anyone, though. Barbie looked as beautiful as ever, lying dead in her casket. The mortician did such an incredible job on her face that I wanted to go up and kiss her. Surprisingly, there were only about twenty or so people there. I saw Tony walk in wearing an Armani suit, accompanied by Skippy and several other gay friends. And then I saw Barbie's parents and siblings for the first time, at least I think it was them. They sat down directly in front of the casket and were doing most of the crying. I also saw Brian, looking more clean-cut than usual in a cheap suit. But he still had the scruffy beard and horn-rimmed spectacles, and his long hair was slicked back in a ponytail.

After sitting through a long-winded preacher and a bunch of sappy songs for over an hour, I followed the procession to the cemetery and hung back a ways, sitting up against someone's tombstone, drinking a pint of whiskey I had stashed away in my jacket. I listened to the preacher eulogize over Barbie's remains some more and then stood up to watch them lower her into the ground. The last time I saw her, she was so full of life... well, full of spirits and opiates, anyway. And now she was worm food—if those little fuckers could find a way to get into her vault.

Once her casket was no longer visible, I set my sights on Brian, standing in back of the small crowd. If anyone could tell me what happened, it was him. I hurried back to the car before everyone else did and waited for him to leave. He was driving an old Volkswagen bus, appropriately enough, parked just two cars ahead of me. I watched him step into the vehicle and drive off and then took off right behind him, keeping tight on his tail.

He pulled into the Mama Jo's parking lot, just three blocks away. *He must be ticklin' the ivories for 'em again,* I thought. I parked several rows behind him and watched him go inside. I went in two minutes later. He wasn't anywhere in sight, so I walked straight up to the bar and sat down. Hank was still working behind it, but he didn't seem to recognize me in my clever disguise. He eyed me suspiciously, though, as I ordered a screwdriver. The mean, old bastard looked exactly the same, except his Jheri curl was a lot grayer.

Brian walked in from the dressing room in back, wearing his regular shitty clothes. He took one look at me as he headed toward the bar and said, "Hello, Benjamin... are you following me?"

I was taken aback, but immediately shook it off.

"I need to know what happened," I said while he sat down next to me. "Why did she come back? How did she die?"

"You want the whole story?"

"Please."

"Bring me a Heineken, will ya?" he said to Hank. Then he told me all about his and Barbie's adventures in the big city, talking more than I'd ever heard him talk before. "Good gigs are hard to come by there in the five boroughs," he said. "And rock and roll bands are a dime a dozen. We ended up workin' in a shitty old dive, much like this one... makin' barely enough bread to afford our shitty old apartment in Brooklyn." He laughed to himself. "It didn't go quite the way we expected," he said. "Let's put it that way. We were back to doin' smack in no time, seein' how it's much cheaper there and easier to come by. Just don't let the boss catch you doin' it... unless it's ol' Hank here. Right, Hank?"

"Right," he said, and rolled his eyes as he was busy pouring himself a drink.

"The club manager caught us shootin' up in the dressin' room and gave us the boot," Brian explained. "Next thing you know, we're bein' booted out of the apartment—livin' on the street. Barbie's turnin' tricks to support her habit and I'm robbing convenience stores. Then, one morning, she got on a bus and took off without me."

"You mean, she came back *here?*" I said.

"That's right."

"How long ago was that?"

"Almost five years ago," he said. "I stuck it out for another three before *I* called it quits."

"Five fuckin' years!" I moaned, deeply frustrated. "I don't believe it! Where was she stayin' at?"

"Her parents' house," he said.

"Their trailer house?"

"No, man," he said, "they bought a real house near here. It's still a dump, though. She turned her life around, too. She went to rehab and got clean. Then she started goin' to church."

"Church?" I exclaimed.

"Yeah," he chuckled. "I couldn't believe it either! She became a born-again Christian and everything!"

"Jesus!" I gasped.

"She wouldn't let me come anywhere near her when I came back," he said resentfully. "I guess I was a bad influence on her."

I could just picture her sitting alone in a crowded pew, one last, desperate attempt to belong to something, only to be reminded once again that people like me and her didn't belong anywhere—except with each other.

"How did she die?" I asked him, rather hesitantly.

"Killed herself," he said. "She slit her wrists in her parents' bathtub."

"Why?" I asked.

"Why do people *usually* kill themselves?" he said. "She was depressed, man! She felt hopeless, insignificant, unloved! Only, for her it was ten times worse... 'cause she was bipolar."

"So turnin' to God didn't help, huh?"

"I guess not."

"She wasn't unloved," I said. "*I* loved her."

"Yeah, well... she thought you was gone," he sneered. "You *told* her you was leavin' in that letter."

Oh, yeah... the frickin' letter, I thought.

"You told her you was movin' to LA," he said, "to be in the movies or somethin'."

"I never went," I confessed. "I was right here the whole time... just fifteen miles away. I hoped she burned that letter."

He shook his head. "She kept it. She said it was all that she had to remember you by."

"All *I* had was her picture," I muttered.

"She thought it was quite brilliant, actually," he admitted. "I mean, for a fuckin' letter."

"Yeah, it was some letter," I sighed.

"She also felt that you had every right to be angry with her," he said. "She regretted the way things ended with you."

"If only I'd known she was back," I said, shaking my head. "I would've fixed it—made things right!" I slammed my fist against the bar, causing Hank to scowl at me and suddenly recognize who I was, it seemed. "Goddamn it!" I exclaimed, frustrated. "Why did she have to go and kill herself?"

"At least she was thinkin' about you when she died," Brian sneered.

"You think so?" I said.

"Honestly?" he said. "I think she died *because* of you. That's why I can barely stand to look at you right now. I'd rather not see you anymore after this... if you don't mind."

I nodded and said, "I'll finish my drink and go."

Then we sullenly looked at ourselves in the mirror behind the bar, both of us sad and heartbroken. It was my foolish pride and drunken folly that did her in.

The next day, I called the T-Bone and asked for Tony, but the assistant manager said he wasn't working there anymore. So I drove all the way to Norman and went straight to his mansion by the lake, having to climb over the stockade fence to get in. An extremely handsome young man in tight pants and a Henley t-shirt answered the door and let me into the house. Following the sound of loud techno music, I found Tony dancing inside his chic, Tuscan-style living room with two other young and handsome, tightly-clothed men. They all looked like they could've been models. And, looking outside through the glass wall, I saw more of the same—two gorgeous hunks sunbathing by the pool in bikinis and another one doing the backstroke. Tony appeared to have discovered the fountain of youth. He hadn't aged a day, and he was at least five years older than me. He stopped dancing and looked surprised when I walked up to him.

"What up, B?" he shouted over the music.

"I tried to get ahold of you at the restaurant," I explained to him, "but they said you don't work there anymore."

"I'm retired!" he said proudly. "I invested Neil's money in the right stock and doubled it."

"Looks like you're livin' the life... partyin' it up!" I remarked. Then I got right to the point. "Why didn't you tell me she was back?" I said.

"Who?"

"Who do you think?"

"Sorry, B," he said. "I had no way of gettin' ahold of you. You just flat out disappeared."

"You could've looked me up in the phone book—left a message on Matt's answering machine," I said.

"I'm not about to call *him!*" he laughed.

"I bet you became really good friends again, didn't you?" I scowled. "You got to talk to her—spend time with her! You could've at least told her I was here! It might've given her some hope! Time was on our side, for once! We could've been together, finally! But you didn't want that. If you and Matt couldn't live happily ever after, why should *we?*" I shook my head at him and laughed. "Some kind of friend *you* are."

"You've got it all wrong, B," he said.

Then one of his boy toys stepped in, getting up in my face and gently slapping me on the chest backhanded.

"How dare you!" he snapped. "You should apologize to this man... and then get on your knees and beg for his forgiveness." He stepped up to Tony and put his arm around his shoulder. "This here's the sweetest man on earth," he said. "There isn't a vindictive bone in his body... never gets angry or raises his voice—"

Another boy toy walked up and stuck a pill in my face. "I've got just what you need," he said, and rubbed my arm. "Take it, my round friend."

I just glared at him.

"Take it, B," Tony said.

Both young men started dancing very close to me.

"C'mon, dance with us, guy!" one of them said.

The third man walked up to Tony, meanwhile, and *they* started dancing. I simply turned and walked off.

***

There was much brooding over Barbie in the following months. I sat next to her grave and talked to her for hours on the weekends, often bringing a bottle of wine or a pint of whiskey with me. Yet the conversation was always one-sided, and there were three important questions left unanswered. Why did she choose to end it all? Where was she at right now, and should I join her? I went to see a clairvoyant, hoping she could connect us long-distance. It seemed necessary, in fact. Barbie was a spiritualist herself, and was probably trying to reach me from the great beyond. I entered the old woman's house and she took me to a little, dark room in back, with purple curtains, long candles, a small table with a purple tablecloth over it and a candle-lit chandelier hanging down—everything but the crystal ball. She even put on a purple robe to make *herself* look more authentic. I truly wanted to believe she was the real deal, so I left my skepticism at home.

I told her all about Barbie and how much I loved her. Then she summoned Barbie's spirit in a matter of seconds. I was so ecstatic to be able to speak to her through the old woman. She told me that she loved me and that she killed herself because she thought she'd lost me for good and felt so alone. She also assured me that she was in a much better place and felt perfectly at peace. I asked her if I could come with, but she told me that I needed to stick around here for a while—that I had a lot more living to do and so much more to accomplish. That's when I realized that the old lady was a total fraud. Yet I kept playing along because I was enjoying every minute of it—and I could at least pretend that I had all my answers now. It was money well spent.

Now it was time to move on with my life, as Porsche suggested. Being obsessed with a dead girl was clearly not the way to go. I needed to find a living, breathing creature to obsess over—preferably a woman! Having replaced my word processor with a computer a while back, I decided to put it to good use and gave online dating a try.

I began my search locally, but then I received a mysterious e-mail and attachment from a young Ukrainian woman named Olga. She looked like she could've been a supermodel. She said it was her lifelong dream to come to America and meet an older American man, and I felt a strong obligation to help her achieve this dream.

We started sending e-mails back and forth, which grew more and more affectionate, sentimental, and downright schmaltzy by the day. I was actually falling for her, even though we were oceans apart and all I had were her lovely words and a bunch of sexy photos she kept sending me. I couldn't wait to get home from work just so I could read her letter and respond it. I never knew love could be so easy! Though I'm sure it probably helped that we were both hungry for it and wanted it right now, this very second. I was prepared to go overseas, put a ring on her finger, and bring her back to the States.

Then, all of a sudden, she asked me to send her money, which instantly burst my bubble. *What does she need money for?* I wondered. *Wouldn't she rather me just come over and get her the hell out of there?* I suddenly felt very sick, thinking that I'd wasted weeks of my life getting all lovey-dovey with a fat, middle-aged man from Arkansas. *I should've known better!* I thought. *Love never comes that easy... and I ain't ever gettin' a supermodel in this lifetime!*

"Now what?" I asked myself out loud, only to realize that it was time to stop pretending—no more fraudulent mediums or "women" online!

If I wanted to be loved and adored, I needed to put in the effort, lose all the weight and become completely healthy and diabetes free—not half or three-quarters of the weight this time, but every single pound. I always had the terrible feeling that Barbie would've stayed if I'd been a slender man with a healthy penis. So, with that in mind, I dug the stationary bike out of the closet, dusted it off, and put it back together. Then I pulled my dumbbells out of storage, which I hadn't used since high school, and went right to work—four sets of military, bench, and curls and an hour on the bike. In a matter of weeks, I'd graduated from the twenty-five-pound dumbbells to the thirty-fives and was on the bike for an hour and a half straight, followed by another hour and a half just before bedtime. And this was after a full day at the grind!

My diet consisted mostly of baked skinless chicken or fish, broccoli with a slice of melted, low-fat cheese on top, and a can of green beans at work. I never exceeded twelve hundred calories in a day.

While I was busy sanding a wall at work and getting a face full of sheetrock dust, I had an idea. Why not write a story about Barbie and immortalize the bitch? Better yet, I'd write a story about our relationship. It'd be an honest, detailed account of what took place, with a few embellishments here and there, dealing with themes of love and obsession and expanding over fifteen years—from the first time we met 'til her untimely death. And I was thinking a novel instead of a screenplay. Since I couldn't come up with an extraordinary plot or create elaborate, imaginative worlds, like a Stephen King or a JK Rowling, I'd simply write about my experiences here on this stinking planet—write what I know! I wasn't quite sure what to call the book yet. *Chasing Barbie, Manhood, The Gay '90s, Coming Out, Once a Dancer, Stuck in Nowheresville, Natural Born Liar, The 45-Year-Old Virgin,* and *The Endless Ramblings of a Love-Starved Party Machine* were just a few of the titles I had kicking around in my head.

***

July 9, 2011—I went to Homer's funeral. He died at seventy-four, just three years after retirement. The old man was a superhero in my book, working clear into his seventies! He continued to visit us regularly after he retired, but mostly just to gloat and show off the expensive toys he'd bought with his retirement money—like a brand-new RV. Yet, for the last year or so, he'd been bedridden with severe respiratory problems and finally succumbed to silicosis, a lung disease common among construction workers after breathing in drywall dust and insulation fibers day in and day out, week after week, year after year. My eight surviving coworkers and I knew it was just a matter of time before *we* were dragging around oxygen tanks, and we weren't afraid to joke about it. We sat in back of the church so no one could hear us making wisecracks or snickering at the preacher, who obviously knew zilch about Homer. Decent, lovable, kindhearted, loyal, hardworking... those were just a few of the adjectives he used to describe the man as he stood over his casket. At least he got the last two right.

"I guess y'all know I'm next," Tim whispered, who was now close to retirement age. "Whatever you do, don't let 'em put me in the ground! I'm claustrophobic."

"You want us to cremate you?" I asked.

"Nah," he replied. "Just prop me up beside the jukebox, like the song says."

"We'll put a smokin' jacket on you and stick a pipe in your mouth," Sean grinned.

"Yeah, the Hugh Hefner look," I concurred.

"Who's Hugh Hefner?" said the Kid, a man in his late thirties now.

A few of us laughed at him, causing my father to turn around and look at us disapprovingly. He was sitting up front with Mom and Homer's girlfriend, Sheila. She was still quite the looker at forty-eight.

"How did Homer end up with such a hottie?" the Kid whispered.

"Are you kiddin'?" said Ron the Biker. "Homer was a stud back in his day."

"Maybe she likes guys that chew tobacco and cuss a lot," Sean remarked.

"Yeah, and tell dirty jokes," Tim said.

"And kinky stories," I added.

"Oh, man... he had a ton of those," Tim laughed, and proceeded to retell the one about the Taiwanese hooker who could open a beer bottle with her vagina.

We all had a good laugh over it, which prompted my dad to turn around and scowl at us again. But, all joking aside, I was really going to miss ol' Homer. Sure, he could be crude, stubborn, and downright mean sometimes, but I knew he cared about me. And he was always there for me when I was in a pickle. Like it or not, construction was my life, and these fellow laborers of mine were my brothers.

The following Monday was just as grim. My cat, Lisa, was dying of lymphoma—a form of cancer. For the past six months I'd been feeding her expensive medicine, hoping it'd make her feel better. But it seemed that all it did was keep her alive. She used to be so energetic and playful. And now she just wanted to be left alone, lying on her little blanket all day, looking sad and miserable. She slept a lot, ate very little, and vomited constantly. Miss Kitty was usually by her side, keeping a watchful eye on her or sleeping with her. Sometimes she'd bring her cat toys to her, hoping she'd play with them. But those days were long gone, it appeared. Finally, I decided that my little girl had been through enough. It was time to put her out of her misery. Miss Kitty moaned when I reached down and removed her from her blanket.

"Sorry, ol' girl," I said solemnly. "I've gotta take her."

I put her in the pet carrier and took her to the vet. After parking in front of the building, I looked toward the passenger seat and caught her staring at me through the carrier with sad eyes. I immediately opened the carrier door, pulled her out, and held her in my lap, suddenly bursting into tears as I gently stroked her fur.

"I'm so sorry," I said, and leaned down to kiss her little head. *How can life be so beautiful one minute and so unbearably cruel the next?* I thought. It wasn't fair! We were a family!

A whole hour passed before I took her inside. I stood over her and continued petting her while the veterinarian injected a sedative underneath her skin.

"Now she'll just go to sleep," Dr. Abbasi said to me consolingly. "No more pain."

I watched her slip into unconsciousness, then quickly fled the room before he administered the euthanasia solution to stop her heart.

Miss Kitty was sitting in the entryway, waiting for my return. She looked noticeably dejected when she saw me walk in with an empty carrier.

"It's just you and me now, sweetie," I said.

***

After five years of dieting and exercising, with plenty of backsliding and rededication in between, I looked totally different, having lost a grand total of a hundred and fifty pounds! I went from three hundred and twenty-five pounds on the Michael Keaton's Batman scales to a hundred and seventy-five pounds! And I had only thirteen percent body fat, which was considered athletically fit. I wasn't diabetes free, as I'd hoped. But my blood sugar was in the 110/120 range for the first time in years and would remain there as long as I stayed on a low-carb diet. I threw the glipizide and insulin out with the garbage—their services no longer required!

On the downside, I'd just celebrated my fiftieth birthday. Yet I didn't fall off the face of the earth, surprisingly enough. To the contrary, I was happier than I'd ever been. I felt more confident. Barbie was becoming more and more of a distant memory, and my novel was almost finished. I never imagined that my life would change for the *better* at fifty!

Now that I was at my ideal weight, it was time for the detail work. I'd already seen a specialist about my ED problem and was currently giving myself penile injections three times a week. The less said about that, the better, except that hopefully I'd have my dick back soon!

The next doctor on the list was the plastic surgeon. He removed all the excess skin on my belly, my chest, and underneath my arms. Then he designed me a prosthetic toe made of silicone rubber and attached it to my foot with a special prosthetic adhesive. I was amazed at how natural and life-like it looked for a fake, rubber toe.

Finally, I went to a hair restoration clinic to see what could be done about my thinning hairline and ended up getting a hair transplant. According to the hair doctor, it'd be thick and wavy again in no time. I was determined to look normal no matter what the cost. And I could almost afford it, since recreational drugs were no longer eating up my savings.

Ironically, as I was doing my high-dollar makeover, a new normal was taking the country by storm. The gay and lesbian population was on the rise, demanding acceptance; more and more Americans were becoming obese, and type 2 diabetes had already reached epidemic proportions. It was a brave new world, it seemed. Bellies were in, everyone was on insulin, and it was cool to be gay! And, in my desperate attempt to be perfect, I was still completely out of step with the times—still a freak! I was one of those fifty-year-old freaks, going through a mid-life crisis and spending tons of money trying to beat the clock. Tomorrow, I'd probably be wearing a ponytail and driving a Ferrari!

On a brighter note, I now enjoyed shopping for clothes. Buying six pairs of jeans with a thirty-six-inch waist was quite the adrenaline rush! Plus, I bought a stunning, gold Hugo Boss three-piece suit and had it custom-made to fit my slight frame. Then I went car shopping and traded in the Volkswagen Rabbit for something a little more appealing—not a Ferrari, but a black Ford Mustang Shelby GT500 Super Snake. And I put one of those Austin Powers vanity plates on it that read "SWINGER." Now I was ready to come out and show off the new me! I called Matt and Sean on my cell phone Saturday night, asking them if they wanted to party. They both turned me down flat.

"I don't do that shit anymore," Sean said bluntly. "And even if I wanted to, the wife wouldn't let me. I gotta go now, Big B. I'm takin' her and the kid to Chuck E. Cheese." *Click.*

Matt's excuse was that it was too much of a hassle trying to find a babysitter. But I sensed that he'd rather just stay home anyway—with his kids and his OxyContin.

"My boys are my life," he explained to me. "Nothin' else in this world matters to me now."

I could respect that. I thought it was downright admirable, in fact, choosing to stay home and take care of the kids while his wife was getting fucked-up somewhere.

But then he went on to say, "B... you'll never know what love is 'til you have children of your own."

Well, now you're just rubbing it in! I thought to myself angrily, for that was one experience I'd most likely never have. I cut the conversation short before he made me even more depressed.

"How do you like that?" I said as I clicked off the phone. "All my rowdy friends have settled down."

I used to think I was Pinocchio, but now I was Peter Pan, the boy who never grew up and couldn't get the old gang back together again!

I ended up going to Porsche's that night and she and her friends gushed over me and my new look. Though it felt good, I had to keep reminding myself that these weren't real women, and not to get too carried away like I did with the Ukrainian gal. We all got in our separate vehicles and went to Heaven for a while. It'd been years since I'd set foot in the club—or any club, for that matter. It was quite painful, to tell you the truth. There were so many fond memories inside that place and they all came back to haunt me, reminding me of what could've been—or *should've* been, rather.

As I stepped up to the dance floor, I saw Barbie's ghost smiling down at me from the balcony. Yet she quickly faded away, and all I saw were a bunch of new faces surrounding me—youngsters, mostly. She was ancient history, a product of a bygone era—the gay nineties! I didn't see anyone from the past, except for Porsche's gang. It just wasn't the same. I *did* recognize one familiar voice, however.

"Now there's a face I haven't seen in a while," my old DJ friend said over his microphone.

Somehow, I knew he was talking to me. I looked up into his dark booth and raised my margarita glass to him.

"Good to see you again, big guy," he said. "Or little guy... I should say."

Porsche and Kaneesha practically had to drag me out onto the dance floor, even though I'd taken a pill earlier. I was afraid that I'd lost the gift, especially since I was still walking with a slight limp. But it magically went away the moment I broke into my little soft-shoe routine, much in the same way people lose their stutter once they start singing. Before I knew it, I was dancing like a wild man—only not sweating near as much. *Still got it!* I thought with a sly grin as Porsche and I joyfully danced together.

"Look out, boys and girls," said the DJ, just as the techno song ended. "He's back!" Then he started playing "Dancing Queen," by ABBA. "This one's for you, my friend," he said.

I looked up at him and winked. And, within twenty seconds of the song, I broke away from the group and went off on my own, hogging the dance floor, as Barbie referred to it. It was the best night I'd had in a very long time! But, when it was over, I thought, *Here I go again, livin' a fantasy... dancin' with shirtless men and guys in wigs!* I couldn't even look at the few real women in the place, out of respect for Porsche. I needed to hit the straight clubs for a change. And I needed a new wingman.

I went home and googled Ritchie Dickerson, my old nemesis who became my best and only friend back in the day. I was happy to find that he was a social media junkie. I skimmed over his Facebook page, read his tweets, looked at several of his photos and videos on Instagram, and even read his profiles on a couple of dating sites. He was an insurance sales agent; he'd been married three times, had four kids, and was currently single. *Perfect!* I thought.

The next day, I drove to his house in Edmond. From the looks of the place, he was doing quite well for himself. And I was surprised to see how well he'd aged when he answered the door, still long and lean with a handsome face and salt-and-pepper hair, like mine. His Facebook and Instagram photos didn't do him justice!

"May I help you?" he said, as if he was talking to a complete stranger. Although, it *had* been thirty-two years since he saw me last.

"Hey, there... Ritch!" I exclaimed. "It's me, Ben Oldman!"

"No, you're not," he scoffed. "That guy was a mountain."

"Not anymore!" I said proudly.

"Well, hey... buddy!" he exclaimed. "Long time, no see! Get your butt in here! We've got a lot of catchin' up to do!"

He let me in, showed me into the living room, and got us a couple of beers. Then he immediately tried to sell me some insurance. I told him that I was pretty well covered, so he started talking about himself and told me what he'd been up to for the past thirty-two years, which wasn't much. And I had even less to say on the subject. Of course, I left out the part about Club H and all my gay friends, knowing our history together. Finally, I got around to asking him about his social life.

"So, you gotta special lady in your life?" I asked.

"Hell, yeah... ladies," he laughed. "I'm not interested in wife number four, if that's what you mean! I like 'em all... tall, short, round, big-breasted, small-breasted! Hell, I'll fuck anything on two legs."

This is gonna be a cakewalk! I thought.

"How 'bout you?" he asked. "Married or single?"

"Single, definitely," I said.

"Oh? Do you party?"

"Are you kiddin'?" I laughed. "I'm a party machine!"

"Well, heck... buddy!" he exclaimed. "We need to hook up! Do you know where we can score some blow?"

Bingo!

We did an entire eight ball at his house that very same night, compliments of Porsche. I told her it was all for me. Ritchie's name was never mentioned. Afterward, we drove from one straight club to the next, ending with Shenanigans. We looked like a pair of old studs, sashaying through the joint in our fancy suits.

"Two hotties at twelve o'clock," Ritchie said to me as we approached the two young females sitting at the bar. "Hello, ladies," he said. "I'm Ritch... this here's Ben." His eyes were focused on the blonde. "Care to dance?" he asked her.

"Sure," she said, quickly getting up from the stool and walking off with him.

It suddenly felt very awkward, being stuck all alone with the dark-haired girl. She looked far too young for me—early twenties. Yet she was quite beautiful. She even favored Barbie, with her green eyes and fair skin. If only she was ten years older—or more!

"Do you wanna dance?" I asked her, just to be polite.

She shook her head and said, "I can't dance to this song."

It was "Blurred Lines," by Robin Thicke. Apparently, the live band was on break. I simply nodded at her and started to walk off.

"Wait!" she exclaimed, quickly reaching out and grabbing the back of my suit.

I slowly turned back around.

"That wasn't a rejection," she said. "I just don't like the song. I don't like any of the songs in here."

"To tell you the truth, neither do I," I laughed, stepping up to the bar and sitting down on the empty stool next to her. I extended my hand to her and said, "Benjamin."

"Stephanie," she said, and shook it.

I noticed that her glass was almost empty. "Care for another one?"

"Yeah, thanks."

I summoned the bartender over and asked her, "What you drinkin'?"

"A strawberry daiquiri," she replied.

A girl after my own heart! I thought, and gave her a big smile.

"Two strawberry daiquiris," I said to the bartender as he walked up.

He set them down before us a minute later and I paid for them. Then we both leaned over and slurped them up with our straws. We looked at each other, smiled, and rolled our eyes as the DJ began playing Katy Perry's "Last Friday Night."

"I know a place that plays *really* good music," I said.

"So do I," she replied.

I studied her curiously. "Heaven?"

She nodded and laughed.

"Do you go there often?" I asked.

"Not as often as I'd like," she said. "Kelly doesn't like it there! She says it's for gay people... which it *is!* But I really like the music... and the people."

"Most of my friends are gay," I said proudly. "My other best friend's a drag queen, actually... Porsche. You'd like her! And I think she'd really like you." We just smiled at each other for a few seconds, encouraging me to pop the question. "Do you wanna go there?"

"Heaven?"

"Mmm-hmm!"

"What about them?" she asked, pointing at Ritchie and Kelly, who were practically having sex on the dance floor.

"Did she drive?" I asked.

Stephanie nodded.

"Then I don't think they're gonna miss us," I said.

We both laughed and jumped up from our stools. She walked straight up to Kelly as she was dancing, however, and told her we were leaving. There was a bit of an argument, but Stephanie got her way in the end. And Ritchie probably thought I was doing him a favor. Now Kelly would have to drive him home. He even winked at me from the dance floor.

"How old are you?" Stephanie asked me curiously as we shot off down the road in my Mustang.

"Forty-seven," I lied.

"You look younger," she said.

"That's what they tell me," I sighed.

"I'm twenty-three," she said.

"I figured," I said, not wanting to dwell on the subject.

"Age doesn't matter to me," she said. "Ageism sucks! All the -isms do... racism, sexism, socialism, capitalism, skepticism.... Stop me, will ya?"

We glanced at each other and laughed, just as I drove into the Heaven parking lot. The floor show was coming to an end when we stepped inside. We sat down at a table, had a couple more drinks, and I got to know her a little better. She worked as a waitress in some swanky restaurant I'd never heard of. Like me, she didn't care much for her job—nor did it define her. Also like me, she preferred the rain and gray weather to warm, sunny days. And she liked all kinds of music—blues, jazz, classical, opera, classic rock, alternative, and even a few Johnny Cash tunes.

But most importantly, she loved movies. She was into film noir, horror, Westerns, Hitchcock, Fellini, Bergman... and she adored musicals, *West Side Story* being her favorite. She was also into tattoos, apparently. She rolled up her blouse sleeves to show me the multitude of gray-and-black roses and skulls on her arms. That she chose to keep them covered up was very telling. They weren't for everybody's eyes.

We could've sat there and talked movies for hours but her favorite song, Erasure's "A Little Respect" began to play and we both got the sudden urge to get up and dance. I was very restrained on the dance floor, afraid I might lose her if I turned into Gene Kelly all of a sudden. *Stay cool!* I kept telling my feet. *Don't blow it for me!* The song ended and we just stood there looking at each other, both of us wondering if we should stick around for the next one.

"I'm gonna do a slow one this time," said my DJ friend over the microphone. "Just one! This is for all you lovebirds out there."

"Always," by Atlantic Starr, started playing. We both shrugged and laughed slightly. Then I stepped in closer to her, gently placed my hands on her waist, and we slow danced. It felt so good, so right! People were staring, of course, not because I was some fat guy in a fancy suit but because I was an old geezer dancing with a woman less than half my age. But, no matter... I was on cloud nine. Heaven truly was a gay bar!

CHAPTER NINETEEN

Stephanie and I spent the next few weeks double-dating with Ritchie and Kelly. I was at Shenanigans every Friday and Saturday night, sitting at the bar with Steph, watching Ritchie and Kelly tear up the dance floor while we sucked up strawberry daiquiris and endured the God-awful music. Ritch and I usually did a bunch of coke beforehand. Despite being a bit of a Goth girl, Steph was smart enough to avoid drugs. And Kel was an anti-drug fanatic. If she knew what Ritch and I were up to she'd dump him for sure, and try to keep Stephanie away from me. So we kept our coke habit hush-hush, though I was much better at concealing it than he was. He had a permanent sniff and was always extremely talkative and energetic. The girls and I could hardly keep up with him. He was also going to the restroom a lot. One time, he came out with a trace of white powder on his nostril, but luckily I caught it before the girls did and gestured for him to wipe his nose. I felt certain that he'd give us away any day now!

I also knew it was just a matter of time before Steph and I went all the way and the penile injections weren't going as well as expected—only partial boners and no morning wood! So I had my urologist prescribe me some Viagra, hoping it would give me that extra boost. I popped one in my mouth as soon as I drove home from the pharmacy and, after staring at internet porn for five minutes, I stepped up to the bathroom mirror stark naked with a stunned look on my face and a stiffy like I'd never seen before. It was sticking straight out, hard as a rock and a good six inches long. I could've hung a flag on it!

"Now it works," I scoffed.

Clearly, Viagra was my new drug of choice—the mother of all magic pills! I kept the bottle with me at all times. I ran into Laura at the liquor store on a Friday night. She'd aged significantly since I saw her last. She looked haggard, and was a little plump, but her big, sparkling blue eyes were unmistakable.

"Hey, Laura!" I exclaimed as I approached her in the vodka aisle.

She had trouble recognizing me. "Do I know you?" She smiled.

"It's me, Benjamin," I said.

"Oh, God... it is!" she exclaimed.

"I lost a lot of weight."

"Yes, you did! You're lookin' good!"

"So are you," I said.

"No, I'm not!" she snapped, and slapped me on the arm. "I'm hideous... and you know it! You're still the charmer, I see."

"Well, you look good to *me*," I said. "It's good seein' you again."

"Why don't you drop by the apartment," she said excitedly, "so we can talk? You still remember where it is, don't ya?" She sensed my reluctance and noticed the daiquiri mix in my hand. "Oh, I guess you've got somewhere you need to be—"

"No, I've got time!" I said. "Let me go pay for this right quick and I'll follow you."

"Great!" she grinned.

As we walked up to her apartment together, she warned me that she had eight cats now.

"I run a hotel for stray cats," she joked.

"I've got one at home," I said. "So is Mr. Peepers the hotel manager?"

"Mr. Peepers is no longer with us," she said as she unlocked and opened the door.

I walked in behind her and immediately got a strong sense of what my apartment would've been like if I'd kept all eight of *my* cats. It smelled atrocious, the furniture was in even worse shape than I remembered, and the place was crawling with cats—big, ugly ones! She grabbed the black tabby sprawled out on the loveseat and tossed him onto the floor so we could sit down.

"You know," I began, once we were seated, "I never got around to askin' you what you did for a livin'."

"Back then, I did a little of everything," she said. "I was a store clerk for about a week, a waitress at one time or another, a card shark, pool hustler...."

I assumed she was joking about the last two. Yet, with her, there was no telling.

"But now I'm retired." She sighed. "Well, on disability... actually. I've got lupus."

"I'm sorry," I said.

Then I told her about the diabetes and the ED, just to make her feel better.

"You fucker!" she snapped. "You should've told me! I was so mean to you!"

"Well, I've got the ED under control now," I said. "Thanks to a little blue pill."

"You got 'em on you?" she said excitedly.

"Are you kiddin'?" I laughed. "They're right outside in my glove compartment."

"Go get 'em!" she exclaimed. "I wanna see if the shit really works." Again, she sensed my reluctance and played the hideous and undesirable card. "Never mind," she said with a sigh. "I'm not fuckable anymore."

"You're still as cute as the first night I met you," I said.

"I'll take cute." She shrugged.

"Let me go get 'em," I said, quickly jumping up and heading for the door.

Minutes later, we were sitting up in her bed together, both of us completely naked. I was busy massaging her breast and kissing her neck. She kept staring at my cock the whole time, waiting with anticipation.

"I think it moved," she said for the third time.

"No, it didn't," I said. "Just be patient and help me out here, will ya?"

"Maybe you should've taken two," she said.

Within the next couple of minutes, we were suddenly filled with awe and wonder as we watched my pecker rise and stand straight up in the air like the giant monolith in *2001: A Space Odyssey*. I even heard Richard Strauss's "Also sprach Zarathustra" playing in my head.

"Hello!" Laura laughed excitedly. "Let's get to work before we lose it."

We scooted down on the bed. Then I got on top of her and experienced coitus for the very first time. Although I wasn't quite sure it was worth the wait, it felt pretty good. I hated to just leave her lying there when we were through, but I was due at Stephanie's apartment at eight.

"Don't be a stranger," she said as she watched me throw on my last article of clothing.

"I won't," I said, and swiftly left the room.

So Laura was my first, I thought as I drove away from her apartment. It seemed a bit odd, but I was okay with it. Love the one you're with, as Stephen Stills used to say!

I pulled up in front of Stephanie's building and took another pill before I stepped out of the car. I had a hunch that tonight would be the night, and my hunch was correct! It was almost the same exact scenario, in fact. Steph and I sat up in her bed completely naked. And while I was busy rubbing her crotch and kissing her shoulder, she kept her eyes on the prize and began to have doubts.

"You think one was enough?" she asked. Suddenly, my penis came to life and she said, "Oh, here we go."

We watched it grow and then I crawled on top of her and penetrated her flower. I was amazed at how much better it felt to be inside someone I actually had strong feelings for. It was definitely worth the wait! As I rolled off her and lay there catching my breath, I noticed my fake toe staring right at us at the end of the bed. *I guess it's time to tell her,* I thought. I probably could've kept my mouth shut about it since it looked so much like the real deal. But she already knew about my crippled hand, the diabetes, the shrunken nut, and the ED, of course. I figured I might as well let her know about all my abnormalities.

After I told her the whole humiliating story, the first words out of her mouth were, "Take it off! I want to see it."

"No way!" I said. "It's too much of a hassle tryin' to glue it back on. Besides, it's grotesque."

"A missing body part isn't grotesque," she lectured me. "It's different! Different and grotesque aren't the same thing." She reached over and bopped me on the head. "You'd think you would've figured that out by now."

She pretended to let it go and started talking about something else. But then she crawled out of bed and told me that she needed to go pee, swiftly walking to the end of the bed, yanking my big toe off my foot, and tossing it in the wastebasket against the wall. It felt like a tight Band-Aid being ripped off the skin.

"Ow! That fuckin' hurt!" I exclaimed. "And that's a five-thousand-dollar toe you just threw away!"

"Shhhh! You don't need it," she said softly, getting down on her knees and rubbing the smooth area where a toe used to be.

Then she leaned in and kissed it, which instantly brought tears to my eyes. I dug the toe out of the trash can before I left, however. The damned thing cost five thousand dollars!

***

August 2013—My father was a carpenter, like his father before him. He started his own company in 1980. In the early years, it was just him and an old high school buddy, remodeling people's houses here locally. Sometimes I'd help, usually in the summer or during spring break, even though I was never good with a hammer and didn't care much for carpentry myself. I really didn't care much about anything when I was a kid, except dreaming up stories and watching a lot of TV.

By word of mouth, my father's business grew and he eventually ventured off into commercial work—where the big money was. Now, thirty-three years later, Oldman Construction was closing its doors for good. Dad had just turned seventy-three and felt it was time to retire so he could spend more time with Mom and they could travel more. It made perfect sense to me. He'd already made his millions. Now it was time to sit back and enjoy his wealth. Since he didn't have a dutiful son to take over the business and keep the family name alive, he was forced to sell it. He and I both knew that with my lack of business sense I'd probably run the company straight into the ground. And we were already struggling anyway, thanks to the housing market crash and Mexicans coming over here illegally and stealing our crappy jobs. I think the only reason he kept the business going for so long was so that I could have a place to work. After he told me we were shutting down, he assured me that he'd find me a job somewhere else.

"Just let me talk to my subs," he said. "I'll see if they got room for another painter, carpet layer, or whatever."

"That's okay... I'm gonna go work for Matt," I replied, and left him sitting there at his desk completely befuddled.

The following week I was on Matt's jobsite, tearing down walls alongside Sean and several Mexicans. Every now and then, Matt would come to check up on us. It was a lot more laid back working for him. He let us smoke pot during breaks, and every Friday he'd take us to Hooters or the Red Dog for lunch.

***

I took Stephanie to meet Porsche and the two hit it off almost instantly, even though Porsche wasn't quite herself. Just seeing her alone in an empty house on a Friday night was cause enough for alarm. She was sitting on the sofa with a blanket wrapped tightly around her, shivering and sweating a little, watching *Casablanca* on the big screen TV for the millionth time. Steph went straight to the kitchen to make her a cup of hot chocolate while I grabbed a thermometer out of the bathroom and checked her temperature. She had a fever of a hundred and three!

"You need to get to the doctor," I urged her.

"Yeah, I will," she said.

"I mean it."

"First thing Monday."

"No, tomorrow," I insisted. "I'm takin' you to one of those twenty-four-hour clinics."

Stephanie and I sat down on either side of her and snuggled up close to give her warmth. Stephanie even put her arm around her and rubbed her shoulder. I was so proud of my Steph!

"You know, maybe it's just my time," Porsche muttered to me grimly. "The party's gotta come to an end at some point or another."

"We'll wait and see what the doctor says," I said fearfully. "It's probably just the flu."

"What are we watchin'?" Stephanie asked curiously.

We both turned our heads and gave her a strange look.

"Oh, I'm simply gonna have to rewind this thing," Porsche said emphatically, and pointed the remote at the screen. "Just sit back and enjoy it, baby," she said to her. "You're in for a real treat."

Stephanie was sound asleep on Porsche's shoulder before the movie ended. Porsche pointed it out to me and we laughed to ourselves.

"She's a doll," Porsche whispered. "And very young."

"Twenty-three," I nodded, and sighed. "Around the same age as Barbie when we met. Only now I'm a *really* old man."

"You're not *that* old," she said. "Besides, gettin' old's a good thing. You should appreciate every birthday."

"Yeah, whatever," I scoffed. "I guess I'd better be takin' her home soon."

"Go on," she said.

I just sat there looking at her.

"Go ahead, I'll be all right," she assured me. "I ain't plannin' on dyin' overnight... if that's what you're worried about."

"I'll be back at eight o'clock sharp," I said, slowly lifting myself up from the sofa.

"I'll be here," she replied.

It was actually seven thirty in the morning when I returned. I could hear the music blasting before I even stepped up to the front porch. I knocked furiously for about a minute and then just went on in. Everyone was there—Daphne, Jasmine, the other two Supremes, and even a few faces and wigs I'd never seen before. Some were dancing up a storm on the living room carpet, others just sat around, talking. Porsche was flirting with a group of young men next to the entertainment center, in full Diana Ross attire.

I walked up to her and shrugged. "What the hell's goin' on?"

"Haven't you heard?" she said in a drunken slur. "It's the end of the world! And I ain't goin' out with a whimper, by God!"

"But I'm supposed to take you to the doctor!" I said.

"Fuck doctors!" she exclaimed. "I've already takin' my medicine." She raised her whiskey glass, then nodded toward the kitchen. "Go help *yourself.*"

I give up! I said to myself, and headed for the kitchen.

I was still partying that night, but with Ritchie. He wanted me to bring over an eight ball, so I did. We sat at his dining room table with a mound of coke between us, both of us wired to the gills.

"God, I'm glad you came over," he said. "Had another shitty week at the office. Then I called Kelly last night and she tells me she wants to take it slow... which is code for 'go fuck yourself.' I wonder what turned her off all of a sudden. Eh, fuck it." He bent down and snorted up his last line with a rolled-up dollar bill. Then he howled like a maniac. "Wooooooo! I am ready to par-tay!"

"Easy there, tiger," I said, a bit concerned, noting the beads of sweat running down his red cheeks. "You don't wanna overdo it."

"Oh, yeah, I do," he said with a wild-eyed nod. "I must."

He scooped up some more powder with his credit card, placed it directly in front of him, and made one huge line, quickly leaning over and sucking it up his nose like a human vacuum cleaner. *I guess I'd better stop,* I thought. *One of us needs to be able to drive.*

"I'm gonna take a piss," I said, and got up to go to the bathroom.

When I came back a couple of minutes later, his head was on the table with a face full of coke.

"Ritchie?" I said, hesitantly walking up to his chair.

His eyes were wide open and lifeless, strangely reminding of Janet Leigh, lying dead in the shower.

"Oh, God!" I cried out in a state of panic and shook him profusely, hoping it would jolt him back to life.

Yet I realized it was no use. His fifty-year-old heart simply gave out on him. *Now what do I do?* I thought. *I could be in a shitload of trouble here! I can't go to jail! I'm fifty years old! Imagine my dad havin' to bail me out now!* It suddenly occurred to me that prison would most likely be my punishment, serving anywhere from a year for possession to twenty-plus years for manslaughter, seeing that I supplied the dope. Trying to remember everything I touched, I frantically went all over the house with a dishrag and dusted off my fingerprints. Then I got the hell out of there!

I kept a close eye on the local TV news and newspapers for the next few days, but it actually took two weeks before his death made the third page of the *Daily Oklahoman. Two whole weeks before anybody discovered him... and only the third page,* I thought as I read. *And to think that he was Mr. Popular in high school. I guess bein' an asshole will only take you so far!*

It was time to tell Stephanie the news, but Kelly had already beaten me to the punch. Steph called me just as I was keying in her number and told *me* what happened.

"Kel suspected that he was a cokehead," she said. "That's why she dumped him. How 'bout you? Did you know about it?"

"No," I said. "I'm as shocked as you guys!"

I sensed that she didn't believe me, though. There was an awkward pause, which compelled me to change the subject. *That* probably made her even more suspicious. I told her we were good friends since high school!

That night, I took her to the Winchester Drive-In Theatre, the only drive-in still alive and kicking in the Oklahoma City Metro. I'd told her that my parents used to take me and my siblings to the drive-in theater all the time when we were kids, and now she wanted to go. It was just another wonderful thing she'd missed out on, being a millennial. The only problem was that the movie sucked. It was the latest Adam Sandler stinker, *Grown Ups 2*. We kept looking at each other disappointedly as we sat with our seats tilted back in the Ford Mustang.

"I should've known," I remarked. "I mean, it's Adam Sandler. What d'ya expect?"

"You haven't said one word about Ritchie," she then pointed out to me.

"What do you want me to say?" I said. "You play with fire, you're gonna get burned... simple as that."

"I thought he was your best friend."

"He was... my best and *only* friend," I said. "But now he's dead, so what are you gonna do?"

"I haven't told you this," she said, "but when I was in Porsche's kitchen a couple of weeks ago... I opened her cookie jar and it was full of pills."

"Maybe it was aspirin." I shrugged.

"I know what ecstasy looks like," she said. "Just because I choose not to do the stuff doesn't mean I'm naïve."

"I don't think you're naïve," I said.

"No, you think I'm young and stupid!" she snapped.

"I don't think you're stupid, either," I said. "But you're definitely young. Do you realize there's almost twenty-five years between us?"

"Don't start that again," she huffed. "Just tell me the truth."

"About what?"

"Are you doin' drugs?"

"Oh, come on, Steph," I protested, "just because my friends are doin' them?"

She continued staring me down with those beautiful, piercing eyes.

"No... I'm not," I bluntly replied, and looked her straight in the eye.

But then my resolve wavered and I lowered my head in shame. I started to tear up, in fact.

"Oh, baby," she said, and reached over to stroke my hair. She was in tears as well. "Please tell me you'll stop," she said. "I don't want you to end up like Ritchie! Please... I'm beggin' you! Will you do it for me?"

I simply nodded, suddenly bawling like a baby. She leaned in further and threw her arms around me.

***

She'd been begging me to go with her and meet her parents for weeks, and I finally gave in and did it. I figured I owed her at least that much for lying to her for so long. Plus, I wanted her to see just how committed I was to the relationship, even though two people were about to become very angry and disappointed—and perhaps keel over from a heart attack! She assured me that she'd told them all about me, but I believe she left out one "minor" detail. And I guess I didn't look as young as I thought.

They were noticeably unsettled when they let me into their big, beautiful house and she introduced me to them. Age is just a number? Try telling that to the parents of a young daughter with a fifty-year-old boyfriend—or forty-seven, rather! I still hadn't come clean about that. Even they looked younger than me— early forties, perhaps. And they were an attractive pair, like their daughter. They tried to be as polite as they possibly could under the circumstances, at least at first. They told us to sit and offered us a beverage of our choice.

"No, thanks," we said almost simultaneously, and sat down on the sofa together while they stared me down from their recliners. It was even more uncomfortable than I imagined.

"Benjamin took me to my first drive-in movie... the other night," Stephanie began, and tried to relay the experience to them.

"I'm sorry," her mother, Charlotte, interrupted her and looked straight at me. "I don't mean to be rude, but how old are *you?*"

"I'm forty-seven," I said, without batting an eye.

Both parents just looked at me like I was a cradle snatcher.

"And what do you do for a living?" Charlotte asked.

"I'm in construction," I said.

"Oh, you own your own business?" said her husband, George.

"No, just a worker bee," I said with a nervous laugh.

"I see," he said, and cleared his throat.

Now the couple looked at me like I actually was a bee—or some other lowly insect.

"So, what are your intentions?" George asked me very sharply.

"Intentions?" I replied.

"Do you plan on marryin' her?"

"Daddy!" Steph playfully scolded him. "We're not that far along yet."

But I was beginning to see things from her parents' perspective. It simply wasn't going to work. Stephanie deserved someone closer to her own age, someone who could easily provide for her and take care of her with his six-figure salary—and, most importantly, someone who could father lots of children. And her parents deserved a more suitable son-in-law to spend their wedding money on. Even if I was able to have children—the jury was still out on that one—I'd probably be dead before they graduated. And, once we got hitched, was she just going to move into my shitty little apartment with me, or vice versa? I clearly didn't think things through. Laura would be a more practical choice for me, even though I didn't love her. At least we could wallow in misery together.

I felt like I'd just been torn apart by the Spanish Inquisition when Steph and I left her parents' house.

"Now it's your turn," she said as we were driving away.

"Huh?" I said.

"I wanna meet *your* parents."

Hell, they'd probably be thrilled to death, I thought. *But it's never gonna happen!*

Stephanie called me on my cell phone several nights later, asking me what I was up to. *Okay, this is it!* I thought as she rambled on and on about her shitty day. *It's now or never! Break it off!*

"Stephanie," I suddenly interrupted her. "We're gonna have to call it quits. I'm sorry."

"Call it quits?" she replied. "What the fuck are you talkin' about?"

"We've gotta stop," I said. "It's not working."

"What, us?" she exclaimed. "You're fuckin' kiddin' me, right? Is this about you bein' too old for me?"

"It's not just that," I said. "Well, no... it *is* just that, actually. It's another thing I've been lyin' to you about... my age. I'm fifty."

"Just three years older," she said with a chuckle. "That's nothin'! Women lie about their age all the time! My mom's been thirty-six for eight years—"

"Do yourself a favor, Stephanie," I said. "Find someone who's more age-appropriate. When you're my age, chances are, I won't be here."

"Fuck that," she said. "I live for today... and so should you! Hell, we'll all be dead soon enough."

"It's not gonna work, Steph," I persisted.

"Bullshit! Stop sayin' that!" she shouted desperately. I could hear her tears through the phone. "We love each other... that's all that matters."

"I don't love you," I said sternly, which was probably my biggest lie yet.

"Yes, you do!" she exclaimed. "You've said it a million times."

"I lied," I said. "Our whole relationship's been based on *lies*. I'm gonna have to let you go now."

"Don't you dare!" she cried. "Don't hang up on me, Benjamin!"

I immediately clicked her off, yet she kept calling hour after hour, day after day. It got to where I had to shut off the phone for a while. Her constant ringing alone was making me sick to my stomach. Saturday morning, I went to visit Barbie at the cemetery to give me strength. Her tombstone read, "Here rests our sweet, beautiful daughter. Sleep well, my darling."

"Okay, you win," I said as I sat by her grave in total defeat. "You were the one... the love of my life. There'll never be anyone else." Then, with a slight laugh, I added, "C'est la vie."

I sat with her for a couple of hours with my trusty pint bottle by my side to help kill the pain.

***

October 16, 2013—I let Miss Kitty out at two o'clock in the morning and she never returned, which was so unlike her. She was usually back and scratching on the door within a couple of hours, after she'd had her fill of rolling around in the tall grass and chasing jackrabbits. I probably shouldn't have let her out at all. She'd been acting a little sickly lately, and yet she was sitting by the door and waiting for me to let her out like she always did. I thought a little fresh air would do her some good. I went out looking for her when I got home from work and found her lying in the bushes the next building down from me.

"No!" I exclaimed, seeing that she was panting really hard.

I pulled her out of there and swiftly carried her back to the apartment, holding her tightly to my chest.

"Please don't die on me," I said to her over and over again.

The Chicano gang members living directly below me were hanging out in the downstairs breezeway. They snickered and sneered at me as I carried her up the steps. I couldn't help but think that they did something to my girl. All my neighbors seemed to hate me for letting her come and go as she pleased. The most likely suspect, however, was the old lady who still lived next door to me. I could see her looking at me through the crack in her door. I glared at her as I opened *my* door and quickly stepped inside. I came out seconds later with Miss Kitty in the pet carrier and ran back downstairs, rushing to the vet as fast as I could and hurriedly walking inside.

"I think someone poisoned my cat!" I said to the lady at the front desk.

I said the same thing to Dr. Abbasi as I walked into the examination room and pulled Miss Kitty out onto the table.

"How was she poisoned?" the Iranian doctor asked me. "I thought she was an indoor cat."

"I let her out at night," I frantically explained to him. "And she didn't come back this time."

He looked at me disapprovingly and then gave Miss Kitty a thorough examination, listening to her heartbeat, checking her eyes, mouth, and ears, and asking me questions the whole time.

"Any difference in her behavior lately?" he asked. "Loss of appetite, fatigue, vomiting, incontinence—"

"Yeah, all of those," I said.

"She wasn't poisoned," he said.

"What is it then?"

"Old age."

"Really?" I said. Somehow, that never even crossed my mind.

"She's seventeen years old," he said. "That's eighty-four in human years. Animals don't like to be around people when they're dyin'. That's why she didn't come back. She went away to die."

"There's nothin' you can do for her?" I said pleadingly.

"I can make her transition quick and painless," he said. "It's just like goin' to sleep."

"Not quite," I sighed. Seeing that she was still having trouble breathing and wasn't acknowledging anyone, I said, "Do it."

"Would you like to spend a little time with her?" he asked.

"No, just do it quick," I said. "Put her out of her misery."

I stroked her fur one last time and left the room.

***

That weekend, Kaneesha called and said, "Benjamin, you should come over. Porsche wants to talk to you."

Those words should've filled me with dread. Kaneesha wasn't in the habit of calling me up on the phone just to pass on a message. But, strangely, I didn't think much of it. I figured they just wanted me to come over to party. It was about that time after all—two o'clock on a Saturday afternoon.

I got there at two thirty, and Kaneesha showed me to Porsche's upstairs bedroom. I'd never been upstairs. And I sure as hell had never been in her bedroom. She was lying in her brass, queen-sized bed fully covered, hooked up to an oxygen tank and IV machine, a nurse in white uniform sitting by her side. On the other side of the bed sat Mo'Nique, Jasmine, and Daphne. Jasmine, the pint-sized drag queen, was crying. I slowly walked up to the bed. The nurse gave me her chair and left the room for a minute. I'd never seen Porsche look so listless and, even though her skin was very dark, the large, purple lesion on her left cheek was quite visible. But her wig was still intact and she was wearing her pink lipstick and mascara. She was still Porsche.

She took off her oxygen mask and said in a faint, wheezy voice, "Well, at least it wasn't AIDS that did the old lady in. It was cancer... Kaposi Sarcoma. AIDS-related, though. Hopefully, it won't be long now. I can't stand bein' laid up on my deathbed."

"Jesus, Porsche," I said, and suddenly burst out crying.

I honestly had no idea that the end was near. I *did* happen to notice that she'd lost a little weight. But other than that, she'd done such an incredible job of hiding her cancer from me. She pulled her hand out from under the covers and grabbed mine.

"Stop your cryin'," she said, and looked toward the other three. "You too, Jasmine." Focusing on me again, she said, "I've had a good life. Wish I could stick around for a little bit longer, but oh well. I've been here long enough... and no regrets... except maybe one. I wish I'd traveled more... seen the world. It's not like I didn't have the money or the time. All *my* time was spent partyin'— gettin' fucked-up." She tried to laugh and then held my hand tighter. "See the world for me," she pleaded. "Be my eyes."

"Where am I supposed to go?" I said. "This place is all I know."

"And that's what's so sad." She nodded. "You've been stuck here for far too long. The world is so big... and this place is really small. That's why we party so much. What else is there to do?" She tried to laugh again, as did I. "Get the hell out of here, Benjamin," she said.

I started to get up.

"No, not this room," she said with a wheezy laugh, continuing to hold onto me. "You big dummy. I meant the state... Oklahoma. Many of us have tried to escape and couldn't... at least not physically. It's up to you now."

As much as I would've loved to obey her dying wish, I wasn't about to gallivant all over the world, going from one adventure to the next—especially at *my* age. It just wasn't me, and she knew it. She must've been suffering from dementia! I visited her throughout the following week, her health declining more and more with each visit. It got to where she could barely talk or keep her eyes open, let alone breathe. And she seemed a little disappointed whenever she saw me walk up to her bed. The first words out of her mouth were always, "You're still *here?*" and I wasn't sure if she was joking or not.

Finally, on Sunday evening, she pulled off her oxygen mask, gently grabbed my hand, and said in her faint voice, "Please don't come back here anymore. I don't want you to remember me this way."

I started to cry.

"Just one last thing before you go," she said. "I want you to know that you were the only man I ever loved."

I'd always suspected it, but it was still a shock to hear her say it—and also quite puzzling.

"All I ever talked about was Barbie," I said with tears running down my face. "It was always Barbie this, Barbie that. Why would you even put up with that? Why did you help me?"

"I wanted you to be happy," she said. "I wish I'd been born a woman... instead of just pretending to be one. Then maybe I could've taken your mind off her for a little bit."

"You did," I assured her.

She smiled and nodded toward the door. "Go now," she said. "Go and join the living." As I slowly turned and began to walk away, she added, "It was a pleasure knowin' you, Benjamin Oldman."

"You, too," I said, and forced a smile.

She died four days later, on October 31, 2013—Halloween. She was tired of hanging on, so she had Mo'Nique and Kaneesha make her a suicide cocktail full of lethal drugs and the three of them had a little

Halloween/farewell party before she departed this world. She didn't want me to be there—thank God!

There must've been over a hundred drag queens at her funeral. Plus, I saw Tony, Skippy, and even Laura—all gussied up in a dark-blue dress. All the old faces came out of the woodwork to pay their last respects, as one would expect. Everyone loved and adored Porsche. She was like royalty in the gay community—a true queen! Yet, oddly enough, she chose not to be buried as Porsche or any of her stage characters. She wanted to leave this world the same way she came in, according to Mo'Nique and Kaneesha. She'd spent most of her life living a lie—rebelling against God and her nature. But her fight was over and she wanted to make peace with him. Thus, she—or he, rather—lay in his casket as Michael Jerome Whitney, looking very sharp and angelic in his white tuxedo.

A few days later, Kaneesha came to my door and handed me a large, yellow envelope.

"She wanted you to have this," she said, gave me a hug, and left.

Inside it were a *Hollywood Musicals* CD and a smaller, white envelope that read in black magic marker, "Travelin' Money." I opened it to reveal a large stack of five-hundred-dollar bills, amounting to fifty thousand dollars.

Wow, this is a shitload of money! I thought after I counted it all. Yet I took it that she only wanted me to use it if I chose to leave, so I stuffed it in my little closet safe, along with the CD, and didn't give it any more thought. I didn't want her money or her things. I just wanted *her* back!

***

November 6, 2013—I finally completed my five-hundred-page manuscript and mailed the first five chapters to over a dozen literary agents. Originally, it was supposed to end with Barbie's demise. But, alas, it took the death of my dearest friend for it to reach its rightful conclusion. And I had to change the title from *Chasing Barbie* to *Me and the Drag Queen.* On the one hand, I was extremely proud of it. It was by far the best thing I'd ever written, and it felt good to get Porsche's story out there. But I also hated the story. It hit too close to home. Hell, it *was* home! If I ever decided to write a second book, it'd definitely be set in an alternate universe or a different time period. And it would either feature dwarves, dragons, and fairy princesses or steely-eyed gunslingers, cranky old sheriffs, and scroungy bank robbers with hearts of gold—no matter how much it sucked. At least I'd enjoy writing it. Then again, maybe there wouldn't have to be a second book. Maybe this one was my *To Kill a Mockingbird* and it'd sell over a million copies. Who knows?

CHAPTER TWENTY

November 21, 2013, Thursday—It was my fifty-first birthday *and* an end of an era. I'd spent some time with Laura the night before and she told me that Heaven was closing its doors for good after this weekend. The owners were fixing to tear it down and replace it with a Whole Foods store for the gay community. *Eh, good riddance!* I thought, through with the party scene for good. It was time to put away childish things and act my age. I had no plans to do any celebrating that night. I told my mom that I didn't want any more birthday parties and she reluctantly agreed to it. Yet, around six o'clock in the evening, I received a surprise visit from Stephanie, standing at my door with a card and a birthday cake. I was furious! I distinctly remembered telling her that we were through! Yet she was still calling me every now and then and leaving text messages. *Fuck it,* I thought, and let her in.

"Happy birthday, sweetheart," she said, kissing me on the cheek and handing me the birthday card. Then she rushed over to the dining room table, set down the cake, and removed the lid. "You got any candles?" she asked.

"No," I said and thought, *Thank God!*

"Oh, well," she said, walking into the kitchen and quickly returning with two small plates, a couple of forks, and a spatula. She cut off a big piece of white cake with the latter and thought about putting it on a plate. But then she just grabbed it with her fingers, carried it up to me, and tried to cram the whole thing in my mouth. She managed to get about half of it in there. "Good?" she asked as I was busy chewing.

"Mmm-hmm." I nodded.

She ate the other half and licked her fingers one by one—rather seductively, I might add! Afterward, she stepped up very close and licked the crumbs off my lips.

"Stephanie, you shouldn't be here," I said once she was finished.

"Shush," she replied. "You're not gonna get rid of me that easy. I'm willin' to fight for you if I have to. We were meant to be together." She gently caressed my cheek. "Now, you can either just give in and go with the feeling," she said in a smoky voice, "or prepare for a massive battle."

"Are those my only choices?" I asked.

"Mmm-hmm." She nodded.

"Okay, then... I guess you win," I said with a sigh, and led her toward the bedroom. "Just give me a sec," I said, slipping into the bathroom first.

After an hour of foreplay and a minute of actual sex, we just lay there on our pillows, thinking of something to say.

"We should go out tonight and celebrate!" she suddenly blurted out.

"Our favorite spot?" I said.

"Yeah, or anywhere," she replied. "We don't have to go there."

"Well, it's now or never," I said. "Heaven's shuttin' down for good after Sunday night."

"You're kidding!" she exclaimed.

"Nope."

"Where did you hear that?"

"An old friend told me the news," I said. "You wouldn't know her."

"Well, I guess we'd better go there then," she said. "It'll be our last dance. It's kinda sad, actually."

"Yeah," I concurred.

She gave it more thought and said, "Eh, it's just a club."

"Yeah," I concurred.

We got to Heaven at ten o'clock, both of us dressed up like we were at the ball. We ordered a couple of daiquiris and sat down at our favorite table. As we sipped our drinks, I noticed one of Matt's old connections walk past, a big, fat guy in a trench coat and a fedora, named Tuna. I was surprised to see that he was still around.

"I gotta pee," I said to Steph, quickly getting up and following him into the bathroom in back.

I stepped up to the urinal next to his. "Oh, hey there, Tuna," I said as I unzipped my fly and pulled down my pants.

"Hi, guy," he said, appearing not to recognize me.

"It's me, B," I said.

"Really?" he said. "You look different."

"Yeah, I lost some weight."

"Oh, yeah? What's your secret?"

I told him my secret, and then asked him if he was carrying.

"I'm always carryin'," he said.

After we finished doing our business, we went to the corner stall and locked ourselves inside. It was a good thing that one of us slimmed down a bit, though it was still a little tight.

"So what d'ya need?" he asked.

"What d'ya got?"

I ended up buying a gram of coke and two hits of ecstasy. I chewed up the pills, did several key bumps of coke, and went back to the table. Within ten minutes, I was ready to dance, and so was she. I started putting on a show for her a quarter of the way through the first song, which kept her entertained for a while. Yet, by the fifth song, she was ready to leave the dance floor. I really wished I could've bought her some E so we'd be on the same page!

"Just one more," I mouthed to her and raised my forefinger.

She shook her head and laughed and kept on dancing. Three more songs flew by without me even realizing it, and she was still right there with me. But she looked a little pissed. Finally, she stopped and grabbed ahold of my suit sleeve.

"Come on, let's go!" she shouted. "You need to take a break!"

She tried to pull me off the floor, but I swiftly jerked away.

"Fine!" she shouted angrily, turned, and walked off.

I couldn't fathom why she was so upset in my current state. But I thought, *To hell with it! Now I can really cut loose!* I did the Electric Slide and added a little flavor to it, the Cupid Shuffle, the wobble, the running man, the robot, and even a pretty decent moonwalk. She was still standing on the edge of the dance floor almost thirty minutes later, staring right at me with tears streaming down her cheeks. *Oh, don't be sad!* I thought, wanting to run over there and throw my arms around her. But I knew that the best thing I could do for her was flat-out ignore her tears. *Please go away, Stephanie,* I tried to communicate to her telepathically. *Go away and forget about me!* Then I turned my back on her and quickly disappeared into the crowd, dancing to the other end of the floor. I was rolling so hard that I started doing key bumps right there in front of everybody while I continued dancing.

"Put that away, young man," my DJ friend said to me over the microphone. "This here's a respectable joint."

I looked up into his booth and nodded, then did exactly as he said. Suddenly, I noticed Tony dancing with a boy toy nearby. All differences aside, I was glad to see he'd made it out to bid our beloved watering hole a fond farewell. And he was wearing his black leather pants and shirtless vest! Only a fifty-six-year-old man of his stature and build could pull that ensemble off. Dancing straight up to him, I stood completely still and just smiled at him. He smiled back and stopped dancing. I stepped in closer and we hugged.

"You're lookin' good, Slim," he said into my ear.

"I really miss her, man," I said into his.

"Me too, B," he replied. "Me too."

As we separated and went back to shaking a leg, I realized that I should've told him which "her" I was referring to. But it didn't matter. I missed them both. Peering toward the sidelines, I noticed Stephanie was still there, and Kelly was standing with her to console her and hopefully give her a ride home. The two began arguing and Kelly tried to pull Stephanie away. I could pretty well imagine what Kelly was saying to her. "Fuck him! He's no good." And she'd be right. They started to walk off together. But then our song began to play, Erasure's "A Little Respect," and Stephanie turned back around and stared at me pleadingly throughout most of it. I pretended not to see her, yet finally looked at her as she turned and walked away for good. *That's my girl,* I thought, and smiled for her.

Starting to come down, I danced over to Tony again and asked him if he had anything on him. He reached into his pocket and pulled out a baggie with several pills in it. I dug into *my* pants pocket, but he gestured me to stop.

"It's on me, B," he said with a wink and a smile.

"Thanks," I said, immediately opening the baggie, pouring them all in my mouth at once, and swallowing them whole.

"Wow! You really *are* a wild man!" he laughed.

I laughed and went right back into action. Soon, I was sweating bullets and my suit was all wet, just like old times. There was no turning back now! I was determined to go down with the club. Why not? The women I loved were gone, the cats were gone, and I didn't have to take care of my parents. They were still taking care of me! I'd be doing them a favor. Even the DJ kept egging me on.

"That's it," he said. "Dance, boy, dance... harder, faster! Push that envelope! Push it!"

His voice sounded deeper and more sinister now, as if he was the grim reaper himself. Maybe he wasn't even real to begin with, just a voice inside my head. I looked toward the balcony and saw Barbie smiling down on me, just as the evil bastard played Depeche Mode's "Enjoy the Silence."

"I'm comin' for you, girl," I said. "Any second now."

I could already picture us dancing in the clouds. Right next to us was Marilyn Monroe, grinding on Abraham Lincoln. He and I looked at each other and grinned. Plus, I saw Socrates doing the shimmy with Plato, Bob Fosse doing jazz hands with Michael Landon, and Emily Dickinson twerking on Elvis! But the most glorious sight of all was seeing Porsche dancing with Jesus. There were so many other familiar and unfamiliar faces, all of us dancing without a care in heaven—the real heaven! All of a sudden I collapsed, and my life faded to black.

***

Sadly, I didn't wake up in front of the pearly gates but in a hospital bed, hooked up to an IV machine with my parents sitting by my side. I was surprised to learn that it wasn't the drugs that almost did me in but the diabetes—or perhaps a little of both. My blood sugar was severely low and I slipped into a diabetic coma for several hours. I wasn't sure how much my parents already knew, but I decided to come clean about the ecstasy, coke, crystal, crank, crack, smack, acid, pot.... Did I leave anything out? They were extremely disappointed, to say the least.

"I thought you was through with all that!" my father exclaimed. "Jesus, Benji! You should know better than to be doin' that crap with your diabetes! Are you *that* stupid?"

"Stan, calm down," my mother said.

"Well, Carol... he's got me worried about him!" he said.

"Me *too*!" she argued.

"We could've just as easily been at the morgue right now," he scolded me. "Do you know what that'd do to your mother... and *me*... to see you go before us?"

Then Mom suggested that I move back in with them so they could keep a close eye on me. I assured her that it wasn't necessary, that I was through with all that shit for good.

"Watch your language, dear," she said.

"Sorry," I replied.

Perhaps I could've phrased it another way, but it was the truth. I *was* through with all that shit. Benjamin the Party Machine was dead. I took his depravity to the extreme and pushed him over the edge. And now, by the divine grace of God, I was born again. Porsche was right. I needed a change of scenery to go with my fresh start.

"I wanna get out of here," I said to my parents, "go somewhere else for a while... see the world."

"You mean travel all over the country?" Dad said.

"Yeah," I replied.

"Oh, son," Mom said with concern. "Where would you go? You need to have *some* destination in mind."

"New York, maybe?" I shrugged.

"That's not a good idea," she said, vehemently shaking her head. "Not in your condition—"

"Oh, I don't know," Dad interrupted her. "It might be the best thing for him. He's fifty-one-years old and never been anywhere."

"We took him and the other two to Six Flags once," she argued.

"Well, yeah," he scoffed. "But I doubt he was old enough to remember it." Then he turned to me and said, "Me and your mom's been just about everywhere. We've been to the Rocky Mountains, the Ozarks, Hawaii, Alaska, California, to see your brother, of course.... We've even been abroad... Europe, Canada...." He added with a frown, "Then there was New York. Maybe we'll go back there someday... when the world isn't in such a mess."

He continued telling me about all the places he and Mom had seen, seemingly growing more and more convinced that I should see them as well.

"Oh, you'll love it there," he kept telling me.

I just lay there, smiling. *Wow, I'm actually gonna do this!* I thought. *I'm going on a journey!*

Mom and Dad came over to the apartment on Sunday to help me move out. I gave what little things I had to them for safekeeping and spent the night at their house. They saw me off the very next morning. I hugged them and said good-bye, then hopped into my Mustang, started it up, and buckled my seatbelt.

My mother leaned into the window and said, "Don't forget to call us as soon as you get to a hotel."

"I won't," I said.

She leaned in further and kissed me on the cheek. "Bye, baby," she said, almost on the verge of tears. "Have a good trip. Drive safe."

"I will," I said.

She stepped back and I slowly drove off. I could see them holding onto each other and waving at me through the rearview mirror. *Say good-bye to your lifeline,* I thought, both excited and a little apprehensive. All I had in the trunk was a suitcase full of clothes and a toothbrush. And in the passenger seat was my cell phone, Porsche's traveling money, and her show tunes CD.

As I approached the state line, heading east on I-40, I decided to give the CD a try. I opened the case and out fell a small sheet of paper, which read in Porsche's handwriting, "Benjamin, listen to track three! It reminds me of you." I slipped in the disk, went straight to track three, and listened to a deep, gravelly-voiced Lee Marvin belt out, "I was born under a wand'rin' star," from the movie *Paint Your Wagon. How ironic*, I thought, and laughed while passing through the Oklahoma state border into Arkansas. I had just entered the unknown, having absolutely no idea where I was going or where I'd end up. But I thought I might take a gander at that big island on the East Coast everyone was raving about. Hell, I'd probably be back home in a week—or two!

ABOUT THE AUTHOR

The gay scene of the 1990s—or the Gay Nineties, as author Bryan Foreman fondly refers to it—is a world and time period that he's well-acquainted with. He went from a clueless twenty-something to a clueless thirty-something in the early nineties and most of his friends were gay, even though he's hopelessly heterosexual. He lost a lot of those friends to the AIDS epidemic, sadly enough. They were an amazing group of people and he feels incredibly honored to tell their story. A native of Oklahoma City, Foreman graduated from the University of Oklahoma with a bachelor's degree in professional writing. With a strong passion for storytelling and inspired by such literary giants as Mark Twain and Emily Brontë, he is currently at work on his fourth novel, another semi-autobiography spanning from his childhood to his late twenties and also focusing on LGBTQ issues, family relationships, love, and friendship.

Dear Reader,

Thank you for reading *Heaven Is a Gay Bar*! If you enjoyed the book, would you please do me a huge favor and write a customer review on Amazon? Reviews can be tough to come by these days and I need all the help I can get. So if you have the time, please go online and visit my author page at http://www.amazon.com/author/bryanforeman

Thanks again for reading my book and for spending time with me!

In gratitude,

Bryan Foreman

www.ingramcontent.com/pod-product-compliance
Lightning Source LLC
Chambersburg PA
CBHW020329180626
46812CB00001B/107